Odin was on his feet, fumbling for the hilt of his sword. Loki crouched by the throne, malice glittering in his dark eyes.

She cried out, "Have you no response to me but this? I have my own magic! Save your steel and let me show you fire . . ."

Fire flowed through her outstretched arms. One white hand reached toward Odin and the flame licked around him, touched him with a spark that limned each nerve in light.

Swiftly he came to her; she saw a new fire glowing in his eyes. And as he came she saw the face of Michael Holst laid over his like a mask.

"BRISINGAMEN is exciting; it brings ancient and powerful myth into the lives of modern people."

—*Poul Anderson*

"Vivid, gripping, magical."

—*Evangeline Walton*

"A truly positive approach to magic which does not treat the unknown as horror. I love it—I wish I had written it myself!"
—*Marion Zimmer Bradley*

DIANA L. PAXSON
BRISINGAMEN

BERKLEY BOOKS, NEW YORK

BRISINGAMEN

A Berkley Book / published by arrangement with
the author

PRINTING HISTORY
Berkley edition / November 1984

ISBN: 0–425–07298–3

A BERKLEY BOOK ® TM 757,375
The name "BERKLEY" and the stylized "B" with design are
trademarks belonging to Berkley Publishing Corporation.
PRINTED IN THE UNITED STATES OF AMERICA

ACKNOWLEDGMENTS

I would like to thank Frank Fraga for providing me with resources and insights into the Viet Nam war, and Paladin for designing, operating, and repairing the motorcycles used in this book. I also wish to acknowledge my debt to the unknown compiler of the Poetic Edda and to Snorri Sturlusson, who composed the Prose Edda in the thirteenth century and thus preserved so much of what we have of the ancient lore.

Grateful acknowledgment is offered also for permission to print excerpts from the following:

The True Critics by Paul Edwin Zimmer, © 1979 by Paul Edwin Zimmer
MacDatho's Dog by Paladin, © 1979 by Paladin
Requiem by Paladin, © 1976 by Paladin
Lightning, Lightning by Robert C. Cook, © 1978 by Catherine Cook

For all those whose faces
I could not see,
And whose voices
I could not hear.

1959–1975

IT SHALL NOT HAPPEN AGAIN!

PROLOGUE

Already smoke was eddying through the Hall, dimming sight and tormenting the lungs. Thorgerda coughed and worried the point of her knife beneath the coffer's copper lining. From outside came laughter—the sound that men will make when they torment a captive or bait a bear. Metal clashed as Yngjald and the others tried to break free. And underlying all those other sounds was the constant crackle of the fire, like the gnawing of the Serpent at the root of the world.

Gasping, Thorgerda gave the metal a last wrench and looked down at the white, mute face of her daughter, huddled on the floor where the air was still clear.

There was a shout from beyond the doors. "Yngjald, will you take the King's mercy? Swear to receive the White Christ and come out of there! Already Hell's flames rise around you, do you want to burn for eternity?"

Thorgerda grunted. "The mercy of Olaf—the pity of the White Bear!" In Iceland men had voted to accept the new faith a generation ago, but here in Sweden, Olaf Lap-king was following the example of his son-in-law the King of Norway and enforcing conversation with fire and sword.

Yngjald laughed. "What kind of god would want servants who are forsworn?" He added an obscenity. "Tonight we sup with Odin and feast in Freyja's Hall. But on the day of Ragnarok when the fires of Surt devour the world, we will fight again, and the gods themselves will be our allies!"

"Then send out your women now—"

Thorgerda sighed. She had expected this, but not so soon.

1

"Freydis—get your jewelry—quickly now!"

As the girl crawled toward her bedplace, Thorgerda tugged a leather bag from the bosom of her gown and spilled out a golden necklace that seemed to shine in its own light.

"Brisingamen . . . " breathed Freydis as she returned to her mother's side and saw what she held.

For a moment the living gold swung from Thorgerda's hand. Then she kissed the necklace reverently, pulled off her silk kerchief to wrap it, and thrust it into the space between the copper lining and the coffer's floor.

"Brisingamen the Beautiful—" Thorgerda echoed as she pressed the copper down. "But Freyja will wear her necklace no longer. Her image is cast down and her worshippers scattered. Soon none will remember the ceremonies. But the necklace must not be destroyed! While it exists, no matter what name men call upon, the power of the Goddess will work in the world! The womb will swell and the fields will bear. The wolf age of Ragnarok will be held at bay. Remember that, Freydis, and guard it well!"

The serving maids were twittering before the great door like a flock of frightened hens. Swiftly Thorgerda scooped the shoulder-brooches and arm-rings and chains of gold that were her daughter's dowry into the coffer and forced the latch down.

"Go now—" For a moment she clutched Freydis against her, memorizing her daughter's firm body, the wild hay scent of her hair. Then she pushed her away.

Freydis picked up the coffer and took a step, then stared back at her mother. "I can't leave you here!"

A laugh tore at Thorgerda's throat. "I have served the Goddess all my life—do you think I will abandon Her? And even if I sought Olaf's mercy, how long do you think he would let me live? No, my love, you must go meekly. Let them sprinkle you with water and name you anew. Perhaps they will marry you to some man of Olaf's and give him this land to hold for the King.

"Live, Freydis! Do what you must to survive. But when your daughter comes of age, show her this coffer, and she will tell her daughter, and when this wood decays they will make other chests to be Brisingamen's hiding place."

The girl swallowed, nodded. Fire blazed through the roof and her hair shone like red gold. Thorgerda struggled to her feet and together they moved toward the door.

"Remember," she whispered, "I entrust Brisingamen to you with my dying word. You must guard the necklace, you and your daughters after you, until it is time for the power of the Goddess to manifest once more."

Thorgerda's eyes were streaming. Women surged around them and she let Freydis go. The fire roared like a wild beast, and even if she had wished to say more the girl could not hear. Freydis crossed the threshold, stumbling past grinning warriors toward the foreign priest on the white mule.

Yngjald limped to his wife's side. Blood dripped from his spearhead and darkened the grizzled gold of his hair. Behind him stood Thorgerda's sons and the other men who had remained faithful to the end. A roof beam crashed behind them; sparks arced glittering through the air. The heat seared her lungs. For Thorgerda, Ragnarok was now, but her daughter would carry the power of the Goddess into a new world.

Through the heat-shimmering air she saw Freydis look back, and lifted one arm to salute her. Then Thorgerda and Yngjald turned away and walked back into the fire.

1

Hear my words now, for I know them both,
*   forsworn are men to women;*
We speak most fair when most false our thoughts,
*   for that wiles the wariest wits.*

                    THE SAYINGS OF HAR

"Karen, I have to talk to you . . ."

Fire scalded her eyelids. She struggled against the folds of cloth that stifled her, suddenly afraid. Yngjald . . .

"Karen, wake up—I have to go."

Karen moaned; he was shaking her; she reached out and her hand closed on fine cotton. For a moment she held her breath, awakening consciousness sorting the feel of tangled bedclothes and the soft mattress beneath her from her memory of the heat and the reek of the fire. But it was not firelight, only the pale light of morning shining through her closed lids. The dream was disappearing like smoke dispersed by the wind. She drew a long shuddering sigh and opened her eyes.

"Roger?" In the half-light by the window she saw him in silhouette.

"Maybe I should have told you this before," he said softly, "but I didn't want to spoil our night together." His voice was muffled as he tucked in his chin to knot his tie. The fine shape of his head and the line of his shoulders were blocked clearly against the glow from the window; she did not need to see his

4

features to know him, she had memorized every angle of him in the two years since he had brought her home from a faculty party one night and stayed until morning.

He turned to face her. "I talked to Joan yesterday. She sounded different. She's changed, Karen, and she needs me. She wants me to come home."

Karen shivered suddenly and pulled the sheets around her. She heard what he was saying, but the words made no sense to her. With a burp of static her clock radio came on, an undercurrent of strings and the deep calling of horns. Her awareness began to follow the music, was called back to the present, this room, as he spoke again.

"It's not as if you and I were anything permanent—we always knew that." Roger reached for his jacket. "It's been good, Karen, and I'll always have good memories of you, but—well, Joan *is* still my wife." He shrugged into his jacket and patted his pockets automatically. Then he reached out to pick his cigarette lighter from the Victorian overmantle that dominated the bedroom, though it only guarded a gas log now.

Other things were taking shape in the growing light—piled books; photographs of her parents on the ranch; her brother still in uniform, the day he got back from Viet Nam . . . the discomfort in Roger's face.

"Roger—" One word only, one concession to the clamor that was beginning in her brain. She clutched at the sheet as if she could squeeze a protest from its folds.

He had said he was done with permanent ties. He had said he loved her because she was a free spirit. Like him. They were companions. Neither would ever make the other feel guilty or tied down. And Karen had believed him.

Music swelled, burst in a shower of descending chords, and faded to the stillness of exhaustion after some great storm. "And that was the overture to *Gotterdamerung* by Richard Wagner—" came the voice of the announcer, impossibly cheerful. "And now for a word—"

"I don't think I've left anything here." Roger looked uncertainly around him, glanced at Karen and away. "You will be all right . . ." It was not quite a question.

Why? she thought in anguish. *What did I do? I only tried to be what you wanted me to be. . . .* Her head moved in bewildered pain, but he did not see.

"Goodbye, Karen—maybe I'll see you at a party sometime. . . ."

They had met at a reception for a University lecturer whose topic, nineteenth century Symbolism, was supposed to relate to Roger's specialty in Art History and hers, which was Romantic Literature. Or was intended to be—she had a job with Dr. Walter Klein of the Department of Comparative Literature while she was supposed to be working on her dissertation. Secretary, research assistant, reader for his classes; she supposed she had become too valuable to him. At least he never asked her how her work was progressing anymore.

Roger had liked having a lover who knew his world, but somehow Karen understood that he would not have liked her to acquire too much status there on her own.

He bent over the bed to kiss her, just as if it had been any ordinary day. His lips touched hers and she reached for him, her fingers tightening on his shoulders as he began to pull away. He tried to straighten and she saw on his face the twitch of panic, the beginnings of distaste.

He is afraid I will make a scene, some distant, cold voice said. He would never let her touch him in public, had never kissed her where anybody could see. Obediently her fingers loosened, and she let him go. The brisk, unfeeling measures of a Haydn symphony buzzed in the room.

Roger turned with a relieved sigh, moved to the bedroom door and lifted his hand in farewell, a darker shadow in the dimness of the alcove. Then he was gone and Karen stilled, all her being focused to a single sense, listening for the final latching of her front door.

The radio cut off automatically—eight o'clock, though that meant nothing now. In the silence she could hear too clearly the sound of his car starting in the street below. As the motor roared and receded, a moan tore from the depths of her belly to become a shout of denial that rattled the blue glass pitcher on the windowsill.

"No! You bastard, you *used* me!" Words erupted—all the words she had not been able to say when Roger was there. "I was just someone to pass time with—what I did made no difference at all!"

Gasping, she fought free of the bedclothes' constrictions,

grabbing for the window ledge as if to fling herself through. Her hand struck the blue vase, shattered it, and a shard pierced her palm.

With a shocked whimper Karen pulled the glass from her hand, watching her blood drip to the floor. The thick drops shone like garnets in the morning light.

"Never again!" her lips' harsh whisper barely stirred the air. "By my own blood I swear it—I will find out what I am meant for in this world. If I suffer again, I am at least going to know why! Do you hear me?" She was shouting now, though she did not know to whom she cried. She lifted her arms in entreaty and for a moment the room glowed gold. Or perhaps it was only that her gesture had moved the curtain to admit the sun.

Pain shot through her palm. She pressed it to her mouth to stop the bleeding and collapsed back onto the bed. She burrowed against the pillow, trying to muffle the agony, but Roger's scent was still on it. Finally, hopelessly, she began to cry.

Roger had not been her first lover, but he had been the first one to stay with her. She had built her life around the knowledge that he would be there. He had been the first man to whom she had felt any physical response at all.

And for two years she had worn Roger's image of her like a garment, as models lose their personalities in the fashions they showed. But she had lived for twenty-two years before she met him—she must have had an identity then. *Not much of one*—the humor was bitter. *At college no one could ever remember my name.*

At least she had been someone with Roger—the slim, quiet girl who wore misty colors to complement her pale hair, disguising diffidence with an aloof, slightly amused smile.

But that was Roger's Karen . . . Karen Ingold . . . Karen Ingold. . . . Who is she now? But she was nobody and nothing, and to be nothing was to be dead.

For a moment Karen longed for that red darkness that would engulf all pain. Roger would not be so smugly sure that she was "all right" then. Even his sophistication might be shaken if they found her body with a letter to him in her hand. And Joan . . . Karen had met her once, remembered only a sweet, unsure face. What would Joan say to her husband when she knew what he had done? Would Joan suffer? Did it matter? Let the whole world go up in flames since her world was gone.

Her hand was throbbing dully now. Remembering the pain, Karen knew that she would never be able to use a knife on herself. But there was aspirin—no, she had finished the bottle and had not yet bought a new one. And even in her agony Karen knew that once she had dressed and gotten herself to the store life would reclaim her and her tenuous resolution would fade away.

I don't even have the courage for suicide. . . . There's nothing I can do to make Roger feel even a fraction of this pain.

A babble of young voices swelled and receded in the street below—children passing on the way to school. It was getting late. Everyone would wonder if she did not get to the office soon.

Karen pulled herself up and stumbled to the window. Fog still lay heavy on the Berkeley hills, and she was obscurely glad. In the San Francisco area, August was a month of mist, and the skies were as grim as her soul. She could not have borne her pain beneath a cheerful sun.

I could call in sick . . . will they give me sick leave for a broken heart? she wondered with bleak humor. *How can I work when I feel this way?* But here, every piece of furniture still bore the impression of Roger's body.

Walking like an old woman, Karen went to the closet and pulled out, almost at random, a pair of faded jeans and a knit top in muted brown and grey. The first shoes she found were an old pair of black flats; they did not match her clothes, but she could not be bothered to look for something more appropriate.

She winced as she turned on the light in the bathroom, caught sight of her face in the mirror on the medicine chest, and stared. Her eyes were rimmed with red, her cheeks looked like badly kneaded dough. Light hair hung lankly down her neck. Karen shook her head, eyes stinging with returning tears.

"I'm ugly—" she whispered to the distorted image in the glass. "No wonder Roger left me. . . ."

Mechanically she pulled the stiff brush through her hair and tied it back, washed her face and put lipstick on. The cabinet was full of eye-shadow and pencils and liners—all the devices a busy cosmetics industry had invented to make grey eyes and pale brows visible—but Karen shut the door without touching them. Eye make-up would smear if she began to cry again, and then she would look not only plain, but slovenly.

Karen knew better than to attempt breakfast. Her feet carried her up Telegraph Avenue toward the campus without direction from her. The Campanile was already ringing out the hour as she threaded her way among the students taking advantage of the end-of-summer break for extra study and passed beneath the rustling plane trees in the plaza before Dwinelle Hall.

Dew from one of the broad leaves dropped onto the back of her hand. She took a deep breath, blinking back tears. *Even the trees are weeping! I've got to control myself, not let anyone know. . . .* She forced herself to stand straighter and went in.

After years of second-class status in various outbuildings, the Department of Comparative Literature had achieved the dignity of offices in one of the major buildings devoted to the Liberal Arts. Karen walked along the worn linoleum of a corridor decorated with bulletin boards covered with announcements for summer study in Europe, University clubs, a symposium on the legacy of Viet Nam—she had read them all long ago. Soon it would be time to replace them with a fresh papering of class announcements for the fall semester.

The door of the Department Office was already open. Karen stumbled as she went through, reached her desk, and collapsed into the chair, letting her handbag slide to the floor.

"Hey, for once I beat you in here—what happened, did you and Roger have too big a night on the town?"

Karen stiffened. She had hoped for a moment to get some coffee, to get her bearings among the familiar jungle of hanging plants and the bland familiarity of the yellow plastered walls before one of the secretaries said something that would strip her pitiful secret bare.

But why did it have to be Micaela, who had left her native El Salvador behind her without relinquishing her birthright of Latin charm? Micaela never had problems with men. . . .

Karen turned away, but the easy tears were already welling from beneath her shut lids. A chair scraped, she felt the other girl's arms around her, then Micaela let her go and pressed a tissue into her hand. She heard the sounds of the other girl making coffee and took a deep breath, trying to get control of herself again. The other two women in the office looked up with covert curiosity, but no one spoke to her.

After a few minutes Karen blew her nose defiantly. Micaela had perched on the corner of the desk and was gazing at her with unexpected compassion in her dark eyes.

"What did he do?"

"He stayed the night and then told me he's going back to his wife," Karen said baldly. It sounded so paltry, stated that way. She shook her head angrily. "I don't know why I'm letting it upset me. He's . . ." she could not go on.

"He is a *cochino*! You gave him everything—he should not be allowed to treat you this way." Her eyes flashed.

Karen felt a pang of envy. If Roger had treated Micaela like this her cousins would have been waiting for him with knives—if Micaela herself had not been first with the blade. A *cochino* minus cojones, he would be, and serve him right, too! She could understand now the Latin compulsion to fill the aching void of loss with violence. Her hand throbbed dully where the glass had gashed it and she remembered the exquisite release of pain. But there was nothing within her that could initiate action anymore.

"It's no use. I'm not what he wants now."

"Is he what *you* want, Karen?" Micaela lifted a pile of summer session exams from the chair and gathered the crimson flounces of her skirt to sit down. With her head tilted to one side, dark eyes sparkling with indignation, she was like some vivid tropical bird.

"Does it matter what I want?" asked Karen.

"Well, if you do not know, how do you think a man will give it to you? You have to know who you are and make them desire it. You have to use your power!"

The phone rang and Micaela reached for it. Her voice grew crisp—someone important must be on the line. Micaela worked for the Romance Languages side of the Department, and was convinced that the rest of the University underestimated them.

I wish I could do that—I sound like a serf when someone from the Dean's Office calls. Karen wondered if that were another reason she had stopped working on her degree, and why she had been so grateful to Roger for wanting her.

Power. . . . Is there a power that a woman can exercise? Not

*just the power to say yes or no, but to make things happen?
Micaela does that. When war destroyed her home she forced
fate to bring her to this country. When she wants to leave this
job I am sure that things will arrange themselves to offer her a
new one.*

"Karen—can you read this?" Sara Thomas came heavily
across the room and laid a sheaf of papers on Karen's desk.
She was an older woman, working to put her children through
college. "It's Dr. Klein's article for *Speculum,* and he's got all
these notes in the margin and I don't know what he wants me
to do."

Karen sighed. Walter should have known not to give the
paper to anyone but her—reading his handwriting was a spe-
cialized skill related to the deciphering of palimpsests. Sometimes she thought the real reason Dr. Klein had hired her was
to read his scrawl.

"Let me take this. You still have Dr. Walberg's annotated
bibliography to do anyway, don't you?"

"I sure do. Thanks, Karen. Dr. Klein did say something
about waiting for you to do it, but he was in a hurry, so I said
I'd try. He was hoping it could get done before he got back
from the planning meeting so's he could look it over and
maybe mail it off today."

Karen nodded and picked up the papers with a sense of
relief. Surely the complexities of Old Norse would distract her
from her own problems. Here, the only uncertainties were
whether Walter had meant an umlaut or merely wanted her to
repeat a phrase, and centuries of scholarly squabbling had
worn all the emotions away.

*In the most ancient material there is what might be viewed
as an evolutionary cycle from divinity to humanity and
back again. Dead kings of the Swedes are raised to demi-
gods; the Frankish king Sigeberht becomes a grandson of
Odin while his queen, the Visigothic Brunehilda, attains
the rank of Valkyrie. At the same time, Snorri Sturlusson
(as well as more modern euhemerists) reduces the war between the Aesir and the Vanir to a tribal conflict. One
senses a continuing struggle to comprehend and define
the proper relationship between men and the gods. . . .*

The lunch hour was half gone before Dr. Klein arrived, just

after the mail, colliding in the doorway with a battered crate labeled in Swedish and English, HANDLE WITH CARE.

"It came a few minutes ago—Karen signed for it." Curiosity shone blatant in Micaela's eyes. She hovered, looking over Karen's shoulder, though Sara and the others had gone to lunch long ago. The corridor outside echoed with chatter and the clatter of footsteps.

Dr. Klein folded his tall figure downward to peer at the label. His fair hair had begun to grey early; silver strands glinted in the light from the eastern window as he bent his head.

"It's from Professor Freiborg at the University at Uppsala, but what on earth can he have sent me?" Walter looked around him uncertainly and Karen handed him the screwdriver she used when the metal desks the office had been supplied with gave way. As he wrenched at the slats the crate teetered and crashed to its side. He looked at the label informing them of the fragility of the package and shook his head ruefully.

"Let me—" said Karen. The lethargy that had held her at her desk was gone. She needed activity, a physical struggle on which to spend the hopeless anger that burned within. She had grown up on the pig-ranch in Sonoma that her brother took over when he got out of the service, and her father had taught her how to handle tools.

She worked the edge of the screwdriver under a slat and levered it up with a swift sharp movement as if she were rending Roger, and with an almost human groan the wood came free. Without pausing she attacked the next, while Walter pulled away the paper and excelsior inside. It was the old-fashioned kind—a mass of sweet-smelling curls of wood, not the styrofoam turds American companies used for packing now.

Karen ripped off the last slat and as Walter brushed the excelsior away they saw a wooden chest with an envelope taped to it.

"Perhaps this will tell us what it's all about."

Karen scarcely heard him. The chest fixed her attention as she gently stroked the dust away. One corner of it had been wrenched askew.

"Dr. Freiborg says that this piece was in his grandmother's house outside of Uppsala. Apparently the land had been in the

family for generations, but the last old aunt died a year ago."
Walter scanned the letter.

Karen's fingers were exploring the damaged corner of the
chest. The wood seemed sound, smooth with the patina of
age. She had always been clever with her hands. Perhaps she
could fit the pieces back together again.

"It's a thank-you gift . . ." Walter's fair skin grew pink
with pleasure. "He wants me to have this in return for my
hospitality when he visited last year."

Micaela peered down at the chest. "Does he say what it is?"

Walter glanced back at the letter. "According to family
tradition it was a bridal chest handed down from mother to
daughter for several hundred years. It's an eighteenth century
piece, he says."

"Yes," said Karen. "Here's the date carved on the lid—
1752."

Walter put the letter on her desk and maneuvered himself
down beside her to see. "If the date is there I suppose it must
be eighteenth century, but this carving looks much older."

The chest was built from slabs of some hard wood strengthened by narrower boards whose carving was intricate but
clumsy, as if the design had been copied by an inexpert crafts-
man or defaced and distorted by age. The wood was darker
than the rest, and Karen wondered if perhaps the carved
boards were older than the body of the box.

"These pictures are very strange—" said Micaela. "See, all
these funny creatures biting their tails."

Karen followed her pointing figure along the interlace out
of which the faces of fantastic beasts peered and disappeared
again.

"They're called gripping beasts—" said Walter musingly.
"But the Borre style flourished in the tenth century. It's
odd—" He shrugged. "Family tradition, I suppose. What
shall we do with it? Dr. Freiborg thought it would be a nice ad-
dition to my office, but it should be repaired, and I don't
know whom to trust it to."

Karen was still kneeling with her hands on the wood, drawing strength from its solidity. "Let me try . . ." she found
herself answering. "I've done this sort of thing before." It
had been a sort of hobby with her for a while, but she had not
thought of it . . . for how long? Since she'd met Roger, she

realized. His image of femininity had no room for sweaty struggles with fabric and wood.

"I'll bring some tools in here and we won't even have to take it away," she went on.

The crease between Walter's pale brows eased. "If you want to do that, I would be grateful." He looked at the wreckage strewn across the office floor with faint alarm. "However, we should probably move it to my office . . ."

"I should think so!" Micaela was losing interest now. "There is not so much room here to begin with, and this thing is blocking the door."

Together they managed to shove the chest down the hall and shift enough piles of books from the floor of Dr. Klein's office to make a place for it.

Karen looked back gratefully as she went out, but four pages still remained of Walter's paper. Tomorrow, she thought, she would bring in her tools. Tomorrow she could sink herself in the comforting discipline of manual labor and forget the gnawing pain of thoughts with which, like the contorted creatures in the carvings, she fed upon her own flesh forever unsatisfied.

2

Wroth then was Freyja, and with anger chafed,
all the Aesir's hall beneath her trembled:
In shivers flew the famed Brisinga necklace.
                        THE LAY OF THRYM

By the time Karen got home fog was sweeping through the
Golden Gate and across the Bay to cover Berkeley like a damp
shroud. Shivering, she turned up the radio. But the apartment
was no refuge. Every wall had become a backdrop for memories of Roger. Swearing at her own weakness, she took down
the pictures he had chosen and threw towels over the chairs to
change their color.

It was well after midnight before she dared try to go to bed,
and in the end it was only after finishing Roger's bottle of
Scotch that she slept. But in the morning Karen remembered
the Swedish wedding chest, and that thought gave her the
strength to endure her aching head and the sharper ache of
despair, and to gather her tools and go back to the University.
If she could restore the chest, then perhaps she could believe
that some miracle might make her whole again.

After watching her make her preparations, Walter had
hastily gathered up a set of proofs and left the office, murmuring something about the library. Karen scarcely noticed. She
knelt on the floor and then, very carefully, raised the lid of the
chest.

Its interior had been lined with thin sheets of copper,

green and corroded now. The metal on the bottom had been
wrenched when the corner was knocked loose in shipping
—that would have to come off. Once Karen was able to see
what was beneath she could decide whether to replace it or
insert new wood for strengthening.

She picked up a small chisel and began gently to worry at
the edge of the copper. Age had hardened the wood rather
than disintegrating it, and the chisel scratched the gleam of
brass from the dull surfaces of the nails. Would she have to
pry them out to get the copper off?

Considering, her unfocused gaze fixed on her own slender
fingers, pale and ringless against the dark wood. Then, momentarily, she saw the wrinkled skin of an old woman's hand,
then a farm-woman's rough and reddened fingers, a girl's
hand—pale and smooth but plumper than her own, a sequence
of women's hands laid upon the ancient wood of the wedding
chest and ending with her own. Suddenly she found it hard to
breathe.

Fancies! Fantasies! Could she find no peace even here? She
dug the chisel into the wood, but the old craftsmen had built
for the ages, and the two inch slabs were reinforced with heavy
ribs of oak. She wrenched at the metal, and its corroded edge
tore in her hand.

With unexpected frenzy Karen worried at the metal until the
last bit of copper came free. She sat back with a sigh, wondering how long it had been. A large spider made her tentative
way up from the dark space between the slabs of wood, then
scurried over the side of the chest and across the floor.

Karen recoiled and swore. "Did you come all the way from
Uppsala?" She peered into the chest suspiciously. What else
had found its way into those crevices in two hundred years?

She reached for the flashlight. The dim beam showed her
old spiderwebs between the bottom ribs of the chest, but nothing that moved. Relaxing a little, she took the whisk broom
in her other hand and began to brush the cobwebs away. The
bristles met resistance; something clinked and fell back as she
snatched the broom away. There was a brief rattling as it came
to rest, then silence once more.

Cautiously Karen shone the light into the crevice. There
was a dark lump—no, several, which had been dislodged from
a mass of decomposing wood, as if something had been
wrapped carefully and hidden there. The light trembled as

Karen stabbed downward with her tweezers and lifted the dark object out.

It was a metal bead. Rubbing it against the soft cloth of her jeans, she saw a yellowish gleam that might be tarnished silver or perhaps gilded bronze. She turned it in her hand, finding it lighter than she had expected; it was hollow, the surface rough with ornamentation encrusted with the remains of its packing so that she could not make out the design.

She felt a pulse begin to pound in her throat, dropped the bead into the toolbox drawer and peered back into the chest. One by one she plucked into the daylight other beads, some like the first, some larger, some pendant pieces with tops rolled for stringing, bead after bead, until the drawer was almost full.

"How are you doing?"

Karen gasped and dropped the bead, then had to track its rolling until it fetched up against the file cabinet and she could pounce and pop it into the drawer with the rest. She looked up. Walter was standing irresolutely in the doorway, as if at a word he would have fled back into the hall.

"You're back!" She got her breath again. "It's all right— you can come in now . . ."

"I didn't mean to startle you." His long fingers shuffled the stack of letters in his hand. "Can you repair it?"

"No—it's okay." she said again. "I was concentrating so hard I didn't hear you, that's all. And the chest is in good shape—it's jointed at the corners and if I knock them back together it should last another two hundred years. But the metal lining is shot"—she indicated the pile of metal fragments on the floor—"and we should probably replace it if you want to store anything inside. . . ." Her gaze went involuntarily to the drawer where she had put the beads.

Walter set down the letters on the scarred top of his oak desk and bent over the toolbox. His motion reminded Karen of the deliberate stalk of the white herons that fished in the flats beside the Bay, saved from comedy only by the birds' fair dignity.

"What did *you* find inside?" Behind the thick glasses his eyes were suddenly acutely focused on her face.

"I don't quite know . . ." she answered slowly. "Someone seems to have been hiding her jewelry. It could be valuable. What do you want me to do with it?"

"Jewelry?" Walter peered dubiously at the bead Karen handed him. "It doesn't look like much." As he dropped it back into her hand Karen felt a quiver run through the floor, as if something heavy had been dropped on it, or a very large truck and gone by outside.

"Earth tremor . . ." said Walter. "Loki's struggling again." Karen stared at him, then realized that the remark had not been a non sequitur but a scholarly reference to the legend that the gods, fed up with Loki's treacheries, had bound him where a serpent would drip venom incessantly on his head. His faithful wife holds a cup to catch the poison, so that it is only when she goes to empty it that the venom sears him and Loki's agonized struggles shake the land.

"Only a small one . . . " Walter added at last. He looked down at Karen and smiled. "If you can do something with the pieces you're welcome to them—your labors deserve some reward, and I certainly don't have any use for jewelry!" He looked faintly alarmed, and his eyes grew vague again.

Karen repressed a smile. Departmental gossip had long ago exhausted the question of why Dr. Klein had never married and what, if anything, he did instead. With women he used an abstract courtesy, no matter whether they were students or secretaries, seeming to really see them only when the conversation turned to some obscure point of scholarship, or better still, to the meaning behind it.

But as she considered him, Karen realized that it was only in scholarly discussions that he focused on anyone. She had long ago concluded that an awkward adolescence had probably disillusioned him with his body, or perhaps the life of the mind had always been more attractive to him. His long fingers moved with certainty only on the stops of an instrument, and playing the French horn in a chamber group was Dr. Klein's only known recreation.

Now that Karen's concentration on the chest had been broken, she realized that the light that filtered through the window had turned gold. Somehow the afternoon had passed. *Roger* . . . gingerly she tested the memory, as one will touch tongue to a bad tooth to see if the ache is still there.

Immediately his face was before her, closed against her in the dim morning light. But now the vision was outside her, and the pain of it had begun to dull. Faintly she glimpsed a future in which it might be possible to deny it all of the time. She tried to smile.

"Thank you, Walter. I'd like to clean the beads—at least to see what they are. But I still think we should check it with customs, or a museum, or someone . . . "

"Oh dear—I'm sure Dr. Freiborg would not have done anything illegal, and I would hate to get him in trouble. If you want to, take it over to the Lowie Museum. The anthropology people may have some ideas. But let us not involve the government!" He was sitting on the edge of the desk, hands thrust into the pockets of his worn jacket, shaking his head.

Karen nodded and picked up one of the pendants, turning it between her fingers as if touch could read what was hidden from the eye. Yes, she could take it home. She understood then how afraid she had been to repeat the night that had just passed and she felt a sudden rush of gratitude.

"Well . . . I'm done for the day." Walter picked up a brief-case whose leather was scuffed and seams burst by the weight of the books he habitually carried in it. He looked at her as if he wanted to say something more personal but did not know how. "Don't stay too late . . . " he got out at last. "There's no reason why the chest must be fixed right away. And remember to lock up when you go home."

"Yes, I will." Karen looked after him, wondering if Micaela had told him about her and Roger. Maybe that was why he had been so thoughtful, but it was hard to imagine how even Micaela could find a way to get the conversation to that point. No, she concluded, it must simply be Walter's usual abstracted kindness. And even if he had wished to help her he could not have known the chest would arrive just then, or that there would be pieces of jewelry inside.

Karen peered into the chest a last time, probing with the screwdriver to make sure she had found all the beads. There were twelve of the kind she had found first, and perhaps twice as many smaller ones. Among them lay the nine pendants, of which one was the largest—obviously the center of the neck-lace. . . . Yes, it must be a necklace; suddenly she was sure of that.

She got to her feet, stretching painfully as muscles cramped by her hours of work began to complain. In the drawer of her desk was a plastic bag that had once held trail-mix. She found it and dropped the beads in, then knotted it securely. The clouds had finally cleared, and through the long windows of the office she saw sunset striking fire from the glass windows of houses in the Berkeley hills and touching the summer-bleached grass with the deep shimmer of gold.

She shrugged into her sweater and looked around her, trying to remember if she needed to stop by the grocery store on her way home. But she was too tired.

She thought, *It doesn't matter what I fix for dinner . . . I'm only cooking for myself, now.* But she would have the necklace to work on—she must remember that. She slid the plastic bag into her purse, slipped the strap over her shoulder, and went out the door.

By the time Karen's footsteps echoed on the sidewalk of her own street, the light had faded to rose. Her flat was located in the upper half of an old brown shingled house on Oregon Street, in one of the sycamore-shaded blocks between Telegraph and Shattuck Avenues south of the campus. She had chosen it because the rent was reasonable, and the place was old enough to have some character. Roger had liked it because the neighborhood was a quiet one. Karen realized unhappily that her life would be even quieter now.

Suppressing the thought, Karen climbed the stairs. *Don't think about it,* she told herself, *don't think about anything—just keep busy!* But still she stood for a moment in the center of the sheepskin rug, hands twisting uncertainly, before she went on into the bedroom to kick off her shoes and replace her pants and jersey with an old robe.

The beads . . . she reminded herself. *First I should try to get that gunk off of them. An ammonia solution should do it, if I don't leave them in it too long.* She padded into the kitchen, mixed ammonia and water in a glass bowl, and carefully dropped the odd pieces of metal in. In a few moments bubbles began to form on their surfaces and she knew that the chemical was beginning to work.

Now for some tea . . . Karen put the kettle on and took the box of teabags from the shelf over the stove, then looked around for her favorite stoneware mug. It was not in the sink or on the blue-tiled counter, nor could she see it on the formica table by the window. She must have taken it into her bedroom.

She found the mug on the little table next to the bed, picked it up and then stood, her fingers rubbing compulsively at the rough glaze, remembering. She and Roger had come in late that night, after dinner and a film at Ghirardelli Square in San Francisco. Roger had wanted a nightcap and poured himself some Scotch, but Karen made tea, since alcohol always made her sleepy too soon.

They had come into the bedroom, she still carrying the cup of tea because Roger had finished his drink by the time the tea water had boiled. She had sipped at it, laughing as Roger began to undress her, and had finally put it down half-full for fear of spilling it on him. And after that she had used her lips for better things than tea.

But the remainder was still in the mug, dark and muddy with a little scum already forming. *No one will keep you from finishing your tea tonight. . . . No one will ever stop you again.* . . . Grief rose like bile in her throat. Gasping, she threw the mug across the room. It crashed against the bureau and rebounded, spraying dark liquid like drops of blood across the floor.

Karen collapsed against the bed, shaking, whispering denial as all that day's anguish washed over her again. She could not move. *I thought I was past this. Is this what my whole life is going to be?*

Like a call from another world she heard the teapot's wail, forced herself to visualize the pot vibrating furiously on the burner and the jet of white steam, saw the counter beside it, and on it the glass bowl.

"The beads!" Shock shattered her despair. "There'll be nothing left of them!" She thrust herself away from the bed and dashed for the kitchen.

Ignoring the screeching kettle, Karen took the bowl to the sink and emptied it, then set it under the faucet with cold water running before returning to the stove to turn off the gas. Resolutely she lifted another cup from the shelf, dropped in a teabag and poured in the water, waiting until it became suffused with the rich brown of the tea before summoning her courage to return to the sink and see what was left of the treasure she had found.

Ammonia was excellent for dissolving corrosion. The only trouble was that if most metals were left in too long the ammonia would begin to interact with the metal itself, forming salts that would destroy it. Silver might hold up, but if those beads were bronze. . . . Apprehension tightened her throat as she looked down.

There, sparkling through the running water like the Naiads' treasure in the bed of the Rhine, she saw the seductive gleam of gold.

With almost any other metal, ammonia would react, but not with gold. . . . Of all man's treasures, only gold resisted all dissolution. Though it might be soiled and hidden, it would only grow fairer and brighter with cleansing. She saw specks lodged in the ornamentation that would need jeweler's rouge and some sharp tool to remove, but it was clear now that the beads and pendants that Karen had rescued from the Swedish wedding chest were crafted from fine gold.

A kind of terror shook her then. With gold at its current price, the pieces must be worth a fortune. Their age and work-manship might well make them unique, a treasure indeed. When Walter had told her to keep them he could not have ex-pected this! She must tell him tomorrow, give them back to him. She wondered what he would say.

But first she should finish the cleaning, and perhaps the beads would be easier to handle if she strung them as well. From the number and size of the pieces it was not hard to see what the form of the necklace would be. Karen could almost see it indeed, shaping itself against the shadows of her mind as she had seen Roger's face not so long ago.

Working quickly now, she spread newspapers over the din-ing room table, gathered her tools and spread the gold pieces out to dry. Her tea grew cold, but she sipped it anyway, obliv-ious to the passage of time.

With dentist's pick and jeweler's cloth she worked the abra-sive rouge into each crevice and out again. The pieces were astonishingly intricate, their flat surfaces ornamented with a wealth of abstract or zoomorphic interlace laid on with wire, and glittering beadlets of gold. Even the smallest beads were dotted and spiraled with gold until they sparkled like tiny suns. The larger pieces held stylized forms within the design—here a sow with piglets so tiny that Karen had to use a magni-fying glass to identify them, next two cats, a falcon in flight, a swan, a rearing mare.

They warmed to her touch as she worked over them. Her tools moved more surely; she found herself knowing even as she uncovered it what each image would be. And as she completed each one she laid it upon a clean cloth, and as she had envisaged it, the necklace grew.

She left the pendants for last. There were nine of them, graduated in size, and each bore the face of a woman. One of them rose from flowing water, another wore on her forehead a jewel like a star. One had the face of a woman and the breasts of a sow, one a warrior's helm; one was winged, another on horseback; one bore a spindle in her hand and one a hood that covered her eyes.

The ninth pendant Karen left for last. It was the biggest, obviously the centerpiece, about two inches long. As she worked, the figure emerged from its encrustations—the whole body of a woman this time, long-legged, with little conical breasts and upraised arms. Her hair streamed out around her and behind her were scattered what might be stars, or flowers.

Karen gave it a final rub, then set it shining in the last gap in the circle of gold. A treasure . . . she hardly dared to speculate on what it had been. Surely such a necklace could be no less than the dowry of a Queen. What tragedy must have caused it to be hidden so carefully, and what chance had brought it to her to be cleansed and made whole again?

Slowly, almost reluctant now to complete her task, Karen took a roll of brass wire from her jewelry-working kit, looked again, and found a heavy clasp from a necklace whose beads had scattered long ago. Carefully she measured two lengths of wire and began to thread them through the double row of beads, joining them as she came to each pendant, then separating them as she added round beads again. When all the pieces had been strung she twisted the wires tightly into the clasp and clipped them short.

"There, now you are whole again!" Karen realized she was addressing the necklace and began to laugh. The compulsion which had driven her to finish it was gone. Her shoulders ached and her fingers were sore. And she was hungry. Still smiling, Karen went to the refrigerator and reached eagerly for the leftover chicken and an apple in the vegetable tray.

How silent it was! The clock on the stove told her it was almost midnight, and except for the distant, intermittent wail of a siren, the neighborhood was still. She heard the rattle and hum as the refrigerator came on again, and the regular drip from the kitchen tap into the sink. Her shoulders sagged; she thought in wonder, *Tonight perhaps I will sleep soundly after all*. But she wanted to make sure. Taking a wine glass from the cupboard, she went back into the dining room.

The necklace lay where she had left it. Involuntarily, Karen's fingertips reached to caress the shining gold. It was so beautiful . . . she had never seen anything so fair. She could not keep it—in the morning she must take it to Walter. And yet—Karen wondered suddenly how she would look in the necklace of a Queen.

If I had been beautiful, Roger would not have left me. Karen told herself bitterly. *No piece of gold is going to change that!* But already the necklace was in her hands. With a thrill of almost sacrilegious fear she clasped it around her neck.

It was heavy, and cold—no, not so cold, the metal absorbed her body heat so rapidly; after a moment her breast began to accept that golden weight as natural. She peered into the silvers of mirror set in the sideboard, but only glimpsed the glitter of gold.

For the first time since Roger had left her, Karen went into the bedroom without thinking of him. She turned to face the long mirror on the closet door and flicked the light switch on.

But the necklace was half-hidden by the collar of her robe.

Karen tried to fold it back, then in exasperation let it slide to the floor. That was better—the inner edge of the circle of gold followed the curve of her collarbone. The metal glowed against her pale skin and her hair seemed to have picked up some reflection of its glory.

But now the tawdriness of a pinned bra strap became an irritation not to be borne. Staring at the image in the mirror, Karen slipped off her bra, then pulled off her underpants as well.

She was not thinking now. Some other impulse compelled her, as if she sought to recreate some image whose form she only dimly knew. Impatiently she tugged the elastic from her hair and brushed it until static electricity drew it away from her head in a cloud of gold.

Yes, that was closer . . . that was almost right, now. Slowly Karen lifted her arms in salutation to the image that glimmered before her, illuminated by the golden necklace's refracted light.

She saw the form of a maiden, slim and straight, hips swelling smoothly above the golden triangle of pubic hair. Her breasts were small and perfectly rounded, their rosy nipples tilting upward as if the bra had been only a formality. The face was a white mask whose only expression came from the darkened eyes. But they were not *her* eyes.

The hair rose on Karen's arms as she realized that the face was not hers either, now. It belonged to Someone Else who gazed around Her with wondering delight.

Karen forced her shaking fingers to loose the clasp. She pulled off the necklace, grabbed a scarf from the dresser and wrapped it before thrusting it into her bureau drawer. Quickly she turned off the light, averting her eyes from the mirror in which she had seen . . . what *had* she seen?

Still naked, Karen cocooned herself within the blankets, but as she hid her face against the pillow and felt sleep close over her like the waters of some warm and welcoming sea, still her eyes and her mind were blinded by the dazzle of gold.

3

*Not for all of England's earth and kingdoms
Would I forgo the golden-braided girl,
Nor yet for Ireland.*

                      KORMAK'S SAGA

There were trees around her—many trees, whose needles glistened in a pale sunlight that revealed each detail of bark or foliage, of lichened rock or forest flower, with stark clarity. The bowl of the sky was the sun-washed aquamarine of the far north, and from somewhere nearby she could hear the soothing murmur of the sea.

Karen saw these things with the wonder of one to whom they were new, and the content of one seeing them with long familiarity. She was wearing a grey woolen gown beneath a linen apron fastened at the shoulders by brooches, her body was swollen with child. *Who am I*, she wondered, *what am I doing here?* But that other part of her knew that she and the other women in the grove had come for the ceremony.

They were singing and dancing around a treetrunk that had been carved into the form of a woman. It was draped in a beautifully woven robe. A pitcher of milk and a platter of fine white bread rested on the pile of stones before it, with a wooden dish of honeycomb. Karen danced with the others. Her feet moved joyously.

An old woman was standing before the image. Her cloak of heavy blue wool flapped around her in the cool wind; a catskin cap covered her greying hair. As she lifted her arms, gold glinted between her hands.

"As it has always been, so shall it be—Lady, receive Thine own!" The shout echoed from a dozen throats, re-echoed from the trees as the crone bound about the neck of the statue a necklace of gold that flashed in the sun . . .

. . . gold sparkled, gold dazzled the eye with a thousand points of light . . . light glowed, grew radiant until the entire image shone . . . and changed to golden flesh that joined in the dance. . . .

Karen flung up her hands to protect her eyes from that glory, cried out and realized that she was awake, and that the room was glowing with the golden light of dawn. Somewhere nearby a cat was meowing, loudly, with a lordly insistence that assumed satisfaction would be forthcoming soon.

She sat up, blinking, separating the trees of her dream from the familiar furnishings of her room. *That was really something!* She rubbed her eyes. *I dreamed that I*—but already the details were fading. She retained only a recollection of the taste of wonder, and the certainty that the golden necklace had been there.

Hastily, Karen swung her feet over the side of the bed, pulled open the bureau drawer and felt for the hard shape of the necklace. Then, still dazed with sleep, she padded into the kitchen to put the teapot on. It was already boiling before she realized that she had not thought about Roger until now, and that even now, the thought of him brought regret and anger, but not pain.

She was sure a whole chorus of cats must be voicing their demands outside. Curious, Karen opened the door to the back porch. With an air of "What took you so long?" two large golden cats stalked in.

Karen stared at them, noting that there were none of the usual marmalade markings. One was the deep amber of a pendant her uncle had brought her from Russia, the other the pale gold of the star thistle honey they made on her brother's ranch. She wondered if their mother had encountered a wildcat somewhere in the Berkeley hills.

"Why me?" she asked as she took the boiling kettle from the burner and filled the teapot. "You're both well-nourished and healthy—you must belong to somebody. What are you doing here?"

One of the cats arched to her feet and padded forward to wreathe about Karen's ankle.

"I suppose that good condition needs a lot of feeding—" Now that the cat was on her feet Karen was struck once more by her size. Shaking her head, Karen opened the refrigerator door. Words of warning echoed in her memory—"Once you have fed them they will never go away. . . . " But the cats were so beautiful, and there on the top shelf was an open can of tuna almost past its prime, and it would be cruel to withhold it once the cats had smelled it. . . .

They ate daintily, almost condescendingly, as if the favor had been theirs. Watching them, Karen lost track of time and had to rush into her clothes. As she rummaged through her drawer she uncovered the necklace and remembered her strange experience with the mirror the night before.

She had fallen asleep as soon as she had taken the necklace off, but she had dreamed. If only she had thought to write it all down as soon as she woke—but would she have understood it any better then?

At least it's a change from agonizing over Roger, Karen thought wryly.

The necklace swinging from her hands drew her gaze. Whatever else it might be, it was valuable. She couldn't leave such a thing unprotected here. Even her purse would be too vulnerable. Skin twitching with apprehension, Karen put the necklace on.

But there was no strangeness. The beads settled snugly around the column of her throat. Beneath the turquoise silk of her shirt collar she glimpsed only a gleam of gold. *It was just the thought of its value that bothered me,* she told herself. *It's only metal, no matter how beautiful. . . .*

Karen spent part of the morning finishing the repair of the wedding chest and oiling the old wood until it shone. Then, regretfully, she settled down with the scrawled list of references Walter wanted available for the next semester's classes, dividing those which were already in the University library and could be immediately reserved in the Undergraduate library or the Humanities Graduate Service there, from those which could be borrowed from other institutions, and those which they would have to battle other faculty members at the budget meetings in order to buy.

Nobody commented on the necklace, though Karen was

constantly aware of its warmth and weight. But both Sara and Micaela told her how well she was looking and asked if the blouse was new.

The mail came just before lunchtime, and the boy who delivered it spent a full half hour hovering about Karen's desk, making conversation about a prospective shift in the schedule for delivering mail. By the time she got rid of him it was well into the lunch hour. With a sigh Karen turned back to the list of references.

"What are you doing here so late?"

Karen looked up with the paper still in her hand and saw Walter standing in the doorway with his jacket over his arm.

"I was on my way to lunch and heard you in here—have you eaten?"

"I just wanted to check a publication date before I wrote to U.C.L.A.," Karen explained. "I hadn't noticed the time—" She pushed back the chair and glanced out the window, decided it was still too warm for a sweater, and picked up her bag. It seemed natural for her to fall into step beside Walter as they went down the hall and out into the sunlight.

As they crossed Sproul Plaza Karen lifted her face to the sky. She fancied she could feel her skin absorbing the sun's warmth until she was filled by a golden glow. She felt the energy of the people around her—students sunbathing on the steps of the Administration Building and beside the fountain or reading under the sycamores that lined the open avenue to Sather Gate. From the steps of the Student Union, a congo-player sent waves of rhythm pulsing through the still air. Karen straightened, letting her body respond to that rhythm. Her blue-print cotton skirt and the ruffled petticoat under it swirled about her knees like the waves of the sea.

I'm alive. . . . The awareness throbbed in her mind as the drum throbbed in her bones. In this moment, she could not even imagine the despair that had ruled her three days before.

The shadows of the "Bear's Lair" seemed Stygian after the bright air outside. Karen stopped short, blinking. She felt Walter's hand on her elbow, and let him steer her through the gloom. As her vision adjusted she saw that the worst of the lunch crowd had gone—an advantage of coming in late, she supposed—but still she was surprised by how quickly the waiter came to take their orders.

As she leaned forward to return the menu, a strand of her hair caught in the necklace and she remembered why she had wanted to speak with Walter.

"You remember those—bits of metal—I found in the Swedish chest?" she began. He murmured some reply. "I cleaned them up and strung them into a necklace," Karen went on.

"Hmm?" Walter focused on her finally. Karen pulled her collar away from her neck so that he could see. "It looks very well on you."

"Walter!" she whispered. "These pieces are real gold. They must be worth a fortune, artistic value aside. I can't keep this —I was even afraid to leave it at home. You've got to send it back, or something!!" She reached back to unscrew the clasp, but her fingers slipped. She took another grip on the tiny bit of metal, but somehow she could not get the right angle, or perhaps the clasp was stuck. Without seeing, it was impossible to tell.

"Can you undo this?"

Walter looked dubious, but in a moment Karen felt the light touch of his fingers at the nape of her neck and the tug of the necklace as he manipulated the clasp.

"It seems to be jammed—" he said at last. "And if I break it, we'll spend the rest of the day looking for the pieces in this gloom. You can cut the wire when you get home."

Karen stared at him. The clasp had never given trouble before. Certainly last night it had opened without difficulty. *It's almost as if the necklace doesn't want to go.* . . . With the thought came an instant rejection—that was superstitious nonsense; if she went on like that, soon she'd be like the kids who read tarot cards for tourists on Telegraph Avenue on warm afternoons.

The waiter's return with their meal was a welcome distraction. Karen stabbed her fork into the depths of her salad, forcing herself to concentrate on the food.

Someone called Dr. Klein's name. Three men were coming toward them, carrying mugs of beer.

"You know Paul Haden and Randy Gonzaga, don't you? And this is Artur Shiller of the German Department." Walter moved his chair to make room for them.

Karen nodded and smiled. The two graduate students were in the Comp. Lit. Department. She probably knew more about them, about their academic histories at least, than they might prefer. Dr. Shiller's nod had the air of a bow as he settled himself on her other side.

"How is your dissertation coming, Randy—or should I ask?" Walter grinned.

Randy shrugged. "Oh well, you know how it is. You come up with a great theory, but as soon as you start to apply it, all sorts of side-issues come snarling out at you and you lose track of your argument beating them back." He looked appealingly at Karen, who produced an encouraging smile. His eyes widened.

"Maybe I should spend more time in the Department Office. It might inspire me . . . "

"What is your dissertation topic?" Dr. Shiller asked politely.

"Courtly love—" his friend Paul answered for him. "Maybe you can help him with the minnesangers. I forget, Randy, are you planning to go into the German stuff at all?"

"I hadn't intended to, but who knows?" said Randy gloomily. "I am *trying* to explore the idea of *domina* as *dea*—the Lady as goddess, based on the cult of the Virgin with references to Aphrodite." he explained.

"Awful, gold-crowned, beautiful Aphrodite . . . " Without intending it, Karen murmured the opening lines to the great Homeric Hymn, memorized for a course in lyric poetry and never forgotten. All three men looked at her and she felt her fair skin flushing.

"Gold-crowned indeed!" Paul Haden's eyes were on her hair. "Perhaps, Randy, you need some contemporary study."

There was an awkward silence while Karen read in their eyes a tribute which, if she had ever before received, she had not recognized. She caught a glimmer of gold beyond them and saw in the dark marbled glass that covered the wall her blurred reflection. But as it had been the night before, it was not entirely her own image that she saw. They were seeing not Karen Ingold, but Aphrodite, some immortal beauty for which she was the imperfect mirror as she herself was mirrored by the wall.

And suddenly, aware of her power, she felt for them a kind of compassion. "Why is your study so complicated?" she asked Randy.

"Well, take the figure of the goddess—" he started off, the

relief in his tone rapidly becoming enthusiasm. "Aphrodite is supposed to be the goddess of love, but she's described as everything from a maiden to a whore, or even a goddess of war. So is the Virgin Mary, for that matter—remember how King Arthur rode to the battle of Mount Badon with her image painted on his shield? Sometimes the Goddess is every man's dream, and sometimes she's a nightmare. Just when you think you've defined her, something new turns up and you have to rework it all!"

"It sounds very Jungian," commented Dr. Shiller. "As I recall, they divide the goddess-archetype into Good Mother, Terrible Mother, Virgin and Witch."

Karen suppressed a smile as the conversation began to follow the traditional academic pattern of point and reference, as formal as a dance.

"In the Middle Eastern mythologies you get Mother Goddesses who are either generic creators or queens of the gods—and the younger daughters, or rival goddesses, who do just about everything except bear children. Remember the bas-reliefs of the Lady with the two lionesses, riding to rule or to war?"

"Freyja . . . " said Walter.

"What?" the others turned to him.

"I never realized it before, but Freyja, in the Norse mythology, fits precisely into that pattern," he said. "We think of her as goddess of love, but she seems to have governed the fertility of all nature. She also shared with Odin the pick of the battlefields, so she was probably expected to lead them when Ragnarok came."

"Sort of a super-Valkyrie?" asked Randy.

Walter smiled. "You might put it that way."

"Isn't that your answer, then?" asked Karen. "As the ancients saw all the contradictions as aspects of one goddess, couldn't the courtly lover see aspects of *The* Lady in whatever mistress he might choose?"

"That might work. . . . " Randy frowned abstractedly. "I'll need to do a bit more with the psychology, but you could certainly make a case for this kind of a goddess figure being a recurrent necessity for human males."

And what about human females? Karen wondered then. *What was She to them?* Now she remembered—in her dream, women had been worshipping.

Walter looked at his watch and pushed back his chair. "I'm

afraid that for me student conferences are a recurring necessity, and I'm almost late for one now!''

Karen got to her feet too, and the other three men stood up.

"It's been nice meeting you." said Paul Haden. Dr. Shiller nodded.

"That's an understatement," added Randy. His bow managed to be both medieval and Latin. He brought her hand to his lips and she knew she was blushing again.

As Karen followed Walter to the door she realized that the others were still watching her, frowning as if they found it hard to keep her in focus. She paused in the doorway, feeling the sun's radiance behind her while her face was in shadow, and waved goodby.

"Good for you—" said Walter as they passed from light to shadow to light again up the stairs. "That suggestion was just what he needed to get going again."

"But I don't know anything about it! I only did courtly love in a medieval survey course, and I know nothing about ancient religions."

"This may sound like academic heresy, but it's not mere knowledge of facts that makes a scholar. No matter how learned you may be, you can't remember everything. You have to be able to define problems and solve them, and you have to know where to look for the facts. What you said just now required not knowledge, but perception."

But I never had that kind of intuition before, either. . . . Karen reflected as they went on. *Neither those comments, nor the courage to make them, came from me.* Her hand went unconsciously to the necklace, fingering the golden pendants as if to reassure herself of their reality, while her internal dialogue continued—*When those men looked at me it was not me they were seeing . . . no man has ever looked at* me *like that! They saw something else—maybe the same thing I saw in my mirror . . . or Someone . . .* an even deeper level of awareness formed the words. But that was crazy—she thrust the thought away, and realized that Walter was still talking, saying something about her own abandoned academic career.

"You really must go on, you know—you'll always feel incomplete if you don't, and besides, it would be a waste of a good mind."

Karen looked at him in astonishment, and he colored a little.

"Not that I don't value your work for me, Karen, but I feel

as if I were using a sword to cut cheese."

Karen hadn't really worked on her dissertation since she'd met Roger—she only retained academic status to keep her job. Had she feared he would dislike competition, or did she merely want to leave herself free to be formed in his image? But it was her mother's ambition that had sent her to college in the first place. It had not been hard for her to give up a goal that was not her own.

She sighed. "I don't mind doing odd jobs, but you're right. It's not what you could call a career. But I don't know what I want instead. Why bother with a degree if I'm not going to need it?"

"That's true. But don't wait too long to decide."

Karen found herself grinning and turned her face away, not wanting to try to explain. Just now men had looked at her as if she were Aphrodite—who knew what she might become?

"I almost tried a career as a musician, you know . . . " Walter went on as if he were talking to himself. "People told me I had talent, and it gave me great pleasure. But I loved digging around in obscure languages and literatures too."

"How did you finally decide?"

"I went to my old music teacher, who told me that *he* had once wanted to be a dancer. But he found that he could put off practicing dancing, but not the music, so obviously that was what he was supposed to do."

"And that's how you made your decision?" Karen asked.

"Partly, I suppose. But it's also true that however greatly music adds to the joy of life, once the echoes die away the music is gone. In scholarship, there are insights to be gained and mysteries to be solved, and one's work becomes part of the cumulative knowledge of mankind. It didn't look as if I would ever make much of a difference in the world by playing my horn . . . "

Karen glanced sidelong at his face. His lean profile was turned away from her, but she saw a hint of extra color beneath the fair skin. *He has never told me so much about himself before*, she thought. *How hard it must be for him—he must be nearly as confined within himself . . . as I am. . . .*

"But nothing that I know how to do can change the world, so how can I choose?" she asked.

Walter looked at her. "Sometimes one is chosen instead."

•   •   •

Mentally reviewing her shopping list, Karen walked home.

Some hamburger, if the price is good—there's a can of spaghetti sauce in the cupboard somewhere . . . I think—no, better get some while I'm in the store—the sky was glowing like beaten gold, gold edged the leaves, sparkled through the crystals suspended from the rack of the street-merchant on the corner, touched the faces of the crowds on Telegraph Avenue with the beauty of angels in some Renaissance fresco. *And maybe some wine, too. And cat food—*

Karen's mind continued to work on two levels as she threaded her way down the street. On these warm summer evenings, the Avenue was like a fair. On one side, a belt-maker was fitting a unicorn buckle onto a length of tooled leather. Down the street a girl sold ceramic dragons—one almost expected them to roar. Jewelers, potters, woodcarvers, and people selling prints or tie-dyed T-shirts lined the street. She paused, admiring rows of earrings crafted from beaten copper and silver and brass, then her hand went to her neck. There was nothing there worthy to be worn with the necklace. She pulled herself away and went into the little grocery store.

Holding the paper sack awkwardly against her breast, Karen continued down the street. A red light stopped her at the corner of Haste and Telegraph. She stood on the curb, her attention caught by the mural of the Berkeley riots painted on the wall of the restaurant across the street—a confusion of running figures, police in gas masks, boys weeping over the body of their friend—local history becoming legend. As the sunset glow intensified the colors, she thought of ancient frescoes again.

She had been in junior high school when the riots were going on. She remembered distorted fragments of film in the news. But it was hard to imagine what Berkeley had been like then. The war was long over, and there was nothing to protest anymore.

The light changed. Still looking at the mural, Karen stepped down from the curb.

"Look out!"

Brakes screeched. Karen looked up; a car skidded toward her. She saw the driver's face shift from blank surprise to glee; the car leaped forward as the brake released. Light flared from chrome fenders and slanted windows, the dark bulk expanded explosively.

Disbelief froze her in place.

Hard fingers closed on her shoulder, but the roar and rush of the car were all she could see. In one breath, a jerk backward, a buffet of hot wind and a blow. The hard pavement rose to meet her and Karen fell into darkness.

When she could breathe again a confusion of faces surged between her and the sky.

"Did the car hit her?"

"Someone call an ambulance!"

Karen pushed herself upright, trying to bring the world into focus again. "Please, I'm okay." she said faintly.

"Typical Berkeley pedestrian—the light was red."

"No, it had just turned green—the S.O.B. was speeding down the hill."

"Did anyone see the license number?"

Karen managed to shake her head. "I'm not hurt! Don't call anyone, please. She remembered the light turning green, but her most vivid memory was of the driver's face, shock overlaid by a mindless malice as he tried to run her down.

"What hurts? Did you hit your head?"

The low voice spoke at her ear. Karen realized that someone was kneeling behind her; she was only upright because he supported her. She turned her head and saw a face with the austere severity of a sword, dark brows knit, grey eyes inspecting her impersonally. Or rather, one grey eye, for now she realized that his right eye was dull, half-hidden by a scarred and puckered lid. She looked away.

"I . . . don't think so." Her heart was racing. She drew a deep breath of soft summer air. Her shoulder throbbed where he had gripped it and her arm and side were beginning to sting. She rubbed at her shoulder. "Just got the breath knocked out of me when I fell."

"Sorry about that." he grimaced. "He was going to hit you."

"He would have—thank goodness you grabbed me!" Karen assured him fervently. Everything around her had an unnatural clarity. The darkening sky had a sapphire purity against which the electric wires made a web that had caught the first star. She had narrowly missed death, and she had never felt so alive. Her hand went to her throat and jerked away, tingling, as she touched the necklace.

It feels as if it were rejoicing in life as well. . . . She flinched from the thought as her fingers had flinched from the gold and looked back at her rescuer.

Now she recognized the deep lines of mastered pain that ran from his mouth into his short beard, and the strands of silver in his dark hair. Yet it was still a young face—he looked as if he were in his early thirties now. But his expression was changing, losing the eagle-look as the excitement drained and he too became aware of who and where he was once more.

"Thank you very much." she tried to smile. "I don't think anything is broken, but if you'd stopped to be gentle I wouldn't be thanking anyone now."

She started to get up, swayed as the world spun around her, and clutched at his arm.

"Come on." He lifted her to her feet.

"I'm sorry. I just need a minute . . . you don't have to . . . where are you taking me?" she protested as he began to bear her along. Someone had gathered up her scattered groceries, and he carried the battered bag under his other arm.

"I learned about shock in Viet Nam. You need something hot with sugar in it."

Karen relaxed a little, aware now of his strength and her own disorientation. "Where are we going?" she repeated as they crossed the street and headed into the next block. But they were already at the door to the "Mediterraneum" coffee house. He pushed it open and led her in.

"Sit down here—it's warm, nobody will bother you."

She leaned back in the chair, waiting for the roaring in her ears to go away. Viet Nam . . . she should have known. She had seen that look in her brother's eyes after he came back, until he had married Sophy and taken over the ranch.

Espresso spiced the air; conversations from the tables around her made a soothing background murmur while her mind ranged free. Two tables away a group was arguing politics. Nearer, a pair of voices negotiated what sounded like a drug deal. Lovers whispered across their *cappuchinos* and laughed. Compared to the vision of death that she was only now beginning to comprehend, it was all equally unreal.

Her mind drifted, superimposing the car, the crowd, the driver's face, over the stylized mural of sea waves and gods upon the wall.

"Drink this—"

Obediently Karen opened her mouth, and as the hot coffee

burned down her throat the world came abruptly into focus once more. "Thank you . . . " she muttered in embarrassment.

His black brows twitched in amusement. "What are you ashamed of? I told you—I know the symptoms. Now eat—these are *cafe mochas,* and the thing on the plate is a Viennese torte. Now you can thank me by telling me your name . . . "

"I'm Karen Ingold—" She took another swallow of coffee, feeling the heat expand through her body. He was wearing a scuffed black leather jacket and stained jeans. If she had seen him on the street she would have avoided him, but the stereotype that went with the outfit did not match the face she had seen.

"And I'm Michael Holst. Do you feel better now?" It was amazing how the grimness of his face eased when he smiled.

"Much better—you were right, I needed this."

"You a student?" he asked after a little pause.

"Not exactly. I work in the Comp. Lit. office." Karen sighed, wondering how long it would take them to get through the obligatory exchange. "What about you?"

Michael shook his head. "I quit awhile ago. I write poetry," he added a little defensively.

Karen sought for an appropriate response and found herself blurting, "Good poetry?" instead. "I'm sorry—" She began again, but surprisingly, he was grinning.

"What poet would say no to that? I think so, and every so often some little magazine publishes a poem so I don't entirely lose hope. I do readings sometimes at the Blue Door Coffeehouse down on Shattuck Ave. Poetry night is Thursdays—you should come."

"I'd like to." She returned his smile. She had never thought of poetry as a performing art, but surely the least she could do would be to listen to him read. "What kind of poetry do you write, anyway?"

"Well, it's pretty revolutionary," he said seriously. "I believe that poetry is an oral art, and if people are going to listen to it, then the poet ought to use rhyme and meter and alliteration and any other damn device that will hit the ear. Did you like poetry when you were in school?" Michael's good eye fixed hers.

A little shamefacedly, Karen shook her head. He had all his lines down pat—he must have given this speech many times before—but she had also noticed how the harsh lines in his face were easing as he went on. Whether he was a good poet or not, he was at least a committed one.

Michael nodded. "Don't be ashamed of that—neither did I. And I doubt you'd find three people in this room who did. Well, maybe Julia—" He waved at a woman in a black-and-gold poncho who had just come in, still holding a jar of soap bubbles and a blower in her hand, "But I'll bet you never got to memorize or read it aloud. That's the trouble—the teachers all thought it just had to look pretty on a page, and that free verse was ordained by God at that, and they killed poetry!" He paused, felt inside his jacket and pulled out a pouch of tobacco and a pipe.

"But doesn't rhymed poetry get boring if it's long?" Karen asked. Her own mental muscles were beginning to function again.

"Well, I don't mean you can't use some imagination, although even ballad meter is good for quite a while if you use a variety of rhymes or set it to music. But the world is full of verse forms and rhythms begging to be used. There's one guy who's written poetry to the beat of the dances he saw in India—it's great stuff—you can almost hear the drums!"

Karen laughed. "I *will* have to come listen, then. The last contemporary poetry I heard was a fellow in the Student Union droning on about the war . . . oh, I'm sorry," she added as she saw his face change.

"No. It's all right." Michael drew deeply on the pipe, then let smoke swirl slowly out again. "I didn't think much of the war myself. Though it pisses me off when I hear some guy moaning about Imperialist tyranny who never missed a meal in his life and can't tell Victor Charlie (that's a Viet-Cong) from Charlie Chan!"

He frowned. "I didn't know why we were over there before I went, and after I got there I found out that nobody else knew either! That was the hell of it—we could have won! We had good men; we beat them whenever we really got to fight. But we never knew what we were supposed to be fighting for, and when we did get anywhere, the brass just gave the territory away again!

"I could have declared myself C.O., but nobody could tell me how to get out of it when it was just this one war I didn't believe in. I couldn't swear that I would never fight—I wouldn't mind getting killed if there was ever a cause worth a damn!''

Yes, I believe you—Karen lowered her eyes, remembering the warrior-look on his face as he had pulled her to safety. He had schooled his features now, but the hand that held the bowl of his pipe was white-knuckled with strain. *This* was not a speech that he often gave.

''But that's not what I meant to say,'' Michael went on more easily. ''I know the kind of poetry you mean, 'laundry list poetry' is what we call it at the Blue Door, not that we hear it much there anymore. It kinda got satirized to death, and some of us have been trying to demonstrate what poetry is supposed to be.''

He looked at his watch and then, with an embarrassed grin, at her. ''How are you doing? I don't usually lay all this on someone the first time we meet, especially on someone who's just been, well—''

''Whom you've just saved from a death worse than fate?'' Karen laughed. ''Even if I hadn't been interested, listening to you talk seems a small enough price to pay.''

''I guess I forgot I haven't known you for years. But it's getting late, and you need rest. If you feel up to it, I'll walk you home.''

As Karen followed Michael toward the door, she thought it had been different for her. She knew that she had not met anyone like him before.

4

Treasure, gold on the ground,
May easily madden any man;
Conceal it who will!
                    BEOWULF

Pain of mind and of body can recur as echoes and aftershocks long after the original trauma is past. Karen stood in front of her mirror, brushing her hair, testing her memory of the accident as she would have tried a broken bone to see if it could bear her weight again. At least it had been a distraction. By the time her bruises healed, the pain of losing Roger was dulled as well.

She no longer woke shaking from nightmares in which she saw the car bearing down on her again. But like the itch of a healing wound, the expression on the driver's face still puzzled her. First it had held horror, and then recognition and a maliciously triumphant grin—but it was impossible. She had never seen the man before; the shock of it must have distorted her perceptions. Slowly she drew the brush downward, let the pale silk of her hair swirl around her face again.

"Mrrwirl . . . ?"

In the mirror Karen saw one of the cats sitting in the doorway behind her, still as an amber lioness except for her golden eyes.

"In a minute . . . " she murmured. "I'll feed you as soon as I finish with my hair."

The two cats had been waiting on her doorstep that night when Michael brought her home, and she had given them the mashed meat that had been in her shopping bag. Apparently this was the equivalent of a formal adoption. By the end of the week she had become resigned to being owned.

When Walter gave her a ride home one evening he saw them crouched among the rosebushes and asked their names.

"I don't know—" Karen had replied. "It seemed presumptuous for me to assign them names as if they were kittens. I am sure they have names already, but there's no way to find out what they are."

"Well of course, *all* cats have true-names which they use among themselves and which no human ever knows . . . " he had said, smiling. "But convenience requires use-names as well. It's a pity that none of the surviving literature gives the names of the two cats that drew Freyja's chariot or I would suggest you use those, but you might try, say—*Bÿgul* and *Trjegul*, which would be the Icelandic for Bee-gold and Tree-gold, close enough kennings for honey and amber—the sort of names a Norseman might choose."

"Freyja's cats? Well, that's certainly a compliment! And the names do seem to suit them—" She was still laughing as she got out of the car, and it was not until she was halfway up the stairs that Karen remembered that she had meant to bring down the necklace to give to him.

And that had been the other odd thing about the night of her accident. When she had started to take off the necklace, forgetting that the clasp was jammed, it had come free easily. She supposed her fall must have loosened it somehow, but it still seemed odd. So she had hidden the necklace beneath her summer blouses in the bureau, and somehow she could never seem to remember to take it out to return to Walter.

Her brush caught in a tangle and abruptly she was in the present again. Wincing, she began to separate the fine strands. Her hair had grown past the shoulder-length bob in which she had worn it for several years. She wondered if she should let it grow.

Karen had never had really long hair. When she was a kid on the ranch her mother cut it short for convenience—even when she was in high school and every other girl had straight smooth hair hanging down her back, hers had fluffed around her ears. She remembered how ugly that had made her feel.

And now all the feminists preached that long hair was a sellout to male fantasies. But there was something so luxurious about the silky brush of it against her bare shoulders, and surely it was not wrong to enjoy the sheen of light that rippled across its gold. Could it be permissible to fulfill her own fantasies, and see herself as beautiful?

She was sure that her hair had gotten thicker, too, and that she had gained some weight. Was she getting fat? A new worry—she examined her body anxiously. Her breasts were fuller, and there might be more roundness to her bottom as well, but her waist was still thin—maybe even smaller in contrast.

If this is the real me—she thought, *why should I be ashamed or want to change it?* In all those years of trying to fulfill other people's expectations, she had never dared believe she was an individual with her own distinct and valid personality, or if she were, that anyone could find her very interesting. Yet Roger had left her. She had only herself to please now.

And what did she, the real Karen, want to wear today? The Indian summer weather had ended early; she stared into her closet, looking for a wool skirt to put on, then pulled out the royal blue flared one her mother had given her for Christmas one year—the one she had rarely dared to wear because the color was so commanding. To go with it she found a camel-colored turtle neck jersey, and a paisley scarf with some of the same blue. She pulled on her brown boots, then looked at herself in the mirror again, nodding approval of the image in the glass. That was better—the blue even seemed to deepen the color of her eyes.

Still smiling, she went into the kitchen for breakfast. Býgul followed her and joined Trjegul in front of the refrigerator. They had far too much dignity to yowl for their meal, but it was impossible to ignore those unwinking golden stares. They waited with a royal confidence that they would be served; she would not have dared to disappoint them.

"If I were Freyja, would you pull my chariot?" she asked as she carried her coffee to the table. "Goodness knows you're nearly big enough." Trjegul's tail twitched and Býgul flicked one ear in her direction, but both cats kept their attention firmly on their food. "That's right—" she told them. "Don't forget your priorities."

And what are my priorities? Karen wondered as she sipped

her coffee and gazed across the scrambled rooftops toward the hills. The dry season had bleached the grass to almost the same pale gold as her hair, bright against the loden green of the trees and the clear azure of the sky. She set the cup down, the internal dialogue that had begun before her mirror continuing, *First, I guess, is finding a reason to be alive.*

She considered the idea. She was not depressed, not on a morning when the world shone in the crisp air as if newly crafted by some master artisan. But she remembered how Walter had told her she must make something of her life. *Something worthwhile—not just a way to make a living, even a good one. I want to do something that will matter to the world.*

The cats looked at her curiously as she laughed aloud. Somehow she could not see herself as a campus radical, always about to save the world with the latest cause. She began to sort the stack of mail that littered the kitchen table, setting aside the bills, throwing out the ads, and taking a moment to fill out a contest coupon before she left for work.

The fall semester had started, and in the Comp. Lit. Office the leisurely pace of the summer was a thing of the past. The in-baskets overflowed with assignment sheets and texts to be copied, order forms, memos, and the perpetual scholarly papers.

This semester Karen was serving as a reader for Walter's *Survey of Medieval Literature.* As the carillon of the Campanile finished ringing out the hour, she picked up her notebook and hurried down the hall. She didn't have far to go, for the course was popular enough to require one of the large auditoriums on the first floor. As she turned the corner she could hear Walter's voice through the open doors.

"Although it has been traditional to refer to the early medieval period as the 'Dark Ages,' to those who lived in them, those times did not seem unusually gloomy—in fact they were probably no more filled with wars and disasters than our own. . . . "

The students laughed politely. Karen eased into her seat at the back and fumbled for a pen.

"As in our own times, life in some parts of the world was undoubtedly traumatic, while in others it was relatively prosperous and serene. But this was a period of ferment and change. Populations were shifting, ideas changing even more.

Literacy was more limited than it is now, but there were men, and women too, of intelligence and culture who saw the need to record the transformation going on.

"It is to these individuals that we owe our understanding of the pagan culture that preceded their own, and although their interpretations are filtered through the lens of Christianity, we should be grateful that they preserved anything for us at all." He paused for breath and turned a page in his notes.

"A succession of historians passed the knowledge down. Much of it has been lost, although Jordanes' sixth-century *History of the Goths* preserved some of it. Other writers include Rimbert and Adam of Bremen."

Karen's pen slowed. This was all material he had covered last year, but she had never really wondered about it before. What would it have been like to live in a world where everyone believed in the supernatural, and where, although new gods might war with the old ones and the goddesses be called demons, no one doubted their existence?

In that early period there were still great forests in the land, and many peoples on Europe's frontiers were still frankly pagan, not to mention those ostensibly Christian folk who followed some rather questionable practices at sowing and harvest times. Did they continue those rituals from fear, or had they actually received some benefit from them?

Karen shivered, though the windows were closed, as if the icy darkness of the north were reaching out to her. For a moment she longed for the comforting weight of the golden necklace, and realized with annoyance that once more she had forgotten to bring it in.

That afternoon, Walter surprised her by offering her two tickets to the opera.

"Actually, they belong to Dr. Feruchetti and his wife—but they're out of town. I was going to take a friend from my chamber music group, but I have to pick up the Zellerbach lecturer at the airport. Please take the tickets—when there's a world-class opera company in your town you should not waste any opportunity to hear them."

"But I don't know anyone to go with . . . " Karen saw the disappointment in his face and went on, "What is the opera?"

"It's *Rhinegold*—you know, the beginning of Wagner's Ring Cycle. I've been recommending it to my students, even though Wagner's use of the Norse material reflects nineteenth-century preoccupations, not ninth-century ideas. Still, it should give them a sense of atmosphere and show them that the old myths still have power."

He held out the small envelope, and Karen did not know how to say no. He smiled at her a little shyly then, and adjusted his tie. In the afternoon light his hair looked lighter. She realized that despite his imitation of the hoary professor, all worn tweed and bulging briefcase, he was not really that old. She wondered if the musician he had intended to go with were female.

I'll do it, she decided abruptly, *even if I have to go alone. Maybe I can sell the other ticket at the door.*

But as it happened, there was no need. As Karen was passing the Mediterraneum, someone called her name and she saw Michael Holst standing in the doorway.

Here's a way to repay what he did for me—Karen thought as she turned to him. *I just hope he likes music!*

The bright clarity of the day had dimmed when Michael came for her. Having been warned, Karen was already dressed in pants and a heavy jacket when she heard the roar of his motorcycle outside. She gave the cats a farewell pat, her fingers lingering on their soft fur, and went down the stairs.

The western sky was a clear and warm gold, promising an exquisite sunset, but the wind was chill. Karen was glad she had dressed so warmly. Michael lounged against his bike, waiting for her, a white helmet dangling by its strap from his hand.

"Here—" he said, "put this on."

She looked at his wind-rumpled dark hair. "But isn't this yours? What will you wear?"

"Mine?" He glanced at the helmet and laughed, his face turned slightly toward her so that she saw the glint of amusement in his good eye. "Honey, I haven't worn one of those things since I took my driving test."

Dubiously she put it on, not daring to protest again. The silver ornaments on his leather jacket and the immaculate gunmetal grey enameled and polished steel of the cycle demonstrated that this was not negligence, but disdain. She must go helmeted, if only to proclaim her novice status.

"It's a beautiful machine . . . " she said truthfully, and was rewarded by his smile.

"It's a Harley-Davidson '46 Knucklehead, at least it started out that way. I've rebuilt it a couple of times and made a lot of changes." As if he had pulled a switch somewhere, the words swept on. "These cylinders, for instance, are from a '57 pan-head. The original cylinders have a tendency to go 'bang,' so I re-machined some later ones to fit." Abruptly he stopped.

Karen peered obediently at the gleaming black mass of fins he was indicating, but already the light was too dim to see much detail.

"Never mind—" Michael laughed. "It's too dark to really see. Tonight all that matters is that this baby really goes! Just as well, I guess. If I really got started talking bikes we'd never get across the Bay. If you're interested, sometime we can take an afternoon and I'll show you the works."

Karen nodded. "I'd like that." She realized that it was more than her natural instinct to be agreeable to an attractive man. His words and manner had the exotic flavor of a traveler from another land. Either he was a highly unusual biker, or she was going to have to do some massive revising of stereotypes.

Michael swung onto the bike and kicked it to life while Karen fastened the chin-strap of her helmet and slipped the strap of her canvas bag over her shoulder. There was a question in Michael's eyes, and she explained that she had packed an evening skirt to change into when they arrived.

He nodded. "Have you ever ridden on a bike before?"

Karen shook her head. "But I ride a bicycle, and horses— I've done barrel racing."

"That should help—it's just a matter of balancing. You sit behind me and put your arms around my waist, lean when I do, and *sit still*!"

Karen nodded meekly and settled herself behind him. For a few moments longer he fiddled with the controls like a musician tuning his instrument, until the motor eased down to a steady drum-like beat. Karen felt the hard surfaces of the necklace beneath her scarf, reassuring herself of its security. She had wondered whether she should wear it, but it was Scandinavian, and what could be more appropriate to wear to an opera about the Norse gods?

Michael engaged the clutch smoothly, and they chugged sedately through the quiet streets until they reached the Grove Street entrance to the freeway. Karen instinctively tightened her hold on him as the acceleration thrust her against the padded seat. They swung up the ramp to the freeway, and the loping beat of the motor rose to a full-throated roar of power.

Commuter traffic still clogged the lower span of the Bay Bridge, but on the upper level the road opened before them like the Bifrost Bridge, and the towers of San Francisco were etched like a new Valhalla against a sunset sky. Karen gasped and ducked into the lee of Michael's shoulder as the wind tore her breath away.

The bridge lifted them skyward, or perhaps they really were flying now. Speeding down a hill on a bicycle, urging her horse toward the finish line in a race, she had almost felt such ecstasy, but this was the reality. The metal beast beneath her quivered with power, and sky, the struts of the Bridge, and the cars they passed, went by in a blur of speed.

Traffic began to thicken as they neared the city and Michael throttled down to a slower pace. Catching her breath, Karen glimpsed a shimmer of water, and beyond it the graceful slope of Mount Tamalpais north across the Golden Gate. They curved above the tangled streets through the city and slipped into the slow procession of vehicles leaving the freeway, then chugged toward the Opera House, looking for a parking place. Karen sat back a little, her hands still resting on Michael's waist, sorry that the ride must come to an end.

"I always think I should disapprove—"

Karen leaned forward to hear as Michael waved at the rococco gilt facades of the Opera House and City Hall. "I like clean lines, materials that look like what they are. Ah—there's a spot!"

Karen clutched at him as they swooped toward a space beside a construction building. Then, at last, they were still. Awkwardly she swung off the machine so that Michael could maneuver it into position.

"Yes, but can you imagine San Francisco without those Victorian frills?" Karen picked up the conversation.

"Yeah—I guess it's the Barbary Coast influence. In San Francisco, even decadence has an innocent charm." He thrust his goggles into the pocket of his leather jacket, pulled out a black velvet eyepatch, and slipped it on. He saw her staring at it, and grinned.

"I used to have one embroidered with the Eye of Sauron, but I couldn't find it. Too bad, it would have been appropriate—"

Karen blinked, then remembered that in both Wagner and

Tolkien everyone was fighting over a magic ring, and laughed.

They walked down Van Ness and Karen's stiff muscles began to loosen. A stream of opera-goers were converging from every side, and Karen realized that she had been silly to worry about what she was going to wear. Formal gowns and mink coats or designer jeans and plastic jackets were equally stylish this year.

If I dress up for something like this, it's not just to impress Michael, though I do want him to see me when I'm looking good. . . . I just want to live up to the occasion!

They presented their tickets and passed inside. Karen hurried across the polished marble of the lobby and around the corner to the ladies' room. Ignoring the curious glances of the other women there, she stripped off jacket and trousers and pulled on the jersey evening skirt she had rolled up in her bag. It was navy, and under her jacket she had on a long-sleeved V-necked sweater of navy interwoven with threads of gold. She straightened, turning before the mirror, and twitched the sweater smooth.

She had been right, Karen thought, surveying herself in the glass. The necklace picked up the gleam of gold in the sweater, and the dark color made the gold shine all the brighter. She took out a comb and did her best with her crushed hair, then touched up her lipstick. *But how will I look to Michael?* she wondered, stuffing the discarded pants and jacket into her bag.

The warning gong sounded and she hurried out. Michael had achieved a somber elegance by taking off his jacket to reveal a black turtleneck that matched his black corduroy pants. His only ornament was the belt buckle of heavy silver in the shape of a wolf's head.

His face brightened as he saw her and he held out his hand, and only then was she aware that she had feared he would appear in his usual tattered T-shirt and the two of them would look ridiculous. The second warning sounded. They rushed to find their seats before the theater darkened and the prelude to the opera began.

"The scene opens in the River Rhine . . . IN IT!" The voice of Anna Russell from the record her college roommate used to play echoed absurdly in Karen's memory as the curtain rose. On the insubstantial surface of the scrim a wavering light began to play, forming patterns like those on the undersurface

of a pool. But the depths beyond this play of light were dim, threatening.

Long ago in the dormitory Anna Russell's ribald summary of Wagner's Ring Cycle had left them all gasping with laughter. Karen realized now that although everything she said was (as Russell herself pointed out), all true, it was only part of the reality.

Already the music was drawing her into its flow like a leaf being whirled downstream. Karen knew that the sounds said more than could ever be conveyed by words: *This is a world of magic. . . . Here, all colors are rich, all sounds have an inner harmony, every deed holds a meaning that transcends time. . . . This is a world whose twin faces are terror and joy. .*

Then the growing light revealed the Rhine Maidens, clinging to their rocks above the fitful gleam of their guarded gold. Michael leaned over to mutter appreciatively that they had finally found some sopranos who looked like water nymphs instead of hippopotami, but Karen scarcely heard. She was Elsewhere . . . There . . . on the edge of another world for which she was homesick although she had never been there before. Her eyes stung suddenly with tears.

The dwarf Alberich, renouncing love, made off with the Rhinegold, and the scene shifted to the heavens where the gods were seeking to get out of the contract that made Freyja the fee for the building of Valhalla. But when Freyja herself entered, blonde, pretty, and hysterical, the spell holding Karen for a moment thinned. Walter had once pointed out that in the Eddas, when Loki proposed a similar bargain to get Thor's hammer back from the giants, Freyja had rocked Valhalla with her rage. Who was this vapid blonde?

From that question came another—why was Freyja such a prize? Did the giants have no women of their own? But Freyja's own brother had been entranced by the beauty of a giant-maid. The following scene, in which the gods, with the help of some blue lighting, dwindled and aged because Freyja had been taken from them, suggested an answer. It was not just sex then or even love that Freyja ruled, but some basic vitality for which the gods with all their powers relied on her. The giants were taking her not only from lust, but as a move in the age-long struggle that will end with Ragnarok.

Although *Rhinegold*, as the closest thing to a "short" opera that Wagner ever wrote, was intended to run in a single act, the director had decided to add an intermission between scenes two and three, perhaps so that people could patronize the Irish coffee and champagne stand on the balcony level or the less elegant concessions on the higher floors. Still dazed from the assault upon her senses, Karen wandered out into the lobby, waiting for Michael to return with the Irish coffee he had promised her.

The dazzle of color and the babble of conversation around her seemed less real than the world on the stage. Wagner's melodies haunted her, familiar as if she had grown up with them, although, except for chance selections on the radio, she had never really listened to Wagner before.

"Your necklace is lovely . . ." said a deep voice beside her.

Karen jerked around, saw a big man smiling politely down at her. For one confused moment he seemed to hulk in furs and leather like one of the giants from the opera and she took a panicked step back.

"Please excuse me. I didn't mean to startle you."

Forcing herself back to present reality, Karen realized that the man's size was not really abnormal, and although hair showed on the wrists beneath the cuffs of his shirt, shirt and suit themselves were not only conventional but elegant. She felt herself blushing.

"No—it's all right. Thank you." She found the presence of mind to respond, then smiled briefly and looked away, a maneuver which usually ended conversations with strange men. But this one did not move away. Karen felt the pressure of his presence even without looking at him.

"With gold of such quality and artistry, the necklace could be a part of the Nibelung's hoard. Have you had it long?" he asked pleasantly.

Unwillingly Karen looked at him again, long conditioning keeping her from rudeness. And here, in the middle of the Opera House lobby, what could he do?

"It's an old piece, I believe. From Sweden." Her eyes swept the crowd, seeking Michael.

The man nodded. "A very rare piece. I am rather a connoisseur. Would you consider selling it?"

"What?" Karen looked at him in amazement, suppressing the impulse to explain that it wasn't really hers and that she should not have been wearing it.

"Sell it—" he repeated. He seemed to grow larger as he bent

over her. "I could offer you four thousand for it, or perhaps even five." Gold winked from his smile.

Gold . . . Karen thought wildly. *He wants the Rhinegold . . . he wants the Ring!* Mute, she shook her head.

"A beautiful piece"—he moved closer—"and such a beautiful neck to bear it. Which is worth more, eh, your beauty or your necklace? Which—the goddess or the gold?"

She stared at him. His expression changed from benign interest to a hideous mingling of lust and greed. She took another step backward and found herself pressed against the wall beside the potted palms. The stranger loomed over her.

"I told you, I know old things, and you would not be wearing this around your neck if it had come into the country legally. It belongs in a museum. . . . Do you have the papers to prove it is yours?" He spoke fast and low, and his eyes—somewhere, but it was impossible—she had seen that look before.

Karen shook her head, denying his words, denying him. *Michael . . .* she could make no sound, *Michael, help me!* The world swam around her; Freyja was being carried off by the giants; the floor beneath her shook to their heavy tread.

"But I will help you—if you keep this thing they will find out and take it away. I will give you ten thousand dollars and take the necklace and no one will ever trouble you about it again. You will have money enough for a vault full of jewels!" He reached into his jacket for pen and checkbook.

His momentary distraction released her. Karen took a step to slide past him into the crowd. But as she moved, his hand closed on her arm.

"Where are you going, lovely?" he growled. "Do you think you can walk out on a business deal with me?"

Beyond him Karen saw a dark shape that moved through the crowd like a shark through shoals. *Michael!*

"Karen! I wondered where you'd gone . . . " Michael's pleasant tone did not match the hard glitter in his good eye.

Karen wrenched her arm free and darted to Michael's side, breathing raggedly. His eyes went from her to the other man and he handed her the two Irish coffees. His stance eased toward a crouch, knees bent and hands ready at his sides.

But the stranger's face was emptying. He looked blankly at Karen, then down at the hand that held his checkbook, as if wondering how it came there.

Michael spoke to Karen in a low voice, not taking his eyes off the other man. "What's going on? Was he hassling you?"

Karen knew suddenly that if she said yes, Michael would leap at him instantly. She could see the big man falling, crashing to the floor in the midst of this elegant crowd.

"No . . ." she said quickly. "I'm all right now."

The big man frowned. "I don't understand—did I bump into you?" He shook his head. "Nice talking to you—" he said vaguely and turned away.

Michael straightened and looked after him in disgust, the almost palpable aura of danger that had surrounded him fading away. "Drunk at the opera!" He took his coffee glass from Karen. "I'm sorry I was gone so long. This place sells Irish coffee like beer at a Cycle Rally. *Was* he giving you trouble?" he asked again.

"Yes . . . well, no . . . at least not the way you'd think. He wanted to buy my necklace."

Michael looked at it, nodding as he noted the workmanship, then glanced again in the direction the big man had gone. "It's pretty, sure, but this hardly seems the place or time!"

Karen shrugged and sipped her coffee, grateful for the sweet warmth and the hint of fire as it went down. She shut her lips against the other thought that had come to her—the expression the big man had worn, at the end, had been like that of the man in the car who had tried to run her down. *Paranoia* . . . she thought, *that's what they call it when you think the world is after you—or after your necklace* . . . her inner voice went on. *But why?*

The lights blinked above them. Hastily, she drained her glass and set it down.

Back in her seat, Karen realized she was trembling, and reached for Michael's arm. She felt his glance in the darkness, then he put his arm around her. *What's wrong with me? Whatever it was, it is over now. . . . I'm acting like Wagner's Freyja, not like the real one!* She forced herself to focus on the stage.

Loki was tricking Alberich into demonstrating the Tarnhelm, and as the music grew more sinister, what was intended to be Alberich-transformed-into-a-serpent uncoiled itself above the stage.

"A rope!" whispered Michael. "Look at it! Can't they do better than that? Wagner must be turning in his grave. Why don't they get somebody like George Lucas to stage a production—can you imagine what Lucasfilm could do with this?"

Karen nodded, her awareness split between realization of the silliness of the thing and the conviction conveyed by the magic. Her fascination grew deeper as the deception was completed and Alberich's curse bore its first fruits in the murder of one giant by the other as soon as the Ring was in his hand. Karen shuddered, remembering how the stranger's eyes had gleamed as he looked at her necklace. *Now I would really be worrying,* she thought wryly, *if I had found a golden ring in that chest of Walter's!*

Now the music soared, shimmering and serene. Karen felt the last of her tensions ease. Donner sang his call to the mists, swinging his hammer to make the lightning blink, and at the back of the stage the glimmer of the rainbow bridge to Valhalla began to glow. One by one the gods ascended it, and as they moved onward the glory increased, momentarily transfiguring them. Then they disappeared into the light.

Karen leaned forward, staring at the stage. It was there—if only the mists would part she would see—she knew what was behind the light, as when she rounded the corner of her street she knew what she would see. The light brightened, dazzling her. Then the curtain swung down and it was gone.

As the house lights came on Karen sat back in her seat, blinking, and found that her eyes were wet with tears.

Silently she followed Michael down the stairs to the lobby, reclaimed her bag and went into the ladies' room to change for the ride home. When she came out, Michael was waiting for her, clad in his leather jacket again.

As they walked up the street toward the cycle, he began to whistle something which resolved itself into Donner's "Call to the Mists."

"Oops!" Michael stopped himself. "Better not sing that if we want to stay dry on the way home."

"What?" asked Karen, intrigued out of her abstraction.

"I have it on good authority that they don't do *Rhinegold* anymore in open air theatres like Santa Fe, because every time someone sings the 'Call to the Mists' it pours. Out of a clear sky . . . " he added with a grin. She looked at him dubiously. "Well, why take chances?"

As they started out again Karen found that she was learning to relax on the motorcycle. The passenger seat thrust her against Michael's back, thighs spread, breast pressed against him. Now she found herself enjoying his solidity, reading in the subtle movements of his body the signals for the bike's balancing so that she could match her own responses to his.

It was like riding bareback on a good horse. *It was like making love.* . . . Karen shunted the inner voice away. The vibration transmitted through the cycle from the road was arousing her, but she did not know him well enough, nor did he know her . . . she had no reason to think he would even want . . .

She tried to stiffen again but the wind was singing in her ears and instead she found herself laughing, intoxicated by the swift flight through darkness.

When they reached Karen's flat the cats were waiting for them, sitting on the front steps like two pieces of brass statuary.

"You're well-guarded, I see . . . " said Michael, helping her to dismount.

"I suppose so," Karen said dubiously. Until recently, she had never needed guarding. Was that why they were here? She was still dizzy from the ride; she realized she was clinging to Michael's arm and let go abruptly. Of course—he was joking. She tried to laugh.

"Really, they are quite friendly. If you want to come up for coffee there's no need to be afraid. . . . "

He grinned agreement and followed her up the stairs, pulling apart the heavy snaps that held his leather jacket closed. Karen fumbled with the key, suddenly regretting that she had asked him to come in, trying to remember how much of a mess she had left in the living room.

When the door swung open she flicked on the light, looking around her for a moment with a stranger's eyes. There were white oblongs on the wall where pictures that Roger had chosen for her used to hang, and the bedspread with which she had tried to disguise his favorite chair was wrinkled. *I should do something with this place; make it more my own!* Sighing, she dumped her bag on a chair and went into the kitchen to put the water on.

Michael had stopped in front of the bookcase. Karen could just see him through the open kitchen door. With a kind of detached appreciation she noted the clean lines of his shoulder and back in the tight-fitting jersey, the balanced economy of his movements as he bent to read the titles on the bottom shelf of the bookcase. Her anxiety about him had vanished—now it seemed natural for him to be here.

The kettle began to vibrate and she reached for the cups, but as the first furious whistle burst from its spout Michael reached past her to lift it from the burner and turn off the flame.

His arm went around her. "I don't blame the giants at all. . . . "

Karen tipped her head to look at him and met his kiss, tentative at first, then harder, claiming her. *Yes . . . if he wants me, yes . . .* she thought dazedly, knowing this for the inevitable conclusion to that ride; knowing that from the moment she had invited him upstairs, this was what she had meant to say.

Somehow she was not surprised that he had spotted the door to the bedroom. With their arms still around each other they moved toward it. Awareness of his body overwhelmed her, all the intimations of the ride and the evening together fusing into a single comprehension of strength and suppleness. How sure he was, and how knowledgeable. How deftly his hands moved over her body. His words of passion and reassurance were murmured so low that she could scarcely hear.

But as they stood in front of the bed, embracing and removing their clothing piece by piece, then embracing again, she began to doubt. This room held too many memories.

Am I doing this to prove I don't need Roger anymore, or because I want someone to take his place? she wondered. *Will Michael run my life the way Roger did? I don't want that . . . but we can't stop now. . . . What can I do?*

As if for comfort, her hands went to the necklace she still wore. She opened her eyes and saw herself reflected in the mirror, naked now except for the necklace and her own golden hair. In the dim light her eyes were dark and wondering.

"Oh, God—" came a whisper behind her. "I didn't realize you were so beautiful. What am I doing? I didn't know . . . I didn't know!"

Karen turned. Michael was half-crouched against the bed, staring at her—at her reflection—with his good eye while he covered the scarred remnant of the other with his hand. Startled, she looked into the mirror again.

That is not me. . . .

Glowing in the light of the necklace, Karen saw the image she had seen when first she put it on. Forgetting the man behind her, she lifted her arms in homage.

"Lady . . . " She breathed, "Who are You? What is happening?"

"I am The Lady—" the Voice spoke within her head quite distinctly. *"Do not be afraid."*

Beauty burned upon the air . . . bright hair that made an aureole . . . breasts whose perfect curves were equalled only by the flowing line from waist to thigh and the mystery hidden by Her triangle of gold.

Then Self and Other merged and with a single will held out Her hand.

"I must not dare—I am maimed, and you are too beautiful." Michael said in a low voice, beginning to back away.

"You are My warrior and My Chosen One. Come to Me!" She commanded. Her hands reached out to bless his bent head, and with a shuddering sob he came to Her, kneeling, and hiding his head against Her thighs.

After a little while Karen moved her hands to his shoulders and raised him, and seeing his image in the mirror knew that he had changed as well. He stood erect now and powerful—more powerful than he had seemed when he was ready to defend her, because now all his force was focused to a single goal. If she was a goddess, now he was a god. With a triumphant smile, She let Him lift Her to the bed.

And after that there was no need for worry or for wondering, for both of them were kindled by a single flame.

5

*The fourteenth (spell) I know, if to folk I shall
    sing and say of the gods:
Aesir and alfs know I altogether—
    of unlearned, few have that lore.*
                    THE SAYINGS OF HAR

Karen turned over in bed, stretched luxuriously, and opened
her eyes. Why hadn't the alarm gone off? Oh, of course. It
was Saturday, and . . . there in the bed beside her, Michael was
still sleeping peacefully. She raised herself on one elbow, considering him, remembering the night before.

At their first climax he had sobbed aloud, and afterward
wept quietly in her arms. And she had been so grateful for the
gift of his passion that she supposed she had been crying too.
Whatever the future might hold, now she had proof that
Roger had not left her because she had lost her attractiveness,
nor was he the only man who could wake her passions.

Although, she realized suddenly, it had not been entirely
she, Karen, who was being loved. She touched her neck, remembering the odd fancy that Someone Else had been there
too, shining through her body like a candle through a lantern
shade.

Michael stirred and murmured something in his sleep.
Quickly Karen fumbled with the catch of the golden necklace
and drew it off, then dropped it into the drawer of the bedside
table. Maybe she should find out what he thought of her

without the glamour of the necklace, now, before they were both deceived.

Trjegul padded across the floor, leaped lightly to the window ledge and began systematically to wash. Karen lay back in the bed, eyes half-focused on the cat's rhythmic movements, her mind following strange by-ways of speculation.

*It's the necklace. . . . Either I'm crazy, or that piece of jewelry is distinctly strange—at least when I'm wearing it strange things happen—the near accident with the car, and the man at the opera last night. Not that the things are always bad ones—*she reminded herself, remembering again the joy of Michael's body against hers.

Something teased at her memory, some reference to a famous necklace that she had read or heard. It was gold . . . for a moment she almost remembered, then lost it again. *Never mind,* she thought then, *Walter will know. I can ask him when I go into work Monday.*

Michael muttered again and flung out an arm. Smiling, Karen moved his hand to rest on her breast. In the morning light she could see the tattoo of a grinning skull crowned with flames on his forearm, and on the right side of his neck and shoulder a tracery of silvery scars. Even the flesh was uneven there, despite what had obviously been some elaborate surgery. That must have come from the same explosion that destroyed his eye.

Then she realized that the hand lying on her breast was no longer relaxed. She held her breath as Michael began to slide the work-roughened palm of his hand across her nipple until it hardened, still without opening his eyes. Then the hand slid across her body, drawing her to him, and she realized that he had grown hard as well.

"Ummm?"

Karen bent her head to kiss him and lifted the covers away so that their bodies could align more closely. "Good morning."

"So it was real. . . . " He slipped his hand down her back until it cupped the curve of her buttock and pulled her against him. She giggled and kissed him again.

"Better make sure."

Yes—thought Karen as he began to make love to her. *I too want this to be real.* On the window ledge, Trjegul finished washing and settled into a patient crouch, dozing in the sun.

It was nearly noon before Karen and Michael got out of bed at last. Karen started the eggs and found some bacon to fry while Michael showered and the cats paced hopefully behind her. By the time he was dressed, breakfast was ready. Karen pulled out one or two tag ends of bacon and added them to the cat food on the back porch.

"—Only way to get them out of the kitchen—" she said, bringing the coffee over to the table and sitting down.

"At least they didn't get into bed with us," observed Michael. "Thank God—those are pretty well-grown specimens."

"Oh, they are far too dignified to get involved." She repressed a reminiscent smile. "Although a friend of mine once had a cat who thought that anything moving under the covers was fair game—*anything*! And when her boyfriend moved in . . . well, anyway, she doesn't have a cat anymore."

"I had dogs when I was a kid—two big brutes that were mostly shepherd with some husky mixed in. I think they decided I was their pack leader, at least I never had any trouble with them, but they weren't as tolerant of other people as your brass lionesses there. . . . " He shook his head, his face darkened by some memory. "When I went into the Army they had to be put away."

"I'm sorry—" Karen began, but he was already smoothing the emotion away. She wanted to tell him it was all right—he didn't have to keep his armor on with her—but she could find no words. The mark of pain between his brows, the bitter lines at his mouth that disappeared into his short beard, had not been put there in a day. Perhaps he had good reasons to maintain his defenses. Only, she remembered his face alive with delight, or open and innocent as that of a boy. *Whatever he says, whatever he does*—she told herself, *I will remember that*.

"That reminds me," he said after a moment. "I've got an invitation from an old Army buddy to see his show at the Flamingo Dancer in San Francisco. It's a nightclub—you know, a sort of cross between Finochio's and the Hungry 'I'—and not quite my usual routine, but it might be interesting. Want to go with me?"

"I guess so—" she answered. "When does it happen, and what kind of show does your friend do?"

"It'll be about two weeks from now, the last Friday of the month." Michael finished his coffee and held out his cup for more. "And actually I'm not sure what the show will be. Duncan's always been a little weird. Over in 'Nam he kept the rest of us going, sometimes, you know—he could always come up with a practical joke or some kind of song. He was into card tricks and juggling and stuff too.

"Of course it was mostly what you'd call 'black humor' . . . well, I guess we were all into black humor over there—fun and games wouldn't have made much sense somehow. I remember one night-attack on a village when we sent out two guys to reconnoitre—Peters and Andreotti, they were—and only Andreotti came back. When we asked him if the Charlies were in the village he said he didn't know, but their fireworks were there . . . and then he dropped his hands and we saw the burns—"

Michael's spoon swirled the black coffee in precise, mechanical strokes while his single eye stared through Karen to some tortured landscape of memory. "And we laughed—" he continued more slowly then. "We went in there and burned the village out, and we were still laughing when we marched out again. . . .

"Anyway—" Michael pulled himself together, drank half the cup in one swallow, and put it down. "We thought Duncan's gags were pretty funny at the time. He used to go around with the Viet Namese holy men too—learning new tricks, he said. But in some ways I think he hated what was going on—what we were doing, even more than the rest of us. . . ."

Karen watched him, but there was nothing she could say. She had just started high school when the war ended. She had been in one protest march, she remembered—just one, and the whole time she had been afraid. Michael was only seven years older than she was, but they were years that held experiences she could never share.

On the back porch the cats were meowing with a nerve-scraping monotony. Karen got up to let them in and when she came back Michael was smiling again. She smoothed back the lock of dark hair that hung over his brow, at once relieved that his mood had lightened, and sorry the moment of revelation was done.

"Well, I'm glad you'll come with me to see Duncan." He reached up to capture her hand, drew it down to kiss the palm and let her go. "I promised a guy I'll help him strip down his bike today, but tomorrow's free. Can I see you then? Want to go for a ride?"

"I would like that." Karen returned his smile, her heart soaring with the realization that this was not going to be a one-night stand, that things were going to be all right now.

When Michael had gone she sat for a while at the kitchen table, gazing vacantly out at the hills and drinking coffee without noticing it had gotten cold. Ideas moved dimly in her mind. Her fingers prickled with an energy she had almost forgotten. When she was growing up she had been so much alone she had never depended on others for amusement— there had always been some project: refinishing furniture, needlework, building toys for her brothers' kids—she had even tried weaving once with homespun yarn.

Karen stretched out her hands, flexing them, wondering if they had lost their old skill. *I feel as if I have been recharged!* The image brought back thoughts of the night just past and she felt herself blushing. Did Michael feel the same energy that pushed her to her feet and moved her restlessly into the living room?

She remembered how dingy the flat had seemed when she opened the door. *It needs brightening up—pictures or something to make it look new.* Now she saw the furniture around her with a different eye, calculating proportions and light sources, searching for the "look" that would complement the varnished redwood paneling and bring out the potential beauty of the room.

Karen moved swiftly back to the bedroom and began to pull on clothes, then found her car keys and headed downtown.

By the time she returned, some hours later, she remembered something else about this kind of project. It was hard to stop. But the day was so beautiful; everywhere she looked she saw colors and textures she wanted to make her own. It was as if a veil had been drawn to reveal a new country around her, or as if she herself had learned to see anew.

It took two trips to bring everything upstairs. Then Karen sat down in the middle of the room with her purchases spread around her, trying to get her breath again. The walls of the living room were grimy as well as bare, so there was a half-gallon of celestial azure paint among her packages and some off-white for the ceiling. To cover the big armchair she had bought a semi-fitted cover of tawny gold plush, and assorted remnants of upholstery fabric, loosely woven in combinations of blue and green and rusty browns and gold, to cover her throw pillows.

"Earth colors . . . that's what they are." Karen told herself as she looked at the pieces of fabric spread out around her. With relief she realized that the muted browns of the rug that had come with the apartment would harmonize nicely.

Carefully she unwrapped her one real extravagance, a large stoneware bowl glazed in swathes of blue and green. And at that, twenty dollars was hardly extravagant for something so beautiful. There had been other things she wanted, of course, especially a wonderful cloak handwoven in shades of blue, but by then the balance in her checkbook was dwindling fast and she forced herself to turn away.

She cleared the mess off the deep ledge before the front window, dug out a sisal placemat, and set the bowl upon it where the morning sunlight would set the glaze aglow. The curtains were dingy too, and she pulled them down, for her packages contained two lengths of a fabric striped unevenly in turquoise and azure and green with a hint of gold that looked as if it had come off of some peasant-woman's loom. About half an hour with the sewing machine would give her new curtains to replace the old.

She should have plants too, though she had never had much luck with them. But now she could almost see them hanging by the window with sunlight glowing through their leaves—ferns and trailing vines, herbs—she could smell the bitter perfume of fertile soil.

Pictures would take longer to find, but she had bought one, an enlarged print of one of Arthur Rackham's illustrations to Wagner's *Ring* cycle which she had bought to remind her of last night's opera. It showed the three Norns spinning out men's fates on a craggy height, bare sky above them, mountains and forests falling away below, the colors almost transparent in the clear Northern air. Those colors and that air . . . a memory stirred of trees in the sunlight and women's voices raised in song. She had been there—she remembered—but that was impossible. It must have been a dream.

Carefully she eased the print into a frame. "Oh, you who spin the futures of women and men, spin a good one for me!" she murmured as it slipped into place. Then she bent down the nails to hold it and after careful considerations found a place for it on the wall.

She spent the afternoon painting, and by evening she was working on curtains and pillow covers. By the time Michael came for her on Sunday it was almost all done, and she was able to tear herself away and enjoy the run on the cycle he had promised her.

He took her up to Tilden Park in the hills behind Berkeley, racing along the narrow roads until she was drunk on rushing trees and blue skies and wind. Afterward they stopped at the Station, a little hamburger place that slathered the burgers with mushrooms and guacamole, then went back to her flat to make love.

When Karen got back to work on Monday morning, she felt ready to take on the world. Fortunately—for with the fall semester in full swing the office was a madhouse of class descriptions, class lists, waiting lists, and requests for changes. Between students with registration questions for her, and students wanting advice from Dr. Klein, it was Tuesday afternoon before Karen had a chance to talk to him.

"Walter, the ASUC bookstore says they've called New York and the copies of the *Volsunga Saga* you ordered are on the way."

"I don't suppose they said when they mailed them?" He continued to shuffle through a folder of lecture notes.

"Are you kidding? That would be giving state secrets away." She looked around and saw that no one was waiting. "Walter . . . I've got what may seem like a silly question."

"As long as it's not about class lists—" He looked up then and smiled.

"It's about necklaces."

"Has something happened to the one you found in my Swedish chest?" he asked. "Speaking of which, why don't you come on into my office and I'll give you the rest of that bibliography. . . . "

Karen followed him down the hall, her eyes seeking the chest as now they always did as soon as she entered that room. When she had finished repairing it, she had cleaned and polished it with lemon oil until it shone. Dr. Freiborg had been right—it did indeed lend the office a touch of class, almost transcending the worn linoleum.

"No—the necklace is fine. Did I tell you that someone tried to buy it from me at the Opera?" Karen sat down.

Walter turned abruptly, his long fingers poised on the handle to the filing cabinet. "You're not asking me to take it back, are you?" he asked suspiciously. After several weeks of argument, Karen had reluctantly agreed to keep it, still unable to decide whether the gift showed Walter's generosity or his dislike of being bothered.

"No, Walter," she sighed. "I've had it too long—I would find it very hard to give it up now. But it has got me interested in Norse mythology again, and I have a feeling there's some famous necklace in the legends that I should remember. Were there any necklaces in with the Nibelungs' gold?"

"Probably, but none that are named. The only necklace I know of is *Brisingamen*, the one that Freyja got from the dwarves."

"Freyja and the seven dwarves?" Karen laughed.

"Well, actually there were only four of them, though it does make one wonder!"

"Can I look it up in Snorri's *Younger Edda* or something?"

"No, although there are references to Brisingamen throughout the legends—even in *Beowulf*. But the only place that tells how Freyja got it is in the *Sorla Thattr*. William Morris translated it in *The Tale of Hogni and Hedinn*—that's in *Three Northern Love Stories*. I can give you the gist of it—"

"If you're going to lecture, I want some coffee," Karen interrupted. "What about you?" He nodded, and she took his cup back to the Department Office to fill, along with her own.

"Fortunately, the story's fairly short—" he said as she came back in. "I have a conference at four." He sipped at the coffee and put it down on his scarred desk. Repressing an impulse to take notes, Karen began to drink her own.

"There is not much information on what Freyja did before she got Brisingamen, although the mysterious goddess 'Gullveig' who upset the Aesir with her sorcery and started the war between them and the Vanir is generally considered to be one of her aspects. At any rate, Freyja was one of the hostages sent by the Vanir to seal the alliance, and she soon became Odin's mistress and instructor in witchcraft as well. It was only later that both of them began to wander the world, having affairs with all and sundry.

"In any case, one day Freyja saw four dwarves forging a marvelous necklace of gold. Naturally she wanted it, and as a goddess who could weep tears of gold she had plenty of money. But the only thing that interested the dwarves was Freyja herself, and the only price they would accept was a night each in her bed."

"The lady certainly got around . . . " said Karen dryly.

"Apparently. At least in the *Flyting of Loki* he taunts her—

> *Hush thee, Freyja, I full well know thee:*
> *All Aesir and alfs within this hall*
> *Thou hast lured to love with thee.*

She was the Aphrodite of Asgard, you might say."

In the other office a phone began to ring. They fell silent, listening, but Micaela answered it and Walter went on. "Anyway, Loki told Odin about the necklace and how Freyja had acquired it, and Odin told Loki to steal it from her. Through some complicated shape-shifting, Loki was able to do so. The *Sǫrla Thattr* version says that Odin would only return the necklace on condition that Freyja set two kings against each other in eternal combat—a reference to her function as a war goddess there. According to Snorri, on the other hand, the god Heimdall went after Loki. The two of them fought it out in the form of seals and Heimdall won and returned the necklace to Freyja."

"Why did Odin want it? Was it just sour grapes and jealousy?"

"Karen, nobody ever worries about the *motives* of the gods. They are like natural forces, and their ways are beyond the understanding of men. But I have always thought that Brisingamen must have had more than beauty. Unfortunately the poets were most interested in Odin, who after all was the poet's god. We know more about Freyja than about any of the other goddesses, but that's little enough. Whatever her priests and priestesses may have known, they didn't write down."

"But do the stories say what the necklace looked like?" persisted Karen.

"Not really. It was made of gold, and it was a collar or necklace with pieces and a clasp. If it was like other Viking jewelry I've seen it might have consisted of pendants and hollow beads—"

"Like the necklace in your chest." Karen said softly. She had thought the golden necklace worthy of a Queen. But worthy of a goddess? *Don't be ridiculous!*

"I suppose so. It seemed like typical work. But we don't really know." He finished his coffee and began to gather up papers.

"What else do you know about Freyja?" she asked eagerly.

"Karen, have a heart! It has been a long time since I tried to memorize the *Voluspa*! Here—" He pulled a tattered volume from his bookcase and handed it across the desk. "Here's a fairly readable translation of both the *Elder Edda* and Snorri's collection. That's the basic source—read it for yourself!"

"I'm sorry, Walter." She hugged the book to her breast, thinking of the necklace reposing innocently in her drawer at home. "It's just that if I'm going to have fantasies about that necklace, I'd rather they were authentic ones!"

"Oh, Karen." He shook his head, laughing. "You've been around this place too long."

"Don't complain." she replied, standing up. "At least my mind is working again!"

And my body, she thought as she strode down the hallway, *and my heart . . . surely that's excuse enough for a few odd fantasies!*

6

*Art mindful, Odin, how in olden days
we blended our blood together?
Thou said'st that not ever thou ale wouldst drink
but to us both it were borne.*

LOKASENNA

"Michael—look! Flamingo Dancers!" Karen tugged at Michael's arm and pointed at the neon sign flickering above them. Shocking pink flamingoes entwined in an endless tango surrounded by a border of glowing palm leaves. Bemused birds and the flowing script of the club's name alternated in syncopated harmony.

Michael zipped his gloves into the pocket of his jacket and grimaced. Three punkers rigged out in purple plastic and safety pins sauntered toward them, expecting them to step out of the way, then took in Michael's worn engineer boots and leather jacket and stepped awkwardly aside.

Karen suppressed a grin as Michael steered her to the door. Flames screamed from a black background on the poster beside it—*"DUNCAN FLYTE: MASTER OF MAGIC!"*, it proclaimed. She peered at the photo, glimpsed a narrow mischievous face whose contours seemed to change with every shift of light. They had come to the right place, but she would not have wanted to come here alone.

Michael muttered their names to the doorman. They passed inside, feeling the vibration of amped music through the tiled

floor even before it hit their ears. Karen looked down, wondering whether the obscenity of the designs on the tiles came
only from her own pre-conditioned perceptions. Blushing, she
forced her gaze back to the potted palms, the Art Deco mold-
ings of the shadowed ceiling, the screens of gilded bamboo.

*It's like something the presidente of a banana republic
might have built for his current light-of-love*, she thought as
she handed her jacket to the checker. She took a deep breath
and straightened her necklace. She had been uncertain about
wearing it, but the more Norse mythology she read, the more
natural it seemed to put it on. Her neck felt naked without it,
now.

Michael beckoned and she followed him past the last of the
potted palms; the door opened, and sound stunned her—onstage a girl in a purple sequined gown wailed something inar-
ticulate and interminable as she writhed beneath a blue light.
The hostess had on a blue dress splashed with yellow hibiscus
that matched her poufed hair. She escorted them to a marble-
topped table near the front with a gilt "Reserved" sign, murmured confidingly into Michael's ear and gazed at him soul-
fully as he replied.

He grinned as he met Karen's stare. "They must like old
Duncan a lot—the first round is on the house. What will you
have?"

In homage to the spirit of the place Karen ordered a *Piña
Colada*, then settled back to watch the singer, since she still
could not understand the song. With a little shock she realized
that although the performer's gown clung to a nicely curved
figure, the forearms were unusually muscular and the hips
rather slim, and that, in fact, the husky voice belonged to a
man.

Startled, she looked around her. The couple at the next
table appeared to be straight, with the self-conscious glossi-
ness of Marin socialites having a night on the town; but
beyond them two men gazed passionately into each other's
eyes, and on the other side was a couple dressed alike, with
cropped bleached hair streaked with orange and blue, whose
sex she could not determine.

Michael laughed at her expression. "Does it bother you?"

"No . . . " After a moment of thought Karen said,
"Although I suppose it should—I was just surprised."

Michael shook his head. "Should!" he exclaimed. "What a

lot that word has to answer for. Do things because they're right, or because you have to, but never because you think you *should*!" He took a long pull of beer.

Karen frowned. At least she was not the kind of woman who kept getting involved with the same sort of man. For Roger, everything had been a question of "should." But what *should* one do while waiting for desire or necessity to point the way?

The singer finished and bowed, showing a degree of cleavage which in the circumstances was startling. A waiter in a red jacket with gilded buttons took Michael's empty glass, assessed the level of Karen's, and brought them more.

The necklace clinked as Karen turned her head, and she realized that the study of Scandinavian myth and legend *had* compelled her. Suddenly, although the presence of so many bodies made the club uncomfortably warm, she was shivering.

"Because you *have* to?" she said slowly. "But where does the compulsion come from, Michael? Is the driving force something inside you or does it come from somewhere else? How can you tell?"

Michael looked up from his drink, his good eye glittering in the shifting light. "Maybe that means I'm some kind of fatalist, but I've always felt that if something was strong enough to compel me, it was worth being obeyed."

"Like the Army?" The words were out before Karen could reject them. She gazed at Michael apprehensively.

His face darkened; for a moment he was still. "At first, maybe. I was from the Midwest, you know, and where I came from everyone thought that any war we were in must be right. I wouldn't have known how to get out of the draft if I had wanted to. But later . . . when we realized what was going on . . . there was a change. We were there; we couldn't get home; but I don't think you could say we exactly *obeyed*." He smiled, not too pleasantly. His hand rubbed his wounded eye as if to soothe a vanished pain.

"Duncan was there—" he went on. "I wonder what he would say—" His gaze sought the empty stage.

Around them, the volume of conversation rose as patrons tried to drown out the between-act disco music. She and Michael would be screaming soon if they tried to talk more. She laid her hand lightly on his and smiled at him, and after a moment his frown eased.

Karen sighed and for the first time really began to look at the room. The theme of the foyer had been continued, with palms along the walls, interspersed with rubber plants and banana trees that looked as if they harbored tarantulas. Tawdry prints vied with the tarnished elegance of the walls. Overhead a brass and mahogany fan turned lazily. At the back of the room a magnificent bar with brass fittings had been installed.

Brass sparkled and faded as the lights dimmed and the music ebbed away. The bas-reliefs of coupling flamingoes in the alcoves to either side of the stage were the last to disappear, glimmering eerily when all else was in shadow. For a moment the murmur of conversation swelled, then it too died away.

The thin treble of a flute challenged the silence, wandering like a lost soul up and down the scale. Then Karen glimpsed a movement of light from the stage—a glowing blue sphere that soared and fell and soared again, was joined by another, and another, and more, until eight globes were swirling in a pattern that dizzied the eye.

While the balls of light swooped and twirled the flute faded, to be replaced by a voice, thin, high, almost sexless as it was apparently bodiless, that echoed the flute's melody, then resolved itself into words. Fascinated, Karen watched the lights perform their ever-changing dance as she listened to the song.

> *In the darkness of the night,*
> *In the brightness of the day,*
> *Light and shadow interact;*
> *I dance in their interplay—*
> *For I . . . am the . . . magician . . .*
>
> *Open-eyed you see me not,*
> *Close your eyes and I am there—*
> *Illusion or reality?*
> *You must choose well, or else beware!*
> *For I . . . am the . . . magician . . .*

One of the balls disappeared and was replaced by something that flashed and glittered through the air. Was it a knife? Before Karen could tell, other items began to appear. A dim red light was growing, and she saw that the balls had been

replaced by a rose, an apple, a sickle, a goblet, and a small
skull.

The light grew stronger. The voice of the singer was supported by the dull throb of a drum. Now the light was pulsing
in many-colored flashes that painted upon the face of the juggler myriad masks.

> *Life and death spin in my hands,*
> *For good or evil what care I?*
> *Only the juggler understands*
> *How the spheres of fortune fly . . .*
> *For I . . . am the . . . magician . . .*

Now the lights were changing too swiftly to identify them,
and a full rock band was making the music. The items being
juggled flashed and sparkled dizzyingly in the changing lights
until not only their positions but their forms seemed to
change. Was that a knife or a bloody sword, a rose or a fluttering butterfly, an apple or a human heart? Volume and pace
of the music and the spinning dance increased.

> *The world will end in fire and ice,*
> *As Life and Death and Nought I roll,*
> *For I play with the Devil's dice—*
> *You hear my laughter in your soul,*
> *For I . . . am the . . . magician . . .*

The music stampeded to a screaming conclusion. Objects
rained through the lights, surely more things than the juggler
had ever put into the air. But he caught each one deftly and
popped it into a black velvet bag. Manic laughter echoed the
music's last wail.

When the air was empty and the music had whispered to silence, the lights resolved to a steady orange glow. The juggler
moved to the front of the stage, his teeth flashed in a wide grin
and his long arms lifted in the gesture of one who accepts
homage. After a moment of stunned silence, the audience
began to stamp and cheer.

Michael swore softly. "Duncan was always pretty good, but
where did he learn to do that?"

"It was certainly a production!" whispered Karen. Now
that the light had calmed down she could see that the juggler

was thin and agile, as if he had been constructed from steel wires, with a shock of reddish hair and glittering dark eyes.

He wore an open caftan of black velvet embroidered with arcane symbols in gold, and beneath it a red satin shirt and trousers with a golden sash. There was a red-and-gold banner on the wall behind him, proclaiming him as "Maestro Duncan Flyte," above the symbol of a skull crowned by flames. Two androgynous assistants in red leotards dusted with gold sequins were wheeling a large box onto the stage.

"Ladies and gentlemen, I welcome you." Duncan's voice was surprisingly rich to come from so thin a frame. "And . . . " he surveyed the mixed crowd sardonically, "gentle ladies and lay-men and all those of you who fall somewhere in between!" As someone started to protest, he smiled and held up one slim hand. "Now, now, no need to be upset—you can be sure that when I mean to insult you there will be no uncertainty! But I meant no derogation . . . this time. As a magician, I thrive on ambiguity. Like you, I live between the worlds, and illusion is my trade!"

He began to walk back and forth along the stage. Reaching into his sleeve, he drew out a red silk scarf which extended as he pulled until he held it at arms' length. A quick motion crushed the material between his hands. When he opened them again a red rose lay there.

"Now you see it, now you don't!" His hands flickered and the flower was a length of silk once more. He continued to play and the cloth assumed a variety of forms. "You have come here to see me do magic," he said. "Rabbits from a hat and card tricks and that sort of thing. And so you will, and more skillfully done than you can imagine.

"But magic is more than mere tricks. Magic is the great transformation. You look and look again and everything has changed . . . but is it the world that has changed or is it you? Be patient, my children, for just a little while, and you shall see. . . . "

He tossed the scarlet silk into the air, and it swirled and winked out like a puff of flame. He motioned sharply. His assistants wheeled forward the box. A roll of drums thundered and died. The guitar picked up the beat with a dancing sort of rhythm and the flute began a minor melody.

The box came to a halt at the front of the stage. The magician unlatched its door, flung it open, then pushed the case this way and that so that everyone could see the empty space within. Suddenly his hand closed on the shoulder of one of his assistants and he pushed him toward the gaping door. For a moment the young man appeared to struggle, then Duncan snapped his fingers and all tension drained from his frame. At a nearby table, someone made a low, satisfied sound deep in his throat. The magician pushed his unresisting victim inside, and snapped shut the door.

Karen had seen this sort of thing on television. She was even familiar with the basic principles by which the trick was done. So why did she feel the ache of tension in her belly and behind her eyes?

Now the magician picked up a large cloth of purple velvet and threw it over the box. He turned it and turned it again until it was hard to remember where the opening had been, then let it come to rest and stepped away. With a theatrical gesture that mocked itself, he raised his wand.

"Lords of Chaos and Chance and Change, translate to another sphere the mortal I have offered you—that soul who is imprisoned *here!*" He struck the box with the wand and there was a flash of light. For a moment Karen felt the floor tremble, and wondered how *that* effect had been achieved. From inside the box came a faint cry.

The magician turned the box around, twitched the covering cloth away, and opened the door. As Karen had expected, there was nothing there. Everyone clapped loudly, enjoying Duncan's presentation, even though the trick was a standard of the repertoire.

Duncan turned to the audience with a strange smile. "It is easy enough to send a man to the other realms, just as it is easy to take a life away. . . . If any of you have been to war, even though you may repress the memory, in your soul you understand that a man's life is a very fragile thing. . . . " His eyes moved across the audience, holding as someone coughed uncomfortably or flushed with anger.

Michael stiffened. "Damn him—what's he doing?" He straightened as he met the magician's stare. For a moment Duncan held his gaze, then his smile became almost wistful and he turned to the box again.

"Let us see if my powers are sufficient to recall the one I have sent away!" He stepped to the box, covered it, spun it around. "Lords of Chaos and Chance and Change, send back to this earthly plane, the creature that I gave to you—send his true form home again!''

Once more light flashed as he struck the box. Then he drew back the cloth and opened the door. There was a gasp and then a ripple of laughter as a monkey dressed in a red leotard jumped out and leaped chittering into Duncan's arms.

"Oh dear . . . '' said Duncan in an aggrieved tone. "I'm afraid I must have been too literal. You must be careful with magic, you know, for what you ask for is what you will get—*precisely* what you ask for. . . . '' He spoke soothingly to the monkey, which relaxed its stranglehold and climbed onto his shoulder, where it perched, surveying the crowd with bright dark eyes.

"Well, well, and what shall we do with you? Do you like being a monkey? You know it's going to be very hard to change you into a man—and are you sure that's what you want to be? Consider unemployment, war, faithless women . . . the human condition is not a very happy one.''

Karen saw no signal, but the monkey turned to Duncan and chittered excitedly.

"Well, then I'll put it to the audience—after all, to please them is our purpose here. What do you say?'' Duncan turned to the crowd and held out his hand. "Shall I change him back?''

"Yes— No—'' the room erupted into ribald shouts and laughter. "He'll be happier as a monkey!'' someone cried. "No, no, bring him back—he had a hot ass!''

"Satan! You're a demon . . . get behind . . . Devil!'' a slurred voice muttered nearby. Karen looked around and saw a young man with glazed eyes trying to make the Sign of the Cross.

Duncan stiffened and his voice cut like a knife. "Satan? Oh no, I am not he. . . . There is no Devil—didn't you know? Men are the only demons in this world! I serve the powers of change that bring all things to an end, but I am only an intermediary!''

"And I serve the powers of change that bring all things to birth. . . . '' It was a woman's voice, and Karen had twisted her head around to see before she realized that she had not heard the words with her physical ears. The necklace seemed unusually warm and she lifted it away from her neck uncomfortably. What was going on?

Michael was sitting with his head resting on his joined hands, frowning. Duncan saw him, shook his head a little, then laughed.

"Well, my friend," he told the monkey, "I suppose we shall have to do something for you. The world is full of unbelievers, and it would be hard to explain where you had gone." He patted the animal, then opened the door to the box and pushed it in. Carefully he adjusted the drape.

"Powers of Chaos and Chance and Change . . . " he intoned a third time, facing the back of the room with lifted arms. "When again I touch this door, let the one I sent to you return, in just the form he wore before!" He bent to the box and appeared to listen. "I don't believe it is working—I'll need help this time. . . . "

All expression left his face. He turned to the northern corner of the room. "Powers of the North, I conjure you, strengthen me!" He waited a moment, and then, clear and high-pitched, another voice responded from the corner of the room. "Master, we hear and obey."

With a short nod, the magician turned to the East. "Powers of the East, I conjure you, inspire my words!" and again the voice replied. To the South and the West Duncan repeated the ritual, and the eerie voices answered him.

"Ventriloquism . . . " whispered someone, and Karen supposed they were right, yet still even the listening made her feel as if she had touched something unclean.

Duncan turned again to the box and appeared to whisper to whatever was inside. Then he stepped back, pulled off the cover, and struck the box with such force that the wand shattered in his hand.

Then he opened the door.

Looking rather dazed, his assistant climbed out of the box. There was a murmur of surprise, and Karen realized that now the leotard the man was wearing was blue.

"Well, well—" Duncan surveyed him, head cocked to one side. "I suppose we can't have everything. I wonder if he really is the same? How do you feel?"

The young man grinned sheepishly and Duncan patted him on the back. "All right, I daresay you will be feeling more yourself soon. You have had quite an experience!" He nodded dismissal and the two assistants, one still in red and the other in blue, trundled the box offstage.

Wondering, Karen took another long swallow of her drink. The monkey had seemed more alert than the man. For a moment her mind played with dark notions of transposition and sorcery. Then she smiled. The act must be successful if it could give her such fancies. Duncan Flyte was only a stage magician after all, and a friend of Michael's at that.

For a time she lost track of what was going on in front of her. She was watching Michael. His face was turned toward the stage, but by now she knew the tilt of his head and the set of his shoulders as she knew his prowling walk, and the contours of his body and the way he made love. Was he the one she had been waiting for?

They were good in bed together, though the act had never again been so ecstatic as the first time. They were good companions at other times as well, and Michael was introducing her to a world she had never known. Memories of Roger were fading like the twinges of a half-forgotten injury.

And yet Karen had no sense of having achieved her destiny. Perhaps Michael was not "Mr. Right" after all, or her experience with Roger might have made her over-cautious. Or perhaps she simply did not want to give up her new sovereignty.

She fingered the necklace again. When she wore it her senses seemed heightened. She was almost painfully aware of the beauty around her, of the pulse of life itself. *The necklace has become my symbol for the new life I'm making, and the new person I want to be....*

Onstage, the magician was performing a seemingly endless sequence of sleight-of-hand transformations—a scarf became a flower which disappeared into an egg which shattered to reveal a fluttering dove which compressed, became a butterfly, was caught, twirled, and turned into a scarf once more. With the tricks came an endless stream of patter—bright and amusing, but with an undertone of malice, or perhaps it was despair.

Duncan finished his tricks, leaped lightly from the stage and began to work the tables, stopping here to pluck a coin from a man's ear, and there to slide his hand insinuatingly across a woman's breast and withdraw a cheeping chick from her decolletage. The waiters were circulating among the tables. Duncan stopped one, set glasses spinning on the tip of each forefinger, then caught and set them before the people who had ordered them without spilling a drop.

"He used to do that kind of thing in 'Nam," Michael said quietly. "I remember one patrol—half our platoon had been picked off, and the rest of us were holed up in a muddy ravine keeping our heads down while we waited for the air cover to come. I guess we sat there being shot at for almost forty-eight hours, and by the end of it I think Duncan's tricks were all that kept us from shooting each other."

The magician continued to wander among the tables, circling until Karen realized he was saving theirs for last. When he finally got to them, he stopped and looked down at Michael with a grin that transformed his face to that of a much younger man. Perspiration glistened on his forehead and at the base of his throat, and the dilation of his pupils turned his eyes to dark holes in his flushed face. Karen wondered if this were just the strain of the performance, or had he taken something to help him along?

"And here's an old buddy of mine—" Duncan's glance flicked constantly between Michael and Karen and the rest of the audience, holding their attention. "He knows all the magician's secrets, but he won't tell, will you, Mike?" He snatched Michael's drink from his hand. Michael made a futile grab and then began to laugh.

Duncan tipped the glass to his lips, leaning backward dramatically until he had drained it, then set the empty on a waiter's tray and signaled for a replacement.

"Oh no—don't you remember when you swore that any time you had a drink I got a share? Besides, I've left you something in exchange. . . . " The long fingers waved over the table and where the beer had been a fresh rose now lay.

But before Michael could react, the magician had turned to Karen. "And where did you find this goddess?" he laughed. "If only you had sworn to share your women with me too! Ah, beautiful—I think you have a very sensitive soul. . . ." He drew one finger lightly along Karen's cheek and she braced to keep from flinching.

The thin finger continued down her neck, but when he touched the necklace Karen felt a shock. She jerked away. He was staring at her, eyes dazed as if he had felt the shock too. "Maybe too sensitive," Karen tried to laugh.

"I don't think so—" Duncan pulled himself together, straightened and gestured gracefully, refocusing the attention of the crowd. "For now it is time for my next demonstration, and I need someone with the right qualities, someone with the psychic ability to assist me in the task . . . and you, who are so beautiful. . . . '' His voice became smoother; his eyes held hers. Karen stared, fascinated, wondering whether he was really dilating and contracting his pupils at will.

"Hey, take Dick here—he's aways seein' things!" someone cried from the crowd, but Duncan still held Karen's eyes.

"Come up onto the stage with me and we will show these fools what the mind can really do—" he said in a low voice, but she saw something leap in his eyes like a little flame.

"No." She shook her head. "I'd rather not."

"It's all right, Karen," said Michael helpfully. "He won't hurt you."

"Karen . . . Karen. . . . '' The magician's voice had become a caressing hum, "Come with me—it's what you really want to do. . . .''

She was still aware of the crowd around her and of Michael watching, but nothing seemed to have significance except the voice that soothed her and the brightness of Duncan's eyes. He was right—she did have hidden abilities that no one had ever known how to bring out before. Why not stop worrying and do what he said? Wasn't that what she had been looking for?

But something held her still, a weight that would not let her take that outstretched hand. After a moment she realized that it was the weight of the necklace. Abruptly her head cleared. She felt the color rise and recede in her cheeks.

"No, thank you." she said clearly. "I'm not into that sort of thing."

His face moved again, and for a moment she recognized the expression she had seen on men's faces twice before. But this time it seemed that instead of a mask put on, that look had been beneath a mask that slipped aside. Her hands went instinctively to her neck and she pulled the collar of her shirt closed to hide the necklace from view.

She felt Michael begin to move beside her, but Duncan was already drawing away, bowing with a theatrical sweep of his velvet robe.

"Alas—then you will never know what wonders I could have shown to you!" He turned swiftly, wove deftly among the tables back toward the stage, pausing on his way to select almost at random a young man who appeared only too eager to play the part Karen had refused.

She slumped in her chair, heart pounding heavily as the magician assisted the young man into a chair and produced a crystal globe on a chain which he began to swing. Gradually the young man's posture eased and he became still.

Hypnotism! thought Karen, *I'm glad I said no! That's not the man I want playing games with my soul!* She hoped it would not upset Michael, but she was realizing that she did not like his friend.

"You have seen me use my powers, but perhaps you suspect that these are only old tricks, clever illusions and subtleties of skill." Duncan told the audience. "Here is the true magic, to speak to the mind and awaken unknown powers within the soul. . . ."

He turned to the man who sat before him. "You hear me, don't you, Joey, and you want to do what I ask of you—"

"Yes, I do . . . " came the low reply.

"Then I want you to stand upon one foot, your right foot, lifting the left one into the air. You will find it very easy to balance, and you will not put your left foot down until I tell you to."

The young man stood up easily and raised one leg like a soldier interrupted in mid-march. When Duncan moved back to face the audience he continued to stand there, obviously quite comfortable.

"You have seen the transformations of the body," the magician said with a little smile. "Now you will see the transformation of the soul. You saw a man in the body of a monkey—now see what can manifest within the body of a man. . . . " He turned again to the young man, who still stood with one leg in the air.

"Do you remember how it felt to be a little child—how freely you could move and how much energy you had? Walk around the stage now as you did when you were five years old. . . . You are five years old. . . . Can you skip? Can you hop? Yes—that's right. . . . "

As the patient voice droned on, the young man's stance subtly shifted. He began to walk, his step becoming more springy until suddenly he was hopping and skipping with the elasticity and abandon of a small boy. Karen shifted uncomfortably in her chair, and yet her reason could find nothing wrong.

"Now, Joey, think of women you've seen—think of a woman's body. . . . It is *your* body now—you can feel your center of gravity sink to your hips, and the jiggle of your breasts as you walk. . . . You are a woman now . . . a whore. . . . You walk across the stage and look at the men, hoping that one of them will take you home with him."

The subject's body changed once more, its balance shifting as if invisible weight had been added to breast and hip and thigh. But more striking was the change in his expression as he looked around the room. Slowly, sensually, he moved his tongue across his lips.

There was a murmur of appreciation. Several men began to whistle and cheer. "Well, my dear, if he's an impersonator he's damn good," said a man at the next table, leaning back so that his open shirt gaped more invitingly across his furred chest. "I think he really has been hypnotized."

"I always knew you had it in you, Joey!" someone yelled from the front row as the young man blew a kiss.

"I could tell him to go down among you—" the magician said softly. "I could command him to fulfill your wildest fantasies. . . . " He smiled a little at the new note in the laughter of the crowd. "But this is a public place, and I suppose some decencies must be observed!"

As the crowd responded with catcalls and boos of disappointment, Duncan made the young man stand before him again. Karen took a deep breath of smokey air and began to cough. Her stomach was churning sourly. Had she had too much to drink? For a moment she opened her awareness to the conversations around her, the emotional atmosphere. No, it was not the drinks that were making her feel ill.

"Michael, I don't feel well. Can we go home?"

"What?" Michael's eyes were glittering, his face set in a scornful smile. In quick succession Duncan had made his subject flap about like a chicken and writhe like a snake along the floor.

"You pride yourselves on being men—" said the magician. "But you see how easy it is for you to become a beast again; how easy to abjure responsibility for what you do. He has delivered his soul into my hand—could a god ask more?"

"Michael, please!" Karen swallowed bile. The emotions around her were like a thick fog, the malice of the man on the stage like a blow. "Michael, I don't like what he's doing up there, and I'm going to be sick if I stay!"

His attention was on her now, but his face was still flushed and his glance was hard. For a moment she hated him.

"All these rich bastards—" Michael said. "He's showing them their rotten souls and they're paying for the privilege. Unfortunately, the show is almost over. Can't you hold out until then?"

Mutely she shook her head.

"Look, if you're going to throw up, go into the ladies' room. I can't leave now. Duncan will be insulted if I don't stay for a drink after the show."

His tone was so very reasonable. Karen stared at him, checking her habitual impulse to agree. She had always agreed with Roger, and it had done her no good in the end. And when she had been with Roger there had never been anything to which she had reacted so strongly as she was revolting against this man, this place, now.

"I'm sorry"—she forced her composure to match his—"the ladies' room won't do. I could still feel the atmosphere. If I stay here I'm going to upchuck all over the table. Don't worry, I can take the bus if you don't want to take me home."

His face changed then and she saw for a moment an ungoverned rage that could have struck fire from stone. Then he mastered himself. His face was the stone, now.

"And now, ladies and gentlemen, let us see if I can put a monkey into the body of a man?" Duncan spoke to his subject, and the young man began to cavort about the stage in a hideous travesty of the little animal Karen had last seen shivering in the magician's arms.

She got to her feet, mentally counting the change in her purse to make sure her threat of going home alone had not been empty. But some machismo point of honor prevented him from letting her do it, or perhaps he simply could not stand for her to walk out on him.

As she followed Michael's stiff back toward the door she realized that he was going to hate her for making him choose between her and his friend. She cast a final look behind her, thinking that perhaps she had been wrong and she could bear it after all, and saw Duncan bringing a lighted candle under the young man's hand. Shuddering, Karen hurried outside.

7

He a high altar made me of heaped stones—
All glassy have grown the gathered rocks—
And reddened them anew with meats' fresh blood;
For aye believed Ottar in the goddesses.
                                    LAY OF HYNDLA

The rumble-buzz of a small motor by her pillow rasped Karen's nerves to wakefulness. She felt warmth against her ear, a warm weight holding down the covers behind her knees. She turned her head on the pillow, trying to ease the sick throbbing behind her eyes, half-choked on fur and struck out.

With an affronted growl Býgul leaped from the bed and picked her way across the strewn clothing on the floor to the doorway, where she sat, glowering at Karen from golden eyes. Karen sat up, rubbing her forehead, felt the morning chill pebble her skin and pulled the blanket around her. Trjegul, dislodged from her own nest in the bedclothes, sprang down to join her twin.

"Oh, Roger . . . " murmured Karen, closing her eyes against inner and outer pain. But that was not right—Roger had left long ago. She was quarreling with Michael now.

But it was my own fault this time— she thought miserably. She had been right; she *thought* she had been right, but she wondered if she could have forced Michael to take her away from that place if she had known she would feel this way.

Michael had taken her home in a silence cold as the wind

that plucked at her clothing. Sitting behind him on the cycle, holding as lightly as possible to his waist, she had remembered the ride over, when they had swung around each curve as a single being—two bodies joined into one. She had fought the desire to cry out it was all her fault, that she was sorry. That they should go back.

But she could not forget her last glimpse of Duncan Flyte's face, demonically illuminated by the candle flame. Her illness had not been of the body but of the soul, but how could she explain that to Michael? How could she tell him this old and dear friend of his must be either evil or insane?

Be patient, she told herself. *Let him cool down. . . .* She repressed a sick apprehension that he would never forgive her, that Michael would not come back at all.

The sky she saw through her window was cloudy, as if nature were sympathizing with her mood. Sighing, she padded into the kitchen to mollify the cats with breakfast, and to begin the weekend alone.

After Bȳgul and Trjegul had eaten enough to forgive her and she had forced herself to consume an orange and a piece of toast, Karen sat down to go through the mail. Trjegul immediately settled herself across her lap like a self-heating lap-robe while Bȳgul sat down beneath the window and began to wash.

Bills and more bills—Karen put them aside until she could get at her checkbook, not wanting to disturb the cat; a post-card from Micaela, on vacation in Las Vegas; a multitude of ads. As she was about to sweep the latter into the wastebasket she noticed that one of them bore a personally typed address and pulled it from the pile.

There was a letter and a check inside. Looking at the letter-head she remembered vaguely filling out a contest form. *But I never win anything . . .* she thought in disbelief. *Five thousand dollars! What will I do with it all?*

Put it in the bank! came the immediate answer, *before it vanishes like fairy gold!*

But as she pulled on her clothes Karen remembered that Freyja, whose very tears were golden, was the goddess of pros-perity. Laughing at her own fancies, she murmured a thank-you.

Once the check was safely deposited, Karen decided to see if the fabric store had anything she could use to cover the last of her throw-cushions. She was turning in the door when a flash of blue from a window down the street caught her eye.

It was the store where she had bought her bowl. The cloak she had been coveting was still there. She hovered in front of the window, almost tasting the rich blue, woven with threads of deep purple and sea-green so that it glowed like a jewel. The cast pewter buttons that closed it gleamed enticingly.

If only . . . she thought. Then she realized that for the first time in her life she had the power to simply walk in and buy. Grinning, she strode inside.

When Michael still had not called her by Sunday noon, Karen felt despair gaining on her once more. An overnight wind had blown the clouds away. The clear air glowed with that exquisite clarity that belongs only to autumn. She had expected to go riding with Michael today, but why should she miss out on all this beauty because of him?

Angrily Karen pulled on jeans and boots and a shirt, and then, with a sense of bravado, added the golden necklace. The wind was chilly, so she picked up the blue cloak as well. Soon she was coaxing her Volkswagen up the winding roads to Tilden Park in the hills behind the town.

It took her some time to find a stopping place. The hills were beautiful even at the end of the dry season, and every campsite had its contingent of noisy picnickers. But she didn't want people, not today. She wanted clean air and a clear trail.

Karen finally stopped at a pull-out where a fire-road led up the hill. Several other cars were parked there, but she could see nothing of their owners. With any luck they would be solitary hikers whom she could pass with a smile. She locked the car, draped the cloak over her shoulders, and strode up the hill.

The first slope was a steep one, and by the time she reached the crest Karen was breathing hard. But as she stood looking out over the tangle of hills toward the blue glimmer of the Bay, Karen felt an abrupt conviction that she had been right to come.

The land around her glowed with the subtle symphony of colors of a California autumn—the pale straw of summer-cured grass and the blazing azure of the sky; the tawny glow of turning leaves and the deeper browns of earth and tree trunks; the shadowy loden-greens of the pines and the furred olive of chapparral, and beyond them, the soft shadings of distant hills

that folded down to the sun-dappled silk of the Bay. The blue
peak of Mt. Tamalpais rose across the water like a sentinel.
Karen took a deep breath, savoring the scents of dry earth and
cured grass, the aromatic breath of bay laurel as its scent was
released by the sun.

Then she laughed aloud and stepped out along the ridge
road that went along the spine of the Berkeley hills. Others
had had the same idea. At every turning, it seemed, she met
couples with children, students with dogs that bounded across
the road, even horsemen from the stables at the other end of
the trail. After nearly being knocked down by a gamboling
Brittany spaniel she began to look for a turn-off.

And there it was, almost as if she had invented it, a narrow,
rutted track half-overgrown with chapparal, winding down
through folded hills whose golden slopes were shaded by dark
clumps of live oak and laurel and madrone.

Once Karen thought she heard singing, but when she
rounded a turn in the path it was gone. She strode confidently
ahead, letting her feet find the way while her body re-estab-
lished its own links with the land. In its own way this was even
better than being with Michael. She was alone, and whole, and
free.

Then she came over the rim of a hill and saw that she was
not alone after all. The path ran down through a cup in the
hills that was partly circled by trees. More trees filled the deepening ravine beyond it. A long table had been set up in their
shade, next to a little fire. The scent of roasting meat came to
her on a momentary shift of the wind.

Here there were no side-trails, but the thought of retracing
her steps exasperated her. Almost in spite of herself, Karen
moved on. A shadow sped before her on the path. She looked
up and saw a red-tailed hawk sail overhead. With dream-like
smoothness the bird soared across the little valley, and with no
perceptible motion of its own was wafted upward on the other
side, where it tilted its wings to circle again.

Perhaps a dozen people were gathered in the grove below,
standing in a circle within the round of trees. Although some
were wearing jeans, most were dressed in Viking tunics or
loose white robes belted with colored cord. In the midst of the
circle a burly young man with luxuriant red hair and beard
stood with upraised arms before an altar of heaped stones.

He looks like Thor, she thought wryly, remembering the

Rackham illustrations to the *Ring. What on earth do they think they're doing?* Then gooseflesh pebbled her skin and she drew her cloak around her despite the sun, for she could hear what they were saying now, and the young man with the red beard was just finishing a long and comprehensive invocation to the Norse gods.

He stepped back from the altar and let his hands fall. A little raggedly at first, then with gathering power, the group began to chant:

> *Hail to thee, day! Hail, ye day's sons!*
> *Hail, night and daughter of night!*
> *With blithe eyes look on all of us:*
> *Send to those sitting here victory!*

> *Hail to you, gods! Hail, goddesses!*
> *Hail, earth that givest to all!*
> *Goodly spells and speech bespeak we from you,*
> *And healing hands, in this life.*

The hymn ended. The leader faced his congregation.

"The summer is done and we have given thanks for a good harvest. Now we gather to welcome winter and to beg the protection of the *disir*, those goddess-spirits who watch over each land and home and individual, during the coming year...."

It's a religious service! Karen could not quite believe it, yet certainly the faces of the people in the circle showed as much fervor and rather more concentration than she had seen in most churches. Nobody had noticed her yet. She stood transfixed, watching them, while the hawk continued to circle overhead.

The young man with the red beard faced the altar again and stretched out his arms. "We honor you and beseech you, oh ye spirits who guard this place—bless the acts we perform here and accept our sacrifice!"

A girl came forward with a pitcher. Karen saw the dark flash of wine as the priest poured it over the stones, covering them until they glittered red and glassy in the sun.

What are they doing? wondered Karen. *Are they Satanists?* But surely no one who worshiped the Judaeo-Christian devil would pour out libations to Nordic goddesses. Besides, there was no feeling of malice or cruelty here. She shivered, remembering the faces of those who had watched the magic of Duncan Flyte. *Those* were the devil worshippers. . . .

"We honor and pray to you, oh spirits who guard our homes and families," the leader went on, "therefore accept these symbols of our respect and gratitude and grant us protection and prosperity. Oh you into whom the maternal love of our ancestresses has passed, watch over your descendents still."

Singly or in families, people stepped forward and laid bread-dough images of horses, pigs, or other animals upon the altar, then carried them to the trees where they hung them from the branches with colored yarn.

Remembering the accounts of the extensive and bloody sacrifices of animals and sometimes of men which were practiced in ancient Scandinavia, Karen suppressed a smile. Given the sensibilities of the present, these people had hit upon an ingenious compromise. But who were they?

She recalled having read in the paper about the Bay Area's neo-pagan groups, but she had gotten the impression that their traditions came mostly from the Celtic lands. It was just her luck to have come upon a bunch of Norse pagans at a time when her own concerns made their ceremonies seem almost painfully significant.

"And above all we call upon the Lord of Earth's abundance, Freyr, and upon Freyja Vanadis of the golden necklace, Lady of Love and guardian goddess of the Vanir themselves! Lord and Lady, look down upon us! Grant us fecundity of mind and body in the coming year! Restore the earth during the months of rest, that life may flourish anew. And as your powers strengthen us, may our praise strengthen you, so that the forces of life will fill the land and Ragnarok be put off for yet a while!" With a shout the priest brought down his hands. The circle echoed with mixed voices raised in invocation or praise.

Karen swayed. The air had grown hot and still. She opened her cloak, pulled at the neck of her shirt so she could breathe. The singing in her ears was louder than the cries of the worshippers.

The scent of roasting meat was suddenly dizzying. She saw two men bring a platter of roast pork to the altar while other men and women brought baskets of bread and fruit, bottles of

wine and cider, pies and cookies, salads and casseroles, and set
them down.

I've had too much sun . . . Karen thought vaguely. She felt
at once acutely aware and curiously detached. A little breeze
lifted the hair from her neck, but she burned as if a fire glowed
within. She put her hand to her forehead to test for fever.

"Let the goddesses be praised!"

"Let the feast be set!"

"Let the celebration begin!"

Shouts echoed from hill to hill. Someone picked up a recorder and started up a merry tune to the accompaniment of a
tambourine. People grasped each other's hands and began to
dance in a spiral around priest and altar and offerings.

As the red-bearded man stood smiling, the hawk that had
been circling overhead swooped downward in a long glide that
carried it a few feet above him and onward in a straight line to
Karen. Startled by the shadow, he looked up to follow the
bird's line of flight and saw her standing there. The hawk cried
out once, then soared upward and over the rim of the hill.

For a moment the young man's face remained open and
smiling. Then his eyes widened a little and he frowned. Hitch-
ing up his robes, he made his way among the laughing dancers,
paused for a moment and slashed downward with his hand as
he passed through the edge of the circle, and started up the
hill.

Karen swallowed. He stopped before her, his blue eyes
bright and measuring in a broad face that was growing pink
from too much sun.

"I'm sorry . . . " she got out at last. "I didn't mean to in-
trude. The path I was following led me down here, and—"
Helplessly she indicated the trail through the grove.

"It's all right." He smiled suddenly. "At least you didn't
blast us with a radio. We don't mind spectators if they're willing to respect our religion. We're celebrating *Disirblot*—that's
our autumn festival. You look like you could use a drink, why
don't you join us?"

She stared at him, but saw only a steady-eyed young man
who was beginning to perspire. "If you're sure you have
enough, and people wouldn't mind. . . . "

"Mind! We've enough for all the disir in Tilden Park!" His
sweeping gesture encompassed the feast. "We call ourselves

the Church of the Aesir and the Asynjur, by the way. I'm
Terry Thor's-gothi—Terry Ritter, that is."

"All right—and thank you." she said slowly. "I'm Karen
Ingold." She held out her hand.

His eyes rested for a moment upon the necklace at her
throat and continued up in the direction in which the hawk
had disappeared. Then he wiped his hand on the skirts of his
robe and extended it.

*I was afraid he might be some kind of religious nut—I
wonder what he thinks of me?* Karen wondered, but the grip
of Terry's callused hand was reassuring, and she followed him
down the hill. At the edge of the circle she felt a curious tingling—she must be more lightheaded than she had realized.
Terry stooped behind her and made a curious motion as if he
were closing a gate, then led her forward.

"Hey, everybody—we've got a thirteenth guest for our
feasting! This is Karen Ingold!"

Except for one girl who was twirling around and around all
by herself, the dancing had come to an end. People were
spreading blankets on the dry grass and reorganizing the food.
They welcomed her with a murmur of greeting. A woman with
brown braids that fell to her waist picked her way over to
them, carrying a silver-bound drinking horn. She held it out.

"Skaal, and welcome to our feast."

"Thank you." Karen suspected there was some ritual response to this, but she did not know it. She took the horn,
admiring its workmanship, and drank. The golden liquid
inside was tart and refreshing. "This is wonderful—" She
grinned appreciatively.

The woman smiled. "It's mead. My husband brews it." She
pointed to the tall man who was trying to carve the roast. "I'm
Nancy Bell and he's Jack. Why don't you come and sit
down?"

Karen eased gratefully down on the quilt beside Nancy, for
she still felt strange despite the drink, and although she was
not cold, she had to grit her teeth to keep them from chattering. *If I'm going to be sick I hope these nice people can help
me home again!*

Nancy held out a paper plate heaped with potato salad,
slices of roast pork, some three-bean salad and a chunk of
homemade brown bread. Karen stared down at it. *Potato*

salad? Just an ordinary church picnic! She fought down an impulse to laugh.

"Besides this, what sort of things does your group do?" she asked politely.

"Well, we try to celebrate all the major festivals as authentically as we can—Yule, and Oestre, and Midsummer especially. A lot of pagan customs survived in folk tradition, and the Church sort of closed its eyes and pretended it didn't know what was going on. Like the Yule log, for instance, and the Easter bunny."

"But why?" Karen put down her plate and looked at the other woman. "I know it's nice to get out in the hills, but you could do that without—I mean—"

"I know what you mean." Nancy laughed. "A number of us go to church or do other stuff as well as this. But the pagan religions were much more positive about nature than any of the modern churches are—it's more philosophically compatible somehow. We do the seasonal ceremonies to sort of bring ourselves into tune with nature, and maybe to return a little of the energy back again. And because most of us had Teutonic ancestors—Norse or German or Anglo-Saxon—we find it works for us to invoke their gods." She began to eat again.

Karen pushed her own food about on her plate. It tasted wonderful, but she had no appetite. She reached for her cup and drank again.

"And then a lot of people are into the Norse gods because of the Viking spirit—you know, fight on through overwhelming odds and laugh at doom—no meek sniveling there! Myself, I don't think power necessarily has to be male. I like having goddesses!" Jack came over with a platter of pork and Nancy speared some onto her own plate and Karen's.

Karen look at it helplessly. Everyone else was eating, grouped in a loose circle before the altar. There were three couples, one with a baby and another with two older children, two other women, and four young men, including Terry. Most of them seemed to be in their twenties or thirties.

Goddesses! Something in what Nancy had said reminded her of what Micaela had said to her once, about female power. She shook her head, trying to understand.

Terry refilled the great drinking horn, stood up and held it out before him, and stretched out his other hand above it.

"Sacred mead, beloved of gods and men, I consecrate you in the name of the Lord Freyr!" He poured a little out on the ground, lifted the horn in salute, and drank. Then he passed it to the man next to him. Slowly it began to make its way around the circle.

Karen drank deeply as it came by, wishing she had discovered mead long ago. The buzz of conversation around her blended with the buzzing in her ears. The detachment that had held her before was returning. On the other side of the circle someone was singing. She could hear the laughter of the children who had run off to play on the other side of the grove.

Again and again the meadhorn was consecrated and sent round. The sun began its downward progress, filling the air with a richer gold. *Like my necklace* . . . thought Karen. The gold around her neck felt warm, as if it had absorbed the heat of the sun. Karen lay back upon the friendly earth, gazing up at the sapphire depths of the sky, and fancied that the ground was embracing her.

"Sacred mead, beloved of women and goddesses, I consecrate you in the name of Freyja Vanadis. . . . " Terry's voice seemed to come from far away. "Blessed Lady, as we drink, fill us with Thy Love. . . . "

How beautiful the sky was, how blue, like a well into which she could fall upward into infinity. Karen breathed in warm air and joy tingled along her veins like wine. The drinking horn came round to her and she drank, then impulsively dipped her finger into the mead and touched it to her brow, her breast, the palms of her hands.

"Goddess bless me. . . . " She *remembered* the Goddess now—had she not seen Her in the mirror when she put on the necklace and later when she and Michael had first made love? She lifted the horn in homage to the heavens and drank again.

As Nancy took it from her hand Karen shuddered suddenly, shaken by a sound, or perhaps it was a sensation, like the long vibration of a deep-toned bell. She stared into radiance, feeling her hair lift on her scalp. She held her breath; the Sound trembled through her again.

And as if a tether had snapped, she found herself free. And yet it was her mind, not her body, that had finally detached itself; herself, Karen observing in serene unconcern as her body got to its feet and stretched luxuriously. But the body was not untenanted, though the soul floated free—it had been filled by Someone Else, as the drinking horn had been filled with mead.

Freyja! She's here! Karen wanted to warn the others that the goddess they had been invoking had come to them, but she had no control over that body's voice now.

She watched as the Lady moved lightly across the circle to the young man with the recorder, bent and asked if he would play again. He looked up at her, and his smile of assent, reflecting the smile that illuminated Her face, was beautiful.

The music began. In a moment the tambourine joined in, setting a beat that lifted the spirit and lifted people to their feet.

The Lady had moved to the center of the circle. As the music got faster She began to turn in place, swaying slightly, stretching out Her hands. As She turned She beckoned, and one of the men came to Her and took Her hands. For several minutes they danced, back and around and forward again, until his face also opened in that expression of wondering delight.

Then She sent him spinning across the grass to draw one of the women into the dance. She turned to Nancy Bell, grasped the woman's hands and whirled her around and around until her brown braids flew straight out behind her. *"Dance!"* She commanded, or did they hear it only in their hearts? *"Everyone dance!"* Power flowed from Her necklace in a blaze of gold.

From one to another the Lady passed until everyone was on their feet and moving to the music. The tambourine player had been swept into the dance, but the recorder player piped like one possessed. The Lady moved among them, brushing lips with a kiss that kindled like swift flame, setting bodies to quivering at yet a higher pitch with a quick embrace.

Now one couple, twirling too fast for balance, fell to the grass, but their dance went on. The young couple with the baby twined around it and each other in a repetition of the embrace that had drawn it into the world. As the piper, mated to his instrument, continued to play, couple by couple, the dancers who had feasted the gods lay down to the feast of love. Only the children, who had wandered beyond the borders of the circle, played obliviously among the trees, unaware of what was happening around the altar of stones.

Terry stood before the altar from which he had invoked the goddess, swaying as if a strong wind shook him. In his expression awe warred with joy. He took a step backward as the Lady came toward him.

She paused before him, Her head thrown back so that the golden necklace sparkled blindingly upon the whiteness of Her breast. She was laughing.

"You called Me—why are you so surprised that I have come? Are you afraid?"

"Yes . . . " he whispered, looking at Her steadily though all the high color had left his face. "When I saw You standing on the hill I knew You, but I did not believe. Yes—I am afraid."

She put Her hands to the front of Her shirt and one by one undid the buttons, then pulled it open so that Her breasts were fully revealed. He began to tremble then and shut his eyes.

Gently the Goddess touched the silver hammer that he wore on a thong around his neck. "You have served the God," She said, "but now you shall serve Me. . . . "

Like a sleepwalker he moved toward Her. She set Her two hands upon his head and drew it down to meet Her kiss. With a groan his arms tightened around Her and She arched against him. The response of his body was possessing him now and his hands moved eagerly, pulling away Her shirt, sliding beneath the waistband of her jeans. The Lady laughed again and, bending, pulled him down with Her to the warm breast of the earth.

Swiftly he dealt with the frustration of Her clothing, his hands at once urgent to reveal Her glory and reverent upon what they found. His loose robe was removed more easily, and when She set her hand upon the erect phallus that made him into an image of Freyr he moaned again and again until the Goddess opened Her thighs and guided him through the Gateway to ecstasy. . . .

And as the Goddess moved Her body in the ultimate Dance, Karen was aware not only of Terry's urgency, but of the delight of Nancy and her husband, and of the other couples who worshipped Freyja upon the grass, and of a buck and a doe mating in the hills nearby and the trees rooting themselves ever more securely in the body of the earth and of Earth herself opening to the rays of the sun.

Gasping, the man cried out the Name of the Goddess, and She moved to meet him, whispering, "For these others what is passing now will become a joyous dream. But you have been My priest, and you will remember. . . . "

And then abruptly She was gone, and it was Karen who received the final flaring of Terry's passion and cried out as her own body convulsed in harmony with his.

8

Cease not, seeress,
'till said thou hast—
Answer the asker
'till all he knows....

BALDRS DRAUMER

Everything was still.

Karen sighed and eased from beneath the weight of Terry's arm. His eyes were closed; on his face she saw a look of astonished peace. He murmured something and reached out as she pulled away from him, but he did not wake.

Even the echoes of the music had faded. The only sounds in the valley were the occasional chirr of a cricket and the peaceful chirping of birds. Karen shivered a little, looking around her at the sleeping couples still locked in full embrace. Even the children were sleeping, curled like puppies beneath the trees.

The Goddess had cast sleep upon them. It was time for her to go.

After this, Karen could no longer doubt that there *was* a Goddess, just as she must accept the fact that by wearing the golden necklace, she had enabled the Goddess to manifest within the world.

"Oh brother (*sister? mother?* her inner voice footnoted), what have I gotten myself into?" She looked down at Terry a little wistfully. Considering their recent intimacy, she wished that she knew more about him. At least the other members of the group were friends already. But Freyja had told Terry he would remember. Karen hoped they wouldn't run into each other somewhere—what could she say?

She struggled into her scattered clothing, then determinedly unclasped the necklace and thrust it into the pocket of her jeans. It was not so much that she regretted what had happened, but she did not think she could cope with more than one miracle in a day.

The sun was continuing its long slide toward the sea and the air had turned cold. Karen was glad for the warmth of her blue cloak as she headed up the path. At the top of the hill she paused for a moment, peering back down into the circle of trees. The figures on the grass were beginning to move. Quickly Karen took the last few steps that would hide her from view and began to run.

The drive down from the hills back to Berkeley passed like a dream. As Karen passed the Claremont Hotel and shops and houses closed around her she began to wonder if what she remembered had been a dream as well. But there was a luxuriant soreness in her body that argued for its reality. . . .

How could it have happened? Had it ever happened before? Was it just the necklace, or did the world hold other talismans that waited to trap the unwary, disguising their power? Walter's books covered the derivation of obscure folk-customs in excruciating, and inconclusive, detail. That group whose ceremony she had just disrupted had probably used such books to cobble together their ritual.

But what could the scholars know of the reality behind the ritual? Dead languages—dead religions—hah! If she told Walter, what could he say? *He would be embarrassed, or think I was trying to seduce him,* Karen decided ruefully. And even if he believed her, he was a desk-jockey, and if not a virgin the next thing to it. She shook her head. There was no help there.

I want an explanation. The light turned green and the little car rattled down Ashby. *Or at least a hypothesis! I want to know why that happened today and whether it's going to happen again! I want someone who won't faint at the idea that the gods are alive and well in Berkeley!*

She turned right onto Telegraph Avenue. Traffic was heavy, and as she waited at the first light she noticed a sign bearing the beautifully painted figures of a man and woman before a luxuriant tree on the other side of the street ahead of her. "EDEN BOOKS" read the sign. The light changed. She sent the car darting forward, wrenched it around in a U-turn and headed back down the block.

There, between the fantasy bookstore and the shop selling Japanese tea, she saw the sign once more—"EDEN BOOKS: OCCULT AND METAPHYSICAL LITERATURE AND MAGICKAL SUPPLIES, ADELINE EDEN, PROPRIE-TRESS." Vaguely she remembered seeing it before, but she had never before had any reason to investigate it. . . .

Against all probability, there was a parking place right in front of the shop. With a sense of fate, she maneuvered into it.

The door to the bookstore opened with a little shimmer of bells. There was a thud as a large lion-colored cat with amber eyes jumped down from a table covered with books and began to pad toward her.

"Trjegul!" The exclamation was out before Karen could stop it, for now it was obvious that this cat was a male—older and larger than her two, and bearing himself with even more dignity.

She turned around and found a small round woman with closely cropped silver hair watching her intently.

Flustered, she tried to explain. "I was surprised by your cat —I mean, I have two just like him, and I wondered if he had ever sired any kittens, or if you could tell me where you got him. . . ."

"I wish I could." The woman's face lost some of its austerity and she picked up her needlework again. "Tiphareth turned up on my doorstep shortly after I opened this shop and has stayed with me ever since. You are lucky to have two of that breed, for I know from experience that against burglars they are better than any dog."

Karen's arm still bore scratches from the last time she had infringed on Bŷgul's dignity. She could imagine. And remembering how she had worried about the safety of the necklace, she was grateful. Had Freyja sent the cats to protect Her property? Was there a supernatural cause for everything? *I'll be taking omens from the flight of ravens next—but Berkeley doesn't have any ravens. Can you read omens from black-birds?*

"That's good." A little embarrassed, Karen smiled and

began to wander around the store, trying to make sense of the closely packed shelves of books on astrology, the secrets of the pyramids, New Age health care, Indian philosophy (Asian and Amerindian), the Tarot and the Kaballah, and psychic development of every conceivable kind. There was an odd scent in the air, as if someone had been burning incense, but if so, it was nothing like the sickly sweet joss sticks the Hare Krishna devotees handed out.

She passed the section on esoteric Christianity, pulled out a volume on Jung, and put it back again. She came to a halt at last before a shelf devoted to female spirituality, feeling panic build. There was nothing here that specifically addressed her problem, and she could not possibly buy them all in hope that one or two would be useful. Her shoulders sagged.

"Are you looking for a specific book or for information on a particular topic?"

Karen jerked around and saw that the store's owner had left her place behind the counter near the door and was standing behind her. There was a certainty in her face, as if she already knew the answer to her question, or indeed to almost any question Karen could ask.

But standing there in her navy skirt and blue sweater Ms. Eden looked like somebody's grandmother. Did Karen dare to tell her the truth? Would she be wise enough not to dismiss Karen's story as the work of a sensation-seeker or a fool?

Karen took a step closer. Through the etching of age and experience the woman's skin glowed. The blue eyes behind her glasses were surprisingly acute and luminous. Impulsively Karen reached into her pocket and pulled out the necklace.

"I want to know about this. . . ."

Ms. Eden's eyes widened a little and she stretched out her hand. But instead of taking the necklace she held it a few inches away as if she were feeling the air around it. She closed her eyes, frowning, and after a moment opened them again.

"Yes—" she said finally, taking her hand away. "I should think you would want to know."

Karen nearly dropped the necklace. "Then there *is* something strange about it! I was beginning to think I was crazy. Ms. Eden, can you help me?"

"Oh do call me Del—" The older woman's eyes twinkled. "As for your problem, I suppose that depends on what you expect me to do. I was just about to close up for the night—"

"Oh. . . . " Karen's eyes stung with disappointment. "I'm sorry. I suppose I could come back. . . . "

"I have an apartment behind the store," Del went on. "Would you like to come have a cup of tea with me while we talk?"

"Oh, could I?" She could almost smell it, taste the hot strength of it going down. Surely neither wonder nor horror could withstand the power of a good cup of tea!

Del Eden's apartment proved to be tiny, superbly organized, and scrupulously clean. As Karen passed through the living room she recognized a Japanese *futon* bed whose foam slabs had been folded up into a couch for the day. There was a small but very fine Persian rug on the floor beside it, and flowers in an antique Chinese bowl beside the door. Breast-high redwood cabinets covered most of the wall space, but there were a few pictures in the spaces between the high windows.

She followed the other woman into the white kitchen and sat down, waiting in exhausted silence while Del moved swiftly about, setting a porcelain pot and two shell-like teacups on the table after she had put the kettle on. The necklace lay before Karen on the table, bright against the worn linen cloth. She touched the links, feeling them hard and inert beneath her hand. In this peaceful room it was hard to imagine the abandon with which she had drunk and danced and made love a few hours ago.

Del poured out the tea, pulled up a second chair and sat down. "How did the necklace come to you?"

"Come to me . . . " repeated Karen. "Yes, you do understand!" Suddenly the words came easily, and as she told Del how she had found and reconstructed the necklace and what had happened when she wore it, everything that had happened took on a new significance, shaping itself to a pattern whose meaning she had to understand.

"When I drove down from the hills today I was convinced that Freyja—the Goddess—had been using my body, and that this necklace I have is Brisingamen! But now—" Karen shook her head. "How could that possibly be true?"

"True in whose terms?" Del asked. "On some level, I am sure that everything is *true.*"

"But how? I've been forced to believe that the gods, whatever they are, must be real. But not physically—Freyja had to use my body—so how could She have a real necklace?"

"There are several possibilities." Del sipped at her tea. "Freyja has no body now, but She could have walked the earth in the form of a woman long ago, permanently possessing a body as yours was taken for a little while. Metal and stones, especially those with high crystallization, can store both energy and information. If this necklace had been worn by a "goddess," it would have absorbed a tremendous amount of power.

"Or it could have been crafted for a statue. Generations of worship in which believers visualized the Goddess and invoked Her power would affect it almost as intensely. When enough people focus their wills and imaginations upon the same image, that image acquires a permanent reality in what you might call the collective unconscious, or, according to another hypothesis, the astral plane. And ornaments like this can act almost like computer chips to store a pattern."

She set down her cup and bent over the necklace again. "Yes—any psychic would tell you the same thing—no matter who made this necklace or why, it has been charged with the power and identity of Freyja, and anyone with any sensitivity may find themselves plugged in, as it were, if they remain in close contact with it for long. For all practical purposes it *is* Brisingamen. . . . ."

Karen weighed the necklace in her hands. "And what about the man in the opera, and the one who tried to run me down?"

"Every action has an equal and opposite reaction." quoted Del. "That is as true for psychics as it is for physics. Brisingamen enables Freyja to manifest in our world. But as you have discovered, power that is not understood or channeled can get out of hand. Although"—her lips twitched with suppressed laughter—"in this case I think your afternoon's companions deserved what, or Who, they got!"

She reached over to refill Karen's teacup and her own. "That may be part of your problem—you have been wearing the necklace as if it were a piece of costume jewelry. It's as if you were to use the Holy Grail for a coffee cup! All that power has been radiating every which way, and who knows what it has awakened?

"Remember, Freyja did not live all alone in Asgard. She had enemies—I seem to remember that Loki was one of them. If She is active, then Her enemies will appear as well, and they will certainly try to capture or destroy Brisingamen. Freyja uses you not only because you possess the necklace, but because you have the capacity to express Her. In the same way, Her enemies will work through those whose personalities, either for the moment or permanently, are sympathetic." She leaned across the table and took Karen's hand.

"Be careful. Do not wear the necklace too often, and when you do, be wary. It may be good for the power of Freyja to act upon this sick world of ours, but the Aesir were not peaceful gods, and Freyja was a major factor in their wars."

Karen held the necklace to her breast as if icy fingers were already reaching for it. She remembered the man in the car, the man at the Opera, and the malice in Duncan Flyte's eyes. . . . Yes, surely Freyja had Her enemies!

"But what can I do?" she wailed.

"Brisingamen came to you—do you know anyone else you would trust to be its Guardian? You are the one who must decide what to do with it. . . ."

Karen looked down at the Tarot card in her hand and sighed. It was the Empress, and for the third time it had turned up in the position indicating an influence on her immediate past. The Tarot deck was one of several items Del Eden had given her at the bookstore the Sunday before. The pictures were pretty, but she was having trouble interpreting the patterns they made.

Del had warned her—"The kind of power that is in Brisingamen is not physical, though it may show itself physically. If you are to use it, instead of letting it use you, you must train your imagination and your will! At first it may be boring, although I suspect that you will get results sooner than most students do, but like a dancer's exercises, it is necessary. . . ."

She finished laying out the cards on her bedspread, wrote down their order and gathered them up again, shuffling them carefully before fitting them into their box. She glanced at the neatly written schedule of exercises Del had given her. She had already done the banishing ritual and worked with the cards. Now it was time for breathing and visualization and then at last she could go to bed. Karen sighed once more. Did other people really go through all this, and did it teach them what Del had called "psychic control"? Or was it all some sort of elaborate game?

There should be some kind of book—*So You Want to be a*

Priestess or some such—to warn people of what they were getting into!

The internal monologue continued, but Karen realized that she had already arranged the cushions for the next exercise and was lighting the candle now. She smiled a little crookedly and sat down cross-legged with her back against the wall.

First, Del had told her, you had to relax. *Your feet, stupid— that's right, curl the toes tight and then loosen them, then the muscles in your calves, and your thighs.* . . . Awareness of the outer world faded gradually as Karen tensed and relaxed the muscles in her hands and arms, her belly and shoulders, and the subtle tensions in her neck and face and scalp.

Now for the breathing—in for four counts, hold for four more while the blood sings in your head, then out for four and four counts of waiting, fighting the urge to breathe in. A few minutes of it dizzied her. Del had told her not to go too fast. But surely tonight it was coming a little easier—her body seemed better balanced, even solider, than before; the constant chatter of thought moved slowly now.

This breathing stuff could be handy to calm me down if I'm angry or afraid, she thought. But surely, as long as she did not wear the necklace, nothing would happen to scare her. Or would it? But in that case why bother with all these exercises?

Abruptly she recognized a train of thought which had already carried her to a dead end too often. She forced her eyes to focus on the candle flame. It was a white candle, translucent with its own light, and the golden flame wavered as it was stirred by the thread of air from beneath the closed bedroom door. But there was a blue flicker in the heart of the gold, like a soul in a body, and shadows that shifted as the flame thinned and twined.

Then the flame was streaming upward in ripples of gold like Freyja's hair. But no, it was only a candle, and Karen saw it as a candle once more, pooling wax upon the hardwood floor. The flame flared at her movement, then stilled. Karen remembered the candle that Duncan Flyte had held beneath that poor boy's hand and hoped that he really was a good hypnotist.

The fire danced as Duncan had danced across the stage. Karen found herself breathing faster and forced herself to control the slow flow of air into her lungs. *Breathe in, and out . . . in and out . . . there is nothing but your breathing, and the fire.* . . .

Duncan Flyte's face leered at her from the flames. *No!* she told herself. *You have to control what you see. There is only the candle flame, blazing brighter and higher before you.* . . .

Was she shrinking, or was the fire roaring up around her? Karen could not feel her body—only flames that darted on every side, heat that seared, light that blinded her.

I am burning, burning! Terror formed the words.

These are not real flames. They are not touching you . . . an answer came from some deeper level. Awareness arrowed toward freedom.

And after an eternal moment the pain was gone. Yet flames still surrounded her. Karen was an observer, as she had been at the festival in the hills. But as in a dream, it was not her own body that she saw. Though this woman's fair hair blazed like the fire it was longer than Karen's and a deeper gold, just as she was taller and more generously endowed.

Freyja! thought Karen. *But what is happening? Who would want to hurt Her?* The body that was and was not hers writhed against the touch of fire. As the flames parted she saw the dark timbers of a great hall, and on the high seat two faces, close, as if their owners shared a single bench. They were twinned in expression too, though one was framed in silver-shot dark hair and a leather patch hid one eye, while the other face was narrow, dark-eyed, with hair like a fox's brush or like a flame.

In those faces glowed a vicious excitement—fear that changed to malice and, as the flames drew away from her nakedness, to lust as well. Her breast ached as if a blade had pierced it. The chains with which they had bound her burned.

Odin . . . *Loki* . . . names precipitated in her awareness. Their arms were around each other's shoulders. Odin picked up the cup that Loki had just set down and drank deeply, then wiped the mead from his beard.

She was bound and powerless before them. No one could help her . . . there was nothing she could do. Like an echo words rang in her memory—*"By my own blood I swear it! Never again!"*

She screamed then; flames recoiled on every side. She burst her bonds and lifted her arms, poised, bright hair tossing in the updraft as if she herself had turned to flame.

Transform—came a voice from another life, *you're supposed to transform what you see.* . . .

Odin was on his feet, fumbling for the hilt of his sword. She glimpsed others moving, caught the flash of bared blades. Loki crouched by the throne, thwarted malice glittering in his dark eyes.

"Nithings!" she cried out then. "Have you no response to me but this? I have my own magic! Save your steel for the Jötuns and let me show you Fire. . . . "

Fire flowed through her stretched arms, darted across the dark hall in tongues of flame. But its touch set flesh to tingling, new energy shooting through the veins, set loins to throbbing with desire. One white hand reached toward Odin and the fire licked around him, touched him with a spark that limned each nerve in light.

His face changed. Swiftly he came to her; she saw a new fire glowing in his eyes. And as he came she saw the face of Michael Holst laid over his like a mask. But Loki wore the face of Duncan Flyte.

And he was afraid.

9

Then began I to grow and gain in insight,
To wax also in wisdom:
One verse led on to another verse,
One poem led on to the other poem.
                    THE SAYINGS OF HAR

Karen rested her elbows on the keyboard of her typewriter and covered her eyes. It was nearly five o'clock of a grey November day, and she was tired. *Too many late nights with cards and candles*, she thought, *and I'm not even winning money! Is lack of sleep supposed to assist psychic development?* But it was not just the exercises. She had been sleeping badly, haunted by dreams of the Goddess, and others in which she and Michael quarreled and made up only to start fighting again.

She sighed and looked down at the Anglo-Saxon poem she was copying as a hand-out for Walter's survey of Medieval Literature:

> *Wulf, my Wulf, my yearnings for thee*
> *Have made me sick, thy rare visits,*
> *A woeful heart, and not want of food. . . .*

and the unknown woman's words of longing for her lover struck her with an almost physical pang.

I have to see Michael again, she thought. *There was some-*

thing going between us, and I can't just let it die. Maybe I was justified, but I started the fight, so I guess it's up to me to swallow my pride. But how can I meet him again without being too obvious?

The poetry in front of her reminded her of the two times she had gone to hear Michael read at the Blue Door. Today was Thursday, and tonight he would probably be there again. Yet she quailed at the thought of just walking in and sitting down in the front row. She needed an excuse, even if it were a transparent one.

She heard someone whistling the solo from the Richard Strauss Horn Concerto in D flat in the hall outside, and began to smile.

"Walter—" she said as he came into the office. "Did you know that there's a contemporary drive to bring back traditional poetry going on at the Blue Door Coffeehouse right here in Berkeley? I'd like to go down there tonight to hear a friend read and I need an escort. Would you go with me?"

"What?" Walter put down his briefcase, stared at her, and took off his glasses to polish them. Without them she could see how fine his eyes were, and how vulnerable.

Suppressing her smile, Karen wondered if Walter had ever been asked for a date by a female, and how she had the courage to do it now. It was because he had given her the necklace, of course. Even when it was safely wrapped in its insulating silk in her drawer at home, she could not forget it, and the secret made a bond between them.

"It's not essential—" She took pity on his confusion. "The place isn't unsafe or anything. I just thought you might find it interesting, and I could use the company."

"Oh—I didn't mean—I had to think if I had any engagements tonight. I would be happy to go with you, Karen, but only on condition that you let me take you out to dinner beforehand!" he replied with a kind of self-conscious courtliness. He thought for a moment. "We could go to the Upstart Crow—that's a literary sort of restaurant. If you can wait for half an hour while I get some things in my office organized?" Hastily he replaced his glasses, gathered up his things, and went out.

"Well!" exclaimed Micaela, who had been watching wide-eyed. "I would not have believed such a thing—the great professor is human. You must tell me your secret!"

Karen laughed, thinking that the secret was that they were all human, women and men too. "Don't get romantic ideas, Micaela—I don't have any ulterior motives, at least where Dr. Klein is concerned! But I thought it would do him good to see that some poets, at least, survived the Middle Ages!"

The Blue Door was, in fact, packed with poets—poets who had already read sprawled in their chairs, drinking beer or coffee, while those awaiting their turn leafed through untidy folders, making last-minute decisions on which poems to do.

An alliteration of poets? wondered Karen as she led Walter among the tables toward the bar, *like an exaltation of larks? But perhaps a "dissonance" would be a more appropriate collective,* she reflected as she listened to the current performer's uneven drone.

Except for the color of its door, the decor of the coffeehouse was the standard combination of unfinished wooden walls papered with announcements for poetry readings and fliers for artistic and/or political events, and a jungle of potted plants. Walter's gaze fixed on the list of offerings chalked on the board over the bar.

"We should drink something, shouldn't we?" He gestured at it. "What would you like?"

"A glass of white wine. . . . " Karen was scanning the tables. She recognized some of the people she had seen when she came with Michael—a blond man as thin as if he had been slammed in a door, wearing a purple jumpsuit . . . a woman with long brown hair, who was trying to tune a small harp over the noise of the room.

Walter handed Karen her wine and grasped his mug of beer like a talisman. "Is there somewhere special that the audience sits, or does one take what one can?"

Karen shook her head, smiling, then stiffened as a burst of sardonic laughter made heads turn. They were looking at Michael, who sat near the front of the room next to Duncan Flyte. The reader faltered, glared at them, and droned resolutely on.

Karen took a deep breath. "Up there—" The look Walter gave her was uncomfortably acute as he followed her gaze, but during their circuitous progress among the tables he made no comment, and smiled blandly at Michael and Duncan when they arrived.

"Hello, Michael—" Karen said brightly. "I don't think you've met Dr. Klein, my boss. Walter, I'd like to introduce Michael Holst and Duncan Flyte." She continued, "Walter is interested in the Renaissance of bardic poetry that you've got going here."

Walter and Michael looked at each other, then at Karen, with the air of two dogs facing a cat who is sitting on the boundary line between their territories. Then Michael's habitual chivalry reasserted itself and he squeezed over next to Duncan so that they could sit down. There were two other men at the table—one of them tall, with bad skin, whose eyes followed Duncan's every move. The other wore an expression of cynicism like a mask, and Karen realized that that was like Duncan too.

She felt herself flushing, recognizing the open amusement in Duncan's eyes, and hoped that the light was too dim for anyone to notice. She controlled her breathing and took a long swallow of wine, then wondered if he had noted that as well.

"The other two guys are from Duncan's magic class in the city—" said Michael after a moment's awkward silence.

"Danny Ortona—" said the sleek man. "Joe Whitson . . . " the tall boy's whisper echoed him. Karen murmured something and ignored their proffered hands.

"Please, Michael, not *magic*—" said Duncan softly. "We deal in illusions and transformations. 'Magic' has become such a tawdry word. Our class meets three nights a week at the Mission YMCA, though I hope to remove it soon to quarters that are, shall we say, less constrained. It's proved quite popular—I have a dozen very devoted students now. Actually I find it rather amusing to pass on a few of the things I know."

Sporadic clapping reminded them that the reader was finally finishing, and they waited while an earnest-looking man whose silvered beard spilled over a T-shirt with the faded legend, "Livermore blockade—No Nukes is Good Nukes," began announcing the featured readers for coming weeks, and a number of other upcoming poetry events.

"Have you read yet?" Karen whispered to Michael.

He shook his head. "We got here late, so I'm pretty far down the list. But there's a lot of good people here tonight. Most of the Greyhaven crowd, like Zimmer, for instance—" He waved at a red-bearded man who had just stepped onto the riser that served as stage.

Walter goggled at the combination of Scottish kilt and samurai topknot.

Michael laughed. "Yeah, I know he looks kind of weird, even for Berkeley. It's his image—if you're going to be a performer you have to stand out somehow."

The red-bearded man adjusted the microphone, focused the attention of his audience with a commanding glare, and began to read. His deep voice carried easily over the buzz of conversation in the back of the room, lovingly stressing the sounds of his words and deftly shifting rhythms as he went on.

> Aesthetic theories come and go
> With ebb and flow of changing times:
> Now rhyme is out, free verse is in—
> Has been since I was young,
> When they sang the best minds of that generation,
>   starving, hysterical,
>   running through negro streets—
> That's right, the Beats!

"You see what he's doing?" whispered Michael. "Even though it's free verse, he's getting in a lot of internal rhyme and little allusions and stuff—"

Walter nodded. "He has a good voice for it." The poem continued, chronicling the changing history of literary fashion from Pope to Pound.

> When in the course of human events,
> The present style has been "in" too long,
> A strong aversion grows up in the young,
> And tongue and pen new theories form and hold:
> The old order changeth, and having writ,
> Its wit and work are left to ruthless time.
> Neither crime nor virtue in "fashion's" eyes
> Will buy it free from time's unbiased trust.
> Rust and moth are the only true Critics:
> Although Aesthetic Theories come and go.

Walter burst into laughter as the crowd applauded the poem's conclusion. "He's right, too! I'd love to post a copy of that on the Department bulletin board. What do you think, Karen? Can't you see Feldman's face, reading that?"

Michael was eyeing Dr. Klein with some surprise and rather more sympathy than he had shown before. Karen took a drink of her wine and began to relax.

The poet had launched into his second piece now and they fell silent to listen to it. This one was based on the Hindu tale of how Rama divorced Sita even though Agni, the sacred fire, had refused to burn her in corroboration of her chastity.

Karen felt the images build within her mind, holy and unholy fires that flickered like the flames in her vision. Across the table Duncan's face moved in and out of focus as it had when she had seen him as Loki in Odin's hall. *My fire versus yours, trickster,* she thought, *and we will see who has the livelier flame!*

"You are not wearing your lovely necklace tonight . . . " Duncan said softly.

Karen sat up straight, fighting free of the words' enchantment. "It's safe at home," she answered coldly. Following Del's directions, she had wrapped it in white silk to insulate its power and hidden it in the bottom of one of her bureau drawers.

One mobile eyebrow arched as Duncan smiled. "Well, my dear, I didn't accuse you of mislaying it, did I?" One of his friends giggled, then stopped abruptly as Michael glared at him.

"Well, that was interesting—" said Walter as the poet finished and stepped down. "I didn't know people still wrote mythological poems, especially about the Hindu gods!"

"Oh, people are writing this stuff, all right, and not just retelling legends." Michael set down his mug and leaned across the scarred table. "There's a guy called Paladin who did a requiem for a bro—a biker he used to ride with. He had him joining Odin in Valhalla— *'Give him to the fire and water, send with him the things he'll call for again! Beer for cheer, and tools for slaughter! Come Ragnarok he'll need them then!'* "

Slowly Walter smiled, his eyes thoughtful behind the thick lenses. "Yes . . . I can see it . . . in spirit, bikers, not soldiers, may be the closest thing we have to warriors now. . . . "

Karen suppressed laughter as a vision of a medieval hall populated by bearded, beer-bellied bikers like some of Michael's friends took shape in her imagination. Then the laughter died, for the bearded Vikings who belonged there were the same kind of coarse-mouthed, hard-drinking men, ready for fight or festival; wanderers who exulted in living close to the edge and whose only loyalty was to their brothers and to their own grim and glorious code. Maybe some of them weren't very nice people, but she supposed, no—she *remembered*—that Odin had never been interested in recruiting "nice guys" for the Einheriar. . . .

The reader had been replaced by the woman with the harp, and the plaintive ripple of bronze strings wove through Karen's thoughts, leaving impressions and images that seemed to belong there—a wandering harper, a woman's lament for a lost warrior.

Michael laughed softly and lifted his mug in salute. "For an ivory tower type, you've got your head on right!" he told Walter. "Karen, now I see why you've stuck with this man for so long."

Walter was actually blushing with pleasure at the compliment, Karen realized that far from enduring the evening for her sake, he was actively enjoying it. *Micaela would never believe me!*

"We had warriors in Viet Nam—" Duncan said suddenly. "We were heroes every day, but nobody gave a damn. The heroes got screwed. The heroes died. And the fakers got the medals and the thieves went home rich. So let's not get all romantic and full of enthusiasm, huh? Nobody wants a hero around, not in real life, not anymore!"

Michael's face changed. Karen recognized the haunted look that always made her want to take him in her arms. She glared at Duncan. Maybe it was true, but what use was it to make Michael remember?

Walter was shaking his head with something like shame in his eyes. "I was 'Four-F,' " he said, taking off his glasses and rubbing his eyes. "Far-sighted, and some other things. I wasn't over there. I never even had to decide. . . . " Harp notes rose and fell with a gentle melancholy and faded to silence.

Chairs scraped suddenly and they jerked back as a figure in purple leaped against them, outstripping the emcee's attempt to announce him.

"Go Serpent!" someone shouted, and the shuttered look left Michael's eyes.

"Listen to this guy—" he said. "I'll bet this is something you've never heard before."

It was the thin blond man Karen had noticed earlier, though now she was aware only of his unleashed energy and the skin-tight jumpsuit whose cutout spaces taunted decency without quite defying it.

"My goodness!" Walter put his glasses back on. But Serpent had already launched into his poem, gesturing broadly and fixing his audience with a challenging stare.

It was something about dwarves, dwarves forging gold. . . . Karen put her hand to her neck as if she bore Brisingamen, but these were not the dwarves with whom Freyja had bargained, and they were not forging jewelry. . . .

> *Fire the furnace; fill the mold,*
> *Then, raise the hammer; beat the gold!*
> *Behold it blaze across the sky*
> *As hordes of foemen, fearful, fly!*
> *And what shall, now, our gold be called*
> *As all the Earth looks up, appalled,*
> *To see the black and empty night*
> *Be rent in shreds with blazing—*
> > *Lightning! Lightning! Lathe the sky*
> > *With fearful flails of flame on high!*

The poet's hand shot out as if he were wielding the lightning bolts and his voice, harsh with excitement, echoed against the wooden walls.

> *Lightning! Lightning's lashing ridge*
> *Before the fabled Bifrost bridge;*
> *To fling against the frozen fields*
> > *of demons dread*
> > *to stay their stead*
> *As Thor his thunder-hammer wields!*

For two stanzas more the poem continued, rising to a crescendo in which words came almost too fast to be spoken. Then he was done, with a final shattering shout that left him panting and the ears of the listeners ringing with doom and glory.

"*That* is what I meant by bardic poetry!" said Michael, smacking his lips, as soon as the applause had diminished enough for them to hear him.

"Yes . . . " said Duncan consideringly. "Even I have to admit that the boy has a certain sense of style."

Walter was shaking his head in admiration. "I certainly never expected to hear anything quite so firmly in my own field!"

All around them people were rising and stretching. A babble of excited conversation filled the room. The emcee, recognizing that it would be impossible to get silence now, called for a break. Michael drained the last of his beer and got to his feet.

"I need another drink!"

"After that, I think I need something too—" said Walter. "What about you, Karen?" She nodded and he took her glass. Duncan was whispering to his two friends and after a moment they stood up awkwardly.

"We're going outside to smoke, okay? See you in a little while."

Karen watched them go, knots of tension in neck and shoulders that she had not even realized were there beginning to ease. Michael was being friendly, but she still could not feel comfortable with Duncan. And his two friends, or students, or whatever they were, were worse, even though they had hardly spoken. Was it the way their fingers had fiddled constantly with buttons or watchbands or lapels that bothered her, or the way their eyes followed their master, watching for his reaction to each poem before they displayed any response of their own?

And yet Duncan was not just Michael's old Army buddy, but a close friend, and he did not demand from Michael the kind of adoration his students offered him. Her lips quirked as she tried to imagine Michael's response if he had tried.

There must be something to Duncan that she had not seen—some depth or sensitivity he would not show her. Or there had been once—if Duncan had changed, if he were no longer the person Michael had loved, what painful revelation would be needed for Michael to see the change?

Karen tried to shake the thought away. This was ridiculous. Duncan was only a man, and his relationship with Michael was no business of hers!

She watched Michael making his way through the crowd

with Walter in tow, stopping at almost every table to reply to someone's greeting or to introduce the professor to some friend. Karen smiled, glad that the two of them had hit it off so well. Michael was presenting the older man as if his presence lent them all some previously lacking credibility, while Walter smiled at them all as if someone had just shown him that Santa Claus was real.

Michael waved to Julia Vinograd, a noted local poet who was also famous for blowing soap bubbles on Telegraph Avenue, and, still smiling, reached their table and sat down beside Karen. His arm went around her shoulders as if they had never quarreled, and Karen leaned against him, understanding that neither forgiveness nor explanations were to be required between them.

Walter smiled benignly, set the wine in front of her, and slid into the place Michael had been occupying before. "You were going to tell me about your work. . . . ''

Michael flushed—Karen was not sure whether it was embarrassment or pleasure. He took a long swallow of beer and set down his mug, watching Walter's face as he replied.

"You have to understand, I started scribbling when I was in 'Nam. I wasn't trying to be a great writer or anything—I just wanted to figure out what I was feeling about everything that was coming down. Maybe I thought if I could describe it I could deal with it. Well. . . . '' He shrugged and looked away. "Maybe it did help me survive.

"A lot of my buddies didn't. Some of them died over there and some when they came home and found out nobody gave a shit what they had gone through." He was trembling and Karen took his hand, trying not to wince as his grip tightened.

"Some guys just spent the whole tour stoned," Michael went on. "I did that too, some, but mostly I wrote poetry. After I got back, out of Rehab, I tried going back to school. But how could I talk to kids who called me a fucking imperialist for having gone over, or else didn't even know there had been a war? So I dropped out."

"But you're still writing . . . '' Walter said gently.

"Yeah. I keep thinking that if I can only put it down on paper right, people will understand that nobody who protested the war at home hated it half so much as the guys who had to fight it over there!''

"That is one purpose of poetry," said Walter, "to express

the things that people don't know how to say, or that they never knew were there . . . to find the meaning of death and a reason for staying alive." His grey eyes were lidded as if even the glasses were not sufficient protection now. Karen felt a swift rush of affection, wondering from what demons Walter sought the protection of poetry.

Michael nodded. "I've even started working on a novel," he added, almost shyly.

"Good luck, brother, but don't hold your breath—how many novels about 'Nam have you seen on the stands?"

Startled, they looked up to see Duncan Flyte standing beside the table with a sardonic smile on his lips and a Scotch and soda in his hand. His two students had not returned.

"More than there were—" said Michael. "Even though most people would rather pretend there never was a war. Maybe by the time I'm done somebody will want to know what really happened over there."

"I would like to read your book. Very much," said Walter quietly. He took the glasses off and Michael grew very still, reading his eyes.

"Yeah? I just may take you up on that . . . " he said softly, then sat back again, his arm tightening as the room quieted and the emcee finally made himself heard. She could feel Michael's heart beating heavily. Walter's words had moved him more than he wanted anyone to know. Duncan took a long drink of Scotch and set down his glass, snapped his fingers at a passing waiter and ordered another one.

Two men whom Karen did not know read next, something not too inspired about love and ecopolitics.

"I don't know why they're so excited," said Duncan in a stage whisper. "Nothing they say is going to make a difference. Nuke the whales!" Michael glared at him and he grinned, but kept silent while an ebullient dark-haired girl got up to read a poem about cats. Karen remembered Býgul and Trjegul waiting for her at home and applauded enthusiastically.

"Say, old buddy, when's your turn coming?" Duncan put down his third Scotch. "I'm waiting to be impressed, and I'm sure your ol' lady here wants to show you off to her professor. When you gonna do your stuff, huh?" He drawled out the words in a parody of Michael's usual conversational style.

Someone at the next table hissed at him to be still, and he

was opening his mouth to reply when Michael gripped his arm—

"Duncan, I think you better shut up and stick to beer. Paladin's on next, and if you bust up his act he'll kick your ass up between your ears! And I'll help him!" He let the other man go. For a moment dark eyes closed with grey—fire and ice opposed and balancing—until suddenly Duncan relaxed and laughed.

"If you say so, buddy . . . anything you say."

Karen had seen Paladin before. She enjoyed watching Walter's expression as the figure with whose wrath Michael had threatened Duncan reached the stage—a small man fashioned of steel and whipcord with a shock of black hair and black boots, jeans and a T-shirt labeled "Helmet laws suck!", its sleeves rolled up to show arms covered with tattoos.

"All right, you fuckers!" Paladin stood with hands cocked on his hips as he gazed around the room. "I understand you wanna hear some po-etry. Well, this is a piece about some troubles they got in Ireland a while ago—" he continued, shading his introduction imperceptibly into a rather startling rendition of an episode from Irish legend.

A farmer there was, one MacDatho by name,
Who had him a dog of the greatest acclaim,
And a pig he had also, of similar worth,
And MacDatho himself was the salt of the earth,
And MacDatho had also a beautiful wife
Who was smarter than he. Oh he had a hard life
And with peril 'twas fraught, for he lived on the border
Of Ulster and Connaught in times of disorder,
Maeve rulin' the latter and Connor the first,
And each to the other was biddin' their worst,
A-slayin' and pillagin' when they were able.
The county line ran through MacDatho's hall table,
And by fire on the hilltop and blood on the bog
Queen Maeve and King Connor each wanted the dog. . . .

While the audience slapped the tables and howled with appreciative laughter, the poet proceeded in his own inimitable style and considerable detail to recount the story of the feast

MacDatho hosted in order to solve his problem, and its bloody conclusion.

By the time he reached the poem's abrupt ending even Duncan was laughing, as if this brand of mordant humor had at last provided an outlet for some of the venom that ate at his soul. Michael was gathering up his papers and getting to his feet as applause swept the room.

"You wanted to hear me?" he said very quietly to Duncan. "Okay—listen! I think that you at least will understand what I'm trying to say. I watched your show—now it's your turn to see mine!" He made his way up to the microphone as the emcee called out his name.

"Well, I guess that's a hard act to follow." He waved a salute to Paladin, who grinned and lifted his beer mug in return. "But I don't believe in long introductions. If a poem's any good you'll all know what it means. . . . "

He waited for them to grow quiet, head thrown back and good eye fixing each one in turn, his body settling to a poised readiness as if he were preparing not to read a poem but to do battle.

Karen leaned forward, holding her breath, as he began to speak.

> *Do you see in my hand this sword?*
> *Wave-edged, light flowing over beaten steel*
> *As water smoothed the sands,*
> *There, where I had it of a little Malay man*
> *By war's strange fortune washed, like me,*
> *Upon that bright, betraying shore. . . .*

Michael raised his arm and in his hand Karen could almost see the blade. He hefted it, turned it this way and that, and Karen blinked at the flash of sun on steel.

> *'This a kris.*
> *Tuan, you its master now—*
> *But take care—*
> *You draw it, it must drink;*
> *It must taste blood before it rest again.*
> *Don't draw for play, don't draw for show—*
> *Your blood will flow.'*
> *I wore it in the jungle*

To wield where modern weapons failed,
Or when they wanted death dealt silently.
And yet it seemed to me
The blade grew thirstier as it was fed:
Sword's rage, spirit's rage, unslaked by widening war,
Shook a fragile sanity
To season madness as my buddies died
For an officer's stupidity, a politician's ambition,
a nation's greed.
Like a million thirsty swords we had been drawn
To shatter or to splatter blood across the land,
Drawn for play, for show.

He paused for a moment, nodding as he saw discomfort and averted eyes, something kindling in his gaze as he met Duncan's black stare.

Oh you who drew the shining sword of war,
Consider well—
We know the taste of terror now,
And we are angry, we are hungry, we are home . . .
Whose blood will you betray this time,
That the kris
May drink and rest once more?

There was no applause when he ended, only a shuddering sigh that was in its own way a greater tribute. They tried to clap as Michael sat down again, but their hearts were not in it. He slipped the paper back into his notebook with a grim smile.

"Now I see . . . " said Walter softly.

"Do you?" hissed Duncan. His eyes glittered in the dim light. "I was there. I waded in the blood that cries out for vengeance in his words. Michael is right, but he is still making it too pretty! And this country is still pretending it never happened while it raises a new generation to do it again! When those who sent us to 'Nam to die and stayed at home to profit drown in the mud as we drowned; when they taste their own blood and choke on their own fear, then the sword may sleep, but only then!"

Karen shrank back, as shaken by awareness of the pain behind Duncan's words as she was appalled by the blast of hatred that bore them. She eyed him with horrified compassion as he pushed back his chair and shrugged his blazer on.

"Good night to you all, you mother-fuckers—" Duncan swayed slightly and as he looked at Karen it seemed to her that additional malice twisted his smile. "Enjoy your nice cozy houses . . . sleep well!" He began to laugh, and, still laughing, wove unsteadily toward the door.

Michael reached for his leather jacket. "He's pretty stoned. I'd better make sure he gets home . . . " he said apologetically. He bent to kiss Karen and for a moment she clung to him, drawing some obscure comfort from the warmth of his mouth with which to counter the chill of fear he himself had raised.

Then she let him go.

10

Have thy eyes about thee when thou enterest,
  be wary alway,
  be watchful alway;
For one never knoweth when need will be
  to meet hidden foe in the hall.
        THE SAYINGS OF HAR

"Karen, are those police cars stopped in front of your house?"

Walter slowed and Karen pushed herself up from the comforting upholstery of the car seat to see. Beyond the line of jagged roofs and bare branches the hills humped dark against the red-grey glow of city lights on cloud. But the street itself flickered crazily in the whirling red-blue-amber flashing of two police vehicles drawn up at the curb.

In front of her flat. Karen peered through the car window and saw an officer talking to someone on the front steps. Neighbors were peeking from adjacent doorways with the avid curiosity people always exhibit for disasters not their own.

"I hope nothing's wrong with Mrs. Owen—" Karen wondered if her downstairs neighbor had finally had the heart attack she was always threatening when the electric bill went up, or when her daughter called to pour out her marital troubles again.

"There's no ambulance." Walter pointed out as he eased the big car into a space across the street. Karen got out, shivering as the cold wind hit her. She began to button up her coat, then stopped, staring. Behind the square figure of the policeman she saw splintered boards—the remains of her own front door.

A spasm of nausea shook her, as if she had been kicked. Her mind flailed blindly—she had nothing valuable, why would anyone break in? And then, as if some mental gear had shifted, she knew.

"Walter—" she said hoarsely, "it's the necklace! I knew I should have given it back to you—"

"Karen, it's all right! You don't have to apologize!" Walter hurried after her. "It's only a piece of jewelry!"

She paused with her foot on the curb. He didn't know—of course, to him Brisingamen was only a piece of jewelry. But what was it to the thieves? What would happen if they tried to melt it down, or sold it to someone who did not know its power? *And what if it fell into the hands of someone who did know what it was for?*

Then she was running up the walk, the cop was turning, Mrs. Owen's torrent of conversation expanded to include her name.

"You're Ms. Ingold? You rent the upstairs flat here?" His words came softly from a dark face. She scarcely heard.

"Yes—" Karen tried to see past him. "What happened? Who called you here?"

"Why, I did, dear, when I heard the noise—" said the old woman. "At first, when I heard the footsteps, I thought it was just you come back from a date with one of your friends. . . . " Yes, she *was* leering! Karen wondered indignantly if her bedsprings squeaked. Just how much had the old lady figured out about her personal life, anyway?

"But it didn't sound like you—" Mrs. Owen went on, "and I didn't think you would be moving furniture about at this hour, and then when the cats began yowling I knew that something must be wrong. For all their size they're generally good, quiet things—they come down to beg a bit of scraps from me when I have fish for dinner, you know, and I've grown quite fond of them—"

"But what happened?" said Karen, anger giving way to anxiety again.

"Well, I had my hand on the phone to call the police when someone came clattering down the stairs, or maybe they fell!

It sounded like someone was tearing the house down, and the swearing"—she flapped her hands to express something for which she had no vocabulary—"then a car screeched away!"

"Ma'am, did you get the car's license number? Ma'am?" The cop resettled his cap with thinly veiled exasperation.

"I told you, young man, I don't move so well as I did, and I was in the hallway trying to phone *you*! I just heard the cats, and the car, and the language, like I said!"

"The cats!" exclaimed Karen. "Are they all right?" Why hadn't they come out to greet her? But no—surely they were only hiding from all the people and the noise. She pushed past the policeman, picked her way around the door, and pounded up the stairs.

"We'll be wanting a report on what's been taken, Miss—" the cop's voice came after her, but she did not reply.

It was the living room that stopped her. She halted in the doorway, her arms going across her breast as if for protection, eyes moving along the trail of shattered glass, books scattered as if they had been swept from the shelves by some angry hand and covered with earth from the hanging plants that had been flung to the floor. The sofa had been overturned; its cushions lay across the room. Karen took a step inside and her foot crunched on glass. She looked down, saw the torn remnants of the print of the three Norns that had hung on the wall, and began to cry.

"Miss, are you all right?" Another officer, big and red-haired, came out of the kitchen, notebook in hand.

Karen hunted through her purse for a tissue, blew her nose defiantly, and looked up at him. "I don't understand—" She waved around her. "Why did they do this, this destruction?" She tried to control her trembling, and the nausea that surged in her whenever she allowed herself to focus on the shambles of the room.

"It happens sometimes," he said tiredly, "when they haven't found anything worth taking. Or if there's a personal motive for the robbery . . . " he went on. "Do you have any enemies? Anyone who would want to hurt you?"

"No, of course not!" she answered automatically, and then stiffened, remembering the malice in Duncan Flyte's smile. But he had been with them all evening, and besides it was ridiculous—he could not object to her relationship with Michael that much. . . .

Karen realized that she was still standing there, when her first thought should have been to check the drawer in her bedroom bureau where she had hidden Brisingamen. *I am afraid!* She tasted the knowledge. *If they did this to the living room— I'm afraid to see my bedroom ravaged and the necklace gone!*

"My goodness!" Walter exclaimed behind her. Karen turned to him and he put one arm awkwardly around her shoulders. "Poor girl, someone certainly had a field day in here! I would have come up sooner, but I thought that if I told the other officer where we had been this evening it would be one less thing for you to go through."

"You had better check the other room, Miss, so that you can tell us if any of your jewelry is gone," said the policeman in a flat voice.

Shuddering, Karen picked her way across the floor toward the bedroom, Walter following her. *That's appropriate*—she thought numbly. *He gave me the necklace—if it's gone he should be the first to know.*

The shards of a broken mirror glittered on the floor, but except for one tumbled drawer and a chaos atop her bureau, the bedroom had not been harmed. Biting her lip, Karen knelt and jerked loose the bottom drawer, feeling with trembling fingers for the knobbly silk-wrapped bundle she had left there.

Her fingers touched softness, closed on it, and with a cry that was half a sob she snatched the necklace to her and it slipped from its wrappings in a glittering cascade of gold. And like an echo came a plaintive meow and Bygul leaped from the narrow space between wall and bureau into her arms. For a moment golden fur and golden necklace were one as she hugged them passionately.

"Bee! Bee! Thank God! But where's Trjegul?" She released the cat, staring around her, and saw the blood smeared across the bedspread and on the floor.

"What did they—?" Karen wadded silk around the necklace and thrust it back into place beneath her nightgowns, then crawled after Bygul, who had slipped around the bed and was disappearing beneath it. She bent, heard a faint mew, threw back the covers, and peered into the darkness.

"Walter, pull the bed back toward the bathroom door," she snapped, reaching under the bed. Her fingers touched fur, the bed groaned as Walter tugged at it and it began to move. She saw a tan shape—Býgul, crouched watchfully by the limp body of her sister.

"Is she dead?" Walter peered over.

"I don't know—she's still warm, but look at her, Walter—they tried to stomp her to death!" Grazed, battered, with one leg bent impossibly, she was like one of those anonymous lumps of fur one sees by the highway. Býgul wailed anxiously and nudged her hand. "What am I going to do?"

"I think the Humane Society has an emergency veterinary office that's open all night," said Walter. "If she's still alive I'll take you there." As he gathered towels and helped Karen to wrap the wounded animal and found a box to carry her in he added, "At least she got in some licks before they did her down—'the female of the species' and all that. Look at her claws, Karen—that blood wasn't all her own!"

The veterinarian looked tired. She shook her head as Karen told her story and peered at the still form wrapped in the blood-stained towel.

"Yes, she's alive. Can't say much more until I've had a good look at her." She motioned to Karen to carry the cat into the office and lay her on the enamel-topped table there. Her assistant was already beginning to lay out instruments on the folded cloth on the counter. They gleamed coldly in the harsh light.

"Of course, I understand. . . . " Karen hovered by the table, ears tuned to the cat's labored breathing. *Trjegul, I thought you were a magic cat, but you're only a poor mortal like me after all, and look what being with me has done to you!*

"It's going to take a while," the doctor said more kindly. The unkind light marked lines in her face and strands of silver in her short hair. "If you want to go home, I'll call you when I finish."

"No . . . no, I couldn't sleep. Can I stay outside until I know?"

The woman nodded, and Karen stumbled back to the drab waiting room and the comfort of Walter's arm.

"It's not your fault!" he said after a little while. "The cat was a stray. Without you, a car might have got her, or she could have starved to death. It's late, and you're tired. And the burglary was a shock to you. . . . ''

"I know . . . '' she replied shakily. "I know all the excuses and all the philosophies. But when I found Tree, for a moment she opened her eyes and looked at me. . . . Walter—go home! I don't want anything to happen to you, too!'' The treacherous tears were running down her cheeks again.

"Don't you think there's safety in numbers?'' he said with an attempt at humor. He held out a tissue, and she swallowed and blew her nose. "I am the one who should feel guilty—I gave you the necklace,'' he went on, shaking his head. "I meant well. I thought that putting it together would amuse you. But I have never known what to do for people, or what to say to them. . . . ''

She turned to stare at him, but his eyes were hidden by the reflection of light from his thick glasses. "You're a professor,'' she stammered. "You make your living talking to people!''

"Lecturing at them—'' he corrected with a faint smile. "It's not the same. A sea of faces flows into the classroom for an hour and goes out like the tide again. The next hour brings another flood, just the same. Semester after semester, year after year. . . . And some do well on their exams and some fail, and I never know if the bright ones would have done just as well by reading at home, or whether the failures were confused by what I said to them.''

"I've heard other teachers say that!'' objected Karen. "Nobody ever really knows!''

"So I'm in good company?'' He took of the glasses then and rubbed his eyes. "But don't you understand? That's why I chose teaching in a university—so that I would never—so that no one would ever know!''

Oh dear. . . . Karen found herself squeezing Walter's hand comfortingly. *At least he's found a way to distract me from my own woes!*

"I did try.'' Walter was continuing as if some door had been unlocked and was now held open by the flow of memory. "When I was in college, and everybody was going on freedom marches, I volunteered for a ghetto tutoring project. The first afternoon there were seven kids there, trading insults, getting up and wandering around the room as if I weren't even there. The second day three showed up. One got up to go to the men's room in the middle of the class and never came back.

The third day nobody came at all.''

And had he tried with women, too? Karen wondered with a peculiar wrench of the heart, and had they also walked past the profferred gift as if it weren't there?

"Well, different people have different talents," she said bracingly. "And there are several thousand other people who made the same choice of a career as you did, so it can't be all that bad. I started out to do the same thing myself! And I seem to remember a speech from you a month or two ago, about using scholarship to increase the total knowledge of mankind."

To her astonishment he blushed, the color of his skin bright against his pale hair.

"How pompous I must have sounded—I'm sorry! I have no right to criticize. Just now I find it hard to imagine what meaning the minutiae of mythology could have for anyone!"

Karen bit her lip. If the burglary had indeed been a manifestation of Loki's presence in the world, knowing mythology might soon be vital for everyone! *But I can't tell him about Brisingamen!* she thought desperately. *If he believes me he'll take away the necklace and put himself in danger. And if he doesn't, which is more likely, he'll think the robbery has made me hysterical and won't listen to anything I say. . . .*

"Walter, you can't know!" she managed at last. "The strangest things can turn out to mean something to someone. And to pursue knowledge, any knowledge, with discipline and integrity surely adds to the stature of mankind."

"Do you really think so?" Behind his glasses, Walter's grey eyes were like a child's. "Well, I must try to believe you—since there is really nothing else that I am fitted to do. . . . ''

And what am I fitted to do? Karen wondered then. When Del had challenged her to protect Brisingamen, she had felt like Joan of Arc at Domremy. But her vision was filled by the picture of Trjegul's mangled body, and her nostrils with the stink of blood. Next time it could be Walter, or Michael. *Next time it could be me. . . .*

"Are you cold?" Walter felt her shiver and put his arm around her again. "I hope the office is warmer than this waiting room." His eyes traveled from the faded print of the worlds' breeds of dogs to the scuffed linoleum floor. "It's not very comforting, is it? I wonder what they're doing in there. . . . ''

As if his questions had been a cue, the door to the office swung open and Dr. Levinthal came out. There was blood on her white smock, but she was smiling.

"She'll live?" Karen croaked.

"Yes, despite several broken ribs and a crushed breastbone. I believe she will. Your cat is basically a remarkably healthy animal, and if she hasn't died already, she should be able to heal. It will take time, of course—a week or two here in the hospital and then careful tending at home. You should go home now—you can call and check on her in the morning."

Karen leaned back against the yielding upholstery of Walter's car, listening with half an ear as he piloted it through the deserted streets of Berkeley. It was a Mercedes—conservative enough in appearance, but built to last, and the upholstery was real leather—a surprisingly luxurious car for him to own.

The anxiety of waiting to hear about Trjegul had left her tired to the bone, but there was a core of tension remaining that kept her wakeful.

"Something else came up this afternoon that might interest you—" Walter paused for a moment as he guided the big car through a left turn, then went on, "I meant to tell you earlier, but this evening has been rather involved, hasn't it. . . . " He cleared his throat. "You remember that exhibit of Viking art that's coming to the Lowie Museum? The Anthropology people have asked me to contribute some notes that show something of the relationship of such pieces to the culture. I think they want to broaden the exhibit's appeal."

Karen opened her eyes. She had heard about the collection of treasures from the Viking Age that had been touring American universities. She wondered if they had anything to match Brisingamen and smiled in the darkness.

"The only problem is, with midterms coming up and the papers I've already assigned for the end of November, I don't know where I'll find the time for anything extra. Will you help me? Perhaps work up some references? We can make final decisions about which quotes to use when we see the catalog. I thought"—he cleared his throat again—"you might be interested in the Viking jewelry."

Karen laughed. "If you think I can do it, I'll be happy to try." Already her mind was reviewing the material she had read for his classes and her own recent studies. With a little shock she realized that she *could* do it—not perhaps as well as he, but certainly better than anyone else available.

He echoed her thought. "I know you can."

"There should be something useful in the *Lay of Volund*. Volund was a goldsmith, after all . . . " she began to think aloud, and the conversation continued through the byways of Norse literature as Walter took them the rest of the way home.

And then she saw the splintered door, roughly boarded up by the police until her landlord could repair it, and realized why she had begun to feel ill again. In her relief at Trjegul's survival, she had forgotten what she would be returning to.

Wordless, she let Walter take her arm and escort her around to the back of the house and up the rickety stairs. She fumbled with the back door key, stepped into the kitchen and stopped, unable to continue into the living room. Walter looked at the shambles and shook his head.

"I don't understand . . . " Karen whispered. "It's only things—possessions . . . but I feel as if I had been violated!"

"At least they left your kitchen alone." Walter stepped past her and firmly closed the door. "Now, do you have any cocoa in the house, and some milk to mix it in?"

In sudden reaction she began to laugh weakly, and pointed to the cupboard.

"Don't you laugh at me!" he said a little sheepishly. "I'm no gourmet chef, but I understand the basics—one of the results of living alone. And something warm with sugar in it is what both of us need right now."

Meekly she sat down. Michael had said almost the same thing to her, after rescuing her from the speeding car; she tried to remember some folk tale in which the hero saved the princess by feeding her hot chocolate. Býgul leaped into her lap and lay there, purring emphatically, as she watched Walter putter about with the pans.

Soon she was drinking the cocoa, and as the hot liquid warmed her she realized that both Walter and Michael were right. It did help, somehow.

"Now I don't think you should stay here alone. Is there anyone you could go to, or who would come and stay with you here?"

"At this hour?" Karen knew people in Berkeley, but no one she could imagine calling at half past three A.M. Except perhaps for Michael, and what had happened would make him angry, and then she would have to soothe him as well as conquer her own fear. For a moment she longed for another woman—for Del, but she only had the bookstore number, and how could she ask a woman of that age to get up in the middle of the night and come here? And Del's apartment was hardly big enough for one—there would be nowhere for a guest to stay.

She shook her head. "No one I'd want to ask to come here, and I don't want to leave the apartment empty anyway."

Walter nodded. "I would offer you my place, but it really isn't fit to be seen. Why don't you sleep in your own bed, since that room was hardly touched, and I'll sleep on the sofa in the living room."

Karen stared at him. Micaela would faint from astonishment if she heard this! "Walter—you've already done too much for me tonight. I certainly didn't intend to get you into anything like this when I asked you to that poetry reading! I'll be all right alone—really I will. That sofa has never been exactly comfortable, and now . . . there's no need for you to miss what little sleep you might get tonight by staying here."

"I would lose more sleep if I went home and worried about you," he said simply. His smile had some of the uncomplicated sweetness of a child's.

Karen realized abruptly that he meant it, that for once he found himself in a position where he could be of real, direct, help to another human being. She must not deprive him of the opportunity.

"Walter—" She shrugged helplessly. "What can I say but thank you?" And was rewarded by a sudden brightness in his eyes.

As Karen settled herself for sleep with the cat curled securely against her side, she thought once more of the comments Micaela and the others would make if they ever learned he had spent the night here. But Walter had not suggested that he might sleep with her, and it had not even occurred to Karen. Had it ever occurred to him? If so, he had given no sign of it, and Karen was at the same time faintly piqued and relieved, for Walter Klein was one of those men who arouses in a woman not even the shadow of desire.

After a time she fell into an uneasy sleep, haunted by dreams in which she waited anxiously in a timbered hall whose pillars were carved and painted with gold, touching her throat as if to simulate the weight of the necklace that should have lain there. Through the window she saw steep cliffs falling away through drifts of cloud. In the distance shone the bright glimmer of the sea.

Freyja . . . she was Freyja now, and she waited in her fair hall, Sessrumnir the Many-Seated, because Loki had stolen her necklace away.

Brisingamen, Brisingamen! her thoughts repeated like a litany, *Ah, Odin, have I not taught you enough of my arts, that you should jealously set Loki to steal Brisingamen? Or was the theft suggested by Loki to you? It must be returned! It holds too much of my power, and without it I know not if I can maintain life in the forests and fields of men. . . .*

But surely it would be returned—her skirts swirled about her long legs as she strode across the floor. Her warriors fought and played on Folkvangr Field outside, but they were no use against Loki—it was Heimdall she depended on— Heimdall the long-sighted, who as Rig was father to the three races of men, who had pursued Loki to get Brisingamen back for her. . . .

Karen woke with heart pounding and sweat running down her back. For a few moments she lay still, waiting for her pulse to slow, remembering who she was now. Then she clambered out of the bed to get a fresh nightgown.

She felt in the drawer and her hands touched silk and the sharp outlines of Brisingamen. *Of course! It's safe—I was only having a dream!* She pulled on the dry gown, and after a moment's hesitation drew out the necklace and clasped it around her neck as well.

As Karen got back under the covers she heard the springs of the sofa creaking as Walter attempted to fold his long frame more comfortably into its angular embrace. She felt a pang of guilt, but she was glad to know that he was there. He had been right. She did need him.

When she slept again, her dreams were happier, for Freyja had been reunited with Brisingamen, and the world shone with gold. She held out the mead horn to Heimdall, he who was called the White God because he was fairest in coloring of all the Aesir, and he turned, smiling, to take it from her hands.

"Freyja, I am the guardian of mankind. Loki's games must not be allowed to place them in jeopardy. You must not thank me for fulfilling my oaths to them. Thor and his hammer are their protection from the Jötun, but it is your power that enables them to flourish. You must always call upon me if you need aid, for you and I, Freyja, are natural allies. . . . ''

He held up the mead horn, and she lifted hers, remembering the times he had helped her before, foreseeing times he would protect her again, and pledged him, returning the smile that lit his grey eyes.

But when Karen woke again her cheeks were wet with tears, for the face that Heimdall turned to her had been that of Walter Klein. And she knew now that he was already linked into the pattern whose center was Brisingamen.

11

Heide they called her, whithersoe'er she came,
The well-foreseeing Vala: wolves she tamed,
Magic arts she knew, magic arts practiced. . . .
                                                    VOLUSPA

Walter was gone by the time Karen hauled herself out of bed
the next morning, but he had left a note ordering her to take
the day off. She was not about to argue, for her head felt as if
it were stuffed with cotton wool, and her muscles ached as if
she herself had been assaulted, instead of her home. Fortunately the landlord found someone to fix the door that afternoon, and by the end of the day her living room, though some-
what barer than it had been, no longer looked as if someone
had been rehearsing Ragnarok there.

On Saturday morning, she was standing in line at the Co-op
to pay for her groceries when someone spoke her name.

Karen turned and saw a strongly built young man with wiry
reddish hair and beard who was looking at her uncertainly.
For a moment she was certain she had misheard, and her face
was stiffening into a conversation-discouraging mask, when
she saw the silver hammer hanging from its thong around his
neck, and realized who he was.

"Karen?" he said again. "I wasn't sure it was you. It's all
right—I mean, I'll understand if you don't want to talk to me
—but I'm glad to see you again."

She found the courage to meet his eyes. "Hello, Terry—

133

don't apologize! I should be relieved you are willing to talk to *me*. . . . After all, you weren't the one who—'' She tried again, "Well, it wasn't me, either, really—not that I wouldn't be interested . . . oh dear, there isn't any way to make this come out right!'' She knew she was blushing. Her inner sight shimmered with images of the field in the hills where Terry's religious group had held its ceremony, and of Terry's face, filled with awe and passion as he came to her.

"Don't you think I understand?'' he said. "Although I have to admit that about half the time since then I've tried to convince myself it was all my imagination . . . but you are real, so I didn't dream it all!''   ·

"No. It wasn't a dream,'' she said soberly, wishing fervently that she could believe otherwise. But her apartment still bore the scars of the robbery, and Trjegul was still on the critical list at the vet's.

The woman ahead of her was checked through. For a few minutes Karen found herself busy transferring groceries from cart to counter and then paying for them. As the last bag was filled Terry touched her arm.

"Can you wait a minute? Let me buy you a cup of coffee.'' He motioned toward the lunch counter. "I need to talk to you.''

Karen waited for him. She was not quite sure why, unless she felt she owed him some explanation. Or perhaps she was simply putting off going home.

"If it wasn't a dream, what did happen?'' Terry asked her when their coffee had arrived. "Were you *trying* to invoke the Goddess?''

Stumbling at first, Karen told him how she had acquired Brisingamen and what had happened since then. "And then, Thursday evening, someone broke into my apartment. My cat was nearly killed driving them from my bedroom, and they nearly tore the living room apart.'' She finished, and looked at him unhappily.

"And you think they were after the necklace?'' He stared into his coffee as he stirred it.

"I don't know what to think anymore. If they were looking for the necklace, how did they know it was there? But if they were ordinary burglars, why didn't they take anything else? My grandmother's silver teapot was on the sideboard, and my typewriter and stereo were in plain view.''

"You can protect yourself from the average break-and-enter burglary by putting better locks on your windows and doors," said Terry. "In fact, I could do that for you—I make my living doing freelance carpentry.

"But if they were after Freyja's necklace," he went on, "you want a different kind of protection. Do you know anything about warding a house, or setting up psychic shields? I'd offer to do that for you, too, but I'm no expert in that area, though I've seen it done."

"No, I don't." Karen shook her head slowly, wondering if this had anything to do with the techniques for personal protection that Del had told her to learn. "But I think I know somebody who could. . . . "

"Well, I advise you to go to him, or her—whoever—and have your place warded right away. And if you ever need any help . . . here's my card. If I'm not there, somebody at that number can usually get in touch with me." He smiled at her then, and she realized that he was offering more than help with carpentry. He did not stir her as Michael did, but as she shook his hand she was aware once more of his strength and solidity.

There might indeed come a time when she would need someone like him, Karen thought then, someone with that kind of stability who did not need to be convinced that the gods were real!

"Thank you, Terry." She slipped the card into her purse. "I'll remember."

And when she had driven home, and put the groceries away, Karen sat down to dial the number Del Eden had given her.

"And this, I presume, is Býgul?" Del Eden set down the bulging shopping bag she had brought and bent with surprising suppleness to caress the golden cat who had slid down from her cushion on the couch to meet her.

Karen watched them with rueful surprise. Generally the cats either dematerialized into the shadows when visitors arrived or held their positions, fixing the newcomer with a hard, topaz stare that effectively discouraged familiarity. She had never known either of them to immediately make up to a stranger before.

On the other hand, Del Eden was not just any stranger. If the force that had drawn Býgul and Trjegul to Karen was the

same as that which had sent Del's cat to the bookstore, it was
no wonder that Bee recognized the older woman as a kindred
spirit. Karen shrugged uneasily at the thought.

What was she doing, and what was this respectable-looking
old woman doing, taking all this mumbo-jumbo seriously?
She stared at Del's shopping bag, momentarily certain it contained groceries, knitting, the *Reader's Digest*—whatever
older women usually carried about. Then Del rose again with
the same smoothness with which she had knelt—more easily,
probably, than Karen could have gotten up—and Karen realized that whatever stereotypes about people older than herself
she might have, Del Eden was undoubtedly an exception to
them.

She probably does an hour of yoga every day! Karen
grimaced. Býgul shook herself and then began to wash.

"Well," said Karen a little defiantly, "would you like a cup
of tea?"

"That would probably be a good idea." Del sounded abstracted. "Indian summer is definitely over, and the wind
out there is cold." Her eyes moved over the bookshelves, the
pictures, the papers piled on the table. It reminded Karen of
the way the cats would pause at the door of a room, checking
it out, before they came in.

"I'll go put the kettle on." She marched into the kitchen,
and as she busied herself with the mundane procedures of preparing food, Karen felt her tension ease. As long as pots
needed washing and water boiled, the world could not have
entirely changed.

But as she measured out tea into the pot she recalled hearing
a friend who had studied Japanese tea ceremony explain how
in the Orient even this homely activity had been developed into
a ritual with almost religious significance. She found her hand
trembling and forced herself to concentrate. Then she sat
back, staring at the gas flame, waiting for the water to boil.

I am afraid. . . . Karen articulated the thought as if to
defuse it. The fire on the stove was one with the flame of the
candles on which she had meditated and the fires of her vision.
The water boiled with the roar of the sea, and the steam that
puffed from the spout of the kettle rose in billowing clouds
that veiled the familiar contours of the room. Even the tea
waiting in the stoneware pot had become a sacrament.
Earth . . . air . . . water . . . fire. . . . The world was dissolving

back into its primordial elements, and who knew what might emerge as they recombined?

No! came the wordless cry, *Stop it! I want everything to be ordinary again!* Karen covered her eyes with her hands and sat shaking as the kettle let out a piercing wail.

There was a quick step on the linoleum and the kettle hic-coughed and moaned to silence as it was taken off the fire. Karen heard the hiss of water being poured into the teapot, the clink as the lid was put back on. Then a gentle hand began to stroke her hair.

"It's all right," Del said softly. "I understand. Do you want to wait and do this another day?"

Karen shook her head. The chair was solid beneath her; the kitchen clock ticked with a rhythm as familiar as the beat of her own heart as the world steadied around her. "No . . . " her voice came muffled through her hands. "If it needs to be done at all, it should be done now!

"I guess that's the trouble—" Karen dropped her hands and looked up at the other woman. "Part of me keeps saying this is all ridiculous—that no amount of chanting or waving candles and incense about is going to bother a man with a gun, and that the other things—spirits or whatever—are all imagin-ation anyway."

"And the other part?" Del's gaze fixed on the cups in the glass-fronted cupboard. She got two of them down, then set the teapot on the kitchen table and went to the refrigerator for a carton of milk.

"There's something else in me that hardly knows words at all," Karen answered her. "I just get images of forces and figures, and right now, this terrible fear that it's all going to sweep me away!" Shaking her head, Karen picked up the teapot and poured, forcing herself to maintain a steady hand. Del followed her example and sat silent for a moment, stirring her tea.

"What you've just said is an excellent example of the dif-ference in function between the conscious and the un-conscious, according to one school of psychology, or between left and right brain thinking, according to another. Whatever the theory, it's generally recognized that we have more than one 'separate side to our heads,' and that the different parts of the mind perceive the world quite differently." She smiled at Karen and took a sip of tea.

Sitting there at the table, with the kitchen light shining on her silver hair, Del looked so *ordinary* . . . Karen felt disorientation returning and checked herself severely. This was no time to get bogged down by preconceptions.

"The trouble is," Del went on, "the two halves don't know how to talk to each other. One purpose of all of the paraphernalia of magic, or of High Church ritual, or grand opera, or a military parade, for that matter, is to manipulate symbols that will speak directly to the unconscious. Appealing to all of the senses at the same time helps the message to get through."

"And what about the unconscious—does it ever talk back?" asked Karen.

"Of course, in the choices we make, and in our dreams."

Karen opened her mouth to tell Del about the dream in which she had seen Walter Klein as Heimdall, then shut it again. Perhaps it was superstition, but she could not help feeling that putting what she had perceived into words would trap him even more tightly in the network of relationships she felt closing around her.

"You make it sound so scientific . . . " she said instead.

Del laughed. "One definition of magic is simply science that hasn't been accepted yet. Chemistry and physics have taken over much of the work of the old alchemists, and psychology has adopted the interpretation of dreams. Perhaps what we are going to do tonight will one day require a license and a degree!"

Karen took a long drink of tea, then set down the cup and looked at Del again. "Yes. Well—what exactly *are* we going to do?"

"The same thing a physicist does when he describes the behavior of a quark or a black hole, only instead of playing with numbers and equations, which are also symbols of an invisible reality, we will be performing a ritual. The ritual will work upon our own minds, of course, but it will also work upon the reality around us. The physicists themselves have discovered that the presence of the observer affects the outcome of an experiment—there are no separate realities. As you learn more about these things you will realize that the human mind, properly trained and focused, can indeed change the world." Del set down her cup and smiled.

Some minutes later Karen found herself putting on the robe of natural linen that Del had given to her and reflecting on what the older woman had said. She had been told to wear nothing beneath it, and she had to admit that the touch of the garment on her bare skin and the silky weight of unbound hair on her back did make her feel different somehow. In her mirror she saw an image that seemed simplified, ready for action.

From the living room she heard music whose tones flowed into one another hypnotically, always melodic, yet never quite resolving into a tune. Del had told her that some of the things they would do tonight would directly affect the fabric of reality, while others were meant to put them in the proper frame of mind for the ceremony. Karen supposed that the gown and the music belonged in the latter category.

She turned out the light and opened the door to the living room, then stopped short, for a moment afraid to go in.

Except for one candle, all of the lights in the apartment had been put out. But that illumination was sufficient for her to see Del Eden, who was wearing an open caftan of glowing crimson silk over a plain robe like her own. As Del turned to face her the garment seemed to catch and magnify the light until it shone with a radiance of its own.

If that is supposed to impress me it's succeeded! thought Karen. Even Del's face seemed different, her face grown thinner and her eyes dark with mysteries. And surely she was taller—for a moment Karen thought she glimpsed the curve of a helmet, and in Del's hand the gleam of protecting steel.

"Come here . . . " Del's voice resonated in the small room. "First we will go through each room to cleanse it. You must walk behind me, carrying this tray, while I perform the banishing. This is very like the exorcism they perform in the Catholic Church—you must not be afraid."

Very carefully, Karen picked up the tray of polished wood on which had been placed a small stoneware bowl of rock-salt, a silver flagon of water, a miniature brass censer from which the pungent smoke of incense swirled, and a lit candle in a holder of worked copper. Still desperately afraid of stumbling or making a mistake, Karen no longer felt foolish. Whether or not it protected her apartment, at least she was doing *something,* and what harm could it do?

She followed Del through the kitchen onto the back porch.

"In the name of Uriel the Archangel and the Powers of Earth, may all evil be gone from here! May this space be cleansed, and may only strength and security remain!"

Something had happened to the pitch of Del's voice—Karen could feel the resonance in her bones. She held out the tray so that Del could take the bowl of salt and, turning counter-clockwise, sprinkle it to the four corners of the porch.

The procedure was repeated in the name of the Angel Gabriel with the water, invoking the harmony of the moon and tides, and then in the name of Raphael, using the censer to send sweet smoke from wall to wall while the blessing of clear thought and inspiration was asked. Finally Del took the candle and held it high.

"In the name of the Archangel Michael and the Powers of Fire, may all evil be gone from here! As this light banishes the shadows and the darkness vanishes away, may all shadow of sorrow or sadness be banished also, and may this house be filled with light."

And as the candle shone upon each corner Karen fancied she could see the light growing, until even when Del turned away her eyes were dazzled by its glow.

Through the kitchen, the bedroom, and the bathroom in turn they moved, counter-clockwise for the banishing and deosil as each room was blessed again. And as the invocation was repeated, its resonance built, echoes gathering until Karen's ears were overwhelmed by their vibrations as her eyes had been dazzled before.

It's only words—she thought numbly, but the incense dizzied her. The shadows around her trembled with the quiver of great wings—living Presences that glowed amber brown and sea-green and blue and flame. How could these tiny rooms contain even the transient extension of Powers clothed still in the splendors of some unimaginably other, vaster plane?

They completed the circuit of the living room. Del opened the front door and swept her arms forward in a gesture that stirred the folds of her caftan like great crimson wings.

"All that remains of evil here, be gone, be gone, be gone!"

Karen staggered in the eddy of a great wind, then Del slammed shut the door and everything was still. Trembling, she set the tray down.

Del bent over a long bundle of red silk that lay on the floor, twitched free its bindings and straightened again. The candle-light glimmered on the polished steel of a short, bone-handled sword.

"Now the cleansing is completed and it is time for the second part of the ceremony. As the angel with the flaming sword barred the way to Paradise, so with this sword we must draw an invisible line which will extend into an unbreakable wall around this place that extends through all the planes." She turned, and candlelight pooled and ran like water down the blade.

"You must help me now." Her eyes held Karen's, glowing as if, like the swordblade, they too held and poured back the candle's light. "Part of the success of this operation will depend on the vividness of your visualization and the strength of your will. As I draw the line you must see with your mind's eye a wall of light flaring up until its edges join and we are enclosed by a golden hemisphere."

Mute, Karen picked up the candle to light their way. But it was the radiance that flickered along the swordblade, not the candle, that was her beacon. Already dazzled, she did not find it difficult to follow Del's instructions as they passed clockwise once more through rooms in which the scent of incense still lingered.

With senses seduced by sight, by scent, by the sound of the music that still played, the busy intellect had at last grown still, a dispassionate observer of the ritual. Doubt was still there, waiting to flood back once this was done, but for the moment Karen was free, in a state where intention and action were one.

"In the name of the Maker of the Universe who informs all things and is encompassed by none, may this place be blessed. May the Powers of the Elements defend it, and the Great Ones who are their Angels. May all evil be repelled from it; may only good enter here. The symbol is nothing, but the reality is all, therefore let that which we have done with our human hands be given substance by the Mind of God. So mote it be!" Del raised the sword so that its tip nearly brushed the ceiling. Light flashed and vanished as she brought it down and hid it in the silk once more.

"Amen . . ." murmured Karen weakly.

Del turned and lifted her hands in blessing, and to Karen it seemed that what she was seeing now was the woman's true appearance, and the comfortable grandmotherly guise of every day was only a personality that Del wore to meet the world. Karen had read once that the Goddess was worshipped as Maiden, as Mother, and as Wisewoman. For the first time she began to understand what the power of that third face of the Lady might be.

Karen reached across the kitchen table for another slice of bread and picked up the butter knife.

"Are you sure you have had enough?" she asked Del, who was sitting across from her with her hands full of bread and cheese. "I had dinner before you came," Karen went on. "I don't know why I'm so ravenous!" She laid a slice of cold roast beef across her bread, added lettuce, and spread mustard on the other side.

Del put down her sandwich and smiled. "Don't apologize—it's quite normal to be hungry after a ritual. This kind of work drains both psychic and physical energy, and the body instinctively tries to replace it as quickly as possible. I would be surprised if you weren't hungry after what we did tonight."

"Yes. But—what exactly *did* we do?"

"Hmmn . . . it's a little hard to explain without using terms which would require more definition still." Del frowned. "Have you ever been in a house where the people have been very unhappy? How did it feel?"

Karen thought of her last visit to an old friend whose marriage was disintegrating. "I guess I know what you mean—" she said hesitantly. "Sort of tense and uncomfortable . . . but I thought that was just my reaction to the people involved."

"Perhaps, at least in part, it was. But houses do develop atmospheres that retain the emotions of those who live in them. Depending on the strength of the emotion and the sensitivity of the visitor, they can be perceived for quite a while. For instance, when I came in, I felt in this apartment traces of fear and anger—yours, and that of the men who broke in here. Therefore, the first thing we did was a sort of psychic house-cleaning."

"Is that all?" asked Karen.

"Isn't that enough?" Del replied. "Don't you feel any difference in the atmosphere? Go stand in the living room for a moment and tell me how it feels."

Feeling rather foolish, Karen went into the other room. Nothing had changed. It was very quiet. In fact, she did not think she had ever known the apartment to be so still. She shrugged, wondering if that was what she was supposed to feel. And then, as she breathed in again, Karen tensed, for she had the distinct impression that there was a strange scent in the room—not the incense, but something crisp and bracing, almost like air freshener.

She looked around her suspiciously. She had nothing like that in the apartment, but she supposed Del could have brought some in that capacious bag. Only, since they finished the ceremony, the older woman had not been alone in the living room. With an unaccustomed flutter in her stomach, Karen stepped into the bedroom and breathed in. And stopped, breath catching in her throat, for that scent of newness was here too.

Karen went back into the kitchen and sat down, reaching for the cookie jar, while Del raised a questioning eyebrow.

"All right, I believe you," Karen said at last. "But what about the bit with the sword?"

"Every action has an equal and opposite reaction," Del quoted then. "Having emptied the place of the mental images it held, we had to replace them with something else or they would have all flooded back again, perhaps with something worse in tow. What we did was to consciously and quickly accomplish what people do inadvertently over a long period of time.

"We blessed the place, and then guarded it with the image of the shimmering wall. People who mean you well will not notice it, unless, perhaps, to feel a special welcome here. But those who come with ill-will are likely to find it reflected back at them. They will either feel extremely uncomfortable or will perhaps find a good reason not to enter at all. *Every action has an equal and opposite reaction,*" Del said again. "If the presence of Freyja's power wakes that of Loki, you may be glad of this protection."

"Oh, Del." Karen shook her head as the sheer unlikeliness of it all overtook her. "How can I believe any of this? How do I know it's not my imagination gone wild?"

Again Del smiled. "My dear," she said, "why does a physicist believe in an electron? He has a hypothesis to explain its characteristics, and when he uses them to set up an experiment, things function as if the electrons were indeed there. . . .

"I can only say that when the job is done properly, the results seem to indicate that these things are real!"

12

No man so flawless but some fault he has,
nor so wicked as to be of no worth.
Both foul and fair are found among men,
blended within their breasts.
        THE SAYINGS OF HAR

The phone was ringing when Karen came out of the bedroom, still toweling her hair. She struggled to twist the loose ends of the towel into a rough turban, then grabbed for the phone.

"Karen?" Ridiculously, Karen felt her pulse quicken as she recognized Michael's voice—deep, with a kind of harsh precision she had never heard from anyone else.

"Are you okay? I just heard about the break-in at your apartment. Look, if I'd had any idea there would be a problem, I'd have taken you home myself. . . . "

"It's all right, Michael. You couldn't have known—for heaven's sake, if I'd known I could have stayed home and there wouldn't have *been* a burglary!" She eased down on the couch and pulled the afghan around her. From outside she could hear the steady drip of rain.

"Maybe," Michael said shortly. Karen wondered whether he was disappointed to have missed a fight. "Somebody said they got your cat?" he went on.

"Well, they certainly tried," she answered. "But Trjegul is pretty tough. They had to kind of glue her back together, but the vet says she'll be okay."

Michael laughed. "I believe you—I wouldn't want to take her on!"

Karen felt her turban coming down and cradled the phone between cheek and shoulder while she tried to twist it up again. After a moment she gave up and pulled off the towel, then sat absently fluffing her hair as Michael continued.

"I wanted you to know—I was glad to see you Thursday night. I've missed you."

Karen made some sound of agreement, but she was thinking, *Thursday—only a week ago!* It seemed as if months had passed. Suddenly her arms ached with longing to hold him, and she realized how much she had wanted Michael to call.

"Are you coming tonight?" he asked.

"I don't think so. It's probably silly, but tonight I don't want to leave the apartment alone. Besides, I just got Trjegul back from the pet hospital, and she needs watching."

"Oh." The disappointment in Michael's voice almost made her change her mind. "Well, do you think she'll be improved enough for you to go out Saturday?"

"Oh, I think so." Karen found herself smiling.

"Will you come out to dinner with me?"

Karen had already begun to agree when he went on, "I thought maybe you and I and Duncan could get together, and the two of you could get to know each other. He's the oldest friend I have in the world, and you—well, it would make me very happy if you and he could be friends."

Karen floundered between her half-agreement and her aversion to Duncan Flyte. If only she had not told Michael she was free—but it would be too obvious if she tried to get out of the date now.

"All right . . . " she answered after a pause which she hoped had not been too long. Over the phone she heard the sound of a motorcycle revving up. Michael must be calling from the shop where he sometimes picked up some extra money doing repairs.

"It's getting too noisy in here for me to talk," he shouted. "I'll call you again and let you know what time, okay?"

"Yes," she said, and when he shouted to her to repeat her answer, she shouted back, "Okay!"

Karen listened to the patter of rain against her window and turned back to her dresser for her paisley wool scarf. It had been raining on and off for the past week, a determined sort of drizzle that darkened the dusty hills and filled the dry creek-beds with gurgling rivulets. The ski resorts must be happy, she thought—by Thanksgiving the slopes of the Sierras would be deep in snow.

She looked around her, wondering if she had forgotten anything. Michael should be here soon. She went back into the kitchen, bent to stroke Trjegul, who still spent most of her time in the basket by the stove, and checked to make sure that the cats' water and food dishes were full.

"There, my lioness—you should be all right until I get back. Stay in your basket, now." The cat's chest was still taped, but the scabs from some of the headwounds had already fallen away. She still looked like a wounded warrior, but a considerable improvement over the mangled thing Karen had taken to the vet's the week before. Golden eyes followed her as she rose to her feet, then narrowed to slits again.

Footsteps echoed hollowly on the staircase, and Karen hurried to open the door. Michael had already reached her landing, hatless, with his leather jacket zipped up to his chin. He shook himself like a dog and she jumped back as water splattered the hall.

"Goodness, Michael—isn't it wet enough outside?" She laughed and stepped aside so that he could come in.

He looked around ruefully and Karen saw Duncan Flyte behind him, his clothing covered by a black trenchcoat, an umbrella in his hand. Karen forced a smile.

"Come on in—I just need to get my coat and I'll be ready."

Duncan paused on her threshold. "No—we've left the motor running—I'd better go back to the car."

Michael grinned as Duncan retreated down the stairs. "That was thoughtful of him." He turned back to Karen, who was buttoning her coat, and pulled her against him. She could feel the contours of his body even through all their layered clothing, and felt an answering warmth in her own. As Michael kissed her she forgot Duncan, forgot the empty weeks since their quarrel, exulting in the hard strength that held her and the purpose in the lips that searched hers. It took her a minute to catch her breath after he let her go, and a moment more before the question that had been forming in her mind when he kissed her surfaced again.

"Thoughtful? What do you mean?"

"Oh, well, he knew that I would want a minute alone with you. The car's all right"—he reached into his pocket—"I have the keys right here."

Yes, of course, Karen thought as she followed Michael down the stairs; Michael always insisted on doing the driving—Duncan was only doing his friend a good turn. But why, she wondered, had she had the momentary fancy that the magician had intended to follow Michael but had been unable to come inside?

Red tail-lights flowered and faded before them as they moved into the sluggish flow of traffic across the Bay Bridge to San Francisco. Sitting next to Michael in the front seat of the Chrysler, Karen missed the closeness of riding the cycle, but in weather like this she was grateful for the protection of a car.

Michael drove with precision, anticipating snarls and compensating for his impaired vision with constant darting turns of the head. Karen sank back into the luxuriant upholstery, listening to Duncan's rattle of conversation and Michael's sporadic replies. For a moment the world seemed shrunken to the capsule that was this car, in which only the three of them still lived, and she shivered. *We're all on our best behavior,* she told herself, *We're going to have a convivial, civilized evening.*

Somehow, perhaps because Karen had admitted to never having eaten Viet Namese food before, they had decided on a Viet Namese restaurant. Duncan knew a place in the Mission District, near where he was holding his classes, called the Bien Hoa. Prices were still reasonable in that part of town, and even on a Saturday night there should be plenty of room.

But he had not guaranteed that there would be a convenient parking place, and they had to walk three blocks through dark back streets before emerging into Sixteenth Street within sight of the restaurant. By the time they got there, water had found its way through an unsuspected gap in one of Karen's boots and her foot was sliding about uncomfortably.

She did not mention it to Michael. Even the little she knew about fighting in Viet Nam included images of sloshing through steaming jungles and rice paddies—he would be quite justified in laughing at her. She was beginning to regret agreeing to come, or at least agreeing to come here. Would the meal

bring back an old cameraderie, or would Viet Namese sur-
roundings raise the kind of nightmares that had so often
awakened Michael struggling and sobbing in her arms?

But the place was quiet, its rice-papered walls and carpeted
floor soothingly conservative in comparison to the garish colors in most of the Chinese restaurants she knew. She stared at
the menu, trying to puzzle out the meaning of the English
translations next to the strange names.

"Order whatever you want." Duncan gestured expansively.
"The Flamingo has extended my run and it's all on me!"

Karen read down the menu—*"Canh bao ngu*—abalone
soup, *gung*—singing chicken in ginger sauce, Ho's steak with
peanut sauce, *Leo xao meng*—pork sauteed with bamboo. . . . " The list ran on, including French dishes as well as
Viet Namese.

"Invisible duck?" she said in astonishment. "What on
earth is that?"

Duncan grinned. "Order it and see—"

Michael nodded. "Go ahead—it's usually pretty good."

"What are you having?" she asked suspiciously.

"Volcano beef—*bo cu lao,* and about three bottles of
beer!"

Duncan was laughing. "Remember that place we went to in
Danang? They musta emptied the curry jar into the pan. You
were running around frothing at the mouth like you'd been hit
by a B-52 with a bunch of cluster bombs." As Duncan leaned
forward the candle on the table underlit his face demonically.
Then he sat back and Karen could see only the gleam of his
eyes.

The waiter, soft-footed on the carpet, came over to take
their orders. He looked about seventeen, self-effacing, wary—
he probably often served vets who came in for nostalgia's sake
or to probe old wounds. Karen wondered how old he had been
when his family came here, what he had been through, how
much of him was now American, and how much still belonged
to Viet Nam.

Duncan was giving their orders in a swift spate of Viet
Namese. The boy nodded and turned away, and in a few
moments brought them cups of a kind of chicken gruel gar-
nished with bits of green that might have been chives or lemon
grass. Michael had started on the first of his bottles of beer,
and Duncan poured out the bottle of good California Riesling

he had ordered for himself and Karen.

"I ran into Hector Santana a few months ago—" Duncan said suddenly. "When I was doing a gig in Phoenix."

Michael looked up. "Old Hector? How's he doing?"

"Oh, I don't know—okay, I guess. He'd split up with his wife and it looked like he'd been hitting the sauce pretty heavy, but he was working."

"Yeah—I'd guess he'd do all right," Michael took a last long swallow of beer and put the empty glass down. "He always swore he was going to get through it without a scratch and he was right, too. I couldn't believe it—him standing up in the middle of the bush with tracers going to either side. He said his mama and all his aunts had a twenty-four-hour rosary brigade working for him, and maybe it was true. You seen any more of the old gang?" Michael went on. "I always meant to keep in touch, after I got out of Rehab, but you know how it is."

"Some. . . . " Duncan's head was a little bowed; his clever fingers played idly with the silverware. "They see my name on the advertisements and they come up after the show."

The waiter brought in the main course—Michael's beef sizzling volcanically on a steel dish set in a wooden platter because it was too hot to hold, and Karen's duck, whose invisibility seemed to lie in the fact that it had been fried in some kind of batter that made it look like Kentucky Fried Chicken. Duncan had ordered *coq au vin*.

Michael set to with chopsticks, but Karen decided that her duck was finger-food, dipped a piece in the sauce, and took a careful bite.

"How is it?" Michael smiled at her.

"Great—and duck is always so hard to get right. But this isn't greasy or dry, and the batter has some kind of spices in it that I'm still trying to identify."

"I think the dip there is peanut sauce—they use a lot of it. It may taste sweet at first, but you'll notice there's a bite to it."

Karen nodded. Viet Namese food looked very much like Chinese, complete with the little dishes of white rice on the side, but once you had taken a good mouthful you noticed that there was indeed a bite to it—the unfamiliar tang of ginger or lemon grass, or the fresh-ironing taste of celantro, and other flavors she didn't know. It seemed to her that the war had been like that too—an apparently simple exercise that held endless and deadly ambiguities.

And you are becoming as fanciful as an old maid on a stormy night, Karen told herself. It was Duncan—he had done absolutely nothing to which she could object, but he still made her nervous as he sat across from her, delicately dismembering his *coq au vin.* Candlelight picked up the silken sheen of his tie and flared from his gold cufflinks as he moved his hands. It was hard to imagine him in a uniform.

Involuntarily Karen's hand went to her neck, where Brisingamen was hidden by her scarf and the high neck of the grey jersey dress she wore. It was illogical to think Duncan might have had anything to do with the burglary of her apartment, and yet it made her uneasy to even think of leaving the necklace unguarded when he knew she was away from home. But she could not bear the idea that he might touch it—even see it—again. So she had compromised by hiding it under the scarf, and as Duncan's eyes followed her movement she saw him smile, and felt a sick certainty that he knew she was wearing Brisingamen. Perhaps he had known that all along.

So what? Even if Duncan does want the necklace, Michael would never let him hurt me! Forcing a smile, Karen lifted her glass in what was intended to be an ironic salute.

"Yes, I've seen quite a few from the old platoon," Duncan backtracked abruptly. "The ones who lived to come home. Of course not all of them made it through the past few years. Tom Bartolini told me that Giorgio jumped out of a window at the Rehab hospital they had him at. And there's Harry Steiner— he O-D'ed in St. Louis three years ago. I don't think there's much point in that twenty-year reunion party we were all planning to have some day."

Karen's fingers clenched on her glass. Why was Duncan doing this? Michael had grown very still, his face hardening in lines she did not recognize, as if he were putting on a mask he had thrown away a dozen years ago. For a moment there was silence. Then Michael took a deep breath and the harsh lines eased.

"I saw one of our guys who survived, and not too long ago. Remember our first medic—Roosevelt Springer?" Michael said. "You should—I seem to remember he pulled you out when that wall got blown up and half-buried you. He got back, and got his shit together, and actually made it through medical school. He's putting in volunteer time at the Free Clinic in Berkeley now."

"He's better off than Gordo, then."

Karen stiffened again. She had heard Michael say that name once in a nightmare, and he had explained that Gordo was the medic who patched him together enough for evacuation when he was hit. Why had Duncan mentioned him now? She looked from one man to the other as if she were watching a fencing match with unfamiliar rules. They were friends, weren't they?

Michael straightened, and as he turned, his good eye was momentarily luminous in the candlelight. "I haven't forgotten," he said gently. "Why do you think *I'm* alive? There were times in Rehab when I didn't want to be. But I remembered that he was sitting on top of that hill working on me when he got it. If someone was willing to lose his life for me I figure I've got to justify it!"

As he stared at Duncan, for a moment the other man's mask slipped and Karen glimpsed in his eyes an unending, uncomprehending pain.

Her own eyes stung with tears and her hand went for comfort to the hard shape of the necklace. *Freyja, here are two wounded warriors*—for they were all wounded, she realized now, whether or not their bodies bore visible scars. *What did you say to the slain warriors you chose to guard your hall? How did you comfort them?*

And for a moment she felt the air warm around her, and a Voice said silently, *"Heal them with your love. . . . "*

Words of pity trembled on her lips and she bit them back. Michael and Duncan did not want pity, but a way back from memory. She managed a smile.

"Thank you both for bringing me here—" she said softly. "You know what they say about San Francisco—when a new ethnic group moves in, people don't ask about their crime rate, they want to know about their cuisine! Now I know!"

Michael stared blankly for a moment, then grinned. Duncan sighed and leaned back against the padded seat of the booth. Then the boy was back, asking if they wanted desert, and normalcy returned.

After the spicy food the cool sweetness of lychee fruit was soothing. They ate in silence like the stillness after battle, but by the time they had finished, Michael's face had lost its haunted look and Duncan had recovered his sardonic grin.

Michael went out to get the car while Duncan was paying the bill. When he had finished he took Karen's arm and they went outside. The rain was only spitting now, but the wind growled like an angry hound, and it had grown piercingly cold. Karen turned up the collar of her coat and peered around her. Scattered puddles reflected an uneasy glitter from the streetlights as wind ruffled them, and the shuttered storefronts and tawdry lights of the bars seemed unreal as the drizzle veiled and revealed them again.

Duncan stood with his head back and his face to the wind. "Cold—" His voice was almost lost as it gusted around them. "At least it is a cold rain. The worst thing about 'Nam was that the rain was warm . . . like blood. If you put on a slicker sweat soaked you worse than the storm."

"It's cold enough now," Karen agreed shivering.

"Winter's coming, with clean pure winds and pure, white snow. . . . " Duncan laughed softly and stepped from beneath the dubious shelter of the awning. "Where's Michael with that car?" He started down the street and Karen followed him.

The door to one of the bars opened for a moment as they went by, releasing a gust of stale air and drunken laughter. Karen walked faster to catch up to Duncan, who had paused at the corner, looking down the alley.

"I was a bit nervous about coming tonight," said Karen, "but now I'm glad I did. It's important to Michael that his friends get along, and some of the conversation—" She fumbled for some way of saying it that would not sound condescending or banal. "Well, it helped me to understand—"

"Understand?" He turned on her, eyes glittering, and Karen skipped back as if he had struck her. "How can you understand, you who lived through it with your eyes on a soap opera and your ass in an easy chair? And as for Michael, you want to be 'good for him,' I suppose? What good will it do him to be lulled by your softness until he forgets all the lessons we learned about what things are really like in this world?

"You think you are safe, but I have seen girls half your age spread-eagled—" Abruptly Duncan mastered himself, but Karen felt lust and frustrated rage radiating from him, as if she stood next to a fire. Instinctively she pulled the image Del Eden had shown her around her—a barrier of light that would reflect his emotions back upon him again.

"Very few people have the will or the skill to mount an intentional psychic attack," Del had told her, *"but the uncontrolled projection of emotion can make you very uncomfortable. This is a way to shield yourself. . . . "*

For a moment Duncan rocked back and forth, buffeted by the wind. The streetlights flickered unsteadily in his eyes. Then he reached into his pocket and brought out a cigarette lighter, fumbled again on the other side, slapped the pockets of his trenchcoat, and swore.

"I've left my cigarettes in the restaurant—I'll be back in a minute. You watch out for Michael here."

Before Karen could answer he was gone. The pent breath went out of her in a long sigh. *Goddess,* she thought, *at least I tried.* A car sped down the street, its tires hissing on wet asphalt, then the road was deserted again. Karen felt raindrops kiss her cheeks and pulled her coat more closely around her. There was no point in trying to open her umbrella in this wind.

The wail of a country western record blared into the night as the door of the bar opened again. Karen heard laughter and an oath as someone stumbled into a puddle, and stepped closer to the streetlight, peering through the rain. The laughter and footsteps came closer. *Late patrons on their way home at last,* she thought. *Where is Michael, anyway?*

Still barriered against others' emotions, Karen did not realize they were near her until she felt a touch on her sleeve.

"Hey, Honee—you waitin' for somebody? You a hot lady—I go with you okay—"

Karen turned quickly. "No!" There were four of them, faces still glowing from the booze they had drunk and the heat of the bar, but their clothes were beginning to darken from the rain. "No—you've made a mistake." She tried to speak calmly.

"You got a car near here, or you wanna go to my place? We all go to my place, okay? How much, huh?" He did not appear to have heard.

Mute, Karen shook her head, gauging the distance back to the restaurant, looking anxiously for some sign of Michael and the car. *Duncan, damn you!* she thought, *You left me here, and*—but that was paranoia. There was no way he could have known anyone would bother her, not on a night like this.

"Hey, don' you like my frien'?" One of the other men had

shouldered close to her now, his eyes more angry and aware.
"You cow, you don' insult us! We offered money—whassa
matter, isn't our money good enough for you?" His hand
closed on her arm and she jerked free.

"Let me go! I didn't mean to offend you, but I'm not—I'm
not for sale. I'm just waiting for a friend!" Karen fought to
keep her voice steady. *You're a big girl,* she told herself, *you
can get yourself out of this!*

"I'm a frien'—" the first man grinned wetly. "Look, I
show you—" He began to fumble with his fly. The other two
were laughing, leaning against each other. Karen could not tell
if they really understood what was going on.

"You're for sale—all you bitches are for sale. Why else you
waitin' in the rain? You with your yellow hair, you think you
too good for us, eh?" Hands closed on Karen's arms, and this
time she was not strong enough to pull away.

"Let me go!" She drew breath to scream and he clapped his
hand over her mouth, callused and smelling of stale beer and
tobacco and other things that stirred nausea at the back of her
throat.

"Come on bitch—you don't want our money, you don't get
it. But you give us a good time all the same. . . . "

Karen tried to struggle as he hauled her into the alley, but
she was dizzy and confused. She could hear the other men
laughing, adding their own obscene comments.

This can't be happening, she thought, *not to me . . .* and
then one of Duncan's gibes echoed in her memory—*"I have
seen girls half your age spread-eagled. . . . "* For a moment
some deep guilt said, *It is just. Why should I be exempt from
what so many other women have borne?*

And her captor, feeling her resistance cease, made a hoarse
sound deep in his throat, halfway between a cough and a
laugh, and gripped the front of her coat.

They'll have you down in a moment, came that cold, mocking voice within. *They'll have you flat on your back in the cold
water with your dress torn open and—BRISINGAMEN!* The
name exploded through her consciousness like a flare on a
dark battlefield. If they tore her clothing they would see the
necklace they would touch it they—the idea of that violation
somehow stirred her where fear for herself had only made her
panic's prey.

The necklace had glowed when she and Michael made love,

but it was unthinkable that obscene hands should paw it, that the Goddess should give herself other than freely, that she, Karen, should be used this way!

"NO!" she shouted, "You *dare* to lay hands on Me?" Her voice rang against the brick walls of the alley and a new gust of wind buffeted them. She could feel Brisingamen burning on her neck—burning, flames were exploding around her. She flung wide her arms as Freyja had burst her chains in Odin's fire, and the men who held her reeled backward.

"You have the souls of the mangy dogs that feed on the dunghill—do you call yourselves men?" she hissed. She drew herself up and saw them crouched far below. "You are vermin, and upon your bellies will you crawl forever if you lay a finger on me! Your *cojones* will wither if you try to touch me—just try it! No food will nourish you, no drink will refresh you—" The alley rang with a torrent of unexpected imagery.

And her tormenters were cringing, whimpering, forcing their feet to motion and careening against the walls of the alley and righting themselves with staring eyes and squeals of fear. Hand still outstretched in malediction, Karen looked down upon them and watched them go.

Running feet clattered on asphalt—a new figure, outlined in lightnings, sending one of her attackers sprawling as he came, whirling smoothly to strike another—but as if that intervention had broken a spell, the men regained their powers of motion and dashed away.

"Karen! I heard shouting—did they hurt you—where—" Michael slid to a halt beside her, panting. At the entrance to the alley she saw the car with its door hanging open and motor running still. Calmly she turned back to look at Michael, almost as tall as she was, with a glow about him that could have been light from the streetlamps but seemed in that dark place something more. His good eye shone.

Is that what I looked like to those men? Karen wondered, but her attackers had disappeared.

"I'll kill them if they touched you—" Michael growled, but already the light around him was beginning to fade. Karen felt the power that had filled her ebbing. She was shrinking; she clutched at the shreds of certainty.

"Where's Duncan?" Michael asked then.

"Right here, buddy. Why, is something wrong?"

Michael and Karen turned. Duncan was standing at the head of the alley. The light of the streetlamp behind him glowed in his red hair. His face was in shadow, but it seemed to Karen that some inner fire still flickered in his eyes.

"Some bastards dragged Karen in here, tried to rape her—"

"I trust you arrived in time to save her from a fate worse than death?" Duncan's voice was colder than the wind. Karen shivered. If he had not arranged the attack—and even now she did not see how, as Duncan, he could have managed it—he was not sorry for it either. Karen glared at him. How could she have ever looked at him with sympathy?

Del had warned her—the first near-accidents with the man in the car and at the opera had been a simple reaction to the presence of Brisingamen, the energy of Loki momentarily possessing whoever was near. But in Duncan Flyte, that energy had found its ideal tool. Consciously or unconsciously he was behind the attempted burglary—she remembered how his two 'students' had left the Blue Door early and was certain of that now—and his spirit had filled the men who had tried to rape her here.

"God damn it, Duncan—" Michael began, but Karen was already answering—

"You would have been happy to see them succeed, wouldn't you, Duncan? You would be happy to see me traumatized and no good to anyone, out of Michael's life so that you can seduce him back to your own vision of Hell! Well, the war's over, Duncan, and I'm not going to let you destroy me, or him!"

"The war's over?" echoed Duncan, as Michael stared from him to Karen and back again. "Is it now? We shall see. . . . "

13

Karen picked a greasy rag from the only chair in Michael's room, dropped it on the floor, dusted off the chair, and sat down. She could see his back and shoulder muscles bunching beneath the thin T-shirt as he torqued down the last of the cylinder head bolts. After a few moments he grunted and sat up.

"Michael, I'm sorry about Saturday night—" Karen began, hoping he would be willing to talk to her now. The rain that had forced him to bring the cycle into his own room for repairs drummed steadily outside; the Grateful Dead wailed insistently from another room. She swallowed. "Michael?"

"Yeah, I know. You two just don't hit it off. I was stupid to try." He picked up the distorted silver vessel that he had told her was the carburetor body, blew bits of the residue that had fouled it onto the newspapers that covered the floor, and set to work with brush and solvent.

"*. . . just don't hit it off!*" Karen bit back laughter that threatened to become hysterical. As a description of the almost primal antipathy between her and Duncan Flyte, it was

157

like describing the Korean War as a police action. She sighed and looked around the room.

She had been here before, but not for long. Most of her time with Michael had been spent at her own apartment or on the great machine that lay dismembered on the floor. Despite the clutter of cycle parts, the place was scrupulously neat. Michael had said once that his neatness was a reaction to months spent in the mud of Viet Nam, months when he hadn't even been able to brush his teeth because he was using his toothbrush to keep his rifle clean. She remembered how he had laughed, and it was the laughter even more than his story that had wrenched at her heart.

Not that he had much to take care of. The room was dominated now by the bulk of the Harley, but the only furniture was a mattress, and a low table with a battered typewriter. And the bookshelf, of course, with the *Oxford Book of English Verse*, a worn dictionary, copies of *Iron Horse* magazine, and journals in which Michael's poetry had appeared. There was also an eclectic collection of fiction—E.R. Eddison next to Donald Hamilton, Tolkien, and a copy of *Njal's Saga* and Frank Fraga's novel about Viet Nam. A poster of Sandahl Bergman as Valeria in the *Conan* movie was tacked on the wall.

And then, of course, there was the sword.

Michael gave the carburetor a final inspection and picked up the polishing cloth. After a few moments' work he grunted in satisfaction and began to bolt the instrument to the intake manifold.

"There on the wall above your bed—is that the kris you were describing in your poem?" Karen asked. "I thought it was only a metaphor—"

Michael began to laugh. "Can't a metaphor be a weapon? The pen is deadlier than the sword . . . but this one is what you might call a 'tangible image,' and it is very real. I read somewhere once that the best symbol for a sharp sword is—a sharp sword!" He set the rachet driver down, swiveled on his heels and reached to take the kris from the brackets on the wall.

Carefully he drew it from the wooden sheath. The overhead light sparkled on the wavy edges of the two-and-a-half-foot blade. It was not as bright as sunlight, but the words of Michael's poem echoed in Karen's memory and something beneath her ribs contracted suddenly.

Because she realized that if the sword was real, then perhaps the other things the poem had said were real, too. With his own hands, with that very piece of steel, Michael had "dealt death silently." She swallowed the questions she had learned not to ask when her brother returned from the war—*Did you kill anybody over there?*

"Yes, it's a kris, though most people think that name belongs only to the wavy-bladed knife that Malay warriors bear," Michael went on cheerfully. "But this is a Moro headhunter's blade." Air whistled behind the sword as he snapped it sideways. Karen flinched.

"Don't worry—" He grinned at her. "I know what I'm doing, but I'll put it away now. Still smiling, he drew the tip of the blade across his arm, then slid it into the sheath. Karen stared as a thin trickle of blood snaked across the flaming skull tatooed on his arm.

Michael set the sword gently on its brackets, turned and saw her eyes on him, picked up a rag and used a clean corner to blot the blood away. Then he reached out for her. Trembling, Karen slid off the chair into his arms.

"Honey—it's all right, it's okay!" he murmured, rocking her. He smelled of sweat and machine oil. "It was just a scratch. I didn't mean to upset you—does blood bother you?"

"No," she managed to say. "I used to kill chickens on the ranch. But *your* blood—yes, I guess that does bother me. Oh Michael, I've missed you so much!"

His grip tightened. His words were muffled against her hair but her body was listening—"I love you . . . my lady, my only love. . . . " His hand moved up and down her back, sending sparks tingling along every nerve. He found her chin and turned her head to kiss her. She clung to him desperately, he tried to hold her closer and they overbalanced and fell into the parts pile.

"God fuckin' damn it to hell!" said Michael, rubbing his leg where the corner of the oil tank had dug into it.

"Hey, Mike, you all right in there?" Someone knocked heavily. "Hey, I gotta six-pack of Heineken's—" The door opened and a wind-burned, bearded face peered in. "Oh, sorry—" The door began to close.

"No, it's cool," said Michael in resignation as Karen turned away, giggling helplessly. "Save some of the brew for me." He leaned over and smacked her lightly on the rear. "Come on—I could use a drink right now!''

Still laughing, Karen got to her feet and tucked her black turtleneck back into her jeans—her tightest jeans, for although it was too cold for a Harley-Davidson tank top, when she visited Michael she tried to put on what a biker's ol' lady was expected to wear.

As she turned she caught sight of her reflection in the window and realized that her jersey must have shrunk in the wash, and with her golden hair falling down her back she came closer than she had intended to a biker's fantasy. Well, as long as she did Michael credit, she didn't care, and no one was going to bother a brother's woman, especially not Michael's woman, especially, she thought a bit smugly, when Michael was there.

And then she remembered foul breath and grasping hands and the damp darkness of a rainy alleyway and grew cold. *Michael can't always be with you,* she thought, *and you and the Goddess must be your own protection then!*

Michael replaced his tools in their box and screwed the cap back onto the oil can, then stretched and took her arm, but the memories of that night in San Francisco were crowding back. She had to talk to Michael about Duncan, but when? There was no place for heavy conversation here.

Beer and pizza had been set out in the kitchen. Karen took some and sat down, smiling tentatively at the long-haired girl with roses tattooed around her wrist who was feeding a toddler. She and her old man lived here, but besides them and Michael, Karen had never been able to count the permanent residents. She suspected it didn't really matter.

"So this guy comes into the shop with a 1961 C.H. with a busted magneto—" That was Jagger, who worked with Michael at Roadway Motors. Karen had met him before, but most of the others were strange to her. She suspected they had been driven indoors by the rain.

"Hey, Mike—" This was a big guy whose massive torso mocked the efforts of his sleeveless jean jacket to contain it. "You got that knuck of yours runnin' again?" Belly—she remembered his name now, a friend of Paladin's.

Michael shook his head. "Spent all afternoon sorting out the top end. The belt drive is still on order. Hope I can get it on the road again soon!"

"I'll bet you're hoping for that, too," the other girl said to

Karen. She finished feeding her baby and set him on the floor. "Last time Jag was fixing his machine he went three weeks without hardly speaking to me, much less doing anything else!" she grinned. "If he spent that much time with another girl I'd have her hide, but by the end of it I guess I was missin' the bike as much as he was."

Karen felt a reminiscent shiver, thinking of the vibration of the machine beneath her, the pressure of Michael's body against breast and thigh and the intoxication of speed as the world rushed by. Beyond all the booze, the drugs, the bizarre clothing and passwords of the bikers' world, this was the bond of brotherhood, the shared addiction to free flight and the open road.

Am I hooked too? she wondered, *or only in love with Michael?* She watched him, lean frame angled against the wall, muscles sliding beneath the tattoo on his arm as he lifted the can of beer. It had been more than a month since they made love, and she wanted him. Did he feel it, too? As if her gaze had touched him Michael turned to look at her and her breath came faster.

The front door slammed and obscene greetings chorused from the other room. Michael peered around the kitchen door.

"Long John! Hey bro, where you been? We heard you was up the coast somewhere. . . . "

The newcomer was one of the tallest men Karen had ever seen. He pulled off goggles and helmet and she saw a seamed face and long, grizzled hair. Most of the brothers she had met went bareheaded around town, but many were willing to put on a helmet when they hit the highway. What they objected to was not *wearing* a helmet so much as being *required* to wear one by the law. They saw themselves as the heirs of the sea rovers and the frontiersmen—righteous, liberty-loving Americans who wanted only to be left alone, even if it killed them. Society saw them as outlaws and a menace on the road whose accidents left living bodies to drain the resources of public medical care, saw in their desire for freedom, irresponsible anarchy.

And which was the truth? If it came to a final confrontation, would they stand on the side of the Jötuns or of the gods?

The thought had taken only a moment. Long John, provided with a toke and a beer, was just settling into a battered easy chair.

"Well, my old lady split, and I was havin' a little trouble with the machine. Parts for an Indian are hard to come by up there, so I thought I'd give the Bay a try." He grinned.

The conversation degenerated into a technical dissection of possible problems with Long John's bike and ways of fixing it, followed by a more general discussion of the relative merits of knuckleheads and panheads, Nortons and Triumphs and Harleys and their motors and gears and frames. Karen sighed, knowing that this could go on for hours.

There was a glow in Long John's eyes when he talked about his bike. She wondered if that was why his woman had left him. "Ol' ladies" might come and go, but a rider's first loyalty was to his brothers and his machine. . . .

And what about Michael? she wondered then. *Will he be loyal to all this, or to Duncan, or to me? I don't want to make him choose, but he's got to understand—do I understand?* She drained the last of her beer and rested her head in her hands.

"Hey, Karen, are you okay? Do you want to go home now?"

As Michael slid his arm around her she looked up and tried to smile. "I don't know—maybe the noise and smoke are getting to me. And I was hoping to get some time alone with you."

He bent suddenly to kiss her, and she saw a pulse beating in his throat.

"Yeah, we'll split," he said a little hoarsely. "I've been cooped up in here all day and I need to get out, even if it's only in that old clunker you call a car."

The weather man said it was only a gap between storms, but as they drove across Berkeley the wind was tearing the clouds into long streamers of grey, tinged now with dirty rose by the last of the setting sun.

"Let's drive up to Tilden," Michael said suddenly. "Park for a while and look at the sunset. God—it seems like months since I've seen the sky!"

He stopped the car in one of the turn-outs on the road that led into the park, and for a little while the battle of wind and clouds spread out before them held them silent. The jumble of houses in the flatlands were a dim mosaic, but the parting clouds splashed the water with streaks of silver, and above them the sky was translucent, jeweled with the first stars. The mountains across the Bay were like an illusion as the swirling mists revealed and then hid them again. Then the streetlights and bridge lights began to flicker on in sparkling lines, and the wasteland was transformed to Faerie.

"It's so beautiful." said Karen at last. "It is hard to believe there's evil in the world. But I've met it, Michael, and I'm afraid."

His face hardened as he listened, but he kept silent as Karen tried to make sense of the events that had followed her discovery of the necklace, and her growing conviction that Duncan Flyte was somehow involved.

When she was finished, he stared at her for a long time and then sighed.

"Look—I know you're afraid I'll say you're crazy, and God knows I've been close to the edge often enough that I can't throw stones, but can you hear what you're saying? Gods and magic necklaces and Giants trying to run you down?"

Karen swallowed. "Do you have a better theory? Will you at least admit that something weird is going on? Goodness knows I've tried hard enough not to believe it, but if the Goddess isn't real, I'm going to have to revise my notion of reality, and if She exists, then couldn't other powers also be looking for people on their wavelength, so to speak, to work for them?" She felt tears burning in her eyes and tried to blink them away.

"Oh, honey, I don't want to lay a trip on you. If Freyja is real for you, then She's real, and if She's made you what you are to me then I'm grateful to Her, too." He slid over on the seat and drew Karen against him, and for a moment the security of his arms around her was enough. She had seen him when a god was in him—the first time they made love and in San Francisco when he raced to her rescue. But he did not recognize what had happened to him, did not remember it, and so he could not believe.

"But you've got to get over this thing about Duncan," he went on, and she stiffened and pulled away.

"Why?" she asked sharply. "Why are you so convinced he

couldn't be doing his bit to help Armageddon along?''

Michael leaned back against the car seat, felt around in the pocket of his jacket and pulled out his pipe and tobacco pouch. He struck a match and for a moment his features flickered mockingly. Then he got the pipe going and blew out the flame and there was only the dull glow of the pipe and the dim oval of his face in the fading light.

"I met Duncan when I had been in-country about three months. He was a replacement, a skinny, red-headed kid from Chicago with his face sunburned almost the color of his hair.''

Karen held very still, aware that now the time had come when Michael could open to her at last.

"The captain put him on point, same as always with new men—new guys almost always did the scouting—either they got hit fast and out of it or they learned to survive, and then it was safe to get friendly, though after you've seen somebody you were just bullshitting with in little red pieces all over the jungle a couple of times it gets kinda hard to open up and be friends. . . . '' The glow of the pipe pulsed as he drew in deeply, then he exhaled, and the pungent smoke eddied about him like the smoke of artillery fire.

"Still, after a while we got to know each other pretty good. Duncan relaxed a little, started showing us his magic tricks— I've told you about that—and we went on a few R & R's. There was one time I remember, when we liberated a jeep from the Officer's Club and picked up a couple of girls and drove down to Saigon, and—well, that doesn't really matter. The thing is, we were buddies—shared booze, money, clothes, whatever we had.'' Michael took another pull at his pipe, then went on.

"Well, that was usual enough, and there were other guys I hung out with too. But Duncan could talk, real serious talk— not just the bright patter you've heard. He was the only person I would let see my poetry. We used to get a couple beers and sit up half the night rapping about what was wrong with the war, what was wrong with the country—what was wrong with the whole damn world! Mostly people just turned their minds off —some of them tuned out the whole year they were in 'Nam. But talking to Duncan I'd feel maybe there was some point to it all—maybe we could learn something so it wouldn't all happen again. I may not be every Mama's idea of a success in life, but at least I'm still in there trying, and if it hadn't been for

Duncan—well, hell! If it weren't for Duncan I wouldn't be *here*!"

He stopped suddenly and for a moment Karen wondered if he was done. She watched him as he stared out the window of the car and saw that he was holding his hand over his ruined eye as if to soothe a vanished pain.

"It's all right—" she whispered, "you don't have to tell me any more."

Michael sighed. "It shouldn't bother me," he said. "It was a long time ago, and I want you to understand." He reached out and she took his hand.

"We got shifted up into the highlands, near the Cambodian-Laos border. It's bunchy, closed-in country up there—not much mud, but green stuff, vines and all that, so thick you think they're going to reach out and smother you. Gives you claustrophobia after a while, especially when you don't know what's hiding there!

"Anyway, we hadn't had any contacts for awhile, hadn't lost anybody either, so there were no new guys to put on point and we were rotating it around the platoon. There was this day it was my turn, and I got careless—I was getting real short, only a few weeks left on my tour, and I guess I got to daydreaming, thinking I was actually going to go home. Or maybe it would have happened no matter how sharp I had been."

Karen nodded in the darkness. "Somebody fired at you?"

He gave a bark of laughter. "It was grenades, like the sky falling. My partner was in pieces all over the trail and I thought my head had been blown off. Between shock and concussion my hearing was gone too—I lay there looking at a bamboo leaf and wondering how long it would take the jungle to eat my bones.

"The next thing I saw was our medic, Gordo. His lips moved, like he was swearing, but I couldn't hear. By then the firefight was exploding all around me—I could see the wind as the shit went past. I tried to tell Gordo to get the hell out of there before he bought it too, and then of course a round smashed him and he was gone. . . . ''

Michael sat very still. Karen tightened her grip on his hand. "And Duncan saved you?" she asked.

He nodded. "My vision was coming and going like an out-of-synch film, but his red head is pretty distinctive. He crawled in there and hauled me bump-ass in the mud all the

way back down the trail. I saw the Medevac comin' down like
a bird on its nest and that's all I saw of anything for a pretty
long while.''

Karen was trembling. In his terse account there had been a
whole landscape, always potential but never before seen, like
the dark side of the moon. It was the face of Chaos, the face
of her enemy. And as if she could shield him from past danger
that had become present through memory, Karen threw her
arms around Michael's body, her lips searching his face as if
her kisses could heal his wounds.

It seemed a long time before he moved, as if his spirit had
been far away. But finally the lips she was kissing began to
warm and Michael lifted one hand and very gently traced the
curve of her forehead, her cheek, moved down the smoothness
of her neck and then across the tightly stretched jersey to cup
her breast.

Life! she thought urgently. *Feel the life in me reaching out
to make you whole! Goddess, work through me now!* She
must assure herself of all of him, cover all of his body as
Brynhild's magic had enchanted Siegfried against harm. But
she would leave no hidden vulnerability. Her lips moved down
the strong column of his neck, her hands went beneath his
T-shirt, relearning the contours of the strong muscles of his
back and tracing his ribs and shoulders and the pectoral
muscles where his nipples were as hard as her own.

Michael moaned softly and lay rigid against the seat, waiting for her to go on. The cramped space of the car and the
steering wheel were only momentary impediments, for Karen
had found the fastening of his jeans and freed him, resurrect-
ing his already wakening manhood, adoring it. . . .

The grip of Michael's fingers on her shoulders was bruising,
though she did not know it then. She had never felt such a
floodtide of emotion, an ecstasy of giving that poured through
her to him as he cried out again and again.

And then at last he was still. With a long sigh Karen rear-
ranged herself. She drew him into her arms with his head
against her breast, and the tears that were sliding silently down
her cheeks were lost in the darkness of his hair.

They must have slept for a little while then.

When Michael moved at last, wakening her, it was almost
midnight by the car clock's glowing dial, and it was raining
again.

"I feel as if I have just awakened to the morning of the world," he murmured against her breast. "You are the sun and the moon and the stars . . . I call myself a poet and I can find no words."

He straightened. Karen tried to move and groaned as the circulation in her arm began to return.

"Good grief!" Michael looked at the clock. "No wonder we're turning into pretzels. I should get you home!"

He turned the key, let the motor idle for a few minutes, then eased the car smoothly into gear and turned it in a tight circle out of the pull-out and down the hill. He took it slowly, because the rain had increased the danger of rockslides, until they came to the crossroads. It seemed to Karen that the car slid a little at the stop sign, but the road was muddy. She nestled closer to Michael, her left hand resting on the top of his thigh.

Michael turned down the canyon that led to the flatlands below, upshifting from first with the same care with which he would have ridden his Harley. They sped through darkness, the car leaned into the first curve, and Michael touched his foot to the brake. Karen could feel no reaction. She stiffened as he pumped it once, again, swore, and grabbed for the gearshift. The transmission groaned as he tried to wrestle it down, and the car was going faster, faster, spinning down the steep, winding road. Michael hauled on the handbrake and the car lurched and began to skid. Then the handbrake too gave way and they hurtled on.

Karen clutched at the edge of the car seat. Her heart pounded furiously but her throat was locked against a scream. This was not real. She was still asleep with Michael in her arms and this was only her nightmare. The car swerved and she was thrown painfully against the other door.

There was a terrible grinding of gears as the transmission caught at last and they began to slow, but they were already going too fast, skidding on the slippery road as Michael fought the wheel. A white-painted curve barrier loomed up at them, then disappeared as he spun the wheel. They darted forward, she sensed dimly that there were trees looming on either side, then she gasped as a light shone in her eyes and Michael swerved left across the road.

They were rolling upward! Disoriented, Karen tried to see through the windows, felt the car slow, pause, and then begin to slide stiffly backward again. Then the angle beneath them changed and they came to a halt. Shaking, Karen saw a street-lamp set at the corner where a secondary road angled off from the canyon and continued up the side of the hill.

Michael was swearing, very softly, a stream of meaningless profanity, his hands still white-knuckled as he gripped the wheel.

It had been a moment. It had been an eternity. Karen looked at the clock and saw that little more than five minutes had elapsed since Michael had started the car.

"I had the brakes checked out just two weeks ago." she said at last. Her voice seemed very far away.

Michael grunted, carefully detached his fingers from the wheel, and began to massage them. "Got a flashlight? I'll see what I can do."

She knew better than to protest as he got out into the rain. She heard him scuffling about behind the car and felt the vibration as the flashlight knocked against something below.

After what seemed a very long time he hauled himself out from under the Volkswagen, opened the door, and climbed back in.

"Well?"

"The hydraulic lines to the brakes were sliced half-through. They'd hold for a while, but the first real pressure on them finished the job." He flicked the flashlight absently on, then off again. "All right!" he went on as if she had answered him. "You've got an enemy. But you'll be okay—I'll take care of you." He began detailing ways of checking the car, precautions to take if she was walking alone. He would come home with her. Until the danger was over he would stay.

But Karen was remembering Duncan Flyte's laughter, and she knew that Michael still did not understand. As long as she held Brisingamen, she was in danger—Duncan was in danger of being used by Loki as well. And the necklace was threatened simply by being in her hands.

She would have to find her own way of protecting them now.

14

I have never heard tell of a worthier treasure
In the hoarding of heroes beneath the sky
Since Hama bore off to the shining city
The Brosing's jewel, setting and gems.
                                    BEOWULF

"They say that the *hauga-eldrinn,* the were-fire, used to burn above the barrows where treasure was buried. There must be a regular three-alarmer going over Lowie Hall right now!" Walter stared around him in awed appreciation. The exhibit room was still awash with crates and packing, but one by one the display cases were being filled. The air glittered with gold.

"Too bad the archeologists can't see the fire—it would save them a lot of time." Karen laughed.

Darcy Miller, who was responsible for the exhibits, saw them standing in the doorway and motioned them inside the museum.

"I'm afraid we're still all at sixes and sevens." She wiped her hand on the side of her jeans and offered it to Walter and then to Karen. "We should have been all set up by now, but the stuff didn't arrive until this morning, and how we're to be ready for the preview party this evening I really don't know! I'm dreadfully afraid we'll mismatch the labels on something and no one will ever notice it!" Her cheerful laughter gave the lie to her greying hair.

"Don't believe her, Karen." Walter grinned, "By eight

o'clock everything will be perfect; I've served on committees with her, and she always complains this way!''

''Why don't we just wander around and set up the cards with the quotations wherever we can,'' said Karen. She fished in her totebag for the packet of cards. She had tried to match quotations from old European literatures with the catalog descriptions, but the magnificence of the reality was distracting. Four governments had released treasures to form this exhibit—it must be the most impressive array of goldwork to be amassed in one place since the dragon Fafnir curled himself around his hoard.

A phone began to ring near the entrance to the hall. Darcy nodded distractedly and darted off to answer it.

''Look at the workmanship on those neck and arm-rings.'' Walter pointed to a gleaming array from Tiss in Denmark. ''What do you have to go with them?''

''A bit from *Beowulf*—my richest source, really, for references to gold.'' Karen flipped through her cards. ''Here it is. 'Then the cup was offered with gracious greeting, and seemly presents of spiraled gold, a corselet, and rings, and the goodliest collar of all that were ever known on earth.' ''

''There's another collar over there, from Sweden.'' Walter pointed to a case where a necklace of five concentric rows of cylindrical beads formed from red gold foil glittered against black velvet.

Karen stared, wondering if there was anything here as beautiful as Brisingamen. The necklace lay safely hidden in the corner of her bureau, but for how long? Freyja's necklace should be a force for good in the world, but it seemed to be a focus for conflict right now. She thought, *I don't know how to use it or how to protect it, and nobody, not even Michael, can do it for me.* . . .

She remembered his disbelief with a sick anxiety. Her car was still being repaired, but even the certain evidence of tampering had convinced him only that someone—some human being—had booby-trapped her car, and after spending a few nights at her place he had moved back to his own room. Duncan had left no fingerprints to advertise his complicity, and as for Karen's theories about Loki—mythology was all very well in poetry, but this was real life!

Karen remembered how Michael had first come to her, when the Goddess had looked out through her eyes. After that, how could he doubt that the gods were real? But then, like a gulf yawning before her, she had seen the danger of reminding him. If it was Freyja's power that had drawn Michael into her arms, where was his freedom? She would lose him for certain if he thought that they had been bound together by magic!

Karen hugged herself, suddenly chilled despite the loose-knit white sweater and heather-blue pleated skirt she wore. Walter was lost in contemplation of a display of Byzantine coins and Viking pendants. With his fine eyes hidden behind the thick glasses, he could have been miles away.

I am alone! she thought desperately. *I must put the necklace somewhere it will put no one in danger!*

Darcy was coming back, swearing as she tripped over a packing case, stopping to help somebody attach a blown-up photograph of the door panels from the church at Hylestad in Norway which showed scenes from the story of Sigurd. Karen had several lengthy quotes from the *Volsunga Saga* to go with that one. She gave them to Darcy, then went on to put beside a group of reindeer-horn combs some lines from *Kormak's Saga*—"*To me, cleansed, there came with comb the Freyja-of-the-hair-shaft: warm the welcome was to skald then given. . . .*"

The people of the North had been interested in art less for its own sake than as a way to make items for everyday use beautiful. And in an age where war was the natural occupation of a nobleman, considerable effort went into the ornamentation of arms. Here, for instance, was a case holding the remains of a helmet banded in gold which was crowned by the figure of a boar—just the sort of helmet described by the Beowulf poet.

It was from an Anglo-Saxon burial in Derbyshire, the only such helmet that had actually been found, though there were numerous references in literature. She wondered if the boar on the helmet was meant to represent Hildisvini—"Battle-boar," the favorite mount of Freyja when she was not using her cat-drawn chariot, or perhaps her brother Freyr's boar Gullin-bursti, whom the dwarves had fashioned of gold that lit the air around him, a mount that could outrun any equine steed. Odin may have been lord of the battles, but the Vanir held their own. She had a sudden, ludicrous vision of a golden-snouted porker showing up at her back door as the two cats had done and she began to giggle in spite of herself.

Still laughing, Karen moved on to the next case. Here, for a change, the ornaments were made of silver—several ring brooches and a Baltic necklace with cabochon rock crystals set in pendants. "*. . . though fair women and brow-white, sit on bench: let the silver-dight one not steal thy sleep, not lure thou women to love.*" That had been the advice of the Valkyrie Sigrdrifa to Sigurd in the Eddic version of the tale. But perhaps when Gudrun seduced him she had worn gold!

Karen moved from one case to another, feasting her eyes on chains of woven gold and twisted arm-rings, intricately carven panels of wood whose interlaced vegetation and tail-biting animal forms drew the eye endlessly into their complexities, a motif that was repeated on flagons and bowls, on the borders of manuscripts, on stones.

"No wonder the family relationships in the sagas are so complicated." Walter paused beside her, echoing her thought. "These people had naturally contorted minds! Look at that thing—" He pointed to an elaborately decorated dragon head from the Oseberg ship burial. "That's the 'old twilight foe, the naked hostile dragon who seeks out barrows, flaming as he goes. . . . ' Did you know that the Vikings always took down their dragon-prows when they neared home? They didn't want the dragons to frighten the land-spirits and make the crops fail."

They were at the end of the last of the filled display cases. Karen looked around to make sure she hadn't missed any, and nearly tripped over a half open box which glittered as a tangle of golden necklaces inside caught the light. You could lose a necklace like Brisingamen in there and never notice a thing. . . .

Karen started to go on, then stopped short. Could that be her solution? The exhibit was certainly well-guarded, and people would be able to appreciate the beauty of the necklace without danger. And even if someone eventually did notice that the hoard had grown, like the ring Draupnir that dropped eight rings as good as itself every ninth night, how could they dare admit it? She looked cautiously around her, wondering how she could sneak the necklace in.

Walter shuffled through the debris behind her. "What do you want to do now?"

Karen frowned, thinking. "I should change clothes before

the party. Why don't we go back to my place and eat something now? By the time we get back here the rest of the exhibit should be ready and we can put up the rest of the cards!"

He nodded, and she realized abruptly that she would have to tell him what she meant to do. Walter had given her the necklace and he had a right to know if she got rid of it. And besides, if she didn't tell him, he might recognize it in the case and give her away.

"I must say, your apartment looks a lot better than it did the last time I was here." Walter took an appreciative sip of jasmine tea.

Karen looked around her. The herbs that hung in front of the windows were flourishing, a little paint had covered the marks on the walls, and she had found new prints to replace the ones that had been destroyed. She probed the pot of rosemary on the window sill, found it dry, and reached for the watering can.

"Yes . . . " she answered slowly, "but I'm still nervous about keeping that necklace here."

"Shall I take it back?" he replied before she could go on. "I've been feeling rather guilty about putting you in danger—"

"And how do you suppose I'll feel if I give it back and something happens to you?" Karen retorted. "No, I have something rather different in mind." As persuasively as she could, she began to explain, but long before she had finished Walter was shaking his head.

"Karen, don't be ridiculous! If it bothers you that much, I'll put the thing in my safe deposit box, or send it back to Professor Freiborg in Uppsala. Will that do?" He set down his teacup and looked up at her. His glasses had gone all misty from the steam of the tea and he took them off to wipe them. A sudden rush of affection for him shook Karen as she watched him, loose-limbed and diffident in his worn tweed jacket, with the watery sunlight of late afternoon slanting past the ivy in the window to glint on his fair hair. How could she convince him?

With a sigh, Karen left him to his tea and the newspaper and went into the bedroom to take her shower. But the problem continued to worry her as she slipped into her blue velveteen robe. Michael had not believed her, but he had "met" the

Goddess several months ago. Perhaps his perceptions had been edited by memory.

Unless Walter saw the Goddess too, how could he believe in Her? Could Freyja manifest Herself just long enough to make him understand? Karen set down her hairbrush and pulled open the drawer where the silk-shrouded necklace lay.

It was heavy in her hands. She weighed it, biting her lip anxiously. Before, the Goddess had come to her unawares, and what had followed had been Freyja's responsibility. Karen had never dared to consciously invoke the Goddess before.

"Freyja—whatever You are—Whoever You are—listen to me," she whispered. "Help me to convince this man that You are real. I don't want to hurt him—I just want to keep Your necklace from doing any harm. Freyja Vanadis, Bride of the Vanir, come to me, please!" She brought the central pendant to her lips and kissed it, and then, with trembling fingers, put on Brisingamen.

Karen took a deep breath, then another. Her pulse drummed in her ears. Was this going to work? What would she do if it did not?

Then she felt the air around her growing warmer. She strove to breathe against the sense of a Presence too great for earth to bear, for the room to contain. She gasped, swaying. *What are You waiting for?* Her heart's voice called. But there was still too much of Karen in her consciousness. She fought to make her breathing regular and to empty her mind as she did in Del's exercises.

And like water from a broken dam, like wind through an opened door, the presence of the Goddess rushed in to fill the vessel that had been prepared for Her.

For a moment Karen's spirit swung homeless. Then her senses began to return to her, clear, but distant, as if she were looking through the wrong end of a telescope. She was not a detached observer as she had been in the hills. However minimally, this time she was a participant in what must happen now, and now she began to understand why men sought the companionship of the gods: The colors in her room had never been so rich; the ivy hanging in the window glowed; she heard—could almost understand—the singing of the birds outside.

And these new senses were not limited by the walls of the room. As her spirit quested outward Karen recognized the life dormant in the leafless plane trees outside the house and in the gardens up and down the street, and the great singing symphony of life in the Berkeley hills. But the song was muted now, the strength of nature rested in the rain-soaked soil. She felt power pulsing within her, waiting for the time of its flowering. She felt the presence of the man in the other room.

Karen's feet moved, and it seemed natural that Trjegul and Býgul should wreathe like drifts of cloud around them. Karen could not have stopped the Goddess now if she had wanted to. She opened the door.

The chair scraped as Walter got to his feet, growing pink with embarrassment as he realized that the robe was all she wore.

She touched the necklace at her throat. "The gold must be preserved—it is Brisingamen . . . " a Voice which was not Karen's purred. "You—word-warrior, do you understand? Do you know Who is speaking to you?"

For a moment Walter stood still, his fingers whitening on the table's edge. Then he sighed, very deliberately took off his glasses, and set them down.

> *Ave formosissima, gemma pretiosa,*
> *Ave decus virginum, virgo gloriosa,*
> *Ave mundi luminar, ave mundi rosa,*
> *Blanziflor et Helena, Venus generosa!*

He was chanting very softly, and it took a moment for Karen to recognize one of the Goliard lyrics used by Orff in the *Carmina Burana,* for even as he spoke she felt herself changing, and realized that though the Lady of Nature had come to him, Walter himself was invoking her as the Lady of Love.

She remembered something Del had told her—*"The gods create us, but we create them as well; the spirit calls forth those aspects of the Divine for which it hungers, and they come. . . . "*

But did Walter understand that this was no literary exercise? The Goddess was already responding to his salutation. Karen had not intended to seduce him—she did not want to bind him to her this way! She tried to shake her head, to warn him, but already he was lifting his hands in the ancient gesture of prayer.

And then abruptly something in his posture shifted, and in

his face she saw an astonished self-awareness, a flowering of joy. He spoke.

"Lady, I have waited all my life for Thee. . . . "

The Goddess was smiling, and Karen, appalled, began to realize that perhaps Walter, steeped in the imagery of the ancient literatures, *did* know what he was doing, knew precisely Who was standing before him now. She could sense the need in him, a capacity for passion so long suppressed and channeled that it had become like a transparent flame.

In her heart love and pity mingled; the last restraint Karen had on the Lady's power misted away. Still smiling, She held out Her hand.

"I am here, my beloved. Come to Me!"

Michael had taken her like a warrior, and Terry with the force of a summer storm. Walter came to her reverently, like a child opening a long-desired gift very slowly, to make the moment last. He removed his clothing layer by layer, as if he were stripping away the shells of his soul. His body was very smooth and white, its basic balance blurred by lack of exercise, but her altered eyes perceived the strength in him, the delicate perceptions of Heimdall, who could see and hear all that passed in the world. Now all his senses were focused upon her glowing body. He loosed the tie that held her robe and let it fall away.

They lay down upon the bed. His eyes were the deep blue of the heavens seen from a mountaintop where the last veils of air mist away.

"Behold you are beautiful, my love, behold, you are beautiful. . . . " He bent to kiss her and she felt his smooth fingers move along her neck and down across her breast. "Your two breasts are like two fawns that feed among the lilies. I will hie me to the mountain of myrrh and the hill of frankincense. . . . " His gentle fingers strayed lower. His sensitive lips, trained to virtuosity by years of practice upon the horn, closed on hers. His agile fingers drew forth her music.

Woman and Goddess breathed faster, glowing, growing like a fire fed by the pure worship he was offering Her. The air burned. His hands upon her body were surprisingly sure, as if he had dreamed this moment many times before.

"You are all fair, my love; there is no flaw in you."

She sighed, and her arms tightened around him, drawing

him to her, opening to him, welcoming him home. She could feel the beating of his heart as he moved upon her, and she knew, as she had known with Michael on the mountain top, that this was the greatest gift of all—to hold the very life of a man between the palms of her two hands.

"Of course I will help you with the necklace. . . . "

Karen propped herself up on one elbow to look at Walter, alarmed at this abrupt capitulation. They were lying upon the bed side by side. The glory had departed and Karen was herself again, but it seemed to her that Walter's face still shone with its afterglow.

"Walter!" she exclaimed helplessly, "You don't have to agree with me—just because we—" She broke off, searching for words.

He looked at her at last, reached out and gently touched the central pendant of Brisingamen—"You have ravished my heart with a glance of your eyes, with one jewel of your necklace . . . " he quoted from the *Song of Solomon* once more. "I know that, and you need not fear I will make demands upon you, just because . . . " He smiled.

"I can guess what the Departmental gossip has said about me," he went on. "Women were just one of my failures. I tried, Karen, but I could never carry the act of love all the way through. You have already given me more than I ever expected to know."

"Damn it, Walter!" she gripped his hand, "Don't you realize that was a gift to me, too?"

He nodded. "That is why I will help you to hide the necklace. All my life I have studied the stories of the gods, never quite daring to believe in them. But when I saw you—Her—standing there, I *knew* that this time I would have the power. Unlike Anchises, I lay with an immortal goddess knowing what I did quite clearly. And if Freyja/Aphrodite is real, then why not the spirit of Loki? I did not have all the evidence when I refused you before. Now that I think about it, the atmosphere surrounding the other pieces in the exhibit may be powerful enough to mask Brisingamen. It is the "Purloined Letter" technique, and it is worth a try."

Karen lay back with a sigh. Distant as memory, she heard the Campanile at the university begin to chime. Five o'clock—she had journeyed from Niffleheim to Valhalla in barely an hour. They should get back to the museum—the rest of the exhibit must be in place by now. And then there was the party to get through. The moment of magic was over. Karen bent to kiss Walter's shoulder, then got up to start running the shower.

"... *for your word's guerdon I'll give you a necklace ...*"
Micaela read carefully. She looked up at Karen, her dark eyes shining with reflected gold. "What does it mean?"

Karen forced her gaze away from the glittering display of beads among which she had placed Brisingamen and glanced at the quotation.

"It's from a story about a girl called Hervor who wanted to get a magic sword out of her father's grave so she could avenge her family. Those lines are spoken by a herdsman who is trying to persuade her not to go, though where he would get necklaces I really don't know!"

"So what happens?" Micaela took off her bright shawl and folded it over her arm. The exhibit room was full of faculty and their guests, and it was getting warm.

"Well, I don't think the Norse believed in happy endings. . . . Hervor disguises herself as a warrior, and takes the sword and gets revenge. Then she gets married, and the sword is eventually responsible for the death of her son." Her voice died away. Across the room she had glimpsed Roger's familiar head. Frowning, she watched him wind through the crowd like a snake through a field of grass.

Micaela followed her gaze and made a small disgusted sound. "Do you want me to turn him off?"

Karen raised one eyebrow and Micaela laughed—"You know what I mean—make him go away!"

"No," Karen answered slowly, "I can't spend my life avoiding him. But thank you for offering."

Micaela grimaced, and then, as Roger approached them, turned with a swirl of bright skirts and walked away.

"Karen, you *are* looking well! I was hoping I might see you here—how have you been?"

One of the students hired as a waiter for the party came by with a tray of champagne. It should have been mead, but one couldn't have everything. Karen took a plastic glass and sipped, wondering how to reply. She knew that her dress suited her—a long, loosely fitted tunic of teal-blue wool jersey whose shoulders were ornamented with appliqued interlace in gold. She had a heavy gold bracelet to go with it, and to show off her earrings of smoky blue tourmaline in twisted gold she had put up her hair.

Yes, between the dress and the afterglow of this afternoon's lovemaking she knew she looked her best. Roger, with the lines of discontent deepening around his mouth and eyes, did not. She considered him and could find no trace of the passion that had possessed her a few months ago.

"Oh, I've been fine . . . " she said at last, *No thanks to you!* echoed her mind. "I've applied for a transfer from the English Department to Comparative Literature. They said there should be no problem. My English M.A. fulfills part of the requirements, and I'll get credit for some of the work I've been doing for Dr. Klein. It will take more time, of course, but I should be ready to start my dissertation in another year."

He nodded benevolently, as if he had been responsible for her accomplishments. Nettled, Karen unleashed the full radiance of her smile. He swallowed, and she noted a sudden brightening in his eyes. *I could get him back if I wanted him—* Karen looked down demurely and took another sip of champagne. *I could lead him on long enough to obsess him, and then drop him the way he did me. . . .*

"That sounds wonderful, Karen. I always thought you should finish your degree," Roger said warmly. "Why don't we get together for lunch sometime and talk?"

Beyond Roger, Karen could see his wife watching them with the beginnings of anxiety in her sweet, unsure face. Karen smiled at her and waved, then motioned to Michael, who was swooping through the crowd like a raven among parakeets.

"I'm afraid that between work and study I'm going to be pretty busy," she answered cheerfully. Michael came up to them and she slid her arm through his. "Michael—I'd like you to meet an old friend of mine, Dr. Roger Hyde. Roger, this is Michael Holst. He's a poet."

Karen watched Roger take in the somber jersey, the silver belt buckle, and the eyepatch Michael had donned in honor of the occasion, trying to reconcile it with his image of a man who wrote poetry.

"I'm glad to meet you," said Michael pleasantly. He shook

the older man's hand and Roger winced. Karen, biting her lip
to keep from laughing, saw the glint of amusement in
Michael's good eye.

"Yes, well, I think my wife wants me now," Roger said
quickly. "Karen, it's been good seeing you again. Mr.
Holst—" He nodded and began to retreat toward Joan.

"I don't think you'll have any more trouble with *him*,"
Michael observed dryly.

Laughing, Karen reached up to kiss him, and as she turned,
she saw Terry Ritter watching them fixedly from beside the
case where the silver-banded spearpoints from Välsgarde in
Sweden lay. She took Michael's arm.

"There's somebody else I want you to meet," she told him.
"I think you two will get along."

Terry's beard flamed above the grey suit into which he had
forced his stocky frame, but his Thor's hammer glittered defiantly above his conservative tie. He belonged in jeans, or in
the tunic in which she had first seen him, Karen thought. This
was probably the only "straight" outfit he owned.

She introduced him to Michael, watching for the subtle flexing of muscles as they tried each other's grips shaking hands,
the assessment in their eyes. Clearly Michael was finding in
Terry the kind of man he understood, wishing they were all
someplace where they could relax and get to know each other
over a can of beer.

But Karen had seen how Terry's eyes widened as he took in
Michael's eyepatch—it was the same look he had had when he
first saw her in the hills. Suddenly she realized how he must be
interpreting the eyepatch and the wolf's head on Michael's
beltbuckle, and the appreciation with which Michael was eyeing the spears. Let him learn that Michael wrote poetry as well
and he would be hailing him as Odin here and now!

"It's great to see you, Terry—how did you end up here?"
she said quickly.

Terry recovered himself and gestured around him. "Do you
think I'd miss a chance to take a close look at Fafnir's hoard?
There's a guy in the Art Department I help out with metal-
work sometimes—" His bicep strained the sleeve of the suit
jacket as he mimed a hammer blow. "And I got him to bring
me along."

"You work with metal, huh?" said Michael. "There's this
part I need for my bike, and nobody seems to have it in stock,

not that the commercial stuff is any good anyway. I've been thinking I might do better to machine it myself, and I wonder—"

Karen shook her head as the conversation disintegrated into metallurgical technicalities. They were getting along, all right —they had forgotten she was there.

"I think I'll go get us all some more champagne!" she said brightly, and headed toward the refreshments.

She heard Walter's voice, and found him talking animatedly in the center of a mixed group of Comparative Literature and Anthropology instructors and their husbands or wives. If she herself was looking well, Karen thought, then Walter looked radiant, as if their experience that afternoon had broken down some barrier that separated him from the rest of the world. Light flashed from his glasses as he gestured, and glowed on his fair hair.

At least I accomplished one good thing with Brisingamen before I had to hide it away . . . she thought wistfully. *Or Freyja did!*

She looked around the room, from Walter to Michael and Terry, from them to Roger, still hiding in his corner with Joan, and began to laugh. She had just remembered how Loki had taunted Freyja when he was insulting the gods in Aegir's hall—*"Hush thee, Freyja, I full well know thee: all Aesir and alfs within this hall thou hast lured to love with thee."*

Of course she hadn't slept with everyone in the room, but all the men whom she *had* been involved with recently were here. Only her Loki, Duncan himself, was missing from among those who had a connection with Brisingamen. Vividly she remembered his haunted eyes and mocking smile. But now the necklace was safely hidden with the other treasures. She would tell Michael to let Duncan know that it was gone.

She had been touched by magic, but all that was over now. Karen felt her neck, remembering how the warm gold had clasped it and missing its weight already, but for the first time in weeks her mind was at ease.

She was safe at last.

15

I ween the first war in the world was this,
When the gods Gullveig gashed with their spears,
And in the hall of Har burned her —
Three times burned they the thrice reborn,
Ever and anon: but still she liveth.

VOLUSPA

The rain had set in again, a dismal, dribbling sort of rain that matched Karen's mood. All the color seemed to have drained out of the world. She trudged down Telegraph Avenue, clutching her book bag against her with one arm while she used the other to maneuver the umbrella.

Once she got back to her apartment she would have to figure out what she wanted to take home for the Thanksgiving holiday. She might even have time to pick up a couple of bottles of wine to contribute to the feast. She hadn't promised her brother that she would come to the ranch to be with them, but maybe a change of scene would boost her out of this depression.

Could the loss of a necklace cause withdrawal symptoms? Karen recognized that this sense of emptiness had been growing in her since she'd left Brisingamen in the case in Lowie Hall. But it had been the right decision—she had to believe that now, and probably high time, too, if it could make her feel this way.

Someone honked loudly and, startled, Karen looked

around. The sound was repeated. A long dark car was pulling up by the curb. A rear window rolled down an inch and someone shouted—"It's wet—do you want a ride home?"

The car's windows were misted. Karen stepped closer to the curb to see who was inside.

The door began to open, "Come on, Karen! I'm blocking traffic!"

It was a man's voice—somebody from the Department? He was right—it was no day for walking. She bent, the door swung wider, and she glimpsed a strange, smiling face that watched her with avid eyes.

Karen did not know him, and she did not like that smile. She straightened, shaking her head, but suddenly he was out of the car, reaching for her. Books scattered as he gripped her arm and jerked her into the car; her umbrella wheeled away. The scream that was building in her throat was cut off abruptly as a hard hand covered her mouth. She struggled, felt her elbow connect with someone's face and heard him swear. Then a damp cloth was pressed over her nose. She gasped at the sickly, sweetish smell, and began to gag as the fumes penetrated her lungs. Then consciousness shuddered and wailed away into a grey wasteland that seethed with troubled dreams.

She was going to be very, very sick, and very soon.

Karen felt nausea building, tried to sit up and fell over. Her hands and feet were tied. Someone turned her head and she vomited into an enamel bowl.

"Okay, bitch—you done? We don't want your upchuck smelling up the place—"

Karen shook her head, groaned, and retched again and again until there was nothing left to come up but stomach acids that burned her throat. She forced herself to stop and lay back again, shuddering.

She could see a rough wood wall above her. Hanging from nails on the cross beams was a collection of particularly hideous masks. She grimaced and closed her eyes. It was cold here. She felt bruised all over, and hideously vulnerable.

"Come on, come on, baby—we went to all this trouble to get you here—ain't you even gonna say hello?"

A sharp pinch sent pain radiating through Karen's arm. Her

eyes blinked open. There were three of them, one looking like
a preppie who had forgotten to wash, the other two scruffier,
with roached haircuts and eye makeup. But there were hard
muscles under their torn T-shirts. They could have over-
powered her easily even if she had not been bound.

She had never seen any of them before.

She tried to speak, croaked, swallowed painfully and forced
air through her throat again. "Water?"

One of them laughed, but the preppie type opened a can of
beer, then pulled her upright and held it to her lips. Beyond
him she could see brick walls with shelves piled with boxes. A
few of them were open—she glimpsed bright gauze and the
glitter of gold trim. It looked like a warehouse—a theatrical
warehouse, perhaps. What was she doing here?

"She can't answer any questions if she can't talk, can she?"
the preppie said over his shoulder to the other two.

Questions? About what? What did she know? The only
questions she could think of were her own. The beer was
bitter, but she swallowed eagerly, then coughed, and he took it
away.

"Who are you and why am I here?"

"The gold, cunt! Did you think we wanted your fair white
body?" He laughed. She saw that he had a streak of purple in
his hair. "You just tell us where the necklace is and we'll get
along fine."

Oh God, Brisingamen! Karen had thought that getting rid
of the necklace would protect her, and now things were even
worse than before. They were staring at her, bright and avid-
eyed as three crows. Behind them scenery flats were stacked
awkwardly against a wall. She could see a classical background, and a section of pianted forest. In one corner a
wooden halberd was leaning, and a silver-painted spear.

"Well? We're *waiting....*"

"I can't tell you," Karen whispered. These weren't mug-
gers, or burglars after quick money. Michael was the only one
she had told she no longer had the necklace, and heaven help
her, she had asked him to let Duncan know. This was his
response.

A sinewy arm snaked out to pinch her again.

"Careful, Lownie—*he* doesn't want her marked!"

The third boy giggled. "*He* won't need to mark her—he'll
just look into her eyes and she'll tell him all she knows!" He

picked up a matchbox, added two colored balls from his pocket, and began to juggle them. Karen's empty stomach twisted as she remembered where she had seen such expert juggling before.

"For her sake, I hope she does," Lownie replied. "Duncan learned a lot of ways to make people talk when he was in Viet Nam. If he gets pissed with her there's no telling what he'll do." He laughed.

"So where's the necklace?" the preppie addressed Karen directly. "You heard them, didn't you?" He leaned closer and added conspiratorially, "I'm not like them—I don't like to see people suffering. I don't want to see what the Magus could do to you."

Karen sighed. Wonderful—she was supposed to betray Brisingamen to spare his sensibilities. If he had any; she remembered reading that pretending to sympathize was a classic technique of interrogation. Her bound wrists hurt, but it was pointless to ask them to loosen the ropes.

"I'll talk to your 'Magus' when he gets here," she said finally. "I don't have anything to say to you."

He shrugged and moved back to the others. One of them lit up a joint and began to pass it around. Karen continued her examination of the warehouse. At the back was a sort of loft with ladders for painting scrims. Nearer, she could see racks of costumes, a workbench covered with cans of paint, pots of glue, an assortment of tools. There was a battered sewing machine, and scraps of fabric and wood shavings littered the floor.

She turned her head and saw that the corner where she was lying had been fitted up with a rug and big cushions. On a low table a candle was burning before a bronze statue of Satan in the form of a satyr. The uncertain light flickered on its hairy legs and cleft goat-hooves, the jutting phallus, and the curving horns above its leering eyes.

Oh, sweet Pan, what have they done to you? Karen closed her own eyes to evade that insolent gaze. But her memory of the laughing and lusty horned gods of the pagan religions—Pan and Cernunnos and Freyr—was distorted by the demonic perversion of their power that stood on Duncan's altar. Its image danced behind her eyelids; she whimpered, opened her eyes, and found herself gazing up into the sardonically smiling face of Duncan Flyte.

"You should have come to me when I first met you," he said very softly. "Things would have been easier for all of us. . . ."

"Duncan, let me go," Karen said in a low voice. "Let me go now, before this goes too far. They said you want the necklace, but it was never mine to give, and I don't have it anymore. Let me go and I promise not to tell Michael what you've done to me."

He sighed, squatted down beside her, and gently lifted away a strand of hair that clung damply to her brow. "You won't tell Michael? No—I think you'll be too ashamed to tell Michael when I have finished with you."

"Are you going to rape me?" Karen swallowed sickly, remembering how the men had pawed at her in the alley.

He put his hand on her breast and suddenly pinched her nipple, hard. "Rape you? Don't flatter yourself, my dear. Rape shows so little imagination, and once it's over, what can you do? I'm sorry to disappoint you, but your body holds very little interest for me."

"Then *why*?" Her breast was still throbbing painfully. "Are you trying to scare me away from Michael? If you don't want me, is it him you're jealous of, or are you just a thief after the gold?" With the memory of his fingers still aching in her flesh, it was hard to think of him as more than a man. Surely she could reason with him—

"Your groupies were asking me about the necklace—did you have them break into my apartment to steal it? You're not starving—why do you want it enough to do this to me? Why, Duncan, *why*?"

He sat back on his heels, his dark eyes focusing on something far away. "Why . . . why does a man become obsessed with anything? When I first saw you in the nightclub with the necklace shining on your breast I knew that it was important, perhaps the most inherently important object I had ever seen. Ever since Viet Nam I've been looking for something—not money, money and sex can both be useful tools, but they are illusions. I want something else, the power at the heart of things. After that night the necklace began to haunt me. I would wake sweating from dreams of fire and splendor, and always that necklace was there.

"You were there too, and Michael—" He turned on her suddenly, and startled, she could not pull her gaze away.

"Why, Karen, *why*?" he mimicked her cruelly. "What is it that my unconscious already knows? That too is one of the things you are going to tell me soon. . . . "

Karen heard movement and knew that the other men were watching them, but her gaze was captive. He set his two hands on either side of her shoulders and lowered his body over hers in a parody of an embrace.

"Karen . . . Karen, don't fight me—why should you fight me? I don't want you to be hurt, and power is always danger-ous. The necklace is powerful—does anyone else understand that as you and I do? But you cannot guard it—let me take it and it will be safe. Come, Karen, tell me about it—you want to talk about it, don't you?"

His voice had gone sweet as honey, smooth and comforting as a mother's arms. It carried her awareness away. She could still see Duncan's eyes—she knew who she was and where, but it didn't matter. She was entering a state where these surface questions were irrelevant, as they were in meditation when she achieved the stillness she was aiming for. There was some reason she should resist him; she reached for the knowledge but it eluded her. His voice was like the embrace that follows love.

"Beautiful—so beautiful—" that seductive voice went on. "How brightly the gold gleams . . . where shall I find it? How shall I name the bright gold?" His eyes drew her gaze inward, her thoughts echoed his words—surely he had no need to ask; surely he heard—

How brightly the gold gleams . . . how brilliantly it shines. It lights up the heavens, bright as the fire of love. Brisingamen, Brisingamen. . . .

"Brisingamen . . . " Karen whispered aloud.

He heaved himself away from her and in one motion was on his feet. Spell broken, Karen screamed. What had happened? What had she said? Brisingamen—but surely he had known that—

No. Duncan had not known what the necklace was. She could see the pieces of the puzzle falling into place in his mind, the shape of the pattern becoming clear. Obviously he knew enough mythology to recognize the name and to begin to understand its significance, and that flaw in him which had left him open to Loki's manipulation was a conduit for com-plete illumination now.

Duncan looked down at her distractedly, then motioned to the others. "Strip her, then tie her again. No molestation, though—remember." He turned abruptly and strode to his altar, folded his long legs into meditation position, and closed his eyes. Michael had once told her how Duncan made friends with the Buddhist holy men. He would know the technique then—but what power would he contact now?

Loki . . . now that Duncan knew the name of the game they were playing he would know where to look for support. All that had happened so far between them was play—the inaccurate fumbling of a fool, but now—

And it is all my fault! she thought wildly. *I couldn't leave well enough alone! Freyja, forgive me—I've betrayed you, but I didn't know, I didn't know!*

Grinning, the three youths began to pluck at her clothes, holding her legs while they pulled off her jeans and pants, jerking her upright so that they could remove her shirt. Lownie tweaked her breast as her bra was torn off, and began to fumble between her legs until his hand was slapped away.

When they were done she drew her knees up toward her bound hands, shivering as the cool air touched her bare skin. If they didn't mean to use her, why strip her, she wondered dismally, and then, as they stood over her grinning, Karen began to understand the curious vulnerability of nakedness in the presence of those who are clothed. She could not meet their eyes. Compared to this, rape would have been a positive and natural thing.

Desperately Karen looked up at the skylight, but it showed only darkness now. *How long have I been here?* she wondered. *How long will they keep me prisoner?* They had grabbed her books and purse and umbrella after they snatched her—in Berkeley there would be no evidence of foul play. Her brother would simply assume she had decided not to come up to the ranch for the holiday, while everyone else would think she had gone home for Thanksgiving after all. It could be days before anyone wondered what had become of her.

"Where's the necklace, Karen?" asked Lownie conversationally.

Karen shook her head. She had done enough damage already—she would not tell Loki where to find Brisingamen. *Freyja! Help me!* She reached out for that presence that had enabled her to resist the rapists, but there was nothing there.

Can She come to me only when I have the necklace on?

"Karen—tell us where the necklace is!"

The question came again and again, and though she did not answer, they would slap her face to make her look at them. She could not concentrate, could not make contact with that power she had once sensed within. She had one glimpse of Duncan, rigid and enraptured as he dedicated himself to his god, and then they were hitting her again, until she wept helplessly, turning her face against the unyielding floor.

She did not know how long it continued. She did not know if Duncan remained entranced before his image or whether he had gone out and returned again. When she saw him once more it felt as if half the night had worn away. Danny Ortona and Joe Whitson, the two students who had been with him at the Blue Door, were at his side. Even in those few hours Duncan's face seemed to have grown thinner. His hair was rumpled, and there was a flame behind his eyes.

And if he looks like hell, what about me? Karen thought weakly. But she was past vanity now. She must set herself to endure to whatever the unimaginable end of all this might be. Naked and alone, her only weapon was her will. And she had not trained it, she thought despairingly. She had only started with the exercises Del had given her, and once she had gotten rid of the necklace she had thought they didn't matter any more.

"She's too comfortable—" Duncan said abruptly. "There—" He motioned to the square wooden framework for a stage flat. "Tie her to that. This has gone on too long."

Karen tried to struggle, but the last hours had weakened her, and it was no use screaming. They had kindly explained that the warehouse was located in the middle of an industrial area deserted for the holidays. Nobody would hear her no matter how much noise she made.

They wrapped scraps of fabric around her wrists where the ropes had chafed them, looped new ropes around them and tied them to the corners of the frame. More ropes led from the other corners to her ankles. Then they began to pull them taut until any movement would wrench Karen's arms from their sockets and she lay spread-eagled on the cold floor.

"I learned a lot of things that weren't covered in Army training in Viet Nam." Duncan said quietly. "We could keep questioning you, but it might take days for you to break and I don't want to wait that long." He passed his hand above her body and she twitched, although he did not touch the skin. "I have glimpsed my purpose, Karen-Freyja's-friend, and you and I together are going to discover the rest."

Karen sensed that he meant something more than simple information, but at that moment his hand came down to touch a nerve with just the right amount of pressure to send waves of pain cascading through her body with such force she could not think of anything at all.

"You have come to depend too much on that beautiful body—if we had longer I could train you so that the very thought of sexual contact filled you with fear, or so that you could find release only through pain, like this—" Again the expert fingers touched her, stimulating a painful throbbing that to Karen's horror found an echo between her thighs. As she caught her breath she realized that Lownie had unzipped his fly and was fondling his member, watching her.

"What do you want of me?" she whispered to Duncan. "What have you learned? Why is possessing Brisingamen so important to you?"

His hands were constantly upon her, now caressing, now piercing her with pain. She twitched reflexively, her senses confused until either kind of touching brought an equal agony. He leaned over her; his voice was soft.

"Don't you remember? I serve Chaos and Chance and Change . . . I have seen the corruption at the heart of this world and felt its pain. Freyja's power maintains it, preserves and propagates so that a new generation can suffer it all again. They are training the sons of those who died in Viet Nam to fight in El Salvador—and if not there, they will find another battlefield. This world is overdue for Ragnarok—a final ending so that life can begin anew. Don't you remember? Loki fought on the side of the giants at the end!"

He sat back and spoke over his shoulder to one of the others. Karen lay still, breathing hoarsely, grateful for the momentary cessation of pain. The others were sitting in a semi-circle around her, eyes closed, channeling to Duncan their energy to increase his power. She coughed as the scent of some incense that was at once acrid and cloying began to fill the room. *Some drug*—she thought vaguely. *Maybe it will take away the pain. . . .*

"Karen, Karen, come on a journey with me—" She tensed

as Duncan bent over her again. It had grown very hot in the room; he was sweating, and he had taken off his shirt. With a dull wonder she saw that across his belly he had a larger version of Michael's tattoo of the flaming skull. It leered at her as he moved.

"I want you to understand why I am doing this," he said. "You have been sheltered; you must understand what the world really is. . . . You have never been in the jungle, Karen. You would hate the color green if you had been in the jungle for a while. Everywhere around you things are growing, sucking the strength from the earth, living on each other, feeding on the rotting remains of whatever falls. . . ."

She no longer knew if he was touching her, for his voice had trapped her once more and was transforming the world around her into a green hell in which life flourished obscenely; in which bamboo shoots could pierce stone and vines grew a foot in one night and pallid blossoms sprouted from the sockets of dead men's eyes. There was no world but this, and he the only other creature in it. Like the serpent in the Garden, he showed her this new kingdom and behold, it was Hell.

"And what manner of being lives in this world of hungers?" he hissed in her ear, "What kind of creature calls itself lord of creation? Listen to me, and I will show you what manner of thing man does to his fellow-man."

With searing precision, the soft voice of the magician guided Karen through a landscape like something painted by Bosch, in which men saw their friends blown to pieces and incinerated their enemies, tortured and killed from suspicion or fear, a world in which women were raped to death, babies spitted, in which maimed children stared at you from haunted, accusing eyes.

"The VC cut off the penises of men they killed and stuck them into their mouths; and there were Americans who collected the ears of enemies they had slain. Whatever they did to us—sooner or later we would do it to them; nice, God-fearing American boys like your brother, like Michael, like me. . . ."

Duncan was remembering everything now, and she was remembering it with him, with perceptions unanesthetized by anger or habit or fatigue. The world was a place of horror, and men worse than any demons spawned by Hell.

"There was a village we used to visit, before we were sent north—before Michael was wounded and sent home. We used to go down there when we were off-duty and take the kids candy, even teach in the school. And when we came back, they said the place had gone over to the Viet Cong. So we went in there and blew it to hell, and afterward we burned the bodies—and there was a baby there, a baby I had delivered the year before, still sheltered in her dead mother's arms. I picked her up; I wanted to save her—but she died between my hands. . . . ''

There, where she was, Karen could see him holding the dead child, thin, filthy, with the purple bruises of fatigue beneath his eyes. Tears channeled through the grime on his cheeks, and then, abruptly, his face changed and the little body slipped unheeded from his hands.

"It is all illusion . . . it is all suffering . . . let it all be destroyed so that no one can suffer again!"

Karen did not know if he were still speaking or if it was his spirit that guided her through fire and thunder and then the cold that turned the bones to crystal as snow began to sift down over an empty world. It was true—everything that he had shown her was so.

Let it come, they thought, *the fire and ice and stillness after all. There will be peace, then; no blood to stain the ground, no greenery to flourish where earth's hungry mouths feed on the flesh of men, no cries of agony. All the suffering will be done.*

She could feel the peace and the blessed rest that follows pain. It was a world of purity—white ice and azure sky and the sibilant whisper of the wind. How easy it would be to let the final silence in. . . .

This is the blessing of the Jotun-kind—that all shall go back to the primal ice from which it came. And you shall help me, you shall be at my side. Let us destroy this teeming anthill that the gods may create the world anew. You hear me, don't you, and you understand—

She did not know who she was, or where. What was there to understand? This voice in her soul was the only reality.

You are mine, my creature—without me you have no will.

I have no will. . . .

We shall turn life back upon itself like a snake that eats its tail—you will tell me how to find Brisingamen.

For a time she floated, trying to make sense out of his demand. If he knew everything, why was he asking her? *Brisingamen* . . . the name shimmered in her consciousness, lighting the white landscape in which she rested with a golden glow. Gold—yes, it was gold, and surrounded by gold. Images began to form in her awareness, displacing her precious serenity—a room full of people. No! She did not want them desiring, demanding, drawing her back to life again. When the ice came, they would all be gone and she could sleep peacefully. From some past life words came to her—

. . . in times past many a man light of heart and bright gold adorned with splendours, proud and flushed with wine, shone in war trappings, gazed on treasure,
on silver, on precious stones, on riches, on possessions,
on costly gems, on this bright castle of the broad kingdom. . . .

In her sleep she smiled.

"Treasure and precious stones! A bright castle?"

Painfully the voice grated on her ears. Where was the gentle whisper that had insinuated itself into her memories? Karen stirred and moaned.

"The exhibit! The damned viking exhibit—that's where it must be! I should have known!"

Hard hands shook her. Dazed, Karen forced herself to focus and stared into Loki's eyes in Duncan Flyte's face. Pain battered at her from every sense as awareness of her body returned. What had happened? What was she doing here?

"You've hidden the necklace in the anthropology museum, haven't you?"

Karen tried to shake her head, but he was already laughing in triumph, springing to his feet to cavort about the room. Memory pieced itself together through the pain.

She had betrayed Brisingamen.

The pale light of a new day was filtering through the grime of the skylight when Karen regained awareness. She was still tied, but they had released her from the wooden frame and roughly dressed her again. She tried to lift her head and agony stabbed her. *Why did they bother?* she wondered dismally. *I can't even move. . . .*

Perhaps if she stirred again the pain would send her back to unconsciousness, but she did not dare to try. *I'm a coward*— she thought, *afraid of life, afraid of death, afraid of pain. Michael knows how to bear it—he would never have given in;*

*even Walter would have seen clearly through the illusions. I
am a whore and a coward and I have betrayed the world!*

The preppie saw that she was awake and brought her a cup
of water. Drinking made it easier to swallow, but it did nothing for the ache that radiated from every bone. Her head
throbbed, sickly.

The door of a car slammed outside. With a dreadful certainty Karen watched the door to the warehouse swing open,
blinked as the room brightened suddenly and Duncan came in.

But was it Duncan? His walk was springier, and surely his
rusty hair glowed now like a candle flame. Glowed—that was
it. There was a shining in him as if he burned with inner fire.
She saw the feverish glitter in his eyes as he looked at her and
smiled.

"Hail, Freyja—thou art fair no longer. I have taken thy
treasure—see how brightly it beckons! But not for thee!" He
stripped off his jacket and tugged open his shirt collar. She
winced at the flare of gold.

Brisingamen—on Duncan's neck—but he was not Duncan
now. An echo of the Goddess recognized the tilt of his head,
the malicious humor in his eyes.

"Now shall we see if the world grows colder—wind and foul
weather shall serve my will. The fruits of the field no longer
shall ripen; I am their master! Ice shall entomb them. Ah!
Now I shall play you the best trick of all!" He flung wide his
arms and began to twirl, and the pendants of the necklace
shattered the light into shards of brilliance that scattered like
chips of ice about the room.

"Magus, what do you want us to do with the girl?"

For a moment the magician paused and met Karen's eyes.
"Take her back, take her away from here. I am magus and
master now, and she does not matter anymore."

Joe Whitson and Lownie lifted her. The world spun, but
even through the dizziness, all the way out to the street and
into the car, Karen could hear the obscene, ecstatic pealing of
Loki's laugh.

16

He feeds on the flesh of fallen men,
With their blood sullies the seats of the gods;
Will grow swart the sunshine in summers thereafter;
The weather, woe-bringing: do ye wit more, or how?
                                              VOLUSPA

"A freak arctic storm sliced into the Bay Area from the Gulf of Alaska last night. . . . " Static garbled the next words, then the announcer's bland voice continued, " . . . sections of the East Bay reported hail. Six inches of snow were measured this morning on Mount Tamalpais and four on Mount Diablo; five feet of new snow has fallen in the Sierras. Dig out your boots and mittens, folks—we may have a white Christmas after all!"

The radio voice was jovial, but Karen shivered and pulled the quilt closer around her. The apartment's heater was working full-time, but her bones ached with a chill no blankets could keep off. *It is the Fimbulwinter,* she thought numbly. *Loki is bringing the Ice Age down on us and it is all my fault.*

"The National Weather Service predicts lows of thirty to forty degrees and highs between forty and fifty today, while the arctic air mass hovers over the region. The Highway Patrol advises motorists to exercise extreme caution on mountain roads."

I could tell them where that storm came from, thought Karen, *but they wouldn't believe me.* She started to turn over, but pain thrust her back against her pillows again. The easy tears trickled from beneath her shut lids. *Why didn't I die?* she wondered. *Why am I still alive?*

The floor creaked beneath a light step, and a warm fragrance stirred the air. Karen whimpered as deft hands eased forward her shoulders, and pulled pillows behind her to hold her upright. She opened her eyes.

"I think you'll like this," said Del. She was holding out a cup of steaming tea. "Camomile and red clover with a little vervain—"

"To keep the witches away?" asked Karen hoarsely. Biting her lip, she reached for the cup.

Del had nursed her for the past two days, since the phone call she had made with the last energy left to her after Duncan's boys had tumbled her out of the car in front of her apartment and roared away. Then darkness had taken her, and it had been a day before she was aware again. She longed to sink into that comforting well of night once more, but Del's gaze was upon her, steady, serenely confident.

Karen sipped at her tea.

There was no physical damage. Del had brought in a friend, a chiropractor with healing in her hands, to ascertain that no bones were out of place, that there were no bruises that would not heal. It was only the pain of outraged nerves and strained muscles that tormented her now. With time, Karen's body would heal itself.

And what about my mind? Her cup rattled against the saucer and Del took it from her hands as Karen began to shake once more. Again she saw the flaming skull writhe on Duncan's belly as he bent over her. Dimly she heard Del speaking, but she could not recognize words.

She gasped for breath, moaning as a memory of pain plucked at her nerves. Loki's laughter echoed through her awareness, mocking her. *"I will always be with you now—"* he had said. *"You belong to me."* He had not needed to damage her body; he had destroyed her soul.

Then a clear golden light began to dissipate the darkness behind her eyelids; she felt warmth moving along her limbs, dissolving the pain and sweeping it away. Opening her eyes, she saw that Del was moving her hands over her body without quite touching it. It was a sweeping motion, with a flick of the fingers at the end of each pass as if to throw something away. As Del's strong hands drew the pain from her body Karen began to breathe more easily. The tea was soothing, but when the pain struck, this was the only thing that could give her ease.

Del had advised against the drugs that separated the soul from the body's pain—they were the door to nightmare. Though it might mean agony, full awareness of her body was Karen's chief safety now.

"Thank you—" she whispered as Del sat back at last. Beadlets of perspiration sparkled on her brow. *What is this costing her?* Karen wondered. *Why is she doing this for me?*

"Now, try some more of the tea," Del said. "And later I'll give you another rub with oil of camomile and wintergreen. That should take some more of the soreness away."

"Yes, of course," Karen answered obediently. She took the tea, cooler now, and drank it quickly. "Are you sure you don't need it yourself? That couch of mine would put anyone's back out of joint."

Del laughed, her silver cap of hair glinted in the morning light. "I daresay it would, but I brought my mat and my comforter. I'm sleeping just as I would at home. Your friend Michael called, by the way. I told him I would find out if you felt up to seeing him today."

"No." Karen did not even have to think to answer that. Michael was a warrior who had never surrendered to his enemy, and he was Duncan's friend. There was no way he could forgive, or understand. "Don't let him come here. . . . "

The weather report had ended and the radio was playing "The Swan of Tuonela," by Sibelius. Karen sank back into her pillows, letting her consciousness flow into the music's somber harmonies. The river of death flowed slowly, inexorably into the darkness. *I will float with the swan,* she thought. *Like Ophelia I will float down the stream. For I have looked upon the face of madness and seen the world's doom. . . .*

Outside the wind howled. A cold rain was beating on the windowpane. Through her closing eyelids Karen saw the older woman's serenity troubled by a worried frown. But she was too weary to care.

The afternoon passed, and a night of anguished dreams. But by the next morning Del's remedies had worked well enough that Karen was able to get out of bed and make her way to the couch in the living room. While Del bustled about in the kitchen, Karen sat, forcing her fingers through the intricacies of embroidering a hanging she was making her brother for Christmas. The activity was almost enough to keep her thoughts safely on the surface. But it was thin ice, barely covering the dark and bitter waters that churned below.

The two cats had curled themselves against her for comfort. She let her hands sink into soft fur, grateful for the heavy warmth, and the steady purring that promised contentment, however illusory she knew it to be. Her fingers curled down behind Býgul's ears and began to rub gently, the volume of the purring increased. Then stopped. Both cats, with widening eyes and pricked ears, looked toward the door.

The cats had lulled her—she had heard no step on the stair. Frozen, she saw the door open. A dark figure burst forth from the shadows on a rush of cold air, and she screamed.

His heavy boots shook the floor, his black-gloved hands gripped her shoulders painfully, his lips were cold, cold—Karen moaned and struggled, but still he held her, his mouth gradually warming as he searched her face and returned to her lips again. And still he held her hard against him; she could feel his strength, and some knowledge in her body that had not yet reached her brain brought her arms around him as if he were the one unyielding rock in the maelstrom of her fear.

"Honey! Honey—Karen, it's all right now!" His voice was hoarse with restraint.

That voice—Michael . . . of course it was Michael, or the cats would not have resumed their purring at her side. And the strength that held her, his body, speaking to hers. The tension went out of her in a long sigh.

"Karen, don't you know I love you? Love you—God, I don't have words!" he added in despair. "Honey, please will you look at me?" Then, abruptly, he let her go. "Oh God, I forgot—have I hurt you?" He shook his head in frustration.

Karen fought for breath and stared up at him through her tears. "No, not really—it's not so bad now. It's just the memory—please, keep holding me."

Silently he held her against him again. She turned her face to his shoulder, knowing that he was at once the cause of her pain's awakening and its cure. She knew now why she had not wanted him to come and why, she suspected, Del had disobeyed and told him to. Life was pain, and Michael made her alive again.

After a few moments he released her long enough to strip off his gloves and unzip his leather jacket. Then he eased onto the couch beside her, lifting the surprisingly acquiescent cats out of the way, and very carefully he pulled her onto his lap. Her head fitted into the hollow between his neck and shoulder; she could feel the beating of his heart.

"Honey, don't you think I know what you're going through? It was like that for me after I was wounded, once the pain began to go away!" His arms tightened.

"But you don't understand—" She tried to pull free. "It was Duncan, and it wasn't even what he did to me! It was *me*! He broke me, and now he has Brisingamen. After that, how could I face you?

"No, don't ask me if I'm sure it was him—" she went on. "I know his face better than yours now, and that damnable tattoo on his belly. I know what nightmares haunt him; I am infected with his nightmares, Michael. Those men near the restaurant only wanted to use my body, but this—oh, Michael, I feel as if he raped my soul!"

Michael jerked as if she had struck him, but the words continued to pour out, the whole story she had thought she could never tell anyone, bursting like a sewer into the ears of the one man whom it would hurt most. But she could not stop, and he did not let her go.

Only when she was done and he gathered her once more against him, she had the sense that they were clinging to each other for comfort now.

"A man has to stick by his buddy—his brother—no matter what he does. . . . " Michael's voice gave out, then he began again. "And a man has to take care of his woman! I was caught between you and Duncan and I did nothing, nothing, even though I sensed that there was something obsessing him . . . deep down I knew that what you were saying about him could be true. Karen—don't torment yourself! Nothing you did under—torture"—his voice cracked painfully— "could be worse than what I did to you!"

He shook his head, and Karen saw that with his one eye he was weeping. She reached up and gently wiped his cheek.

"We're not all crazy, Karen—those of us who survived. And I was so happy to hear Duncan made it home in one piece and was doing well. . . . But maybe the worst wounds are the ones no one can see. I'm responsible for what happened to you because I did nothing to help him. I'll have to go after him now. . . . ''

For a while they sat in silence, and Karen was aware of a curious sense of safety, as if she were holding to an island in the midst of a storm. The music on the radio finished and the news came on.

"Karen, can you forgive me? Do you still love me?" he asked finally.

She lifted her head and very gently kissed his lips and then the ruin of his missing eye. "Do I have a choice? It's a fact, like the sun—" Abruptly she stopped, for the first time hearing what the radio announcer said.

"The Bay Area is catching its breath after the season's first big winter storm, but don't put your mittens away, folks—another cold front is on the way. Snow is expected down to the two thousand-foot level and winter storm warnings have been posted for the Sierras. Yesterday, mudslides . . . "

Karen caught her breath. "—only maybe there won't be any sun. It doesn't matter if I forgive you, or if you forgive me. Loki is loose in the world!"

Michael stroked her hair, trying to still her trembling. "Karen, it's just a storm. They happen every year."

"Not like this, not in California. Remember! Remember how I wore the necklace when we went to bed that first time? Yes, we love each other, but that was something different—"

His gaze was fixed on a memory, and at last he nodded.

"That's the power of Brisingamen, Michael," Karen went on. "Unknowing, we used it for joy. But Duncan has only hatred, and he knows how to use power. As the Goddess took my body to make love to you, Loki has taken him. Duncan is lost, Michael—Loki rides him like a horse, and with the necklace he can turn the powers of nature around. What happens to California now will happen everywhere. He will bring down the final winter of the world!"

Michael took a deep breath. "Ragnarok. . . . " She could feel him tensing, as if the word had stirred some inner awareness. Now that it was too late, was he realizing what god stood closest to his soul? Ragnarok—that name must be like a battle call. But they had been taken by surprise, and they had no weapon against Loki and the forces of Chaos.

"If that's true, I've got to stop him before it goes on too long," Michael said grimly. Very gently he put her aside and got to his feet. "Karen, get well, okay. I have to go now."

Biting her lip, Karen watched him put on his jacket and gloves. "Be careful," she said uselessly. There was no way to stop him from going after Duncan now. And wasn't that what she had wanted? But it wasn't Duncan that Michael would be seeking now, it was Loki, and how could any mortal be a match for *him*?

"Nationally, winter storms have emptied a mixed bag of blizzards, floods, tornadoes, and freezing rain from Oregon to Massachusetts . . . " came the voice of the radio.

The door slammed. Karen heard Michael's footsteps thundering down the stairs, the roar of his cycle diminishing as he sped away.

She was weeping silently when Del came into the room.

The intensity of the rain was terrifying.

After days of bitter cold, everyone had been relieved when the wind shifted to the southwest, bringing with it the warmth of the tropics and a rush of moist, tropical air. But even the meteorologists had not foreseen that cold and warm air fronts, colliding, would precipitate moisture in an epic deluge that had people talking about arks with not entirely cheerful laughter.

Karen stared at the little black-and-white TV Del had brought in, listening to commentators chronicling deaths and damage, watching films of people rowing boats across intersections, or trains derailed by flooded tracks, washed out roads, flood waters raging through river towns. There had been landslides, and the Golden Gate Bridge was closed. Tonight San Francisco was full of stranded commuters who could not get home.

"They're still calling it a *natural* disaster even though they don't know what natural forces could make the weather act this way!" Karen exclaimed at last. Unable to sit still any longer, she strode to the window and stared out into the pulsing darkness of the storm. From the kitchen she could hear a monotonous plunking as water from a leak in the roof dripped into a coffee can. With each day that passed her body grew stronger, but the world around her shuddered with each new storm. She had not heard from Michael at all.

"Wind and water are natural forces, Karen—" Del answered reasonably. "It is not the elements that are un-

natural, but the way in which they have combined. What did
you expect? A glacier rolling down from the Sierras? Explo-
sions of multi-colored fire? The forces of destruction do not
send a special effects studio to achieve their ends—it is sufficient to shift the balance of the natural order, to distort the
pattern, for just a little while."

"Yes," Karen said softly. "It *is* a distortion—I can feel it!"
She put her hands to her ears, trying to shut out the insistent
pounding of the rain, then jumped as the telephone rang.

"Karen?" The voice sounded tinny and there was a crack-
ing on the line as if moisture were soaking into the wires.

"Michael, I can hardly hear you—are you all right?"

"Aside from being wet through, yeah, I'm okay." His voice
held weary humor. "But they've closed both the bridges, and
I'm not going to be able to get home until the rain eases up."

"That's all right as long as you're safe. Do you have a place
to stay?"

The deteriorating connection garbled his reply, but she
gathered he had friends in the city who would take him in.

"But I wanted to tell you I haven't found Duncan." For a
moment Michael's voice came strongly. "I've searched the
Mission District—there's a lot of art stuff there, but no sign of
him, and nobody he was connected with seems to know where
he's gone. Are you sure the place he took you to was over
here?"

Karen had been unconscious when they kidnapped her, and
blindfolded and half-fainting when they returned. She thought
they had crossed the Bay Bridge, but how could she be sure?

"I don't know, Michael—I don't know anymore—just be
careful!" A burst of static cut her off and when the line
cleared she heard the dial tone. *Did he hear me?* she wondered
despairingly. For a moment the need for his arms around her
was a physical pain.

Then she looked at Del accusingly. "You knew he wouldn't
find Duncan, didn't you? That's why you were so calm."

"Would it have been useful for both of us to be hysterical?"
Del asked tartly. She put down her book, pushed her reading
glasses down on her nose and looked searchingly at Karen.

"Of course Michael couldn't find Duncan. From all I have
heard, that young man could probably have cloaked his
presence even before Loki took him on. Michael could have
walked right by the place and never known it was there—

people who know perfectly well where Duncan was holding his classes would find themselves unable to remember when the question was asked. And they would be quite honest." She went on. "Loki has set a shield between himself and the rest of the world that distorts all attempts to reach him. There are no physical means by which he can be located now."

Karen stared at her. "Not physical—but then how? Why didn't you tell me all this before?"

Something in Del's posture shifted to transform her from a grandmotherly woman with glasses comically askew to the commanding figure Karen remembered from the house-warding ceremony a little over a month ago.

"Would you have been able to understand me before? Can you understand me now?" Del said. "Duncan Flyte who is now Loki can only be tracked by the traces he has left in the spiritual world, and only by you. . . . "

Karen's knees wobbled; she felt for the armchair and sat down. "I see."

"I doubt it." Del smiled grimly. "But perhaps you will. You are wondering why, if I know so much, I cannot search him out for you or even destroy him. And it is true that I have spent some time out on the astral—it is a real place, although no one has ever conclusively defined its reality—but people in that state do not wear their ordinary faces, and even if they did I have never met Mr. Flyte.

"You are the only one who knows the shape of his soul well enough to identify him there. And the necklace is still linked to you. . . . "

Karen closed her eyes, monitoring her body. An occasional muscle still ached with a memory of pain, but it was true that for the most part her body was healed; her mind, though— that was different. Del had nursed her through her delirium; how could Del ask her to go where those nightmares would be real?

"I can't . . ." she whispered. "I can't possibly do that!"

"Perhaps not," Del answered implacably. "But if you cannot, then I know of no one else who can."

There was silence in the room. On the television the commentator was interviewing the neighbors of a family whose house had been buried by a mudslide, trapping three children inside.

If you do not do something, came a voice from somewhere

deep within, *this will happen again, and again. Can Duncan's memories of the past in Viet Nam be worse than what you will see around you in the present if this goes on?*

"How?" Karen spoke aloud at last. "What must I do?"

"My studies have been more in the areas of the Mediterranean Mysteries and the Kabbalah and Yoga than in the mythology of the North," said Del, "but I've been looking through your book collection here, and I have enough background to interpret it. You remember the story of the Volva in *Eirik's Saga* who wore a costume of animal skins and ate a meal of the hearts of a dozen living creatures in order to go into her *seithr* trance and prophesy—"

"I am *not* going to wear gloves of catskin!" interrupted Karen. As if she had understood, Trjegul got to her feet and stalked with great dignity into the other room.

"No—obviously we cannot reproduce an authentic Norse *seithr*—you may recall that even in the *Saga* they had trouble finding someone who knew the right ceremonial song. What is significant are the features the ceremony had in common with the practice of shamanism, and that *is* something I can help you to do. . . ."

The drum beat steadily, drowning out the roaring of the rain outside. The sound was somehow comforting, like the beat of her heart. Karen settled herself more solidly among the cushions on the couch, willing her breathing to slow. *Listen to the drum*, she told herself, *rest in the drumbeat and let it bear you away. The drum is the horse that carries the shaman to the other world.* . . .

She had bathed and brushed out her hair and put on the gown of undyed linen she had worn for the house-warding ceremony. In memory of Freyja's falcon-cloak she wore some feather earrings she had picked up on Telegraph Avenue. Now she sat in darkness, listening to Del beat the drum, trying to loose her consciousness and set it free.

"Freyja, hear us!" Karen jumped at Del's cry, then forced herself to stillness again.

"Goddess of the Vanir, be with thy daughter!" the older woman went on. "Guide her to her goal and guard her from harm. For the sake of Brisingamen and the world's beauty, Goddess, be with us now!"

Karen tensed, because for a moment it had seemed that

there was some other presence in the room listening. *Freyja!* she thought. *You got me into this, you help me now!*

"You are walking along a pathway—" Del began again, more softly. "You follow it until you find an opening in the trees, and you press through. . . ."

Drifting, Karen allowed herself to imagine a forest. The path was thick with fallen pine needles; she walked silently. She felt them yielding beneath her footsteps, and she did not know if she really smelled the pungency of pine boughs, or if Del was burning herbal incense in the room. This was very much like the way in which Duncan had enticed her into his nightmare, but this time she had freely chosen to take this road, and Del was offering her plenty of choices about its branchings. Whatever details came to her would be from her own subconscious, or else from that greater reservoir of archetypes which was the ultimate source of all dreams.

"There is a clearing in the forest. In the clearing is a circle of women. They are singing. You join them, and you realize that they are singing the sacred song—"

And abruptly Karen was there, passing through a gap in the pine trees into the circle, for she had been here before, and now the fullness of her dream was coming back to her. There were the women in their kerchiefs and linen aprons over wadmal gowns, and there the roughly carved image of the Goddess, without its necklace now. But there was no priestess—no, *she* was the priestess, and as she danced she could feel the silky fur that lined her gloves and the swing of beast tails sewn to her cloak.

Her head buzzed—the women were singing—she took a deep breath, sinking further into herself, focusing on the words—

> *Hail Freyja! All hail to the goddess,*
> *Highest and holiest, hail!*
> *Brisingamen's bearer, Bride of the Vanir,*
> *We boldly bespeak thee now.*
> *Whiter thy arms than snow in the winter,*
> *Shining in the sun;*
> *Brighter thy eyes than the bridge of Bifrost,*
> *That bears to Valhalla the gods.*
> *Gefion the giver, gold-bright goddess,*
> *Grant us thy favor now,*

> *There where thou sittest in splendid Sessrumnir;*
>   *Linen-clothed Lady of Love,*
> *Hörn we name thee; Heide the Wise One;*
>   *And Heithrun, she-goat of the gods.*
> *As Syr we salute thee, Hildisvini's rider,*
>   *Boar-Ottar's savior art thou. . . .*

The women circled, around and around. Karen danced with them, reeling as the sky whirled above her and the rudely carved post before her seemed to grow. The song continued,

> *Gullveig the golden, fast bound in the flames,*
>   *Re-forged thou thy fate in the fire.*
> *From thy falcon-form a feather, from thy lions a*
>   *whisker,*
>   *Give thou to keep us from fear.*
> *Mardoll of the waters, mighty thy beauty,*
>   *Mistress of gods and men;*
> *Mare of the Vanir, as Gondul dost thou gallop,*
>   *Bearing kings from the battlefield.*
> *Dealer of death, kind is thy embrace,*
>   *But in the earth-womb's darkness,*
> *Lady of Life, light dost thou kindle—*
>   *Goddess, show us thy glory!*

The women were shouting, Karen was shouting, a roar that split the sky as the pole in the midst of the clearing expanded into a mighty tree that pierced the heavens. Shouting, she ran toward it, set hands and feet into the carving, and began to climb. Faster and faster she climbed, her arms reached, and then it seemed to her they were not arms, but beating wings. Her skin cloak had become feathered pinions that beat steadily, bearing her into the sky.

And then the earth was gone. She was in darkness, buffeted by a mighty storm. Below her she saw hills and valleys half-dissolved in rain, and the faintly pulsing lights that were the huddling spirits of men, for on this plane she saw the real world with different eyes. And seeing, she remembered who she was and why she had come.

But I am the priestess too, she realized. *Why did I never understand that before?*

Then she set aside the knowledge and turned her attention

to the battle raging around her, for the struggle of the elementals shook the night. She saw them as shapes of color striving, the blue sprites that had come down from the north resisting the attempts of the warmer elementals of the southern storm to move them so that they could sweep onward as they had always done before. Counter-clockwise they swirled, building the low-pressure area of the storm.

But their deadlock was mindless; she was looking for the force that drove them, the pattern of the storm. She let the wind lift her and soared above the cloud-forms, seeking a focus of brilliance—there! Like a beacon blazing she saw it, radiating power in lines of light.

Surely she knew that golden glow, reddened now by that other energy that directed it. She flew toward it, desiring its beauty even as her fear increased. She circled, lower, lower, seeking to identify streets and buildings with her transformed vision, seeing them like the negative of a picture, or a satellite-sensed image to whose forms she must find the key.

And then she was buffeted by the touch of another awareness, a mind that enfolded and drew her inexorably toward the blaze of dreadful light. Like a netted bird she struggled, knowing only too well the laughter that grew louder as Loki reeled her in.

Goddess, help me! came her heart's cry, and like an echo, the sound of chanting—*"Lady of Life, light dost thou kindle; Goddess, show us thy glory!"*

And a light too pure for the name of color flared around her, unmaking the net for just the moment it took for her to wing free.

And she knew that light, like a scent or a taste it was familiar now that she sensed it again. She desired it, yearned toward it, followed it far from the reach of the storm to a place where power pulsed like great clouds, and patterns of energy moved among them, distinct as any human personality, yet having no form that human perceptions could see.

But there was one such focus to which she could give a name. Joyously she winged toward it, not caring if in the next moment she would be consumed.

And then she was back in the clearing. The other women trembled and hid their faces against the earth, for the image in their midst was limned in flame. The Goddess was showing them Her glory indeed, and they were afraid.

Karen stood on her feet and lifted her arms in salutation, her wings drooping into the folds of her cloak of skins once more.

"Lady, hear me, for I did not understand how to use your power, and now Loki is unloosing Fimbul-winter upon the world!"

"It is not time—the end of all things is not yet come. . . . " The Voice came from without and within, deep, and angry.

"Then stop him!" Karen cried.

"I cannot—he is working in your world—"

"Then what can we do?"

"We will battle Loki and the Jötun as we have so many times before," the Voice softened, as if it spoke in her ear. *"But this time we must do it through human beings. Find friends who will fight at your side, and we will work through you!"*

17

*Then all the Powers, gods most sacred
Went to their judgement seats, asked one another
Who had involved the air with evil
Or conferred the bride of Od on the ogre-kin.*

VOLUSPA

The Co-op was crowded. People had huddled at home during
the storm; now they were hurrying to replace staples and lay in
supplies for the future. Karen looked down the line of shopping carts heaped with canned goods, matches and candles,
crackers and cereals, and even jugs of purified water.

How do they know? she wondered. *Is there some secret
sense still active in the human psyche that tells them the
disasters are not over, or is this just a normal reaction to the
last storm?*

Karen glanced at her watch and pushed her cart ahead.
Walter was due to arrive at the Oakland Airport in an hour—
she must be there to meet him. He had been attending a conference in Chicago and she had had a hard time getting hold of
him. Was she right to have waited for his return before she invoked the gods? There were so few people she could call upon
for something like this, and Walter had been involved with
Brisingamen from the beginning. The pattern would be incomplete without him, and she and Del had needed time to
prepare. Surely the delay would not make that much difference. . . .

"Hey, Jim—how're ya doing? Wet enough for you?"

A loud voice behind her startled Karen. She turned and saw a tall young man greeting another boy—students from the look of them.

"Don't ask!" Jim replied. "You know my basement apartment? Well it flooded, ruined a shelf of books. I was lucky to get my stereo out of the way in time. I'm staying with my girl now."

The tall boy nodded. "My roommate's parents lost part of their living-room—ground just washed out from under it, and they don't know if their insurance will cover rebuilding or not."

"Wow—that's bad. But did you hear about Andy—" The conversation continued, a litany of disaster.

The woman ahead of Karen was leafing through a magazine. Karen read the headline over her shoulder, *"Killer Storm Racks Bay Area: Meteorologists Seek Cause."* The current theory seemed to be that pockets of arctic air from the first storm had kept the rain from moving on. Over four inches of rain had fallen on the Bay Area in a period of twelve hours, flooding the flatlands and washing out the hills.

Karen closed her eyes. The vision of the battle of the elementals was still vivid in her memory. She had *seen* the struggle the terse terminology of the Weather Service described. Did such dramas take place during every event in Nature, for those who had eyes to see?

But the storm was over now. The waters were receding. The dismal work of digging out, of assessing damage and applying for assistance, of rebuilding ruined lives, had begun. The Red Cross and the other disaster relief agencies were applying their varied resources to the task of restoring life to normal.

But it's not over—Karen bit back the urge to cry out from the rooftops like Jeremiah and warn the people of the wrath to come. *Loki has attacked us with wind and cold and rain. What will he try next? What mischief is he using this lull to prepare?* And from some deeper level came the question she hardly dared to voice—*Can we do anything to stop him . . . in time?*

This storm had been a bad one, yet—despite the headlines—it had been a comprehensible disaster. But what if it were followed by another, and another, until all man's power to aid his fellows was exhausted, and the survivors could only cower in the ruins and wait for the next blow to fall? What if the same thing happened everywhere, at the same time, so that when men called no help could come?

Karen shuddered. The boy behind her nudged her; she forced her attention to present reality and saw that the checker was waiting. She managed to smile her thanks and began to transfer her groceries onto the check-out stand.

When she came out of the store the brisk wind that had been blowing since morning had grown stronger. It had cleared the sky of the tattered remnants of the earlier storm, but as she looked around her, Karen glimpsed dark shapes on the southwestern horizon, rising as they grew closer like marching towers. Gusts shook the Volkswagen as she piloted it through rush hour traffic, and the early sunset seemed pallid, drained of energy.

On the flats by the airport the wind was worse, but when Karen had parked and found the Arrivals monitor, she saw that Walter's plane was still on time. She waited by the gate, her neck aching with tension she had not allowed herself to notice, until she glimpsed his fair hair. Relief flooded through her in a tide of warmth.

Walter straightened from his habitual stoop as he saw her. Karen ran to him and hugged him hard. *Goddess, I love this man*, she thought, gripping his shoulders to assure herself that he was really here. *But you love Michael*—protested some remaining shred of propriety. *Then it must be possible to love two men at the same time in different ways*— she squeezed Walter again, then let him go—*because I do!*

"Karen, are you all right?" His voice was tight with anxiety.

She nodded against his shoulder, wondering just how much he had read into the frantic message with which she had called him home. In her body there were muscles that still throbbed painfully, and places in her mind that were more painful still, but her vision of Freyja had seared the worst of the darkness away. Her fears were not for herself, not now.

"I'm okay—" She pulled away and Walter looked down at her. For a moment he touched her cheek, then let his hand fall.

"You've changed," he said soberly.

Karen stared back at him, wondering what he saw. Did he recognize the scars Loki had left on her soul, or did the glory of the *seithr* vision shine about her still? She had thought that

when this was over they could all resume their normal lives—
but what if things were never again going to be the same? The
thought frightened her, but she managed to smile.

"Let's go pick up your suitcase," she replied.

"If they haven't lost it," he answered dubiously, and his account of the vicissitudes his baggage had suffered over the
years helped her to shut the fear away.

They crossed the parking lot, leaning into the wind. As she
waited for the car's motor to warm, Karen switched on the
classical station, but there was only static there. She turned it
off again and headed the car towards home. They turned onto
the freeway, and found themselves exposed to the full force of
the wind. The car trembled, tugging like a skittish horse at the
wheel.

"They should put out 'small car warnings' on days like
this," Walter observed.

Karen laughed, then her eyes narrowed. Tail lights were
flaring ahead like scattered flowers. She began to slow.

"Something wrong up ahead there!"

Karen nodded. Now she could see what it was—a two-sec-
tion trailer rig that had gone over on its side on the freeway,
probably caught by some freak gust of wind. Two cars had
ploughed into it before they got the flares out. Glass sparkled
like ice on the road. A highway patrolman was directing cars
towards the off-ramp ahead.

Frowning, Walter reached over to the radio, twiddling the
dial until he found a local station that carried news.

". . . and this is the KSFN hotline," came the voice of the
announcer. "Where are you calling from?" Scratchy with
distance, the voice on the other end of the station's telephone
replied, "I'm up in Richmond, and I wanted to tell you we lost
our power about five minutes ago." "Well, you're not
alone—" came the announcer's hearty reply. "They've had
ninety mile-per-hour winds up at the Altamont Pass—
knocked down the seventy-five-foot towers at the Tesla sub-
station—that's two million volts of electricity out, and P,
G&E won't say how many homes have lost power. We only
know that all over the Bay Area the lights are going out. Parts
of El Cerrito went a few minutes ago. Yes?" The phone rang
again.

As Karen drove through Oakland the radio phone continued to ring. She and Walter listened in silence as commu-

nity after community reported their lights gone. Soon she came to a section of road where the stoplights were out, too. A young black man in a running suit stood in the intersection, directing traffic. He grinned at them as he waved them by.

Power outages checkerboarded the East Bay, and once as they drove through a business section they actually saw the moment when the lights flickered and died. It was unnerving to drive on main roads without the familiar patterning of traffic signals, and Karen soon took to the back streets where at least the stop signs could be depended on. The deepening dusk was only sporadically broken by the lights of the twentieth century now. Block by block the years slipped away. Karen had never seen such darkness in the city before.

"And so night falls across the world . . . " said Walter solemnly. A Dark Age, or an Ice Age, or something worse? wondered Karen. She sighed gratefully as they turned up Telegraph and she saw the familiar streetlamps still lighting the way.

Michael's motorcycle was parked in front of her apartment, and behind it a battered pick-up truck that must belong to Terry. With a little lurch of the heart, Karen realized that they had all answered her call. She picked up her bags of groceries and squinted into the windy darkness. Her heart was beating like a warning drum.

Then she took a deep breath and followed Walter up the steep stairs.

"I've never been to a seance before—what're we supposed to do?" Michael grinned and pushed his plate of spaghetti aside. Karen braced herself against the weight of four intent stares and put down her glass. Her own plate was almost untouched—the nausea that had troubled her all week was worse now. *Stage fright*, she thought, *and surely no one ever had a better reason for it than I!*

"In the first place, it's not a seance—" she answered a little more severely than she had intended. "As I understand it, the closest practice to what we are planning is Voudoun."

"Norse Voodoo?" Michael echoed disbelievingly. "You're going to sacrifice chickens in your living room?"

Karen shook her head, recognizing in his flippancy an unease he was too proud to show. It was only natural, she supposed, but she wished that he did not feel so defensive.

"To be truly faithful to the Norse tradition we should sacrifice horses, or thralls!" Walter commented dryly. "But if I understand what Karen has told me, what we are trying to do is to become vehicles for the action of the gods."

"Possession?" asked Michael dubiously.

Karen nodded. "But only if you are willing—" She looked around the table at the others. "You have to understand that all this is voluntary. I've explained my theory that the god, or pattern of energies we call Loki, or whatever you want to name it, has taken over Duncan Flyte in order to attack our world, but I can't prove it. I can't even prove that there are such things as gods, or Jötun. . . . "

" 'But they might be giants—' " Walter quoted softly. Terry grinned at him.

"Giants are supposed to be my specialty—" He gripped the Thor's hammer that hung around his neck. The lights flickered, then strengthened again, and his face hardened. "I believe that there are forces that do the work of the Jötun in our world. And all of us have seen the Goddess in a woman's form—why is it so hard to believe in the gods?"

Everyone looked at Karen. She blushed, remembering the circumstances in which Freyja had appeared to each of the men in the room. *But I'd sleep with all of them here and now if that would do any good*, she thought. *If only it were as simple as that!*

Michael's gaze swept over the others and then fixed on Karen again, his good eye burning. *He is wondering how many times, and when* . . . Karen thought with a sinking heart. *I should have told him—I should have known how he would feel.*

It was a point of honor for a biker to be able to hold his woman, and deeper than that lay Michael's fear that his maiming made him unworthy of her. In his face she could read the struggle between his desire to accuse her now and the greater purpose that had brought them all here.

"I thought we were meeting to decide what to do about Duncan Flyte," he said at last.

"No—" Del answered gently. "That is not for us to decide. We are here so that the gods can judge Loki, and perhaps to be their instruments."

"You have to understand," said Karen. "I can't guarantee that this will work, or that the gods will protect us if it does.

Norse history makes it very clear that the purposes of the gods
do not always coincide with the needs of men. I only know this
is the only way I can think of to stop what is going on outside
right now!"

In the pause that followed her words they could all hear the
howling of the wind. A branch scratched at the window as if it
were trying to get in. Eyes met and slid away, lest each read in
the other's the beginnings of fear.

"I am willing," said Walter simply at last, "but is it possible? Karen has manifested the goddess Freyja, but only when
she was wearing Brisingamen. How will we know whom to invoke?"

"I've acted as Thor's priest often enough—I'm willing to let
him use me if he will." Terry held out his big carpenter's
hands and flexed them thoughtfully, then reached into his
backpack and pulled out a short-handled mallet whose
wooden stock was oiled and banded in polished brass. He held
it up for them to see. "This is the hammer I use to represent
Mjollnir in my ceremonies."

They all stared at the mallet gleaming dully against the blue
tablecloth, then up at Terry again. Karen felt her skin prickle
as she watched his eyes grow grim above the red beard. Surely
he was changing even now. With the prospect of giants to
fight, Thor the Protector would surely come.

Terry turned to Michael and spoke in a voice that was already deeper than his own. "And you, warrior and poet—
don't you know yet who you are?"

Michael straightened, his head turned a little so that his
good eye met the other man's stern gaze. Then he grinned
wolfishly. "Do I? Well, perhaps I do at that."

Del nodded. "I will invite that aspect of the Goddess whom
they called Heide, the Vala, to come to me. Let us hope she
will provide enough wisdom for us all." She looked over at
Walter.

"Dr. Klein—you know the myths better than any of us.
What god will you choose to bear?"

Walter closed his eyes for a moment, sighed, then removed
his glasses and put them in his pocket, and looked up at Karen
with a smile whose sweetness transformed his face. "I have
always admired Heimdall, the Guardian of Men. I only wish
that I had my horn."

Karen frowned. There was something about the choice of

Heimdall that bothered her; if only she could remember—

And then the lights yellowed and with a tired flicker winked out. House lights, street lights, all were gone. They were alone with the darkness and the wailing wind; the beginning of the winter of the world.

Music surged through the living room. A chill ran down Karen's back and she pulled her blanket around her. With the heat out, Del had made sure they all had blankets to wrap around them before they sat down. Karen knew that the music was only a tape of Wagner overtures being played on her battery-driven recorder, but in the darkness it seemed part of the wilder music the wind was playing outside. She shivered as she had in the opera house at the beginning of *Rhinegold*, when the city of men dissolved around her and she found herself in a more ancient, primal world.

She took a deep breath. *Now*, she thought, *the ancient world has come to me.*

The music faded to a close. Del got to her feet, a lighted candle in her hand, to begin the warding.

"In the name of Raphael the Archangel, and the guardians of the watchtowers of the East; in the name of Merlin the Archmage and Mercury, swift messenger; and by virtue of all Powers of the Air, may this place be protected from all evil and consecrated to our purpose here." She carried the candle to the eastern corner of the room, bowed, and lit the incense and the blue candle there, and traced the invoking pentacle of Air.

From the east, Del passed to the south, to the west, and to the north, setting each corner of the room aglow. Her movements had a quality that focused the attention. Karen felt herself settling, and knew that already the atmosphere of the room was altering.

Del completed the circle, then returned to her place on the floor. For a moment she lifted her taper high, then bent to touch to life the votive light before her and handed the candle to Walter. He bowed to her as if he had been doing this sort of thing all his life and took it, and as he reached to light his own candle she spoke again.

"From hand to hand we pass the flame, around us burns the sphere of power; the Guardians of Life we name, to ward us in this holy hour!"

From Walter to Terry and from Terry to Michael moved the fire. Karen watched their faces in the uneven light—nervous or dubious, awed or abstracted in turn. Walter looked oddly peaceful, but there was a wariness in Michael's frown as he lit his candle and handed the taper to her. With a short, formless prayer of supplication, Karen set her candle alight and passed the taper back to Del again.

"I have explained our procedure," said Del. "You must still mind and body, and as I call upon each of you, try to envision the figure of the god forming around you, replacing your own. As I am the eldest and most experienced, I will begin."

The older woman closed her eyes, settled herself more solidly on her cushion, and began to breathe, deeply, regularly. The silver ankh on her breast glinted in the candlelight. Then she pulled her black shawl over her head, veiling her cap of silver hair, and abruptly her grey skirt and sweater took on the appearance of a wadmal gown, and the pleasant, maternal face she had worn during dinner became the classic mask of a priestess, an empty vessel waiting to be filled.

Karen waited, listening to her breathing, willing each tense muscle to ease, hearing the soughing of wind in the trees. Around her she was aware of small movements as the others got comfortable, the increasing stillness as breathing steadied and synchronized.

Then, suddenly, the air seemed colder. Karen took a deep breath, and the blood tingled in her veins. There was a strange scent in the air—pine wood burning, and an odd pungence of aromatic herbs. Through her mind flashed the image of the Norns from the Rackham illustration to *Gotterdamme-rung*—three figures darkly silhouetted against a sunset sky. As if the wind had found a voice, a whisper stirred the air:

> *Trembles the towering tree Yggdrasil,*
> *Its leaves sough loudly: unleashed is the giants' child . . .*
> *I tell thee much, yet more lore have I,*
> *Thou needs must know this—wilt know still more?*

Karen recognized lines from the *Voluspa* and wondered if Del had memorized them, or if Somebody else was speaking through her now.

Then Del opened her eyes, and Terry made a small sound deep in his throat, for Del's eyes were wells of darkness, seas of night vast enough to hold all the secrets of future or past. She was the Vala now, peering at their awed faces with a mocking smile and pointing, as the Norn had pointed in the painting, at Walter.

> . . . *at the edge of the earth, etin-maids nine*
> *gave birth and suck to the brightest of gods.*
> *Most high-minded he 'mongst the hallowed ones,*
> *In sib with all sires and sons of earth.*
> *The waters dance; the doom doth break*
> *When blares the gleaming Gjallar-horn;*
> *Loud blows Heimdall—*

The name vibrated through the stillness. Karen felt its resonance in the floor beneath her, in her very bones. Walter covered his eyes with his hands. His breath came in hoarse gasps. Then Karen's eyes were dazzled as if the candles had flared, and her ears throbbed with the endlessly echoing call of a horn. For a moment the sense of a bright presence was almost too much to bear; then, like the shuttering of a lantern, it dimmed.

Fearfully, she looked at Walter. He was sitting very still. Then, abruptly, he let his hands fall. His eyes met those of the Vala in a long stare, then passed to fix those of the others one by one. His fair hair glowed like living gold; to Karen's wavering vision his white sweater seemed to lengthen into a shining robe. And then his eyes met hers, the eyes of Heimdall that saw everything in the world; the eyes that looked upon everything that Walter Klein had been afraid to see.

The Vala nodded and turned to Terry, who swallowed and gripped his hammer as he watched her stern face.

> *The mountains shake: fares Mjollnir's wielder,*
> *Hlorrithi, hitherward;*
> *He will quickly quell the quarrelsome knave*
> *Who mocks both Aesir and men.*
> *Thor, I summon thee!*

The name rumbled through the air like jovial thunder. The bright patterns of Terry's ski sweater rippled as his chest rose and fell. Karen gasped at the pressure on her own lungs, as if some vast presence had displaced the air. Then the breath rushed back on a gust of warm, moist air; and it seemed to Karen that she was a child again, being tossed into the air by her father's strong arms. The patterned yoke of Terry's sweater glittered on his shoulders like a collar of jewels. Grinning like a child on Christmas morning, he swung the heavy hammer high and his deep laughter blended with the rattle of thunder that shook the room.

Karen looked at him with delight. Even to her mortal eyes he glowed, and she understood why Thor had held the central place in the temples of the gods.

Michael was sitting very still, back straight, hands resting on his thighs. He eyed the Vala as a soldier, under orders to hold his position to the end, might watch an approaching enemy. His black jersey gave him a somber elegance; the wolf on his beltbuckle was glittering balefully and the grey blanket flowed from his shoulders like a cloak of cloud. He looked dangerous, even now. Karen remembered the stories about Odin and repressed a shudder of fear.

What verses will you choose to call Odin to our company? What runes will waken the warrior's god? Karen wondered as the Vala locked gazes with Michael and began to speak. But it was the poet upon whom she called.

> *I know for certain, Odin*
> *Where thou didst conceal thy eye*
> *In the wondrous well of Mimir;*
> *Each morn Mimir his mead doth drink*
> *From the pledge of the Father of the Slain. . . .*

Her voice was gentle, but Michael was on his feet before she had finished, crouched as if to spring. Thor half-raised his hammer to protect her, but Heimdall put out a calming hand. Michael stared at them and his fingers touched the ruin of his eye. Why that? wondered Karen, knowing that she must not move or try to comfort him. Why did the Vala remind him of that loss?

For a moment another personality shone through Michael's features, and shadows lifted like dark wings in the corners of the room. Karen heard the dreadful music of the battlefield, and felt the pounding of hoofbeats in the thudding of her heart. Then Michael's teeth clenched, and the Other was suppressed. *He's fighting it*, Karen realized. *Michael, let go!*

His hands clenched and unclenched at his sides; he gasped, and that Other within him drew back his lips in a snarl. He cried out and staggered, staring wildly, and a darkness swirled around him that was shot with the bitter clarity of stars. His lips moved; he answered the Vala, and the sound of that harsh whisper made every hair on Karen's arms stand on end.

> *I know I hung on the windswept Tree,*
>   *through nine days and nights.*
> *I took up the runes, screaming, I took them—*
>   *then I fell back.*

Then he straightened, and Karen saw his face change as he accepted the weight of the wisdom he had won. *Odin*—silently she hailed him, *Master of Wisdom and Poetry, Lord of the Gallows and the Slain. . . .* The shadows precipitated into grey shapes that fawned at his feet and black forms that flapped to his shoulders, whispering into his ear. Staggering beneath the knowledge that had come to him, the Valfather settled into his place again.

Karen bowed her head, knowing it was her turn now. *Why am I trembling?* she wondered. *I have done this before.* She was grateful for the warmth of Trjegul and Bÿgul curled at her side. *Lady, help me! Blessed Freyja, if you want me to serve you, come to me!* She took a deep breath, then another, trying to picture the face and form she had seen in her mirror, transfigured by Brisingamen. The Vala's voice reached her on a wind fragrant with the scent of spring flowers.

> *Freyja is the fairest of all the goddesses;*
> *High-built and beautiful is Sessrumnir her hall.*
> *When she would journey, two cats draw her chariot;*
> *The poetry of love she favors. . . .*

Without Brisingamen it was harder. Karen's body shook—there was something wrong—the Lady of Love was not the aspect she felt overwhelming her. Then a Voice spoke through her, contradicting the Vala's invocation.

> *Folkvangar is where Freyja decides*
>   *who shall sit where in the hall;*
> *Each day she chooses half of the slain*
>   *and Odin the other half has.*

It was the voice of the battle goddess, the face of Freyja that Karen had never wanted to know. Her ears rang, she felt as if she were falling down an endless well. Yet she retained some awareness, like a passenger on the great vessel that was bearing her spirit away. *Freyja!* she cried, and the answer was like the deep, amused purring of a lioness. *"Child—be still. Would you dance upon the wrack of the world? I will teach you another kind of dancing now."*

And Freyja shook back her shining hair, and faced the other gods, and smiled.

With doubled sight Karen saw the room with its worn rug and colorful pillows, and a timbered hall whose walls bore woven hangings and whose pillars were inlaid with an interlace of gold. She saw human bodies in their plain garments, and the rich robes of the gods.

Odin's bowed head lifted. The raven on his shoulder flicked its wings to balance, then was still. The voice of the father of the gods was like clear water rising in a deep well.

"My brothers and sisters, long have we slept. Who draws us now from dreams into an altered world?" He bent forward, searching their faces with the single light of his eye.

"Long have we slumbered, but Loki has wakened. He forces Fimbul-winter before Fate decrees." The Vala settled the folds of her shawl around her like dark wings.

"While you were sleeping, dreaming of battle, I have been wakeful—" Freyja said bitterly. "The world weakens, and I would preserve it. My power's purpose is to nurture men."

"Of thy dealings with men we have some memory—" Odin said sharply.

"And with gods, and with magic—Master of Muninn!" she retorted. "But, thou wolf after women, thinkst thou to master Me?" Light flickered around the room as Freyja shook her bright hair.

"Listen!" Heimdall's whisper stopped them. "From the land, lamentation is rising—" He stilled, staring through the darkness. "With my eyes I see homes harvested by the waters. The children of Mimir rage; who ravages Midgard? Ah, now I see him—Loki is laughing; light flares around him—he bears Brisingamen!"

"Brisingamen . . . " moaned Freyja. "A second time has Loki stolen it! Power pours out of me; my power, perverted— love to hate transforming, growth and life destroying. With the gold he has bridled the winds to his will; now he sends his steeds in mad stampede across the world!''

Wind slammed against the house to echo her words. Windows rattled in their frames fearfully and somewhere there was a rending groan as a tree went down. With their sharpened hearing they heard voices, the warsong of the wind. . . .

> *Pluck branch from trunk and leaf from tree!*
> *We are the broom of Destiny—*
> *We hiss and howl; men's houses groan;*
> *We sweep their hovels stone from stone!*
> *The roar and rushing of our power*
> *The teeming world of life will scour;*
> *The Lord of Death shall enter then*
> *To end the Iron Age of Men!*

The house creaked painfully in the embrace of the wind. Once more the wind-creatures shook it, then rushed laughing on their way.

"Destroy him!" shouted Thor. "You stopped me from dooming him before. For his treacherous head my hammer hungers!"

"He has allies with him," the dry voice of the Vala scratched across the silence. "He has joined with the Jötun; his servants are given to the embrace of the etins. Children of Asgard, I tell you to be careful. They are wise with wickedness, and proud in their power."

"I hammered Hrungnir, though his head was of granite, and into the heavens I hurled Thiassi's bright eyes! Svarang's sons flee in terror when they hear my footfalls; Mjollnir knows the names of all the giant-kin!" Thor's teeth gleamed white in the furnace of his beard as he tossed his hammer into the air, and he laughed as it smacked back into his hand.

"Be silent, boaster." Odin's eye gleamed in the shadows. "The hours are hastening; Freyja's necklace has fallen, and Loki wastes the world. Ragnarok threatens, and we are not ready—"

"If we have not the necklace, let us throw down our weapons," said Heimdall gravely, "for win or lose, after us there will be no new world!"

"Then here we are gathered to do justice on the Jötunfriend, and to find how to bind the father of Fenris again." Odin fell silent, resting his head in his hands.

"Again! Again! Why not make an end of him?" cried Thor. "In every age, Ragnarok rises—let us call Alfs and Aesir, the Einheriar waken. Loki has begun it—Heimdall, blow thy horn!"

"In every era, Ragnarok arises . . . " Odin echoed heavily. "And I harvest the heroes. Tonight will I claim more? Sigfather they call me when I send them victory; Svipal when I claim the sacrifice due by their vows. But *I* do not change! I pursue the same purpose—to be ready for Ragnarok! My foreknowledge tells me the time of our ending. And I know by whom I will fall. . . . "

Freyja stretched out her white hand. "But thou, Odin, wast first the sacrifice."

"Much magic Loki taught me in the young days of the world," murmured Odin. "But my own fate I followed—this he never knew, that I am the spirit of the slayer and the slain!"

"And still dost thou love him?" she whispered.

"Our loving means nothing—" Heimdall's quiet voice interrupted, "if we betray the lives of men. Lest Loki make an ending with us unready, Allfather, arise!"

For a few moments there was silence. The taunting gusts of wind were busying themselves elsewhere now. In the distance a siren wailed like Heimdall's horn.

Slowly Odin got to his feet and looked around the circle, assessing them, mustering the resources he could bring to this fight.

"Loki will battle in the body of a man," the Vala reminded them. "And his allies also. The Aesir are stronger in the world of the spirit, but the Jötun jolt the world!"

"But we're wearing the bodies of mortals also!" Thor stood, his hammer swinging in his hand. "Show me the foe! Warfather, I'll follow!"

"Men's bodies must mend what men's hatred has marred . . . " said the Vala. "It is fitting. Freyja, let us find thy necklace. And when 'tis recovered, teach thy priestess right use of its power."

Freyja bowed her shining head, and Karen, a spark of awareness within her, realized that the gods intended neither to destroy Brisingamen nor to remove it from the world. Did they expect *her* to keep the thing? She buzzed within the pattern of power that was Freyja like a trapped butterfly.

"Earthchild, be still—" For a moment the goddess deigned

to notice her. *"If you survive, then you may complain to Me!"*

A hand touched her shoulder and she looked up into Heimdall's smiling eyes. Was Walter gazing out at her from behind them, Karen wondered, or had he given himself entirely to the god? She knew now why they had named Heimdall the White God, the fairest after Baldur. This was the person Walter Klein had been meant to be.

"The girl has a car that will carry four," said Freyja. "She has seen the place where Loki now works his magics."

"And Michael has a steed whose paces I will joy in." Odin's mood had shifted. He was grinning now, zipping up the gleaming leather of his jacket. "A worthy substitute for Sleipnir's speed. And there is a sword also that I would swing—you must fare ahead, and I will follow."

Freyja reached up to Heimdall and let him pull her to her feet, old allies joined once more to battle an ancient foe. Her other hand she gave to Odin. Thor set down his hammer to link with him and with the Vala who stood on Heimdall's other side. Power flowed deosil through their clasped hands, binding them, building within them until they glowed. The Vala began to chant and the others joined her:

> *Powers of Earth and Sea and Sky,*
> *Ancient when the gods were young,*
> *And holy Fire, be our ally,*
> *Against all foes we walk among—*
> *Upon your strength we dare to call,*
> *For from your substance came our birth—*
> *Be with us, Fire of Life, and all*
> *Ye powers of Sky and Sea and Earth!*

The linked fingers parted, With faces that grew grimmer, they fumbled with human garments, armed themselves against the forces Loki would throw against them. Then the gods went down the stairs into the maelstrom of wind and darkness to seek their foe.

18

Sails a ship from the east with shades from hel;
O'er the ocean stream steers it Loki:
In the wake of the Wolf rush witless hordes
Who with baleful Byleist's brother do fare.

VOLUSPA

"Drive real careful, Miss—the wind's pretty bad up there."
The ticket-taker leaned over the door of his booth and peered
down into the car, his dark face creasing with anxiety.
"They've closed the Golden Gate Bridge to traffic, you know,
and I'm expectin' them to shut down this one any time now.
Gusts of sixty miles and more up there, I guess, and that car of
yours don't have the weight to hold the road. I really
shouldn't let you through at all. . . . "

Karen unrolled the car window a little farther and stuck her
head out into the rain. "Thank you, but it is necessary that we
go to San Francisco this night." Freyja spoke through her,
"We will take care." She smiled, and, dazzled, the man pulled
back into his shelter and waved them on.

Lady, I hope you know what you're doing, thought Karen
as she released the brake and sent the little car forward, *Or this
expedition is going to end in the Bay*. The bridge lights were
swaying on their long poles; the man had been right—it was
not the sort of weather any sane person would go out in—but
then sanity had little relevance to anything that was happening
now.

The car shuddered as the steepening slope of the bridge exposed them to the full force of the wind. If it had been steady, she could have held the wheel firm against it, but it was hitting in gusts, and it took all her concentration to release the wheel just when the wind eased to keep from swerving across the road.

Karen's knuckles grew white as she gripped the wheel. Her own reactions were good, but she had never had the nerve for this kind of driving. A tacit agreement with the goddess had given Karen primary control of the car, but now, as an unexpected gust nearly wrenched the wheel from her hands, she felt panic fraying her concentration. She tried not to notice the queasy trembling of the bridge beneath the car's wheels, not to hear the evil howling of the wind through the latticework of girders that were the bridge-frame, not to see the furious gusts of wind-whipped spray from the dark waters below.

"You fool, do you think that shutting your eyes to your foe will make him go away?" came the exasperated Voice from within. *"Open yourself, feel the forces around you and become one with them—relax!"*

Karen could feel Thor shifting with frustrated anxiety on the seat beside her, the steady support of the Vala behind her, the burning brightness of Heimdall. It was not her own life only that was at stake here; she must master the car, she must—

"Be still and let Me guide you now!"

For a moment panic possessed her, and the wind, whistling gleefully, seized the car and tossed it sideways. The world whirled around her in a chaos of dark wind. The guardrail loomed crazily close—

"Freyja!" Karen screamed.

Something snapped within her and suddenly Karen was a passenger once more. Memories of hurtling through the air with a falcon's wings merged with the reality of the chaos around her. She felt the wind sharply, knew that the deck of the bridge was rippling like a ribbon beneath them, and threw back her head and laughed. For the goddess, it was sport to brave the storm—and there had never been such a storm as this.

She bore down on the gas pedal, fingers gripping the wheel with a delicate strength that responded to each shift in the wind.

The dark bulk of Treasure Island loomed ahead; they caught their breaths for a moment in the brief protection of the tunnel, then they were out onto the suspension bridge beyond, and they could see the cables vibrating like plucked harpstrings as the roadway swung ten feet from side to side.

There was no such thing as solid ground. The little car skipped from lane to lane, rocking once on two wheels and smashing against the railing before the goddess could wrestle it back again. In a moment surely they would be flung skyward and carried over the rail.

Karen felt the shift in angle before she could see it and for a moment thought that the bridge had broken and they were falling into the Bay. Then she realized that they were on the downslope at last, with the few lights that remained in the city twinkling before them.

"We have conquered," cried Freyja. "Loki, thy creatures have failed thee—fear now the rightful wrath of the gods!"

The skyscrapers swayed against the moving curtain of the sky. As they swept down through the city, a flying piece of metal clanged against the hood of the car and a fragment of moulded cornice hurtled past, as if Loki were plucking San Francisco to pieces stone by stone. The few other cars that had braved the freeway weaved drunkenly as their drivers fought the wind. Karen fought her way into the right-hand lane and eased the car down the off-ramp into the relative protection of the streets.

Here, maneuvering the car was less of a battle, but the litter in the road required constant vigilance—a flat tire would delay them as surely as a crash. And they must find Loki soon—all of them could feel the violence of the storm building toward some unimaginable explosion of energies. Karen remembered the pattern of streets her vision had shown her, but she still did not know precisely how to get to the warehouse. She felt her way forward, hoping for some sixth sense to lead her to her goal.

The buildings around them grew meaner—one- or two-story houses of flaking stucco and unreconstructed Victorians that were losing their ornamental "gingerbread," mixed with the warehouses of moribund businesses. For several blocks the neon lights of the bars still flickered defiantly. Then they entered a section where the power was gone and nothing moved but the wind.

And something else—like an invisible light, an impalpable warmth, a song that was sensed, not heard. It was the extra sense Karen had hoped for, and the presence of Freyja intensified. Karen caught an impression of radiance, the warming glow of gold. She turned a corner, the feeling grew stronger. Thor stiffened and gripped his hammer.

"Jötun! I smell them—there they are hiding!" he pointed down an alleyway.

"Yes, there's the stink of sorcery," echoed the Vala.

"I hear Loki's laughter—" Heimdall confirmed.

Freyja nodded, wholly in control now. Brisingamen bloomed in her awareness like a burning flower, and now her heightened sense recognized the turmoil of forces that surrounded it. She stepped on the gas, screeched around the last corner, and skidded to a halt before a frame building whose double doors still bore the remnants of bright paint and gilding.

Both as Karen and as Freyja she recognized it, and for a moment the memory of Loki's magic held her motionless. But Thor flung open the car door, and, more carefully, Heimdall and the Vala went after him. She took a deep breath and let her consciousness slip back into that secret sanctuary where it had waited before. The pride and anger and energy of Freyja surged through her, and the goddess followed them.

The great doors were locked, but a line of light showed beneath them. "We should wait for Odin—" Freyja began, but already Thor's big hands had closed on the crosspiece; he shoved, met resistance, and with an oath raised his hammer and brought it down.

The door split as if it had been struck by lightning. Thor's arm rose again and a section slid back; they stepped through the gap into flickering light and a stench of incense, and the prickling, nerve-tingling presence of power.

The place was just as she had seen it before—the scenery flats, the props and costumes hanging on the walls. Candlelight glowed fitfully on the gold of mock jewels and stage weapons, lent an evil life to masks and hanging clothes. And yet everything was different, too, for this time she came in the fullness of a power that could challenge Loki on equal terms.

Except that Loki had Brisingamen.

For a moment the blaze of the necklace on his shoulders was all she could see. Then she focused on his pale face and brilliant eyes, saw how his hair curled into darting flames as he turned, drawing power and more power from the circle of chanting figures around him.

Her lips drew back in a snarl as she recognized Joe Whitson and Danny Ortona, Lownie and the punkers and the others who had helped Duncan to torture her. There were more of them now, including some women—a dozen in all. His students, she supposed, seduced through that violation of the mind which was the special talent of Duncan Flyte.

But there was no time to wonder how he had enslaved them. Thor was charging the circle, his hammer rising to smash and slay. Freyja and the others dashed after him—

—and met a barrier of invisible energy that threw Thor backward into Freyja's arms. Loki was laughing. With a bellow of rage, Thor strode forward again and struck at the barrier. But the wall held. They should have expected it—they had used the same forces to guard their own circle a little while ago. Duncan had not been able to enter Karen's house after Del had warded it; Freyja could not reach Loki now.

This close, she could feel the constant pulse of Brisingamen, painful as the smell of food to a starving man. And she could read the flow of energies Loki was manipulating. . . . Her heart twisted as she felt the perverted power of Brisingamen spiraling widdershins, adding energy to the vortex of low pressure that was the womb of the storm.

"They are too well-guarded—" shouted the Vala behind them. "Get back into safety!" The barrier was pulsing visibly now.

Freyja grasped Thor's arm and pulled him backward as a reddish light crackled around the circle.

Through its glow they saw Loki beckoning, grinning like Fenris at the sight of Tyr.

"Hail to thee, Freyja!" he mocked. "Hast come for thy necklace? The Jötun thy jewel hold—let thy joy lie in ashes! Too long we have struggled, but I stand the victor. Behold—the unwinding of the world!"

He flung out his arms in ecstasy and began to twirl counterclockwise—always widdershins against the way of the sun—and Freyja felt the power of the necklace turning back upon itself, disrupting the flow of blood in her body, felt the constant countless building of cells blocked, bent, and the first disintegration begin. Dizzied, she drew the others back with her, seeing them already older as their radiance began to fade. Loki's chanting shivered in the air—

> *All that was built shall be broken!*
> *All that has risen shall fall—*
> *The Word of the world is unspoken,*
> *The rhythm wrecked!*

The truncated line shocked her, as Loki refused even the order his verses might have imposed upon the world. More and more powerfully that force of disintegration whirled out from the dancing figure within his ring of power. But if she could not stop him, Freyja must at least try to neutralize his sorceries.

"Our powers cannot penetrate the geas that guard him—" she told the others. "But we must stay his magics, lest they sweep away the world. Go ye to the corners, let us call on the old powers to wall over the barrier, that the evil he raises may rest within."

She hurried to the northern corner of the warehouse and took her stand. She had neither tools nor robes of ritual, but she had no need of them—she was Freyja, and the sight and smell and structure of the earth and all her creatures was an integral part of her identity.

Thor, master of storms, had taken up his position in the east, while Heimdall, who once had fought Loki in the form of a seal to regain Brisingamen, took the western station of Gabriel the Archangel and the powers of the sea. Through the shimmer of power that veiled Loki, Freyja saw the Vala, standing guard over the south with her old hands cupped as if she held the holy fire.

Freyja stretched out her arm and projected a current of energy toward Thor, who put out a hand to receive it and passed it onward through the other hand which held his hammer. From the Vala to Heimdall, and the circle was complete, a slender pulse of power spiraling clockwise to counter the massive impulse toward entropy that emanated from the middle of the room. Freyja set her feet firmly and cried—

> *Powers of Earth and Sea and Sky,*
> *And holy Fire, we call to you—*

Thor took up the chant, his deep voice vibrating in the worn boards of the floor,

> *Though all that we have made should die,*
> *Yet by your law all is made new!*

Across the room, the Vala continued, her trained voice slicing through the discordant chanting of Loki's servants,

> *Life's pattern to preserve entire,*
> *And to fulfill Earth's destiny,*

And Heimdall, picking up the invocation, set the current of power to swirling ever more swiftly—

> *Work through us now, oh holy Fire,*
> *And powers of Earth and Sky and Sea!*

Freyja perceived the energy they were summoning, pale against the murky fires that roiled from the center of the circle. But already Loki's fires were recoiling, beginning to spin more sluggishly as the counter-current the Aesir had established dragged at them.

Freyja sent her awareness deep into the earth beneath her, drawing on the power of Nerthus her mother, the earth-power that was ancient before ever men called upon the gods. Dimly she could feel Thor reaching up to the skies, as Heimdall drew upon the vast force of the sea that rolled behind him, and the Vala reached for the sunfire that burned on the other side of the planet now.

She sensed the unyielding strength of stone, weighty with eons of stability, changing so slowly that the lives of men seemed like those of mayflies. She sensed the fertile energy of the soil, implicit with life, and the longing of each living thing to grow. As if her feet had become roots to dig into the ground, she drew upon that power, sucked it up and poured it out again through her hand to join with the powers the other three were raising until the balanced force of the elements rose smoothly to encase the circle of destruction in a dome of light.

Loki's fires pulsed angrily. Forced to acknowledge the Aesir at last, he ceased his twirling, and it seemed to Karen that the winds paused in their prowling, that everywhere man and nature gasped for breath, wondering if this were respite only or the end of the storm.

"By wind and water have I worked my wrath," hissed Loki.
"With borrowed power upon a witless world I have wreaked
destruction. Do you think you have halted me? Oh ye foolish
gods, you call the elements, and only remind me where my
true power still lies, buried deep in the earth where you yourselves bound me. Let the winds falter! Let the waters fail! I
still have earth and fire!"

Freyja strove to maintain her focus, willed the others not to
listen. Loki's lying tongue had no power over them as long as
they held fast.

"Deep in a dungeon the gods bound Loki. . . . " Softly,
almost wistfully, Loki was whispering now. "Fast in the embrace of Earth they fixed him, with the serpent to pain him,
unless Sigyn catch the venom. But my spirit you could not capture—" Abruptly his voice rose; Freyja could not help but
listen. "Shall I bid Sigyn take her cup away? Then shall I
struggle—then shall the earth shake! Listen! Is it rumbling?
Feel! Does it tremble beneath your feet?"

They had domed a barrier above Loki, but it did not extend
below them, and already Freyja could feel a faint unease in the
earth beneath her, a perturbation in the power on which she
drew.

"Here where I speak, the doom is beginning!" cried Loki.
"On mud stand men's foundations; soon they'll be slipping!
As the earth shakes they will shatter—not one stone shall
stand. In the midst of the wreckage each spark I'll fan to
fury—thus do I doom this land that you have loved!"

Freyja felt her control slipping as the earth power flickered.
After so much rain she knew how precarious was the balance
of anything built upon the soil. Already mudslides had closed
roads and buried houses. If the earth quaked now, mountain-
sides would slip from their moorings and bury the com-
munities below; dams already overstrained by the weight of
water behind them would break, and all below them would be
washed away. Earthquake—the perpetual California nightmare—would bring down buildings as the liquid earth beneath
them gave way. And then, through the ruins, would rage the
greater enemy, fire.

Her awareness reeled beneath the onslaught of images—the
earth exploding in fire and thunder, a rain of metal that tore
limbs from bodies as the fire dissolved flesh from bones.
Buildings, forests, jungles were seared to ash by the holocaust,

and in the midst of the inferno, she saw the uncomprehending dark eyes of a little child.

And in some corner of her consciousness Karen realized that this was the seed of the power Loki was now drawing upon—Duncan Flyte's living nightmare of Viet Nam.

"First, I strike here, but my sway will spread—as this land lies in ruins so will the world one day—disaster upon disaster until men's doom is sure, and gone is the obscenity of green and growing things!"

Loki lifted his hands, then brought them sharply down. Freyja felt the earth crawl like the hide of a horse tormented by a fly. Then Loki bent and placed his palms against the floor, and she sensed the faintest of vibrations passing through the veins of the earth. But it was growing—she felt pressure building as if great hands were closing around her chest.

No! cried her heart, but what could stop it? She reached downward, seeking the heart of the earth's power, and found it already quivering in sympathy with the tension Loki was building, like the tightening string of a bow. *Hold! Oh, my mother, you must hold fast!*

Her spirit quested wildly outward, seeking a power greater than gods or men, but the roaring was all around her, louder and louder until she moaned in agony.

But the Sound that was tormenting her came not from the bowels of the earth but through the air. Heimdall had turned to face it, hands half-raised to defend against this unknown enemy. He whirled, seeking a weapon, and seized a trumpet from a motley assortment of props hanging on the warehouse wall.

Then he tipped back his head and put the thing to his lips, drawing from it, with all his body's skill, a long deep wail that seemed to come from the other end of the earth. Again and again he blew, and even Loki, lost in his incantation, for a moment faltered.

But what help could come to them now?

The deep mutter outside intensified. Freyja stiffened, turned, then motioned to Heimdall to cease blowing, for as in a figure-ground puzzle the hidden pattern suddenly appears, Karen's memory had provided a sudden, joyful recognition. The Sound—the sounds—were as familiar as the blare of Heimdall's horn: the deep drum-roll of Michael's Harley, and orchestrating the air around it, a sharp, staccato bark that must be Dave's Triton, and Belly's Sportster with the echoing, metallic note of its exhaust, and more, the crackling pulse of an Indian Sport Scout, and the purr and growl and thunder of other machines!

The roaring intensified, then stuttered to silence. There was a lull like the pause when men catch their breath in battle, then a crash. The shattered door was flung aside, and Odin and seven of Michael's biker bros burst through.

For a moment he stood poised, keen eye taking in Freyja and the others in their positions, the barrier around Loki and his companions, the conflicting waves of power that pulsed in the room. His men formed up behind him, boot- and buck-knives and chain belts already in hand, faces fixed alike in wolfish grins.

Freyja recognized them; she had seen their kind on many a battlefield. And indeed, as she looked from one to another it seemed to her she knew the spirits that glared from their eyes. Who had they been? Svipdag or Sigurd, Ragnar or Harald—she knew them, the Einheriar who feasted in Odin's hall.

"Hail, Odin—long have I waited—" Loki lifted one hand in a mockery of greeting. Freyja could feel the earth beneath her still trembling, like a whipped horse waiting for the goad to descend once more.

"Hast thou come to challenge, or at last wilt thou join me? Much magic I taught thee when the world was unstained, but now I have knowledge that puts to naught thy wisdom, for I have witnessed the wickedness of this green world." He stood with open hands, his face lit by the mischievous, endearing grin of a child.

For a long moment Odin met his gaze, and Freyja wondered if, even now, he could be swayed by the lust for knowledge and the memory of past comradeship. Then the face of the lord of the battlefield contorted in a terrible smile.

Very deliberately he crossed to the corner where loose pipes and a halbard from some Italian opera were leaning, and with them a long silver spear.

It looked familiar, and some corner of Karen's memory identified it even as Odin set both hands upon it and brought it around before him in an arc of silver. It was Wotan's spear, from the production of *Rhinegold* she had seen. But it was beginning to shimmer now as no stage lighting had ever made it glow.

"Gungnir I name thee . . . " Odin's voice echoed around the room. "Here the runes of Law are written; and thy doom, Loki, and the destinies of the gods! As Gungnir has been given me, so now do I claim thee, and those who thee would follow—the sacrifice of the slain!"

In a single smooth motion he hefted and cast the spear.

19

Brothers will battle to bloody end,
And sisters' sons their sibs betray;
Woe's in the world, much wantonness;
(axe-age, sword-age—sundered are shields—
wind-age, wolf-age, ere the world crumbles);
Will the spear of no man spare the other.
VOLUSPA

The spear of Odin soared like a comet arching across the sky.

It shattered Loki's warding into streamers of bloody fire, curved over the heads of Loki's servants toward Loki, who was startled at last into a swerve to avoid it as it sliced through the circle and out the other side to plunge, quivering, into the wooden floor.

And as the barrier crumbled, the Einheriar launched themselves toward the foe. For a moment the followers of Loki seemed frozen. Then Loki leaped like a flame among them; they rose and scattered, seeming to expand as they moved, snatching stage weapons from the wall that became real in their hands. They had been human, faceless with concentration as they poured out their power for their master. But now they were Jötun, huge and heavy with the strength of giants and the hatred of the etin-kin for the servants of the gods.

Michael's kris flashed in the fist of Odin as the Valfather swung at the largest of his enemies, who had once been Joe Whitson. Now he was something other. He whirled his club

236

like a wand at Odin's shoulder, the god threw himself aside, staggering as the blow grazed his arm, and brought his blade around in a cut that sliced past the Jötun's ear. The floor shook as the giant stepped forward, muscles knotting as the club came up and around once more. Odin leaped backward, seeing an opening, for his sword was too light to parry such a blow.

The Einheriar waded into battle behind him, no longer Michael's buddies, not even their avatars now—their eyes glowed with the feral light of the berserker, their throats were scraped by snarls—but their hands had not forgotten their skill with chain belts and knives, a heavy wrench did terrible duty as a war-hammer, and steel-toed boots were as lethal as paws. But the Jötun outnumbered them. Soon, each warrior was surrounded by misshapen foes.

Thor's hammer smashed through a small table that one of the giants had lifted for protection. Roaring, he strode past him, seeking Loki, but others swarmed around him; he whirled, hammer swinging to keep them at bay. Loki scuttled around him and snatched up a candle; in his hand it became a wand of fire, drawing lines of light upon the air that writhed and became a serpent-tangle that sought to knot itself around the limbs of his foe.

Freyja ducked as a vase hurtled past her. One of the Jötun was snatching props from a shelf and flinging them at her with a juggler's speed. With one arm aching from a blow from a goblet that had caught her as she tried to protect her face, Freyja grabbed for a stage-shield, for a moment held it by its edges before her, then found the straps and slipped her arm through. The impact of crockery striking the varnished surface jolted her—the thing had never been intended to take real punishment.

From the corner of her eye she could see the Vala, who had backed into a corner and was thrusting at all comers with the end of a pole. For a moment one of her opponents hesitated and the Vala stepped forward, her staff blurring. Freyja heard the thwack of the impact, saw the man reeling away.

Then a hand closed on her shoulder and whirled her around. She saw one of the women in Loki's group, face set in a parody of a grin, dagger glinting as she brought it down.

With a cry, the goddess twisted, grabbed the woman's wrist and shoved. The shield caught on the edge of a table and

wrenched her other arm. Her muscles contorted painfully as
she held the descending knife-arm away while she struggled to
free herself from the remains of the shield. Then it was gone;
the breath left her in a gutteral shout as her other hand gripped
the woman's throat. For a moment they struggled, then her
opponent's heel caught on a pile of fabric and she began to
fall.

Freyja came down on top of her, tensing to strike again. But
the impact had knocked the other woman senseless. Gasping,
the goddess grabbed the dagger from a nerveless hand and
began to push herself up.

Metal clashed behind her. She half-turned and saw Heimdall lifting a light rapier to guard as one of the Jötun beat at
him with a spear. The spear-shaft beat the sword away; Freyja
grabbed at the fellow's leg, and the follow-up thrust went
wild. Heimdall grinned his gratitude, then sprang in again, inside the Jötun's guard, pricking at his throat while the enemy
tried to duck away.

Across the room, someone screamed. She saw one of the
Einheriar stagger and go down. A Jötun grinned and turned,
red blood splattering from the edge of his halbard. Odin was
still embattled with his opponent, and now the second giant
lumbered toward them, lowering the point of the halbard
toward Odin's back.

Freyja shrieked at him to watch out, then flung her dagger
at the Jötun's head. Odin whirled, sword flaring before him.
Another of the stage shields hung in tatters from his left arm.
For a moment the three poised like figures in a dance, seeking
an opening.

Freyja gasped for breath and stared around her. The Vala
was pinned down in her corner, Heimdall still engaged with his
foe. From the midst of a knot of struggling bodies she heard
Thor's battle cry, and the remaining bikers were using anything that came to hand against their enemies.

Hauling herself upright, she snatched up a small chair and
held it before her. Where was Loki? There—a flicker of fiery
light showed her his moving figure darting from one of his
followers to another and flashing on. And as she watched, the
character of the battle began to change.

As Loki touched him, one of the Jötun fighting Odin
seemed to grow shorter, broader. Freyja blinked—his form
was not even human now. She saw knotted limbs with quiver-

ing greenish hide, a snouted head from which stained tusks
gleamed. The thing roared and Odin sprang forward, striving
to slice through that thick skin.

She heard snarling, turned, and saw the Vala ringed by
wolves with burning eyes. They snapped at the staff as she
jabbed at them, darting in and out as the wood came down.
Freyja dashed forward and brought her chair down across one
creature's spine.

But even as she touched it the beast was changing, writhing,
extending into a serpent that reared up before her, swaying
dizzily. The goddess swung the chair, and swung it again, but
always the snake darted away, then struck at her head or
hands. She stepped back for a moment; the serpent eyed her
coldly, its red tongue flickering in and out between its fangs.

Then suddenly Freyja was moving, bringing the chair down
to pin the creature and holding it there with one arm while her
other hand groped for the neck of a broken bottle, gripped,
plunged it downward toward the evil triangular head.

And it was a snake no longer, but a man who rolled away
from the blow and jack-knifed to his feet. He came for her
and she brought up the chair one-handed, holding him away.

Two of the bikers, battling back-to-back, were engaged with
a trio of goblins. As one of them darted in, taloned fingers
crooked to slash, another jabbed at the men with a short spear
while the third leaped screeching for their heads. With a shout
of disgusted fury, the warrior flung up his arm, caught the
goblin in the face and hurled it across the room. But the first
creature had reached him and was clinging to his leg, jaws
opening to rend muscle from bone. The man struck down with
his knife; the thing squealed and recoiled, then snapped at his
leg again.

Freyja's opponent grabbed her chair and wrenched it away.
Her attention snapped back, she swirled sideways, slashing at
his arm with the broken bottle. He swung the chair at her, she
ducked, and two of its legs shattered against the wall. He
snarled in frustration; but he was no longer a man, but something fanged and furred with evil eyes. Spittle sprayed from its
jaws as it sprang.

She tried to leap aside, but her foot slipped and suddenly
she was going down with the thing on top of her. Over and
over they rolled. Freyja flailed at it with the bottle while its
teeth sought her throat; her other hand closed on cloth and she

shoved the remains of a costume doublet between the snapping jaws.

Steel flashed above her. The thing convulsed in agony and jerked away. Freyja looked up and saw Odin, for a moment free of his own opponents. He put out a hand to pull her to her feet and they stood, breathing hard, looking around them.

"All Hella's hosts are gathered against us . . . " he said hoarsely. Freyja nodded. Thor's hammer sent an ogre-thing flying across the room, but another was already taking its place in the attack against him. It was hard to tell which of the creatures were Loki's minions transformed, which, illusions he had conjured up to reinforce his attack. No matter how many the gods downed, there were more. The air itself pulsed with distorted shadows.

A thrown spear whipped toward them. Freyja batted it aside, then bent to snatch it from the floor.

"Loki! We must stop him—where is he now?" They searched the heaving mass of men and monsters, seeking the flicker of reddish light that marked their foe.

"Strike with the Spear of Law! Loki's magic will shatter!" Freyja pointed past Heimdall, whose flickering sword was holding at bay a creature like a hag from hell, to where the spear Odin had named Gungnir still stood in the floor.

As they battled toward the spear, Odin caught Thor's eye and the wielder of the hammer fought his way to their side. Monsters surged after them, and worse than monsters now— creatures risen from a thousand battlefields with flesh still shredding from bony arms and rotted back from grinning jaws.

Even in illusion, the perversion of it wrenched at Freyja's gut—that the bones which the clean Earth should have sheltered should come against the living in this obscene mockery! They battled against nightmare and shadow. One by one the lights that had allowed them to see their foes were going out. Now only a single glow drew the eye—a pallid radiance that revealed the figure of Loki, turning toward them as Odin grasped the spear.

And then abruptly it was not Loki they stared at but a great serpent, lifting sickly writhing coils. Thor gave a great cry and sprang at it, recognizing his former and future foe.

Odin swore, the spear still poised in his hand, for already the coils clasped Thor and if he threw he might hit the other god. The hammer swung, they heard a dull thunder and the floor quivered as greasy coils thudded down. It seemed to Freyja that somewhere far below the Earth twitched in answer.

She sensed a shadow rising behind her, jerked sideways and jabbed while Odin danced forward, seeking an opening. The serpent's muscular tail whipped around, sweeping friend and foe before it. As their master's attention was withdrawn, some of the monstrous army began to falter. The gods, striving to catch their breath, paused in their pursuit to stare at the battle taking place in the midst of the room.

Lightning marked the sweep of Thor's hammer, breath rumbled through the cavernous throat of the serpent, echoing the god's thunder. Around and over rolled the glistening coils. It seemed to Freyja that the god was going down.

"The spear! Odin, strike now, before he slays!"

The Warfather drew back his arm and stabbed at unclean flesh. Freyja saw the spear pierce, penetrate and sink in; bloody light rayed and crackled across the serpent's flesh, up the spear and across Odin's arm. Then the snake was gone, leaving Thor's limp body sprawled before them while Odin's weight dug the spear deeper into the floor.

The hosts of shadow rolled toward them again. Loki's mocking laughter rang from roof and rafters. Freyja ran to Thor while Odin whirled to protect them, seeking his invisible foe. Light flickered in the loft above them and they saw the Master of Lies peering down.

Thor groaned and muttered and Freyja helped him to sit up. Above her Heimdall's rapier flickered, and the tattered thing that had been stooping over them flinched away. The other gods drew together around the two on the floor, an island surrounded by obscenity as every mockery of life spawned by Loki's perverted imagination attacked.

Loki had pulled back from the edge of the loft, but they could hear him chanting. Something was changing in the atmosphere of the room; Freyja smelled a heavy acrid odor that choked the lungs, a thickening of the air. What was he doing? This was something more than triggering an earthquake—some deeper sorcery she did not understand.

In the dimness she found it hard to focus. She blinked, but the distortion deepened. The others were shaking their heads in confusion, and she realized that it was not her eyes—the air itself was altering. The sense of wrongness grew ever stronger. Somehow Loki was warping the very fabric of reality.

The earth beneath her shuddered in revulsion. The room danced about her—every fallen prop and piece of scenery bounced, stirred, then began to move of itself in a parody of life. Chairs jerked toward them, lengths of fabric slithered like snakes across the floor. Left and right and up and down distorted; they could no longer be sure what was there and what was the product of their distorted perceptions. The air hummed, thought became a meaningless buzz in the brain.

It could not go on—it *must* not go on. The fear of the human being caught within the goddess shrilled a warning, and the senses of the goddess echoed it; she felt the uncomprehending disturbance of those older powers whose sovereignty Loki was assaulting now.

Karen felt the goddess-form around her fraying, sensed the impending disintegration of all the patterns of the world. The terror of annihilation surged within her, an extinction that would destroy not only her body, but her soul.

And again that existential denial shrieked from the depths of her—*This destruction must not be!*

Desperate, her spirit quested inward, past dimly glimpsed archetypes of goddesses and gods, of all living forms that had preceded her own in the evolution of the world, past all the patterns still implicit in the structure of her human brain. And deeper still—as Loki had reached into his own depths to seek chaos, Karen sought the original pattern that had ordered all the world!

And then, as the other gods began to waver and wink out around her, her stressed spirit found a doorway.

It was Light, so brilliant it blinded vision.

It was Darkness, like an endless, depthless sea.

It was forms for which the three-dimensional perceptions of our world have no names, whirling and wheeling in a Dance whose music was the vibration at the roots of sound.

Karen focused the tatters of her consciousness into a single, silent, cry.

Light and Darkness clapped like two hands around the world with a *kerrack!* that split sight from hearing, and then with a shuddering hiss of withdrawing power, faded away....

There was a great silence, as returning vision showed a

chamber in which nothing stirred, and in which the only light was the candleflame reflected from Loki's astonished eyes.

"So . . . " his whisper floated down to them, a disembodied thread of sound. "For the moment your world is secured. Why wait then to finish me when I am in your power?" He laughed softly, and Odin straightened with a shuddering sigh.

Karen, her senses still dazzled by the vision, felt the pattern that was Freyja forming around her again. The goddess got to her feet and took her place beside Odin. But the others, both gods and Jötun, remained still, shocked by what had been, or mesmerized by what was now to be.

"Loki, thou must be bound," the god said heavily. "Thy malice has mastered thee."

"No—not again!" retorted the trickster. "Never shalt thou hold me. Death thou must deal or leave me free to go. Canst kill me, Odin? I counsel thee—do it, or else be thou wary, for I will work thee woe!"

He laughed again, and Freyja felt unease growing within her, as if the fragile poise of the earth below had been disturbed once more. Loki came to the edge of the loft and looked down at Odin, spreading wide his arms as if to welcome the spear.

"No, thou canst not do it, and I understand thee. What man would slay the brother whom he has loved?"

For so long she had thought of him as Loki, but now the spirit of Duncan Flyte once more looked out of his eyes. He leaned forward, hands braced on his knees.

"Listen to me, for there has been love between us—do you remember, *Michael,* how we drank together? There was a woman on Lamoureux Street—we shared her, thou and I. . . . " The soft voice was like velvet, smoothing all the traumas of the night away. Odin moved uneasily and shifted his grip on his spear.

"No—do not listen—still Loki is lying!" Freyja hissed in Odin's ear.

"Beware of the woman who would now come between us—" came Loki's honeysweet reply. "Long before thou didst know her I was thy brother, closer than flesh. Have I ever betrayed thee? *She* has, with many—"

"Mocker, be silent!" the cry burst unwilling from Odin's lips.

"Tell us, Freyja, the tale of thy lovers . . . " Loki went on, replaying the diatribe of every man who has ever denied a woman's right to give or refuse her body at her own will.

Heimdall, standing on Freyja's other side, quivered angrily. Softly he began to move away from the others, toward the straight ladder at the left-hand side of the loft.

"But what has that to do with us?" Loki ended at last. "What have these tales of gods and goddesses to do with you and me?" Imperceptibly the accent of Asgard had left his speech. The ordinary American twang of Duncan Flyte awakened Freyja's awareness of Karen within her. She could feel a nervous stirring around her and knew that his words were shaking the identities of the others as well.

"Michael, you've got to listen to me—" Softer came the words, and more softly still. "They've all tricked you, tricked us both . . . you've been played for a sucker if you suspect *me*! What's going on, Michael? Why are we here? This is crazy! I'm afraid, and I don't understand!" The magician was kneeling at the edge of the loft now, bending so that his head was only a few feet above theirs. His eyes burned in a face that had become a mask. But which face was the mask? Loki's or that of Duncan Flyte?

Halfway up the ladder, the serenity of Heimdall's fair face was marred by Walter's anxious frown. Next to her Michael trembled uncontrollably, for he was all Michael now. Within Karen, the voice of Freyja formed a warning—*"Do not believe him, daughter, while he bears Brisingamen!"*

Karen gripped Michael's arm. "If it's really Duncan, tell him to give the necklace back—"

He nodded, and managed to get out words in a voice harsh with strain. "Duncan—I want to believe you! Take off the necklace you stole from Karen and throw it down here. In the name of all that's holy, man, do you think I wanted to fight you?" The words came out in an anguished rush.

The man above them put his hand to his neck and they saw the glitter of gold in the light of the candle behind him. *He's going to do it!* thought Karen. *He'll give back Brisingamen and then we can all go home!* Her heart was beating as if it would burst free.

Then the magician sprang backward to his feet. His wild laughter rang against the room. Loki!

"Fools! All of you, fools! A last time have I tricked you!" He twirled exultantly, and it seemed to Karen that once more the air around him was beginning to pulse with a dull glow.

"My powers are returning, but the gods are gone from you! Wretched children of men, what will you do now?"

"Duncan!" Michael cried out as if he would call his friend from the depths of Hell. Walter looked at him with pity, then began to pull himself up the ladder once more. Karen bit her lip, torn between the urge to call him back and fear of letting Loki know he was there. Loki was a god—what indeed could they do now?

Groaning, Michael lifted Odin's spear, drew back his arm, and threw.

In seeming slow motion it arched toward Loki, who deflected it with a casual sweep of his arm.

"Lords of Chaos and Chance and Change, behold the victory I bring to you!" He raised his arms exultantly, and Karen felt around her once again the remorseless gathering of power. She tried to reach out to Freyja, or to that ultimate power that had aided her a little while ago, but for the moment she was empty, exhausted of energy by what had passed. Patiently, Walter continued to climb.

Though his face was glistening with tears, Michael started toward the right-hand ladder. The Moro kris was still belted at his side. Karen watched in horror, knowing that he meant to kill his friend now. The world was doomed if he failed, but if he succeeded he would destroy himself, for how could he live with the knowledge of what he had done?

Loki was motionless, not deigning to notice what the mortals were doing now. His arms were still raised, and Karen could hear the low murmur of his summoning. The ladder creaked as Michael began to climb.

Then she gasped, for she could feel beneath her the first quivering of an answer to Loki's call. He was commanding the earthquake, as he had intended from the beginning to do.

A hollow clatter of footsteps jerked her attention back to the loft.

Walter was running, determination lending his awkward gait a grim purpose as he hurtled toward Loki.

"Walter, no!" Even as the words tore from Karen's throat Walter reached his goal. Loki jerked like an eel as the man's arms closed around him, but Walter had no thought of any fighting strategy, only of holding on. The boards of the loft groaned as they scrabbled for footing, forward nearly to the edge, then back against the rolls of canvas stacked there, kicking over the candle.

Michael shouted and began to pull himself up the ladder with redoubled speed. Loki was cursing in a high-pitched stream of sound, but Walter remained silent. They grappled back and forth, fighting for balance, their struggle bringing them to the front of the loft again just as Michael reached the top of the ladder. For a moment they wavered, then Karen saw Walter smile, as with his last strength he thrust outward and propelled himself and his foe into the air.

Forever they seemed to fall, locked in that parody of Love's unity. Then they struck the piled furniture below with a crack like breaking sticks, flew apart, and tumbled the rest of the way to the cement floor.

With a stifled cry Karen ran to them, while Michael hurled himself back down the ladder. The candle's flame began to lick at the canvas behind him. As if the fall of their leader had released them, those of Duncan Flyte's students who could move scrambled for the door. As it opened, a blast of cold air swept the room and flames ran up the edge of the canvas in a line of fire.

Walter lay sprawled on the floor. In the increasing light Karen could see the shallow movement of his chest and the dark trickle of blood at the corner of his mouth. Numbly she bent over him, feeling his limbs, trying to understand how much was wrong.

As if from a long way away she could hear Terry shouting to one of the bikers to look for a fire extinguisher, but it made no sense to her. Was not the world intended to end in fire? Somebody cried out that they had found a telephone, and she heard Del's voice giving information.

Carefully Karen tried to straighten Walter's crumpled limbs. He must be in shock—she remembered vaguely that one had to keep accident victims warm, and dragged a king's cloak from its hanger to cover him. Flames were eating eagerly into the rolled canvas now.

Terry gripped her shoulder. "We've got to get out of here— I don't know if we can stop the fire!"

Karen shook her head. "Walter mustn't be moved. The ambulance will be here soon—we'll have time. . . . " Terry swore. Then there was a shout and he dashed away.

Someone was murmuring brokenly nearby. She looked

over, saw Michael cradling Duncan's body against him, a dark shape against the growing glow of the fire. The head of the magician hung awkwardly—he must have broken his neck when he struck the furniture. Duncan was dead—had been dead by the time they reached the floor.

"It's all right!" whispered Michael, "The medicopters will come for us—hang on, Duncan, it'll be okay!"

Oh, my poor love—Karen thought distantly, *I should comfort him.* Then she felt movement beneath her hands and her attention fixed on Walter's face. His eyes opened. He drew a painful breath, coughed and swallowed, and fought for breath again.

"Don't move!" Karen said urgently, bending over him. "You're hurt, but we'll take care of you—Walter, please!" she added as he tried to speak, and his eyes clouded with the beginning of pain. The fire was roaring hungrily now. She bent close to hear his words.

"No. . . . " Very carefully he let the word out on a sigh. "Tonight . . . I feast . . . in Freyja's hall. . . . "

"That's not true!" she exclaimed. "It's not fair—you can't—"

He tried to shake his head. "Fate. Heimdall is always . . . Loki's foe."

Karen stared at him, realizing finally why his choice of identities had alarmed her. It was true—it was the ending destined for both of them at the last battle of Ragnarok.

"Walter, we're back in the twentieth century—we've held off the Twilight of the Gods and everything will be all right now!"

Walter swallowed and spoke more strongly. "Each time it happens . . . it is Ragnarok." Michael's head lifted; he watched them with agony twisting his features.

Walter went on, "And finally I have fought my war." In the distance she could hear the wail of sirens like an echo of his horn. His eyes focused fully upon her, luminous in the leaping firelight as they had been when they made love. "I don't mind," he whispered. "I have held a goddess in my arms. . . . " His voice failed, but he continued to smile at her while something in the pit of her stomach tightened as if a fist were twisting there. He was still smiling when his breath ceased to rattle in his chest and she realized that his beautiful eyes were not seeing her anymore.

Very gently, she kissed shut his eyelids, then straightened, trying to remember how to breathe. Smoke made her eyes smart and she blinked. Soon the tears would come. Michael had not moved. Across the still figures of their dead they stared at each other. Then, very deliberately, Michael unclasped Brisingamen from around Duncan's neck and held it out to her.

As Karen's fingers closed on the gold, light exploded around them. The loft was collapsing inward. Pieces of timber crashed around them; burning fragments showered the room. Karen recoiled as her skin was seared by a blast of superheated air. She struggled to breathe.

But she was not afraid. She held the necklace to her breast, thinking, *This is how it ends, but I knew that*—memories of fire mingled with the vision of flame around her, memories of the fire and of Brisingamen. *I have died this way before.* . . .

Then Michael's hands closed on her arms.

He jerked her to her feet. Karen stumbled and his arm vised around her, half-carrying her with him away from the fire. Smoke, acrid and choking, swirled around them and she coughed convulsively. A fragment of burning wood sailed toward them and instinctively Karen thrust out her arm to ward it away. Then other hands were reaching for them, hauling them out of the inferno and into the chill winter air.

"No!" she tried to turn back—"Walter, Duncan—they're still in there!"

"They're dead, Karen—*anyone* who was still in there is dead now. . . . " Terry's voice was tight. He put his arm around her and guided her toward the street. In the distance she could hear keening—there was a song in it—dizzy, she groped to understand the words. She blinked her stinging eyes, trying to see the figures the billowing smoke half-hid.

"Listen to the sirens!" said someone.

Karen shook her head. It was not fire trucks she had heard, but the bitter crying of the choosers of the slain. She drew her arm across her streaming eyes, staring back at the fire. The warehouse was glowing like a lantern now. With a crash, part of the roof fell in and flames leaped skyward, their lurid orange clearing to golden as they fed on the inrush of new air.

Del and Terry stood beside her, brilliantly illuminated by the light of the fire. Beyond them waited five of the bikers who had come with Michael and the only two of Duncan's disciples who had neither died in the battle nor run away.

Those who had fallen remained in the building—warriors burning together in the same funeral pyre. Walter would pass like a Viking King with his enemy at his feet and sufficient panoply of jewels and weapons and furnishings for a dozen palaces in the other world.

Michael stood a little ahead of her, his head bowed, a black silhouette against the flames. More of the roof crashed down. Karen felt the heat even from where she stood, but he did not move.

Cry! she wanted to call out to him. *Cry out and curse the gods! Isn't this how Walter said the world would end?* Red light glowed on the buildings around them. She wondered whether they too had caught fire.

The wail of the sirens pulsed agonizingly around her. Fire engines were pulling up around them; Del drew her out of the way as the firefighters ran out their hoses. Jets of water began to play across the flames, sending up furious clouds of steam.

Del was trying to give the police officers some plausible explanation for what had happened, but Karen was surrounded by a wall of silence. She stood, watching the vain attempt of the fire trucks to halt the destruction of a world.

Then the wind shifted and her smarting cheeks were blessed by a touch of cool air. Michael was walking toward her; she realized that she could see his haggard features even though his back was to the fire. For a moment he looked at her, then he sank to his knees as if his legs would no longer bear him and held out his arms. Without conscious decision, she went to him and he pressed his face against her thighs. She reached down to touch his hair and realized that Brisingamen was still gripped in her hand. Carefully she forced her fingers to let go and slid the necklace into her jacket pocket. Her hand was beginning to throb painfully; she looked down and saw the figure of the Goddess imprinted upon her palm.

Karen sighed, and at last the welcome tears soothed her burning eyes and blurred the sight of the flames. Weeping, she held Michael's head against her. When she could see again, the fire was dying, and behind it the sky was brightening with the silver light of dawn.

20

Lif and Lifthrasir — safe among the leaves,
they will hide in the World-Tree;
The dews of dawn will be their meat and drink;
from them will come the new race of men.
THE LAY OF VAFTHRUTHNIR

The fire crackled as it bit into the kindling, gilding the rough bark of the log. Karen took an unwary breath of aromatic smoke and choked, remembering another fire. But that had been over a week ago—a week, or a century. New pink skin was already forming beneath her burns, but her mind still ached with memories. She forced herself to breathe evenly, to listen to Terry's words.

"Now in the Northland the nights are long—cold, the country cries for warmth. Snow snips the branches until the sun stops, turns, and starts again northward. . . . " The deep rhythms of his voice calmed her, proof of an orderly universe as compelling as his words. Despite (or perhaps because of) everything that had happened in the past few weeks, the winter solstice—Sunreturn—was here. It seemed to Karen that she could *feel* the machinery of the solar system pause, shift, and begin to send the northern half of the planet on its six-month journey toward the light.

Then a log popped in the fire, and she had to force herself to focus on Terry's face, glowing in its ruddy light as he lifted his hands in blessing.

It's only the Yule Fire! Karen reminded herself as the larger logs caught and the sound of the fire became a roar. When Terry had called to invite her to the Midwinter ceremony she had thought she could master her memories. Now she wondered. She felt sweat breaking out on her brow and looked away from the hearth, seeking in the ordinary suburban comforts of Nancy Bell's house in the Berkeley hills an assurance of continuity.

In the leaded glass doors of the bookcase to either side of the fireplace, she saw her fragmented reflection—golden hair a little uneven where the fire had singed it, a thin hand branded, eyes still like charred holes in a blanket, focused on memories.

With a suppressed whimper she shut the vision away. *It is not the world that has changed, it is me.*

Around the circle, faces turned to her curiously, then away. Terry's group had welcomed her warmly, with ready sympathy for her burns and perhaps some confused memories of having met her at their Disir festival three months before. Terry had invited Michael, too, but Michael was gone, no one knew where.

Terry sat back and nodded to Nancy, who opened a lavishly illustrated book of Norse mythology and began to read the story of Freyr's courtship of the giant-maid Gerd. One child squirmed on her lap while another leaned against her, a piece of glittering tinsel twined in her fair hair. There were other children in the circle, eyes wide as they listened to the story or attention wandering toward the Christmas tree.

I have to believe that what we went through was worth it, thought Karen, *so that the kids can look forward to Christmas unafraid.*

The police seemed to have accepted Del's story of a play rehearsal in the warehouse and a tipped over candle. The insurance people might be more difficult, but with so much other storm damage to worry about, the authorities did not have the time or personnel to inquire more closely into the cause of the fire.

Since that night the weather had been cold but fair—the typical crisp, clear climate of California in December. Already other kinds of news had claimed front page space in the papers, and skiers were flocking to the Sierras to take advantage of the abundant snow.

How quickly men forgot, once the visible danger was done! But Walter was dead, and the university had asked Karen to take over the classes for which she had been his teaching assistant until the semester was over. How could she do it? She did not know enough—but as the Chair of the Department had pointed out, there was nobody available who knew more. His letter lay on her table at home, waiting for her answer.

Karen's fingers closed on the teal wool of her dress and she concentrated on the feel of the jersey, anchoring herself to present reality. For a moment she had hung dizzily between the worlds. But though she was here, where was Michael? They should have been comforting each other through this time. The people at his house, involved in their own mourning for the two bikers who had died, could tell her only that Michael had strapped a small bag to the back of the Harley and ridden off the day after the fire.

Once more she tried to still the chill whisper of fear. Michael had loved Duncan—was he blaming himself for his friend's death, was he blaming her? *I have lost Walter,* she thought despairingly, *do I have to lose Michael too?* Imagination tormented her with visions of ways in which Michael might be seeking a final atonement for what had been done.

Nancy's story ended. Terry got to his feet, facing the images of the Lord and the Lady on the mantelpiece.

"Hail the turning sun!" he chanted, and the others echoed him.

"Hail the continuing clan—
"Hail to Freyr and Freyja,
"Lord and Lady of life!"

As the chant ended he smiled at Karen. Instinctively she put her hand to her neck to adjust Brisingamen. Terry had asked her to wear it, and she thought it would be safe—the property was warded, he said, and they were celebrating a sacred festival. But was that true? Would wearing Brisingamen wake the spirit of Loki once more? Perhaps that fear was at the root of her unease. Whatever happened to her or to Michael was essentially irrelevant if the presence of Brisingamen could unleash another such struggle upon the world. She had recovered the necklace, but what was she supposed to do with it now?

The circle broke up and Karen moved out of the way as the children jostled for position as they waited to hang their offerings of animal-shaped cookies on the Christmas tree. For a moment Karen allowed her mind to explore the implications of the little ritual. Was the fir tree with its ornaments an unrecognized survival from the days in which the trees of the sacred groves had been laden with sacrifices? Or was this the Tree of Life whose branches supported the many-tiered worlds —the tree that despite frost and fire and thunder and Ragnarok itself would survive?

Someone started singing the *Boar's Head Carol* as an impromptu procession appeared from the kitchen, laden with pies and bowls of steaming vegetables, Jack Bell's home-brewed mead, baskets of apples and pomegranates and a whole roast suckling pig wreathed with rosemary and bay. Three times it circled the wide living room, then the food was arranged on a table, buffet-style, and people began to line up, chattering eagerly.

Karen swallowed unhappily. She had felt queasy most of the week, and the rich smell of the food made her stomach cramp uneasily. If she came down with the flu it would surely be no wonder, after all she had been through. She smiled apologetically at Nancy, pushed her way through the crowd and eased out through the sliding doors into the fresh air on the deck outside. Jack *had* said the entire property was warded, but instinctive caution made her slip the necklace inside the neck of her dress.

It was just past sunset, and the dull sheen of the Bay still reflected some of the light of the vanished sun. Behind San Francisco's twin peaks the sky glowed like a fading fire. Like a notch on the horizon, the hilltops marked the southern limit of the arc of the sun. Tomorrow it would begin working its way back toward Mt. Tamalpais as the world began a new solar year.

She remembered how, when one was swinging, there always seemed to be a moment of stillness before gravity whirled one down again. She felt that stillness now, as the sun poised before beginning its cycle anew. And *she* was waiting as well, suspended in a kind of spiritual limbo. Walter and Duncan were dead. Brisingamen had been saved. Now she must choose whether to hide it, and herself, away from the world, or else—what? Dimly Karen sensed that there must be another answer, but her mind had no concept of what it could be.

She let the cold air soothe her face, and as she drew the clean wind into her lungs her nausea began to fade. It was very quiet here, poised above the world. Below her the tree-clad slopes of the hills flowed away to the flatlands, dim masses of shadow beginning to glimmer now with the fairy lights of the houses nestled among them. Here and there the lights of Christmas displays sparkled like strings of jewels.

If only I could stay like this—Karen thought dreamily. Her breathing deepened and her body grew still, seeking that moment of suspension her exercises had taught her—that moment in which the mind floated free, a point of silence in the stillness of the world.

A quick rush of tears dimmed her vision, and the points of brilliance below her blurred together in lines of light. For a moment she forgot to breathe, for surely there was more radiance than there had been before, as if she were seeing not the lights of street and household but the myriad flames that were the life-energies of men. Men and women, animals, even plants and trees each had their own glow. The life-light pulsed, there was almost a pattern—yes, it was a shape that resolved itself into the blazing body of the woman who was rising from the land before her.

Karen's hands lifted in adoration, as Terry had saluted the sacred fire.

"Freyja . . ."

The Lady smiled.

This was no dream, nor was it the projected transformation Karen's mirror had shown. This form came not from her own unconscious, but from the larger web of life of which she, Karen, was only one part. Brisingamen burned on her neck, radiating the same energy. With trembling fingers Karen strove to undo the clasp and held the necklace to the glowing sky. This then, must be why she had worn it, why she was here.

"Blessed One—take back your own!"

"Daughter, dost thou not yet understand? Wherever I am, I bear Brisingamen—" The Lady touched her neck and Karen blinked at the blaze of gold. *"Thy necklace is the channel for its power. Bear it, or bury it; guard it, or give it away! But, Karen Yngjald's daughter, know this—Brisingamen is thy inheritance, and thou above all others most fit to wield it in the world!"*

"Oh, no—" Karen began to shake her head, backing away until she bumped into the house wall. For a moment she saw the face of Loki, blazing in an ecstasy of destruction as his strength was fed by the power of the stolen gold. "I'll destroy it, if I must, rather than wake Loki again!''

''Child—'' the voice of the Goddess throbbed with a sadness older than the world. *''Was there ever a power that could not be misused? Love itself, may be a fetter or a devouring flame—wilt thou then forswear love? The price of life itself is the possibility of pain. . . .''*

It was true—the memory of Walter's death bled like a wound, and with it Duncan's visions of hatred and suffering. Better—much better, to retreat from all of it into the uncaring dark.

''Thy choice,'' said the Goddess, *''is between Death, and Me. . . .''*

Abruptly Karen knew she had faced this darkness before. Her hand throbbed, she saw morning sunlight glisten on the drops of her own blood on the bedroom floor. Words echoed in her memory—*''If I suffer again, I am at least going to know why!''*

The golden pendants of the necklace bit into her palms as she clutched it against her. A reason! There had to be a reason for Walter's death and her own suffering! The Goddess was speaking not of the body's death, but of the extinction of the spirit—if Karen chose to reject Her gift, she might never know if there was a reason for all this pain. Seared by the light of self-knowledge, her spirit writhed.

Shrinking, terrified, words formed themselves in the womb of consciousness that lay beyond her will.

"I . . . choose . . . You!"

After a moment, the awful pressure began to ease. Brisingamen pulsed between her hands. Faintly—half-remembered, half-foreseen—images formed in her mind of how the necklace might be used to pour Freyja's healing energy into an ailing world. It must be employed secretly, subtly, not paraded as an ornament. It must be safeguarded, lest its presence create the imbalance that had wakened Loki before, but it must be *used*.

Karen could serve the Goddess, not rejecting all other truths, but complementing them by manifesting a power and a perspective that for too long had been missing from the world.

She held up the necklace once more, no longer in rejection, but in offering.

And the vision before her began to change, its radiance deepening, as its features evolved from the triumphant youth of Freyja to the fulfilled and fertile beauty of One who smiled at Karen with her mother's eyes. And then that vision, too, began to change, the lush curves fined away to the beauty of wind-weathered stone, the eyes growing deep as a night of many stars. Karen remembered the face Del Eden had worn as the Vala, and knew Whom she looked upon now.

And even as She was known, She changed again—visions growing one from the other in a myriad of faces and forms, faster and faster. Karen's consciousness shattered like a broken mirror as all aspects were completed in a Goddess who Herself became One who was neither male nor female, but the single, multiversal pattern of all things.

Gradually, without any sense of transition, Karen became aware that she was standing on the balcony of Nancy Bell's house holding Brisingamen in her hands. The western sky held only a memory of light, and the darkness was filling with stars that glittered like crystals in the clear air. Once more Karen felt herself poised upon a point of stillness, but now it was a fulcrum from which she had the power to move the world.

She could hear music from inside. She should go back to join the others soon. But not yet. Very carefully, she clasped Brisingamen around her neck again.

The door to the balcony opened, and for a moment the singing inside was clear—

> *Now the winter wind blows cold,*
> *Now the turning year grows old;*
> *While the world is held in thrall*
> *Let the Yule fire warm our Hall.*
> *Freyr and Freyja, now we pray,*
> *Bless our Yuletide feast today!*

Karen turned, and with a sense of inevitability recognized that it was Michael who was standing there. The door closed behind him, cutting off the music, and he came toward her. Abruptly she remembered all her fears for him and her hands closed hard on his.

"Michael, damn you, where have you *been*?"

Then his arms were around her, and for a moment she was aware of nothing but the solid reality of him under her hands, his heart beating against hers, his voice whispering her name.

"I had to go—" he muttered, quickly, as if he were afraid that he would never be able to tell her if he didn't get it all out now. "I was going crazy, thinking about Duncan—I needed to get clean away! So I jumped on the bike and rode—I don't know where. All I can remember is the cold wind on my face and the open road ahead of me. But even the Harley can't go faster than Huginn and Muninn—thought and memory are a part of you and you can't run away—"

Karen pulled back a little and stared at him, realizing that in their own ways, he and she had been going through the same thing. "And why did you come back?" she asked him finally.

He shrugged. "Duncan will probably stay with me, one way or another, no matter what I do. Running away didn't solve anything, and when I woke up in the middle of the night I was calling your name." It was not a plea, or a claim, either, but a simple statement.

Michael's arms tightened and Karen relaxed against him. And suddenly, in that wordless moment of content, she became aware of an unexpected discomfort. Her breasts were sore; it was painful to be pressed so hard. *That* was not a symptom of the flu. Some women got swollen breasts when their periods were due, but she had never had that problem. Karen stiffened as abruptly a series of facts she had not had time to notice before clicked into place.

Her period was late, and even the stress she had been under should not have delayed it for this long. Her last period had been in early November. Her breasts were tender, and for the past two weeks she had been feeling sick off and on. But she was on the Pill . . . and that only worked as long as you took it religiously. Could she be sure she had not missed several days, with all that had been going on?

You've been acting as the priestess of a fertility goddess, what did you expect? her inner awareness commented wryly, and she began to giggle unexpectedly.

"Karen? What's wrong?" Michael had felt her tension and released her. He stood, trying to read her face in the dim light.

"I'm pregnant!" she answered in an awed voice. And then, looking at him, was abruptly aware of all the reasons why that had been the wrong thing to say.

Staring down at her, Michael had gone very still. "By me?" She could hear the effort it took him to keep any hint of accusation from his tone.

Goddess, I thought You were rewarding me when Michael came back, but what am I going to do now? she thought as her chain of reasoning continued to its logical conclusion. She knew Michael's potential for jealousy.

When the silence had become worse than an answer, Karen sighed. "I don't know."

"But you said that Duncan didn't—" Michael could not keep emotion from his voice now.

"No!" Karen shuddered at the possibilities *that* would have raised. "But Walter and I—" She tried again, "Well, it was Freyja, actually, but I'm not ashamed. And it was only once—" Her eyes stung as she remembered Walter's radiance. "And Michael—for him it was the only time!"

Another silence, while Karen's stomach grew cold. Then Michael replied.

"Are you going to get rid of it?"

Without thinking, Karen shook her head. She had no convictions against abortion, but faced with the option, she was certain that it was not a possibility for her, even—or especially, if she was carrying Walter Klein's posthumous child. Michael was speaking again, and for a moment she could not understand what he had said.

"Will you marry me?"

Karen stared at him, abruptly reached up to kiss him, then let him go. "Walter killed your best friend—could you act as father to his child?"

Michael shook his head. "Duncan Flyte died in Viet Nam—" he said slowly. "That's one of the things I finally realized when I was away. Besides, I saw Walter's face when they went over the edge. He was smiling at me, Karen—Heimdall did it because he was Loki's enemy, but Walter did it so that I wouldn't have Duncan's blood on my hands!"

Karen nodded slowly, recognizing the truth in that, and knowing that Walter had died exulting in a kind of triumph he had never hoped to achieve.

"We'll name the kid Walter if it's a boy. Besides," he grinned, "statistically there's a much greater chance that the father was me!"

Karen smiled, but an image was taking shape in her mind, the face of a daughter with flaxen hair and Walter's sweet smile. It would be a girl, she was sure—a girl to inherit Brisingamen.

"Well?" Michael drew her into the curve of his arm. "My God, woman, I've actually proposed to you—aren't you going to answer me?"

The thought of Michael as a husband boggled the imagination. He would be jealous of other men; he would go off for days on the bike without telling her when and where; his government aid and the small income from his writing barely supported *him*—she would have to keep some kind of a job. But then, she was planning on going on with her degree anyway; at the very least she could be no worse off with him to help her than she would be alone.

"If I do marry you it won't be just to give the child a name—" she began, but he put his fingers to her lips, silencing her.

"No—" His voice was very sober now. "I know that's not really necessary anymore. But I would have asked you anyway. We've been through so much—it's time to stop drifting and try to build something that will last. It's not just that I'm in love with you, and I know that it won't be easy, but we're connected now. Please, Karen, will you give it a try?"

Karen nodded, thinking that if Michael had asked her an hour earlier she would not have been able to understand. But he was part of the pattern into which the Goddess had woven her, and there had never been any doubt that she loved him, wanted him, needed him, even when misunderstandings drove them apart. As he had said, it was not going to be easy, but if she suffered, at least from now on she would know why.

And as he began very single-mindedly to kiss her, Karen thought of a further advantage to Michael as a husband—at least she would not have to explain to him how she had gotten Brisingamen.

Karen was beginning to wonder whether Michael intended to consummate their marriage then and there, and whether she would put up any objection if he tried, when the door opened.

"Hey, you two—you're going to freeze if you stay out there." Terry paused, considered them more closely, and then grinned. "Well, maybe you won't freeze at that, but you're missing all the fun!"

Breathing unsteadily, Michael and Karen drew reluctantly apart. Now they could hear the music clearly, and the words.

> *Lovely is the evergreen;*
> *Holly's king and Ivy's queen;*
> *Rosemary and fragrant bays*

> *Deck the tokens of our praise.*
> *Of all the gods have given men,*
> *We give a portion back again—*
> *Wheaten bread and honey wine,*
> *Ripened fruit and cornfed swine.*

Terry held out his hand to Karen, and she and Michael let him draw them back into the room and into the dance. Recorder and drum were carrying the tune and rhythm while the dancers, with such breath as was left to them, sang. Sidestepping or weaving in a grapevine step according to their skill, the line of dancers spiraled around the room.

Like a galaxy forming, thought Karen, or the DNA which patterns every living thing, in and out and around went the dance.

> *Lady bless us with your love*
> *As you bless the gods above;*
> *Lord of luck, we sing to you,*
> *Make life leap in us anew.*

Karen felt Michael squeeze her hand, met his eye, and laughed. The energy of their embrace had been transferred to the dance, as if she and Michael and all of them were united in a single act of love. Here was the rhythm of the universe and its harmony, expressed in the intricate, joyous patterns of the dance.

> *Bless the master and the maid,*
> *The child within the cradle laid,*
> *Bless our bread and bless our beer,*
> *Prosper us throughout the year.*

With a shout re-echoed from the garlanded rafters, Terry grabbed the hand of the girl at the end of the line and the swirling figure contracted into circle, spinning deosil, strengthening the sun.

Karen felt the magnetic currents in the earth beneath her flow more easily, felt the fire leap higher and lights all over the city shine more brightly, felt life flowing from hand to hand through the circle as the energy built, radiating out across the land.

Put the darkness now to flight,
Bless the waiting world with light;
Health and strength for each one here
Give us in the coming year.

Faster and faster the circle whirled. The world blurred around her; Karen saw the figures around her glowing golden like the jewels of a necklace, connected by pure energy.

The Dance of Life spun its new cycle—the perfect circle of Brisingamen.